THE NIGHT SHE DIED

THE NIGHT SHE DIED

 a novel by

JENNIFER PATRICK

SOHO

Published by
Soho Press, Inc.
853 Broadway
New York, NY 10003

Library of Congress Cataloging-in-Publication Data

Patrick, Jennifer, 1965-
The night she died: a novel/Jennifer Patrick.
p.cm.
ISBN 1-56947-363-3 (alk. paper)
1. Police–Georgia–Fiction. 2. Women–Crimes against–Fiction.
3. Georgia–Fiction I. Title.
PS3616.A87N54 2004
813'.6–dc22   2003065890

Book design by Kathleen Lake, Neuwirth & Associates, Inc.

10 9 8 7 6 5 4 3 2 1

DEDICATION

To Dad, Mom, and Ian

❧ *c h a p t e r o n e* ❧

October 12, 7:00 A.M.

S TERLING remembered Lara, the first time he'd noticed her. He saw the vision clearly, like she was right there across from him now instead of the police captain with his basset-hound face and red-rimmed eyes. She'd been sitting alone at one of Dairy Queen's red plastic tables, holding a chocolate-dipped cone. He'd watched her bite off the top of the chocolate shell, flick her tongue down inside, then pull it out again, its tip white with ice cream. She was beautiful in a way he'd never seen before.

Her mouth had been puckered like a china doll's. The right-hand strap of her white tank top drooped off her sun-tanned shoulder. Her cut-offs were so frayed that Sterling thought he could pull a loose thread and they'd unravel completely. Sterling thought of the girls at school, their dyed blonde hair frizzed and sprayed to impossible heights. Lara's long dark hair looked soft.

She wore no makeup. Her cheeks were freckled. He got so caught up in staring that it took a moment for him to notice her staring back. Sterling became aware of himself all at once, of his stupid striped Dairy Queen shirt smeared with milky runoff from the ice-cream machine, his work pants stained with hot-fudge sauce. The cap they made him wear drooped over his ears and eyes. He knew he looked like a damned loser. But she watched him anyway, as if he'd been a rare and surprising animal she'd come across in the zoo.

1

Who the hell is she? He'd never seen her before, and he'd seen everybody in town, more than he cared to. He considered smiling at her, flirting some. *But she's older than me. Besides, that might not be why she's looking.* He glanced down. Was his fly unzipped? He touched his face. Was ice cream or chocolate smeared on his forehead?

She'd looked away, her cheeks flushing red. She gathered her big straw handbag, stood, and wandered to the door as if dazed or lost. He figured she was heading from Athens to Atlanta, or vice-versa, and had decided to stop for ice cream because that day in June it was as hot as the devil's dick. *I'll never see her again.*

"Hey." Captain Edgars's voice startled him and the vision faded. "Did you hear what I asked?"

Sterling shook his head. He looked around the small musty room. The upper half of the wall opposite him was a two-way mirror. Sterling could see his reflection, pale in the flickering fluorescent lights. A copy machine hummed in a corner. File cabinets lined the wall behind him, and on top of them Sterling noticed a row of plastic Coke bottles. They seemed strange and out of place. He stared at them and thought about the word *dead,* about how the captain had said it a few minutes ago. He saw it in his mind, huge white letters against a black background. DEAD.

"I asked how you met Miss Walton," Edgars said.

"How I met Miss Walton? Lara? I met her at Dairy Queen."

A day later she'd come back, same time, same order. Chocolate-dipped cone. Again she had sat at a table near the counter, casting quick sidelong glances in his direction, and sometimes he caught those glances and held them, swallowing, his face going hot.

"We got to talking."

"About what?" the captain asked.

"Aw, I don't remember. Just stuff, you know, like I talk about with all the folks that come in there."

But that wasn't how it'd gone at all. As he'd stood behind the register, Lara staring and Jaylee giggling beside him, Sterling decided he couldn't let things go on like this. Setting his jaw, he leaned across the counter. "Is there something I can do for you, ma'am?"

Her eyes opened wide with surprise, and a flush spread from her throat to her cheeks. He waited for her to say something, but she sat frozen, like she'd been caught doing something wrong.

"It's just, you keep looking up here and all," he stammered.

He watched her abashed expression change abruptly to a businesslike frown. As she reached for her handbag and stood, Sterling's heart began pounding. She walked to the register and rested her arms on the vinyl counter so her white cotton tank top hung loose from her chest. He could see the lace edge of her bra. "Could I get a Diet Coke?"

Her voice sounded different from what he was used to, a flat TV-newscaster voice. Behind him, Jaylee laughed. *Damn.* Sterling felt like an idiot. He poured the Diet Coke, took her money, and handed her drink and some change.

"Thanks." She turned to go. Halfway to the exit she stopped, glanced back at him, and muttered "Sorry for looking."

As he watched her push through the glass door and travel across the parking lot with quick long strides, Sterling swallowed hard. "Who is that?"

"She's that weird woman who bought the old Bishop place on Church Street," Jaylee said.

"She *lives* here?"

"Does now."

"Man." Sterling stared at the door as it swung shut. "She's hot."

"No, she ain't. She looked kinda plain, I thought."

"Shut up. You don't know who's hot and who ain't."

LARA. So when did they first really talk? The captain was waiting for an answer. Maybe it was when he'd run into her at the checkout line in Ingles's grocery just a few days later. As he'd approached the register, his skateboard tucked under his left arm, a container of powdered milk in his right hand, he heard a woman arguing in a Northern accent: "I can carry the bags myself." He peered around the candy rack to see Lara engaged in a tug-of-war with the bag boy. At the sight of her, Sterling's heart surged. "Really," she insisted, yanking at the bags, "I can handle them."

The bag boy reluctantly let go, and Lara pulled the groceries to her chest. Then she turned and strode to the exit as if she were angry. Sterling dropped his powdered milk onto the metal rim of the conveyer belt, set his skateboard beside the candy rack, and bolted after her.

Outside, she stood by the curb. The bags rested on the pavement at her feet. She lifted a hand to shield her eyes from the setting sun, which glazed the deserted storefront windows a hot orange. She wore a sleeveless, pale blue cotton dress. Her brown hair was pulled back in a ponytail. She seemed lost, like she'd misplaced her car, or couldn't quite think of how she'd ended up in this parking lot, in this town. Sterling stared at her from behind, at the brilliant sun catching her hair. Her skin looked soft, pink, and damp. The back of her dress was dark with sweat. He took a step toward her. "You want me to carry those for you?" With a start, she whirled around, her hand at her throat. "Sorry," he grinned. "Didn't mean to scare ya."

She took a deep breath and glared at him. "I'm not an invalid. I'm perfectly capable of carrying my own grocery bags." She snatched up the groceries and hurried across the pitted parking lot to wander among the few cars.

He followed her. "Hey, you remember me from Dairy Queen, don't you?"

She paused long enough to arch an eyebrow. "Of course."

"Good, 'cause, see, what I was wanting to know is why you were watching me the other day." She stared hard at each car, as if she'd forgotten what hers looked like. "'Cause I been wondering why," he said.

Stopping in front of a run-down Toyota sedan, she pulled her handbag off her shoulder and set it on the car hood: *chink*. Biting her lip, she groped inside. Coins jangled on the bottom. Sterling walked to the passenger side of her car, where he rested an arm on the roof.

"So I guess you ain't gonna tell me, and I'll have to go to my grave wondering." He put on a sad face and tried to sound disappointed.

She stopped digging in her purse and looked at him. For a moment she frowned. Then her mouth turned up at the corners like she was trying not to smile. It made Sterling grin, and Lara grinned suddenly too, flashing perfect white teeth. "I've been in this town a few weeks, and I have to say you don't look like anyone else here." Her eyes met his. "That's why I was staring. You're strange-looking."

"Well, ma'am, I believe that's the best compliment anyone ever gave me." He winked, wheeled around, and headed back toward Ingles.

"Hey," she called after him.

"I gotta finish buying some stuff." He waved and made a point of not glancing back.

B UT he didn't tell any of that to Edgars. It wasn't the captain's business. Sterling tried to sort out the confused jumble of thoughts in his head. The word *dead* kept floating in front of his eyes, projecting like a movie onto the two-way mirror, but he couldn't quite connect it with anything the captain had asked. He thought it was strange how he didn't feel upset.

Edgars jotted something in an open manila file. Sterling wondered what the file said. Did it mention the night Edgars had caught him and Lacy Williams drinking beer and fooling around behind Wal-Mart? Or the warning he'd gotten for skateboarding on the sidewalk?

Edgars lifted his eyes and studied Sterling's face. "You're eighteen now, aren't you? Turned eighteen this past August?"

"Yeah."

"And you said you did yard work for her?"

"Yeah, and helped fix up her house. She paid pretty good."

"But don't you work down at Dairy Queen and at Eric Teague's place?"

"What, is it some kinda crime to have three jobs?"

"I'm just trying to figure out what you were doing at her house so late."

In the dark, Lara's house was a big, silent shell, the tin roof silvered with moonlight. It always seemed haunted. Sterling thought of leaving Lara last night. He thought of her right hand, her long thin fingers stretched out to him, pale in the moonlight. Ghost fingers.

He looked at Captain Edgars, at the two-way mirror. For a moment, the image of Lara's fingers imposed itself over the bare walls of the police-station interrogation room. Suddenly, Sterling felt as if someone had punched him in the stomach. He couldn't catch his breath. Doubling over, he wrapped his arms around his waist and rocked back and forth.

"Mr. O'Connor?" The captain frowned. "Are you all right?"

Sterling's eyes began to sting. "Is this gonna take much longer? I mean I gotta go. I gotta get to work."

"Do you have access to a gun, Mr. O'Connor?"

"A gun?" The room spun.

"Yes, a gun. Do you have access to a gun?"

"Access?" He wanted Edgars to shut up so he could think.

"It's not a difficult question. Do you have a gun?"

"No."

"Where'd you go after you left Miss Walton's?"

For a moment he couldn't remember. "Home."

"What time did you get home?"

"About nine."

"And did you go back out after that?"

"Nossir."

"How long have you known Lara Walton?"

"Since June."

"And what were you doing at her house last night?"

"Helping her pack. She was moving back to Washington. Today."

Edgars leaned back. He gave Sterling a grim half-smile, exposing a row of small, yellowed teeth. His voice softened. "I know this must be kind've a shock for you. You understand I have to ask these questions. It's my job."

The image of Captain Edgars became blurred around the edges. "So she's dead?"

Edgars paused. "Why don't you go on. You met her at Dairy Queen. Then what happened?"

Sterling swallowed and forced himself to calm down. Lara had come into the Dairy Queen again four days after he saw her at Ingles. Alicia Hopkins, who he'd broken up with three weeks ago, was sitting at one of the booths giving him soulful looks; so when Lara walked in, he tried to act cool. He didn't want Alicia to know about her.

Lara was red-faced and breathless. "Are you from around here?" she asked while he shoved up the handle on the ice-cream machine and watched the thick white stream spurt into the cone.

"Born and raised." He twisted the cone to form a curled peak at the top, then dipped it into the hot chocolate. He watched as the chocolate hardened.

"Do you go to college? Are you home for the summer?"

"Naw. I work here and at Eric Teague's CD store on Highway 29. One-oh-two." She set that huge straw bag on the counter and rummaged, finally coming up with correct change. When she handed him the money, her warm fingers brushed his cold, sticky ones. He fought the urge to grab hold of her hand. He cast a glance at Alicia, leaned forward, and lowered his voice. "So, hey, you wanna go out with me sometime?"

She smiled. "How old are you?"

"How old do you think I am?"

"It doesn't matter how old I think you are. How old *are* you?"

"Twenty-one."

"He's seventeen," Jaylee called.

He scowled at her over his shoulder. "Knock it off, Jaylee!"

Lara laughed. "I'm almost twice your age, kiddo. But hey, I might have believed you were twenty-one, but that's still a little young for me."

"I'm old enough to know what's going on," he insisted.

She cocked an eyebrow. "Is that so?"

Something in her look shot a hot tingle up his legs. When he didn't answer, she took the cone from him, and still laughing, strolled out the door. He glanced at Alicia. She was glaring at him.

Sterling looked for Lara to come into Dairy Queen the next day, but she didn't. He wondered if she'd ever come again. The next day, he was giving himself a hard time about having ruined it with her, when she pushed through the glass door. When he saw her, the hot tingling started in his legs again, only this time it surged higher and got all the way to his face before it stopped. Lara's eyes fixed on him, and he fought the urge to take a step forward. He didn't want to seem too eager. She marched right to the counter across from where he stood.

"Hi."

"Hey."

He heard Jaylee whispering behind him.

"See," Lara started, then stopped. "See, the house I just bought, it's a mess. I had two handles fall off the kitchen cabinets today."

"That sucks," Sterling said.

"So the thing is, I was wondering if you know anyone who does handyman stuff, or if maybe *you* do handyman stuff." She seemed uncomfortable, and he grinned. Jaylee giggled.

"Yeah, I can help you fix the place up."

"I'd pay you well—say ten dollars an hour?"

"Ten?"

"Is that not enough?"

"No, ma'am—I mean, yes, ma'am, that's plenty."

"What's your name?"

Damn, he hated his name. He tried to think of something sophisticated. "Clayton."

"His name's Sterling!" Jaylee called. He flipped her a bird behind his back.

"Sterling, huh?" His name sounded strange in her flat accent. "That's kind of a cowboy name, isn't it?" She paused and frowned as if thinking. Then she stuck out her hand. "I'm Lara. So, Sterling, why don't you give me your phone number, and I'll call you to come do some work for me?"

He took her hand. It was warm and soft. He got to hold it only a moment before she pulled it away. "Call me here," he said. "It's easier to get me here than at home." He didn't want to tell her that his family had no phone.

"Okay, I'll call you here." She paused. "And could I get a chocolate-dipped cone?"

"Your usual, huh? Coming right up."

When she had gone, Chip came out from the kitchen and glanced over his shoulder to see if Bob Waits, the manager, was watching. He elbowed Sterling in the ribs. "Maybe she wants you to mess with more than just her kitchen cabinets."

"That's kind of what I was thinking." Sterling grinned.

⁙ chapter two ⁙

THE phone call had forced Captain Jimmy Edgars out of bed at 3:30 in the morning. He'd driven bleary-eyed through a cold rain toward the Bishop house on Church Street. He squinted through the windshield while the wipers slapped back and forth. As he passed through the darkened neighborhoods, he thought about how he'd left the Atlanta police force to avoid being awakened at ungodly hours of the night. To avoid the shock of seeing carnage when he was still shaking off sleep.

He'd been a good investigator eight years ago, right before he'd left Atlanta; but he was getting older, and the crimes in Atlanta had become more frequent and more brutal. This little town had seemed the perfect place in which to ease his way into retirement.

The town had its genesis in the 1800s when it became a major stop on the railroad between Athens and Atlanta. Local farmers had come from the surrounding countryside to take advantage of the rail line, and the station became a place to buy, sell, and trade crops, cloth, livestock, sugar, salt, building materials, even bootleg whiskey. Shops and eating establishments sprang up around the tracks, and the town was given its name, Winston, after a nearby plantation owner who had put up money to erect a courthouse.

The town wasn't much now. Crop prices had dropped, and the

nearby farmland was practically worthless. The few remaining local farmers scratched meager livings out of soil whose nutrients had been depleted by a century of cotton cultivation.

Winston's young people moved away as soon as they got old enough, and most shops downtown had closed as their customers took their business to Wal-Mart, or drove to malls in Athens or Atlanta. The only enterprises that kept the town alive were the concrete block factory, the poultry plant, and a few service industry chains like McDonald's and Dairy Queen.

The town was a quiet place, too poor, tired, and exhausted to engender much violence as it inched toward its own death. That was why Edgars had chosen it. He wanted quiet. He was tired of violence.

As the captain turned onto Church Street, he saw the Bishop house ahead on his right. From a distance, it looked almost as if a party was in progress. Gold light blazed in the windows and spilled out onto the porch and lawn. Neighbors gathered on the sidewalk. Then Edgars spied the strobing blue lights of the town's two police cruisers parked by the curb.

The group of onlookers followed the progress of Edgars's car as he pulled into the driveway. As he brought the car to a stop, he hoped the inexperienced officers—and all the officers on the Winston force were inexperienced—had kept the scene undisturbed. Investigations were hard enough without corrupted evidence. He turned off the ignition, took a deep breath, and climbed out of his car and into the glare of the crowd. Edgars felt like he'd stepped onto a stage.

"Captain Edgars!" a woman called. Edgars ignored her. He walked around the neighbors and made his way to the house.

Officer Jake Mason motioned to him from the front porch. Jake's partner, Alan Hand, was crumpled over the railing. Edgars saw him convulse and heard him retch as he vomited onto the bushes below.

"What's the story?" Edgars asked Mason as he eyed Alan Hand's back.

"Body's upstairs."

Edgars turned his gaze from Hand and studied the house. "Were all the lights on like this when you got here?"

"No, sir. Only the light in the hall, and the lamp in her bedroom."

"Well, why the hell did you go turning them on? You know better than to do that. No telling what kind of evidence we might have lost."

Mason was pale. "It's a mess in there, Captain. It's an awful mess."

"What about the doors and windows? Were they all closed?"

"The back door was open."

"Who's inside now?" Edgars asked.

"No one, sir. It's really a mess in there."

"Well, when Bill gets here, send him in. The rest of you keep everyone else out, and I mean *everyone*." Bill Hanks was the county crime-scene investigator.

With a huff, Edgars strode to the front door. He pulled a handkerchief out of his pocket, placed it over the handle, then opened the door and stepped quickly inside.

After the commotion out front, the bright foyer seemed still and silent. Edgars stood for a moment in the echoing hallway. A familiar coppery odor made him cringe. Peering to the left into a quaint old parlor, he noticed a wet, dark stain, about a foot in diameter, spreading slowly across the plaster ceiling. An occasional drop rolled from the light fixture at the center of the stain and fell with a loud plop onto the parlor floor.

Blood. Edgars fought the sudden cramp in his stomach. He couldn't let himself get squeamish. He couldn't get soft. He was the only one in town qualified for this kind of work. He turned to the staircase and began to climb.

Lara Walton lay in her bedroom, her back to the door. What was left of her head hung over the side of her futon, which was on a wood frame that lifted it a foot off the floor. The lamp on the nightstand was still burning, and an open book lay on the futon by her shoulder. The captain's thoughts formed slowly. She must have fallen asleep while reading. After all, why would a killer walk all the way over to turn on the lamp when the switch for the ceiling light was right by the door? After taking his handkerchief from his pocket and wrapping it around his index finger, Edgars flicked up the switch. The bare bulb overhead glared.

He turned his attention back to the body, glad he'd never met this woman. Glad he didn't know her. Two shots had penetrated the back of Lara Walton's skull. They had probably knocked her forward so that her head hung over the side of the futon and her blood pooled onto the floor below. Two more entry wounds were visible below the right shoulder blade, and another wound had penetrated the small of her back. The wall that Lara Walton faced was covered with sticky bits of pink, gray, and white, flakes of bone, smatterings of blood. He could see one bullet embedded in the plaster. "At least it was quick," Edgars muttered. There were no signs of struggle, no blood trail, no indication that Miss Walton had any idea she was in danger.

The captain's eyes fixed on the smooth curve of the woman's hip under her thin white nightgown. He could make out the rounded contours of her rear end. Strange, he thought, how beautiful an image it was. It was the only beautiful thing in the gore-spattered room. Edgars stared at her hip as the reality of the situation began to sink in. For the first time in over eight years, he was going to have to investigate a murder.

A N hour or so later, Edgars found himself perched uncomfortably on the chintzy rose-upholstered antique sofa in Pam and Dave Grier's living room. They sat on a matching sofa opposite him. Behind them, above their marble-fronted fireplace, hung an oil painting of one of Dave's ancestors, a young man with a handlebar mustache and the high starched collar of a Civil War–era gentleman.

"So one more time, just to make sure I got it straight," Edgars said. "You thought you heard a noise like gunshots. You looked at the clock on your nightstand, and it was 2:37 A.M., right?"

Pam nodded. She clutched a wadded Kleenex in her hand and brought it up again to dab at her red, swollen eyes. She wore a pink satin bathrobe with a white lace collar, and her brown hair was teased and sprayed. Her makeup had been fresh when Edgars arrived, but black mascara tracks now smudged her cheeks.

"Then you let your dog out at three 'cause she was whining, and she's been having trouble with her kidneys?"

"Bladder," said Pam.

"Bladder. And when you went to bring her back in, you noticed the back door to Miss Walton's house was open."

Pam nodded. "Our floodlight showed it open, plain as day. I went over there and rang the front doorbell, but no one answered. I noticed a light on in the hall and up in her bedroom." She reached for a pack of Virginia Slims and with shaking fingers took out a cigarette, but didn't light it. "So I went around back and called inside, but no one answered."

"So you got worried?"

"Concerned," Pam Grier said. "I went in through the back door and up the hall to the front. That's when I heard the dripping sound in the parlor." Pam pressed her lips together until they turned white.

"Don't you think you've got enough?" Dave snarled at Edgars. "You've been here since five."

The captain ignored Dave, which was a hard thing to do since Dave was Winston's district attorney. "That's when you saw the blood?"

Pam nodded and let loose with a sob.

Dave rolled his eyes. "Lord almighty, pull yourself together. I don't see why you went in there to begin with. Could have been somebody in there robbing the house or whatever. You should have come and got me."

"I didn't think about that at the time," Pam sniffed. "I was just concerned."

"I don't see why," Dave continued. "You never liked her."

"Why didn't you like her?" Edgars asked Pam.

"Aw, she was just one of those liberal, femi-Nazi, environmentalist types from Washington," Dave offered.

Edgars kept his gaze focused on Pam. "What time did you say you saw Sterling O'Connor leave last night?"

"About eight. Maybe eight-thirty," Pam said.

"And you didn't see anyone around the house after that?"

"No." She finally flicked her lighter and held the flame to the cigarette's tip. She took a long drag. Edgars found himself patting at his jacket pocket for his own smokes before he realized he'd left them in the car.

"Did she usually sleep with the light on?"

Pam shrugged. "I'm not sure."

"All right." Edgars heaved himself up. His back was starting to ache from sitting too long on the uncomfortable sofa. "I think that's all I need from you. Give me a call if you think of anything else."

"There is one thing, Captain," Pam said. "I think Miss Walton and that O'Connor boy were involved. They had a fight right out where everyone could hear them. Like a lovers' quarrel. He called her a bad name once, right there on the front yard."

"How long ago?"

Pam leaned forward, eyes intense. "Recently, Captain, within the last few weeks."

Edgars wrote that down in his notebook.

"There was definitely something funny going on over there," Dave interjected. "I saw Eric Teague there sometimes too. Don't know what he'd want with her, seeing as how he prefers boys. But I guess Sterling O'Connor was over there a lot, so maybe that's why."

Edgars tried not to roll his eyes. He would have to question Sterling O'Connor and Eric Teague. He knew Sterling's mother. That family had been through a hard enough time already.

"Thanks for the information. I'm sorry to have kept you up for so long."

Dave followed Edgars to the door. "It's that O'Connor boy for sure. I heard them fighting the other day myself."

"Yeah, well, you know how it goes. I gotta ask a bunch of questions 'fore I can arrest anyone."

"That kid never was any good. He ain't even his daddy's son, the way I've heard it."

Edgars turned the doorknob. Dave stopped him with a hand on his shoulder. "You okay with this, Jimmy? I know it's been a long time since you handled a murder."

"I'm fine," Edgars said. He wrenched open the door and stepped out into the rain.

7:00 A.M.

SITTING in the interrogation room, Captain Edgars studied Sterling's face. The kid was pale and seemed on the verge of tears. His eyes were fixed on the tabletop, and Edgars thought *Not much of a way to start the day, being dragged out of bed at five in the morning and told someone you know is dead.*

Still, there was something about Sterling that unsettled the captain. He tried to put a finger on it. Maybe it was just the way the kid looked. First, there was his hair: It stuck up from his head about an inch, shaved even closer on the sides. The roots were brown, the tips frosted a silver blond that gave them a sheen like an animal pelt. As if that weren't bad enough, he had pierced ears. Edgars was only now getting used to the notion of a boy piercing one ear, but Sterling had them both pierced, and not just in one place. Rows of small gold hoops lined the edges of his lobes like some bizarre sort of armor. *It doesn't help the boy out, looking like this,* Edgars thought.

Sterling cleared his throat and lifted his eyes to look at the captain. "So, are you sure she's dead? I mean, did you check, 'cause sometimes I've heard people can make mistakes."

"Yeah, we checked."

"But what I mean is, did you have a doctor check? Because you cops ain't doctors, you know."

Edgars didn't want to tell the boy that half of Lara Walton's skull had been shattered, that by the time they got there most of her blood covered the bedroom floor in a wide shallow pool, and she was blue-white, stiff and cold.

"The coroner's got her. He's a doctor."

"Because maybe if I could see her. . . ."

"She's not here any more, son. They took her to Atlanta to run some forensics tests on her body."

"But. . . ."

"Son, she's dead and you ain't gonna be able to see her." Patting at his pockets, Edgars brought out a pack of Camels. "You can smoke if you want to."

Sterling leaned back and crossed his arms over his chest. "I don't smoke, and I sure hope you ain't going to, 'cause it's just as bad second-hand."

The captain closed the pack and shoved it back in his pocket.

"How much longer is this gonna take?" Sterling's gaze strayed to the door.

"As long as it has to." Edgars paused. "Did you just work for her, or did you two have something else going on?"

"Work," Sterling said. "I mean, I liked her. We were friends, I guess."

"You all ever fight?"

The boy tugged at an earring. "Why are you asking me all this?" He eyed the door. "I gotta go. I gotta get to work."

Captain Edgars leaned back and ran his fingers over his scalp. Sterling bounced his knees up and down so the table shook.

"When you fought, did you ever get mad enough to hurt her?"

Sterling's knees stopped bouncing, and a forced blankness washed his face clean of expression. "We didn't fight."

"You sure about that?"

Sterling squirmed. "Yessir."

"That ain't what Pam Grier said."

Sterling's face twisted. "Yeah, well Pam Grier never once told a lie."

*   *   *

A N hour later, the captain left the interrogation room, closing the door behind him. Sterling hadn't given him much useful information. The only possible lead was a second-hand story about Dave Grier pointing a gun at Lara Walton. Although Sterling seemed convinced it was true, he hadn't seen it happen, and Edgars knew how rumors could spin out of control in this town.

Edgars turned left down the hall and opened the door to the video room. Reaching up, he pressed the stop button and ejected the tape. He'd have a transcript typed and get Sterling to sign it. In a few days, he'd call the boy back in, ask him the same questions, and see if his answers changed.

A movement in the interrogation room caught Edgars's attention. He watched through the two-way mirror as Sterling slumped in the chair, his head falling forward until it rested against the tabletop. The boy covered his head with his arms, and his body began to shake. *Whoa,* Edgars thought, *is he crying?*

The captain watched Sterling shudder and thought about the boy's mother, Sandy, and his little twin sisters. "What a goddamned mess," he muttered to himself. He knew he should go back in there, go ask Sterling O'Connor why he was crying, but his gut told him he wasn't getting anything else out of the kid this morning. He'd type up the report. That would take a little while. Then, if the kid didn't have anything else to say, Edgars would let him go. He'd call him back in a few days and question him again.

When he returned to the interrogation room with the statement for Sterling to sign, the boy was dry-eyed but dazed. He barely looked at Edgars and didn't speak. He scrawled his name on the statement, then said "Can I get out of here now?"

"Just one more question," Edgars said. "Have you got any idea why Lara Walton moved from Washington, D.C. to Barton County, Georgia?"

Sterling shrugged. "I can't remember if she told me."

Edgars gave an exasperated sigh. "Go on." He motioned toward

the door. "I may need to call you in again, so don't go anywhere far."
Sterling didn't seem to hear and when he stood up he swayed
unsteadily for a moment. "Did you understand what I said, Mr.
O'Connor? Don't be leaving town, now."

Sterling nodded, then whirled and staggered out the door.

Edgars returned to his office and sank into his desk chair with a
sigh. A pink telephone message slip placed on top of a mound of
paperwork said that Henry Jacobs from *The Barton Herald* had called
four times. Chloe Lohman, the receptionist, had scribbled a note
across the bottom in a tiny script, as if she'd been embarrassed to put
it on paper. "Wanted to know how long it's been since you investigated a murder."

Edgars cursed. Early that morning, before he'd started the inter-
views, he'd locked himself in his office and brought out his police
procedural manual to read up on murder investigations. He crumpled up the pink message slip and tossed it into the trashcan.

Most crimes in Winston were kept quiet and covered with
makeup during the day. They involved too much alcohol, poverty,
broken beer bottles, and screaming at three in the morning that the
neighbors pretended not to hear.

"Folks around here are gonna eat this up," Edgars muttered.
Already that morning four people had told him about the town's last
murder, fifty-two years ago. A mob had hanged a forty-year-old man
named Dean Willard from an oak tree outside the Baptist church.
They'd accused him of raping a ten-year-old girl. Dean was simple-
minded, and nobody saw the crime, but the town made up its own
mind without a trial. *Way this place is, I'm sure everybody's already figured out who did this murder too.*

Edgars reached for a manila envelope containing some of Lara
Walton's personal items, bagged in plastic at the scene: a stack of letters, a small booklet that looked like a diary. He took out the diary
and turned to the last page, which contained a long list in a thin neat
hand that began: 1. Chitterlings. 2. Pickled pig's feet. 3. Pickled eggs
(oily pink brine). 4. Fried pork rinds (barbecue flavor). 5. Potted

meat supreme. 6. Smoked hog jowls. . . . He leafed through the rest of the booklet. Other than the list of food, only the first few pages were written on.

"Well, Miss Lara Walton," he muttered. "What the hell were you doing writing grocery lists down here among us rednecks?" He settled back in his chair, turned to the first page, and began to read.

People said, "She's taking it so well." "She's so brave." "It's good she has her job to keep her occupied." "I wonder how she'll handle it. She's always lived such a sheltered life."

A sheltered life.

The voices came through a haze, as if I was looking up at the world from the bottom of a swimming pool with everything blurred by a veil of water. It took a long time, hours, for me to realize that all these murmured comments were about me. When I did realize, the plush room in the funeral parlor came into focus. I heard everything all at once, the drone of conversation, the hum of the lights overhead, the drum of rain on the roof.

I sat near Dylan's polished oak casket with the brass trim. It was closed. Already sealed. At the hospital, when I'd asked to see his body, Dylan's father had put a hand on my arm to stop me and said "No, Lara, you don't want to do that. You don't want to remember him like that."

The Ford Excursion that hit his tiny Miata had been going 85 miles an hour.

Dylan had loved the Miata. He'd loved its gleaming chrome exhaust, the acceleration that pressed you back against the seat. He loved going fast. It was easier to get to his office on the Metro. But he always wanted to drive.

*   *   *

October, 20, 2000

The night he died, I ordered take-out Chinese from the Golden Dragon down the block, and the small paper containers with their metal handles sat on the dining room table, tantalizing me with the smell of Kung Pao vegetables and fried rice. I lay in the living room on our new sofa and eyed the little white boxes with the red Chinese lettering. The vegetables were turning cold, the sauce clotting. I was angry. The least he could have done was call.

Then the phone rang.

My legs were wooden. They carried me to the Metro at a slow, lurching pace. What line did I need? Dylan's parents. I'd forgotten to call them. Would the hospital call them? Why would Dylan never take the damned Metro? And where the hell was the train? I had to hurry. "Critical," the hospital had said. "He's in critical condition."

As I waited for the train, scenes of Dylan played out in my mind, the first time I saw him standing by the blackboard in the American University biology class. Disheveled suit. Curly hair. Flashing dark eyes. The morning we walked along the Tidal Basin with the cherry trees blooming, Dylan holding my hand and whistling "American Pie." The day we'd bought the condo in Alexandria. We'd signed our names side by side on the same line. How long ago had that been? Three months? I'd teased him afterwards. "Does this mean we get married next?"

"Marriage is an unnecessary religious institution meant to enslave the couple in traditional stereotyped roles." But he'd grinned and winked and I ached from being in love with him.

It was a week before Mother threw away the Chinese food. I felt as if keeping it on the table might make everything a bad dream, might mean Dylan was coming home for dinner soon. As she threw it away, I thought, "I'll never be able to eat Chinese food again."

"It's starting to smell, honey," Mother said as she dumped the white boxes unceremoniously into the trash can. "And, sweetheart, don't be offended, but you're starting to smell too."

For days after the funeral, I couldn't work up the energy to bathe. I lay on our sofa and thought of all the things Dylan and I were going to do. Stories I wanted to tell him.

"Take some time off and we'll go to the mountains," Dylan had said the morning before he died. "I'll pick you up."

"But I have to finish this report."

"Workaholic."

"It's the Outer Banks report, the one on the impact of oil drilling."

"So what?"

"So it's important to me. I need to finish it. Alexei wants it Monday."

"So finish it Sunday. Come on, Lara."

But I'd said no.

When I returned to work two weeks after the funeral, I heard the whispered comments. "She's being so strong. She's handling it so well." I was getting tired of people telling me how strong I was, how well I was handling it.

What they didn't know was that instead of sleeping at night, I took Dylan's clothes out of the closet one by one. I ironed them until they were stiff and creaseless. Then I packed them. A box for his white Oxford shirts, one for his blue shirts, one for his print shirts, one for his jeans, one for his khakis. I laid his shoes in neat rows, wrapped them in tissue paper and set them in a box in the storage closet. I labeled all the boxes with a black magic marker and stacked them alphabetically.

I worked twelve hours a day. Then fourteen. Then sixteen. It was after I began sleeping on the sofa in the lounge that Alexei called me into his office.

His pale fingers were folded, his high-cheekboned face grim. I thought that Russians looked very noble when they were grim. Alexei had been a child in Russia during World War II. He was about sixty-five now. His father and older brother were killed during the German siege of Stalingrad. Dylan had introduced Alexei and me.

"Darling," Alexei now said in his rolling accent. I braced myself for the moment he told me how strong I was, how brave. "You look like hell. Have you looked at yourself lately?"

I shook my head.

He waved his hand toward the door. "Go look at yourself. Then come back here and we'll talk."

I went to the ladies' room. The fluorescent lights popped and hummed overhead as I raised my eyes and examined my own reflection. I looked like an actress playing an elderly me, me at fifty, not thirty, eyes sunken, cheekbones too prominent, a crease across my forehead that I'd never noticed. There was a vacant look in my eyes, like there was no one actually living inside me. A sheltered life, *the woman at the funeral home had said.* "She's lived a sheltered life. How will she manage?"

I became frightened. Am I not managing?

I returned to Alexei's office. He motioned to a chair, but I didn't sit. "I think I have to leave," I said.

He frowned. "Are you not feeling well?"

"No, leave," I said. "I mean Washington."

He rested his elbows on his desk and steepled his fingers. "Okay," he said.

"I mean for a while."

He nodded. "You can always come back. Your job will be here. Take the time you need."

"I'm sorry."

"Don't be sorry. You're starting to look like me. That isn't good."

I smiled.

"I miss him too," Alexei said. "But it's been six months. You need to move on. It's time. Dylan would want that."

I managed to turn off part of myself and not think about how Dylan and I had found the condo. How within a week of our moving in, I'd unpacked our boxes and had everything in its place, the clothes hung by color in the closet, the silverware arranged by size and shape in the kitchen drawers. How we cuddled on the sofa and looked out the window at our new view and talked about all the things we'd do to fix the place up.

It took only five weeks to sell.

My parents helped me pack and load my boxes, some still full of

*Dylan's clothing that I couldn't bring myself to give away. I piled every-
thing into a U-Haul that I attached to the run-down Toyota I'd driven in
high school. I hadn't needed a car since high school. I'd always taken the
Metro, and when I didn't, Dylan drove me in the Miata.*

*Early afternoon on June first, I climbed into my Cressida with the U-
Haul trailer behind it. I hit the highway intending to go to my parents'
house in McLean, Virginia.*

*Instead, five hours later I found myself racing south on back roads,
passing peanut farms and tobacco fields, hazy green pastures, pine trees
draped with kudzu. I stopped in a small town on the Virginia–North
Carolina border to call Mother.*

"Where have you been?" Her voice was strained.

"I'm sorry. I just can't come home right now. I'm driving around."

"I've been worried to death."

"I'm sorry. I should have called earlier. I just need to drive."

A long silence from the other end of the line. "Drive then, but call me."

*Now I sit at the rest stop where I made the phone call, and I write down
all of these things. I'm not sure what has made me leave home, my friends,
my family. Maybe it's because of what the woman in the funeral home
said about my living a sheltered life. Perhaps it's just the fact that I can't
bear seeing the places and people that remind me of Dylan. But whatever
the reason, I feel as if I'm beginning over again.*

T HE diary ended there.

"Damn," Captain Edgars muttered. He set the little book on his
desk, then picked up the phone and called Bill Hanks at the crime
scene. "Go through everything," he said. "She started a diary. See if
you can find more of it." After he hung up, Edgars pressed the heels
of his hands against his eyes. *She was grieving, going a little wild. So
what happened when she got here, and why did she decide to stay?*

❧ *chapter four* ❧

June 1

AFTER she'd said goodbye to her mother, hung up the pay phone, and finished writing her first journal entry, Lara had climbed into her car and headed farther south. Every mile, the air got hotter and thicker. Someplace in North Carolina, she passed a brick house with a giant plywood birthday cake sitting by the mailbox. A sign propped in front read HAPPY BIRTHDAY JESUS.

She drove south until she broke down in Barton County, Georgia, early the next morning as the sun was beginning to rise. Actually, her front axle broke down first. *She* broke down two hours later sitting in a torn green vinyl chair in a garage waiting room that smelled of motor oil and tire rubber. When she shifted, the damp vinyl stuck to the underside of her bare legs, then tore off. She began to shake. She looked at the lime-green cinderblock walls, which suddenly seemed very close. *What have I done? I want to go home.* A sheltered life.

Lara's throat tightened. Her eyes stung. She tried to watch a televangelist with unnaturally orange skin and a black toupee on the snowy TV screen. She tried to keep the hysterical voice in her head at bay, but it crept in anyway over the televangelist's emphatic "and the Lawd Jeeesus. . . ."

You're thirty years old. Ten years with him. Ten years and now nothing. You can't start all over again. It's too late. This is crazy. Go home.

But Lara knew she couldn't go home. It would seem too much like giving up.

Swallowing hard to keep from crying, she pushed herself out of the chair and left the garage. She stood on the corner looking down the deserted lanes of Highway 29. The road was girded by power lines and telephone wires, all those wires like spiderwebs flashing in the sunrise.

A sign in front of the ramshackle white building across the street read MEEMAW'S GOSPEL CHURCH. Lara gritted her teeth and crossed to Meemaw's, then turned west toward Main Street, passing a grimy McDonald's with dumpsters spilling plastic and glass into the parking lot. A rolled-up newspaper drifted across the highway like a tumbleweed.

The sides of the old brick buildings on Main Street carried faded remnants of painted Bull Durham and Coca-Cola ads. A few pickup trucks idled at the town's only stoplight. The drivers gaped at Lara as she walked by. One man in the cab of a blue pickup whistled.

"I hate it when guys do that," she'd told Dylan once. "Why do they think they have the right?"

"Patriarchal social prerogative. They think they're entitled to you. They don't understand that you're a goddess."

She'd laughed. "But you do?"

"I worship you, don't I?"

At the thought of Dylan, her throat tightened. But Lara refused to cry. The stoplight changed and the trucks drove on. Lara continued down the empty sidewalk.

On either side of the street, the town rose, dusty and faded: a ghost town. The storefront windows that weren't boarded up gaped dark and empty. Many had FOR RENT slashed across them in angry red letters. The few businesses that were left seemed pathetic, a store selling NASCAR paraphernalia, a tiny gift shop with anemic plastic flowers in dusty blue imitation porcelain vases. Lara paused to stare at the vases. She lifted a hand and touched the cool glass pane. Her fingers left prints.

Ahead of her, the chalky colors of the tiny downtown gave way to rich inviting greens. Lara crossed the street and wandered past tidy brick houses. The air smelled of mowed grass. Looming trees arched above the sidewalks and cast dappled shadows across well-tended lawns. In the humid air, the grass shimmered with dew.

A striped orange cat sat by the curb ahead, cleaning its face. As she approached it, she leaned over, reached out a hand, and clucked. The cat studied her with golden eyes, then walked away, pausing to look over its shoulder. Lara followed it around the corner and watched as it scampered off over a swatch of yellow grass. She studied the weedy, dead lawn in front of her and thought of how out of place it was. She straightened and shielded her eyes to look at the house that went with the lawn.

Her breath caught in her throat. Well off the road, partly hidden by ancient oaks, rose the ruins of a giant Victorian. Surrounded by neat brick homes, it looked like a skeletal beast that might devour its smaller, healthier neighbors.

Lara found herself drawn forward down a cracked concrete walkway. A sign pierced the yellowed lawn. FOR SALE, OPEN FOR INSPECTION. She passed the oaks, and the house's full facade came into view. The drooping roof over the front porch made the old Victorian seem as if it were trying to manage a sad half-smile, putting on a brave face despite its scaling paint and missing roof tiles.

Lara climbed the stone steps to a porch covered with tattered artificial turf. The ancient glass in the front windows was bubbled and distorted. Lara pressed her forehead against one of the panes, cupping her hands beside her eyes. She could make out a large, high-ceilinged room with four windows. Inside that room, sunshine ignited dust motes into a shimmering golden haze. Lara wanted to open the windows so the earthy summer air could flow into the old house. The house needed her to open its windows so it could breathe again.

"Poor baby," she murmured, her fingers running across the glass.

"Have you been left alone to get all dusty and fall apart? What do you look like inside? You might be pretty on the inside." She cast a glance over her shoulder, then tested the front door handle.

T HERE was a sort of grim freedom in owning something that was hers alone. The house was nothing like the condo. It contained nothing to tweak the raw nerves of her memory. The day she'd moved in, she'd walked around the empty rooms murmuring out loud to the faded walls, "I'll take care of you. Don't worry. Everything will be all right."

It had been an easy house to buy. It had taken a week to get the certified check for the full purchase amount from her trust fund, and ten days longer for the realtor, Betsy Bates, to push through termite inspections, paperwork, and homeowner's insurance. Betsy, a businesslike young woman in a neat blue suit, had been as tenacious as a bulldog, and Lara got the sense that she wanted to complete the deal before Lara could change her mind.

June 21

"W HAT now?"
Lara sat in her living room surrounded by unpacked boxes. All of them were neatly labeled. DYLAN'S SOCKS. DYLAN'S SHORTS. DYLAN'S T-SHIRTS. She couldn't stand to think about unpacking those boxes, but she had to do something. After all, she had just asked Dylan's ghost a question.

She saw an envelope on the floor and grabbed it. She dug out a pen and began to write.

"I've been watching a boy at the Dairy Queen. He has bleached blond hair, almost white, and earrings. He is handsome in an innocent way. Today he noticed me watching. Today he talked to me and I talked to him, and now I'm thinking about asking him to help me around the house with stuff I should really do myself. He flirts with me. I like it, and I'm ashamed that I like it. What would Dylan think?"

Lara remembered the first time she'd seen Sterling. The run-down Dairy Queen had faded plastic tables, and that night they were occupied by one or two faded-looking people, one or two teenage girls. The kids at the registers weren't even pretending to work. They slouched against the counter with heavy-lidded eyes, like they hadn't slept in days. Occasionally they spoke to each other in slow drawling accents.

Then Lara saw Sterling. He'd stepped from the kitchen, laughing out loud at something someone had said. Everyone looked at him. He was like a bolt of electricity.

He went over to a girl propped behind her cash register, elbowed her in the ribs as if trying to wake her up, and said, "Come on, Jaylee. I got a contest going to see who can make the most words out of *Dairy Queen*. You know, you can make *daiquiri* out of *Dairy Queen*—well, almost. I guess you'd need more *i*'s."

The girl flushed. She blinked at him as if not sure what to say, but he'd already moved on to a blender, which he turned on and off in rhythm to create a dance beat.

As Lara watched him, she realized she was smiling. *Smiling.* She thought of water balloon fights, skinnydipping, pouring chocolate syrup directly into her mouth from a squeeze bottle. She remembered life.

LARA turned the envelope over and looked around the living room. "This house owns me now," she wrote. "The basement is filled with water and smells like mildew. The attic is musty and full of cobwebs. The whole house needs fixing. So what's wrong with having the Dairy Queen boy come over? The house needs a little life."

For nearly two weeks now, the quiet had weighed on her. She'd been doing online research and e-mailing the information back to her former boss, but she'd had no one to talk to. The last person Lara had spoken with, other than Sterling, was her next-door neighbor Pam.

The previous afternoon Pam had come by. It was the day after

Lara moved in; the pounding on the door had startled her. She looked up from her computer and wondered who it could be.

The front door was huge and had a long window set into the wood, so Lara could see the woman on the porch squinting in. She looked to be in her forties, snub-nosed, round-faced, a going-to-fat ex-beauty queen. Her brunette hair rose bouffanted over just-a-shade-too-dark foundation. She wore a pressed flowered dress with a starched lace collar, the kind of dress a girl might wear to church, and it gave her the appearance of an older woman trying to seem young. Lara opened the door.

"Hi." The woman bustled past Lara and into the hallway. "I don't mean to bother you or anything. I just thought since we're neighbors I'd come and introduce myself. I'm Pam Grier."

Lara thought of the movie star and suppressed a smile.

Pam peered at Lara with dark glittering eyes. "I don't need to sit. It's okay. Hey, this house looks all right on the inside. Well, maybe it needs a little work. Dave and I, that's my husband, Dave, he's the district attorney, our house is the brick ranch. Dave and I were thinking it'd be in pretty bad shape, but it doesn't look too bad at all. Just wants a little TLC, right? And I know you're not from around here. Well, you picked a good place to live. This is a nice neighborhood. I've lived here all my life, and if you ever need to know anything, just come and ask me 'cause I know everyone. I work at the First Union. It's the biggest bank in town. Do you have kids?"

It took Lara a moment to sift through Pam's words and realize that she'd asked a question. "Oh, no. I'm not married."

I'm living with a ghost.

"Not married? Well, I was hoping you might have kids. See, I love kids, but Dave hates them. He'll be glad you don't have any. He's a recovering alcoholic. He doesn't drink any more, though, except for those non-alcoholic beers, but really I think he drinks enough of those to get drunk. I mean, I'm buying four or five six-packs a week. I'm glad you're not Indian. We've had all these

Indians move into town and they live with two or three whole families in one house."

Lara watched the woman's mouth open and close and wondered what to say. Pam seemed so absurd, like some caricature of a Southern belle. Pam glanced at her watch and said "Oh, darling, I'm going to be late for work. It was so nice meeting you. I know we'll be best friends."

But Pam hadn't returned.

July 1

THE potholes in the Ingles' Grocery lot were interrupted by small stretches of pavement so that Lara's car bounced and shivered to a stop in a parking space marked by barely visible white lines.

Sunday night. The grocery store had become her only source of entertainment other than Sterling. Lara had invented a game: find the most disgusting food at Ingles, not to buy, but to note down in her journal. Last night it had been pickled pigs feet, two nights before, chitterlings.

Lara stepped out of her car into the wet air and was overcome for a moment by the heat rising off the pavement. The moisture in the atmosphere shimmered as the sun set, pale orange, behind a deserted storefront across the parking lot. Under her feet, the asphalt was gummy as if it were melting slowly day after day in the scorching sun. Georgia. What had possessed her? Lara picked her way around small damp mounds of chewing tobacco to Ingles's glass door.

Inside, the air conditioning blasted her into goosebumps. She retrieved a cart with a broken wheel that rattled and veered to the left as she pushed it across the dingy linoleum. She felt better with the cart in front of her, a type of protection from this foreign world.

Lara wandered the aisles, spotting canned ham and olive loaf. On a whim, when she got to the snack aisle, she began to toss Cheetos and potato chips into her cart. She grabbed Eskimo Pies and choco-late ice cream. Comfort food.

When she spotted the pickled eggs swimming in pink brine, Lara knew she had her food of the day and, taking a small notebook out of her purse, she carefully printed "Pickled eggs" underneath the previous chitterlings entry.

At the checkout, a girl with chipped red fingernail polish dragged the bags of Cheetos listlessly across the scanner. The bag boy said "Paper or plastic?"

"Plastic's okay." He had blond hair cropped close to his head, and blue eyes deep-set over high cheekbones. For a moment Lara thought of the photos she had seen of Hitler Youth.

"You want me to carry this out for you?" he asked.

"No, thanks. It's just one bag. I can manage." She marveled at this tendency here, how women weren't supposed to lift their own groceries.

"Hey, you ain't from around here, are you?" the kid asked.

"No, I just moved here from Washington, D.C." Lara waited for him to say something more. Just talking to a stranger was good, but the kid turned back to the register. She took her bag and headed out into the sultry twilight. She didn't want to go home yet. She thought about Dairy Queen.

In her mind, she pictured Dylan arching an eyebrow. "You're flirt-ing with him."

"So what?" she said to Dylan in her mind. "If you'd driven slower, I wouldn't be in this mess. I wouldn't be alone in this bizarre little town with only that Dairy Queen boy to talk to." She paused. A pang in her stomach. "I'm sorry. I didn't mean it about the driv-ing. It wasn't your fault."

She remembered how Dylan's father, Ken, had held her back when she asked to see Dylan's body at the hospital. "No, no, Lara honey, you don't want to do that."

He'd just come from intensive care where, Lara imagined, they were wrapping Dylan in a black plastic bag. Dylan's body. The one she had spent so many nights sleeping against. The one she reveled in touching. The least they could do was let her touch him again, but Ken gripped her arm. "No, you don't want to see him like that. Stay here with us."

See him like what?

At the funeral home amid the pile carpet and ornate, yet appropriately somber, furniture, she'd heard one woman whisper to another, "They said you could barely recognize Dylan. That his face was gone."

An acid surge in Lara's stomach had sent her racing to the ladies room where she threw up in the toilet. Then she stayed, sitting on the plush stool in front of the vanity mirror, resting her elbows on the counter beside a crystal bowl of potpourri, trying to recognize her own reflection.

LARA didn't go to Dairy Queen. Back in the huge empty house, she put the ice cream in the freezer, then sat in the living room surrounded by her boxes. She stared at her computer, which rose gleaming from the desk. It seemed so out of place.

Lara felt disconnected and unreal, like some character in a movie. She could see herself from a distance, sitting on a pile of boxes late into the lingering summer evening. Behind the shrieks and laughter from children riding their bikes on the street outside, she heard the murmurs of the faded house, exhausted creaks, the faint scuttlings of an animal in the walls, rasping groans as the wood expanded and contracted in the heat, like some old creature barely breathing.

Night came on slowly. The hot sun hung on the horizon even after the sky darkened. Lara climbed the squeaking stairs in the stillness of dusk, paused on the landing halfway up, and turned for the final flight. Straight ahead was the room she had chosen to sleep in. It had French doors leading to a balcony just big enough for her to set a chair on. She went out and sat in the chair, watching the sun's persistent light and the fireflies, watching blue TV shimmers from houses across the street. She drank cheap red wine out of the bottle with her bare feet propped on the narrow railing. As daylight faded, the evening was filled with the chirping of crickets and cicadas. The honeysuckled air hung damp and heavy around her. She imagined that Dylan stood behind her. That he set his hand on her shoulder.

"Isn't it beautiful?" she said to Dylan's ghost.

❦ chapter five ❧

July 3

STERLING knocked on the front door of the old Bishop house on Church Street. All day at Dairy Queen he'd pictured the moment when Lara would open the door and he'd step inside. In his mind, he came up with different things that might happen, but it always ended up with them having sex, sometimes in the bedroom, sometimes on the floor, once on the kitchen table.

When Lara had phoned him at work earlier that day and asked him to come by, she'd sounded nervous. *That has to be a good sign,* he told himself. He hoped she'd look at him with that expression on her face, the one she'd had at Dairy Queen, like she hadn't eaten in a while and was sizing him up for a meal.

From inside the house he heard a faint call. "Come in." Already things weren't turning out the way he wanted. In his daydreams she always answered the door. Sometimes she was naked when she answered it.

He opened the door and stepped into the hallway. He stood for a moment in the silent foyer, his eyes adjusting to the dim light as the door clicked shut behind him. The house smelled of mildew and dust. Dark water stains fingered down the foyer walls, and plaster scaled off the ceiling. Cobwebs rounded and softened the corners.

Off to the right, Lara and her computer desk rose like an island above a sea of unpacked boxes. "Hi." Her fingers were poised on her keyboard as she looked at him over her shoulder. "Come in. Don't trip."

Sterling wove his way through piles of boxes and stopped beside her chair. He was starting to feel irritated. In his daydreams she'd never been working. He waited for her to say or do something, but she seemed preoccupied with the glowing computer screen.

"Ain't it bad for you to stare at that thing in the dark?" he asked to get her attention.

"I don't know. I never thought about it."

"Whatcha doing?"

She turned so that he could see her profile, the ridge of her nose washed by blue computer light. "Research for work."

"What do you do?"

"I'm an environmental consultant."

He stood silently, not knowing what that meant but trying to think of something to say so he'd sound like he did.

Lara's gaze met his. He realized how clueless he looked.

"You've heard all the talk about economic growth, right?" she asked.

"Uh-huh."

"Washington always wants to see economic growth, but when they measure that growth they leave out its impact on the environment. So what I do for a number of environmental organizations is apply a scale I've helped invent that measures economic growth in conjunction with environmental impact."

Sterling shifted from one foot to another.

"Does that make sense?" she asked.

"Yeah, I ain't stupid, you know."

"No, I know," she said.

An uncomfortable silence. Lara dragged a finger across the keyboard. He stared at the curve of her neck thinking *what now?* He wondered if anything he did would be good enough to impress her and decided to give up trying. It'd be easier just to work, have her pay him, and use the money to get some other girl. But the part of him that got bored with easy things wouldn't give in. *Come on,* he told himself. *Be cool. She was the one watching you at Dairy Queen.*

Sterling reached out. His bare arm came so close to her bare arm that he could feel the heat from her skin. He ran a finger along the plastic rim of the keyboard. "So you can do all that stuff you said right from this computer?"

"Sure." Her voice wavered.

"I messed around on the computers at school some. Didn't have much time to get into it like some folks, though."

"Do you want to have a look?"

"Yeah?"

"Go ahead." She stood and when he slid into her chair, it was warm from the heat of her body. He smelled her baby powder scent.

"What do you want to look up?" she asked. "No naked women, if that's what you're thinking."

"Damn." He grinned. "How 'bout that Mars thing? Pathfinder."

"That's a good idea. I'd like to see that too." She bent her face close to his. "I'll show you how to do a search."

Sterling stared at her long fingers. For a second he thought about putting his hand on hers to see what she'd do, but as he reached out to try, he lost his nerve. Then the pictures of Pathfinder came onto the screen, and for a second he forgot about Lara.

"Man." He leaned forward and stared at Mars's red rocks and dusky sky. "I didn't get to see that much about it when they had it on TV."

"So you're interested in NASA?"

"Oh, yes, ma'am."

She straightened up and took a step away from him. "Don't call me ma'am."

"Why not?"

"It makes me feel old."

He swiveled around in the chair and examined her. She wore shorts and a spotted owl T-shirt. Her hair was pulled back, her pretty mouth pursed. Again Sterling thought she was beautiful, but he couldn't quite figure out why. Her legs weren't really long and thin, her breasts weren't big. But still she was nice-looking, with her gorgeous mouth, her smooth brown arms, her green eyes with long dark lashes. "How old are you, anyhow?" he asked.

She gaped at him and he winked. "Hey, you asked me at Dairy Queen, so I get to ask you."

She smiled. "How old do you think I am?"

"It doesn't matter how old I think you are. How old *are* you?"

"I'm thirty."

He leaned back and stretched his elbows behind his head. "Thirty, huh? Well, that ain't too old for me."

"It isn't? How old is too old for you?"

"Thirty-six."

"Why thirty-six?"

"'Cause that's how old my mama is."

She flinched like someone had poked her with a sharp stick. After an abrupt, military-style about-face, she fled into the kitchen. Sterling sprang up and pursued her as she strode to the refrigerator. He watched while she yanked open the door, bent over, and squinted inside with what he thought was forced interest. Propping his arm on the rim of the open refrigerator door, he studied Lara's face as she examined the iced tea pitcher. He'd been perfecting this technique, where, if he looked at girls in a certain way for long enough, they fell apart and got all flustered and pink-cheeked. So he gave Lara that same lingering up and down look to see what would happen.

"What?" She remained frozen in front of the open refrigerator. "Do you want something to drink?"

He didn't answer.

"Well, I'm thirsty." She grabbed the iced tea pitcher and pushed the refrigerator door closed from underneath his arm.

"Guess I'd best be getting to work." He slouched against the counter as she brought down a glass from the cupboard. "That's what you got me here for, right? To work?"

She poured the tea, refusing to look him in the eye. "The kitchen needs painting," she said coldly and nodded toward two gallon paint cans, and a brush.

"I'll paint the kitchen then."

T HE decision to call Sterling— if it could be considered a decision since it was more an act of desperation—had come to Lara that morning. While sitting at her computer, thinking of the uneventful day that stretched ahead of her and of the silent evening to follow, her hand had reached automatically for the phone book. Within thirty seconds, she'd been dialing Dairy Queen. No conscious thought had been involved. It had been an act of instinct, of self-preservation.

"I sure hope you ain't scared of spiders," Sterling was saying. "I just saw a big one crawl behind the stove."

While he painted, he'd kept up an almost constant stream of chatter. How boring Winston was, and wasn't it funny how old houses all smelled kind of the same, and had Lara lost her mind moving from Washington, D.C. to Podunk Holler?

"Hell, now I'm freaked out." Sterling looked over his shoulder.

"About the spider?"

"Yeah. I mean, it was real big." His shirt was off and he balanced on her stepladder. He eyed the stove for a moment more, then turned back to the wall and stretched taut to reach a high spot with the paintbrush. The way he moved held her attention, the fact that she could see the muscles in his arms flex and relax. His body seemed new and perfect, alive, proportioned by artists, untested in the real world.

"You're ogling him," Dylan said in her mind.

"Shut up," she responded.

A few months after Dylan's death, Lara's body had begun to respond to the absence of what she'd taken for granted for ten years. She caught herself looking at men in the street, men who looked like Dylan with dark curly hair. Thin, slight men who looked uncomfortable in business suits, who seemed disheveled despite dress shirts and ties. She told herself that looking at these men was okay because they looked like Dylan Montgomery.

In weaker moments, she imagined Dylan's pale chest with the curly dark hair in the middle, felt the smoothness of the flesh at his hip-bone, the curve of his back as he arched against her, tasted the saltiness of his mouth, smelled his damp skin.

Sterling began to whistle, and the sound cut through Lara's memory. She stood and walked into the kitchen. "So it went behind the stove?"

"Yeah." He pointed with the paintbrush.

Lara slipped off her shoe.

"You're gonna kill it?"

"Yes," she said. "Otherwise I'll spend all night thinking it's crawling on me." She approached the stove, leaned around and peeked behind it. The spider hung on the baseboard. It was big and sleek.

"You want me to do it?" Sterling asked.

"No." She peered at the spider and felt sorry for it. She set the shoe down.

"Can't get it?"

"I'm going to try to catch it and put it outside." She reached one hand over and behind the spider. She cupped her other hand in front of it. The spider moved quickly, scuttling into her back hand, its legs tickling her skin. She closed her front hand over the back one and sprang up.

"Open the back door for me?"

Sterling leaped off the ladder and ran to the door. He held it open for her, flinching as she passed. On the back stoop she opened her hands and the spider crawled off of her fingers.

Sterling continued to hold the door. His mouth hung open.

"That wasn't so bad," she said as she walked by.

He gave her a look like she was crazy. "I coulda done it for you." He followed her into the kitchen and stood wiping sweat from his face with his arm, looking toward the back door as if he expected the spider to return. "I mean, I ain't *that* scared of spiders."

I've threatened his manhood, she thought, and suppressed a smile. "The wall looks good," she said. "You've got paint on you."

"Yeah, I know." He scratched at a paint speck on his wrist then grabbed his shirt where it lay on a kitchen chair and pulled it on.

"Could I get you to do something else for me?" she said. "Actually, I feel kind of bad for asking, but my basement is full of water."

He slit his eyes at her for a moment, then pulled his shoulders back. "I'll check it out for you."

"Let me get a flashlight."

The flooded basement was the worst of the eerie places in the house. On a practical level, it made Lara worry about leaking pipes and the foundation eroding. But she also lay awake some nights and pictured dark shapes lurking under the murky water. On bad nights, she imagined something sloshing up the steps to her bedroom, leaving a slug-like trail of slime or ooze behind it.

"You don't have to do this if you don't want." She opened the basement door. A waft of cool air rushed up from below as she flicked on the light. The bulb illuminated a rotting wooden staircase.

"Hell, it don't bother me none." Sterling took the flashlight from her, then stepped down to the first riser. The wood under his feet groaned.

"Careful. I don't know how sturdy those are."

The staircase wobbled. "That's okay. I know a good lawyer if I need to sue you." He winked.

She smiled at his bravado.

He eased down the stairs. At the place where the risers submerged, Sterling kept going. When he was on the floor, the water came to his knees. As he sloshed out of sight, Lara saw the flashlight beam play along the pipes overhead. He moved farther under the house and the beam grew faint.

"Hey, are you okay?" she called.

"Yeah!" His voice echoed off the earthen walls. "I think I found the problem. Part of your foundation's gone. Looks like there's been rain coming in here for a long time."

He climbed up the stairs. "Let's go outside and look at it."

He led her through the back yard where, falling to his knees, he shone the flashlight along the foundation until Lara saw the gaping hole.

"You need to get this fixed," he said. "Anything could get in here. Someone could crawl in one night and walk right up those stairs into the house. It ain't safe."

STERLING walked the two miles home from Lara's house in wet tennis shoes and jeans soaked up to his knees. He fingered the twenty-dollar bill she'd given him, which was now crumpled in his front pocket. She'd asked him to come back tomorrow. Maybe tomorrow he'd have the nerve to do more than paint and wade around in her basement.

As he turned onto Hog Mountain Road, he thought about how she'd stood at the door after she'd given him the money. Behind her, the house seemed black and empty. She'd had a strange look on her face, like she was worrying about the hole in the foundation and didn't want to be alone. For a second, he thought she'd ask him to stay.

Sterling looked up at the moon. It was full tonight. As he walked, he forced the damp air in and out of his lungs and thought *Three jobs in one day, no wonder I'm worn out.* He tried not to think about how much easier it would be if his daddy hadn't gone. It had been four years since he'd disappeared, and Sterling wondered where he was. On the road, probably, listening to Garth Brooks, eating super-sized McDonald's French fries out of a carton pressed between his knees. "Thanks, good ol' Dad," Sterling muttered. "Thanks a helluva lot."

When he got home, he stood for a moment outside, looking at the light glowing through the window. He could hear one of his little sisters shrieking. He thought about how the family's truck needed new tires so badly it wasn't hardly stopping on wet pavement.

Up the two steps to the door. The pulpy wood sagged under his shoes. He'd have to find a piece of scrap wood and nail it on before one of his little sisters fell through.

"Hey." His mama turned around from the sink when he came in.

She looked him up and down, frowning at his damp legs. "Take off those shoes. I just mopped the floor."

Sterling slipped off the soggy tennis shoes as the twins rushed over, crowding around his legs like they always did when he got home.

"Ooh," Darlene wrinkled her nose. "You're all wet."

Dayla had a piece of paper in her hand and she pushed Darlene back and shook the paper under Sterling's nose. "Look what I drew!"

He sank onto the chair at the kitchen table, taking the paper while Dayla clambered onto his lap.

"What's that you got there?" he asked. Their drawings always looked crazy; they were six years old. This one was a twisted stick figure drawn with red crayon, a huge misshapen head, uneven limbs, and eyes so big they came off the corner of the face.

"It's a picture of you. See?"

"Aw, yeah, that's good."

"Mama's gonna hang it on the refrigerator, ain't you, Mama?"

"Go on in and watch TV and let your brother eat in peace."

His mother set biscuits, collards, and a dried-out hot dog from the Quickie Mart in front of Sterling. His stomach tightened. Every night his mama came home with leftover Quickie Mart hot dogs or burritos or chicken fingers. Every night she made homemade biscuits or cornbread. Every night he told her she should just buy a can of biscuits at the grocery store to save herself the work, but she never would. Biscuits and red hot dogs or biscuits and dried-out fries, or biscuits and pickled eggs.

"You want some milk?"

"Is it that powdered stuff?"

"Yeah."

"Naw, I'll just have water."

The twins hovered by his chair. "Go on." He kissed each one on the cheek. "Go on and watch TV. I'll come in there in a minute."

The twins clung to him for a second longer, then reluctantly let go and dragged themselves back to the living room, casting long sad glances back at him.

"It's late." His mother set a jelly jar glass of water down in front of him.

"Yeah. I painted her kitchen."

"You got paint on you."

"I know."

"That dish soap might take it off." She paused. "How much longer is she gonna need you?"

"Don't know." Sterling opened a biscuit with his fork and spooned the collards into it. "She pays good. I hope it's for a while, at least." The collard juice soaked through the biscuit and turned it a soggy pale green.

His mother came to stand beside him at the table. She lowered her voice. "Had to buy more of them inhalers for Darlene's asthma today."

"How much'd it cost?"

"One hundred fifty dollars."

Sterling felt even more tired. "I was hoping we could get some new tires on the truck. You know if one of us was to work less, we could maybe qualify for the Medicare."

His mother fell silent for a moment the way she always did when he brought up welfare or food stamps. "You want some honey?" she said. "Dale Dunbar at work give me some honey from his hives today."

"Yeah."

His mother went to the cabinet and brought the honey to the table, saying "If you ask me, I think it's strange her moving down here. If she's got all that money, why don't she go live in Atlanta?"

"Don't know," Sterling said. "She ain't said nothing about why she's here. She's okay, though." He opened another biscuit, poured honey inside, took a big bite. The sweetness slid down his throat. "Man, that's good."

"Dale said he had a hard time getting the comb out of it, but I ain't seen none in the bottle he give me."

He was glad for the honey. Maybe he'd make it through the meal all right. Sometimes he had to force himself to eat because he was tired of the same old thing every night. Mama made good biscuits and good cornbread, but you could only eat so much before they started wearing on you. Still, he had to eat. They both worked so hard to put it on the table, and to not eat Mama's food would hurt her feelings.

He watched her at the sink washing dishes, her thin back bowed, blond hair hanging down the collar of her blue work shirt. She was thirty-six years old and looked fifty—partly because of the smoking, which made her teeth yellow and her skin wrinkled, but mostly because of the last four years. Everything she did seemed tired, the way she moved, the way she didn't bother to put on makeup any more, the way she left the house sometimes without even brushing her hair.

Then there were the nights when Sterling got home and found her in the kitchen using a cigarette to burn holes in some old photograph of Daddy. On those nights, Sterling made his own dinner and stayed away from Mama.

§[*chapter six*]§

October 12

THREE people had already called Eric Teague that morning to tell him Lara was dead. At nine o'clock he took the phone off the hook and sat on his sofa in the sudden silence.

Eric remembered Lara perched on a windowsill in his house, sunlight blazing behind her so that she looked like a holy icon. Her thin white cotton skirt, dyed with small yellow stars, was bunched between her legs, and her bare feet, dusted with powder, rested on the back of an armchair. Strands of hair escaped her ponytail and clung in thin, dark filaments to her cheeks. Lara's arms were always bare and on that day, with their trim elegance, they reminded him of the arms of a marble Athena he'd once seen at a museum.

Lara as the goddess of wisdom or war. Lara in the summer sun.

"So, when are we swimming, Grover?"

She called him Grover, said he reminded her of the Sesame Street character because he was cute and fuzzy, and she wanted to squeeze his face, at which point she did, taking his head between her hands and shaking it gently.

"Can I take some pictures of you?" he asked.

"Pictures?"

"Yeah. You know, photographer, pictures?"

She shrugged. "Sure. I guess."

"Great. Don't move."

When he came back with the camera she was fidgeting. She looked at him with a forced smile.

"No. Just go back to doing what you were doing."

"What was that?"

"Being yourself."

She became bold in that way she sometimes had of changing moods without warning. Sitting up straight, she pulled her shoulders back and pouted at him like a model. Then the fleeting brazenness passed, and she covered her face with her hands, peeking out between her fingers. That's how she looked when he took the first picture.

A copy of that picture hung behind him now on his living room wall, but he couldn't see it from the sofa, and right now he couldn't stand seeing it anyway. Eric sat and listened to the clock tick in the kitchen.

It was after ten when Officer Mason came by, and Eric hadn't moved.

A t ten-thirty, Eric found himself in a dimly lit room at the police station, seated across from Captain Edgars, trying to remember how he had met Lara. The captain wanted to know.

He remembered the day at the store in early July, one guy in the corner, flipping listlessly through the used country–western CDs. Sterling had burst in breathless, dropping a Dairy Queen bag on the counter and sucking on a straw sticking out of a Dairy Queen cup.

"She's coming in here today," Sterling said.

"Ahh. Your mystery woman."

Sterling had been raving about Lara for almost two weeks, going on about her mouth and how gorgeous it was, and her beautiful brown hair and her pretty arms. Eric was intrigued, because these weren't the body parts Sterling usually noticed.

"Just promise you ain't gonna ruin it for me," Sterling said.

"Fine. You want to run around with older women, go right ahead. I'll be here for you when she tears your heart out and eats it for breakfast."

Sterling rolled his eyes.

"Why don't you go write down some order numbers for me while you're waiting on her?" Eric said.

"Okay, but holler when she gets here."

"How am I supposed to know who she is?"

Sterling grinned. "Man, you'll know all right." Grabbing his bag, he disappeared through the office door.

Eric stood behind the counter, looking around at his little store. The building was old and cheap. He'd bought it outright with some money he'd inherited from his grandfather. Buying the store had been a way to prove he was doing something with his life, earning a living instead of just hanging around taking pictures he never tried to sell.

In its former days, the store had been a pawnshop, and it still smelled faintly of cigarettes and gunpowder. He'd put new carpet over the dirty tile floor, painted the walls purple, and erected rows of racks for CDs, tapes, and old albums. It was the only music store in town. During the summer, kids would slouch in after lunch and go through each and every CD, occasionally pulling one out to read the cover as if they hadn't already read it a hundred times.

When the hanging bell jangled and Eric looked up from his account books, he knew that this was Sterling's woman. First off, he'd never seen her before, and he'd have remembered if he had, because she was clearly not from around here. In his run-down little store, she looked lovely and alien, as if she'd stepped in from some wide-open space like the painted desert. Her thick dark hair was wind-blown and tousled, her green eyes bright in her tanned face. She radiated health and brought with her the smell of baby powder and the moist scent of the lush summer afternoon. She wore a man's white T-shirt under baggy denim overalls, cut off into shorts. Eric found himself staring at her bare brown legs.

She paused and glanced at him, then looked around. Eric thought about calling Sterling; but instead, he watched her wander the aisles, running her fingers along the CDs, eyes grazing them with disinterest. Back and forth along the aisles, Eric's eyes moving back and forth with her.

Suddenly she stopped, seized one of the plastic cases and yanked it out. She read the back, mouth hanging open like she couldn't believe what she was seeing. Then, for the first time, she looked at Eric.

"I can't believe you have this."

Rushing forward, she smacked the CD onto the counter. It was The Clash. *London Calling*.

"Wow," Eric touched the plastic case. "Someone finally wants *London Calling*. I've been trying to sell it for five years."

"It's one of my favorites."

"I thought it was a classic," he said. "One of those monumental albums that everyone will always want."

"It is. It's monumental."

"Not here. In this town no one even knows who The Clash is." He picked up the CD and examined it. "I won't be ordering another copy of this, that's for sure." Then he handed it back to her and she clutched at it so that he smiled. "I'm glad I had this one for you, though."

"I'm Lara." She stuck out her hand and he took it. She had a firm grip, not like the limp warm touches of the local women.

"Eric."

A bump, a slam, and Sterling stumbled in from the back room. The boy's face was mottled red, even though he was trying to look at Lara with only the mildest interest.

"Look!" She shook *London Calling* at Sterling.

"Told you Eric had everything."

She turned her bright gaze back to Eric. "Are you from around here?"

"I'm from Athens," he said. "Twenty miles east."

"That's where the university is, right?"

"Yeah." The sudden attention made him self-conscious. He began searching for the CD's price sticker, even though he knew what it said. "Fourteen-ninety-nine."

"Hey." Poor Sterling nudged up against him, trying to get Lara's attention. "Let me see that."

She handed him the CD.

"Sterling tells me you bought the old Bishop place downtown. What's it like inside? Is it falling apart?"

Lara studied him for a moment. "You can come over and see it if you want. I mean, I don't mind. It's driving me a little crazy, actually. It's so quiet."

"Really? I wouldn't want to bother you."

"You couldn't bother me. I don't know anyone here. Come any time. Come tonight."

"Are you sure?"

"Yeah."

"Okay."

"Great. Hey, kiddo," she said. Sterling stood holding *London Calling,* looking abashed. "Let me have that back. I'm playing this the second I get home." She whirled and fixed Eric with the point of her finger. "Tonight."

"Eight-thirty. I close here at eight."

"Eight-thirty. See ya."

She whisked out the door as quickly as she'd whisked in, leaving Eric breathless. The scent of baby powder hung in the room.

Sterling scowled at him. "Thanks a lot, man," he snarled.

"Hey, kid, that's not some high-school girl. That's not one of those rutting-against-the-wall-behind-Wal-Mart girls that you're used to."

"I know that."

Eric found himself grinning into Sterling's face. "I mean, that woman'd hurt you. You're out of your league this time."

"What, you think I ain't good enough for her?" Sterling glared. "I guess you're plenty good enough, though. I'm gonna go finish them orders." He stomped into the office and slammed the door shut.

When Eric opened the door and peered inside, Sterling seemed fixated on the catalogues and wouldn't look at him.

"Listen, I didn't mean you're not good enough for her. I meant you're not old enough. You need to find yourself some sophisticated, smart girl your own age."

"Ain't no girls like that around here."

"Listen, I'm sorry," Eric said. "But it's been a hell of a lot longer since I've had a date than since you've had one."

"Whatever," Sterling growled. He leaned over the order forms and covered his ears with his hands.

July 5

E RIC went by the Bishop place at eight-thirty. Lara threw open the door as he pulled his car into the driveway. She watched him climb the porch stairs, then stepped back so he could come in.

"I've got beer," she said. "You drink beer, don't you?"

"Yeah."

"Good. I was thinking you might be a fundamentalist teetotaler as the words were leaving my mouth."

He laughed. "No need to worry about that."

She got him a Sam Adams, then led him around the house, showing him its grand hallways and parlors, its secret rooms and hidden cubbies. He remarked that it would be a good place for smugglers and asked what she was hiding.

When she was finished with the tour, she put on a Stan Getz CD and they sat on a pile of boxes in the living room and talked and got slowly drunk.

"Who's Dylan?" he asked, shifting on the box labeled DYLAN'S T-SHIRTS, trying to get comfortable.

"Oh." She winced as if the question caused her physical pain.

The music in the background emphasized the sudden silence. Eric decided to change the subject. "So, why are you here? In Winston, I mean. It seems like a strange place for you to be."

"Why?" She sat on her own unstable box, DYLAN'S SOCKS, which crumpled under her weight. "I don't know. Compulsion."

"Compulsion?"

"This is my elephant graveyard."

"What?"

"My elephant graveyard. You know how when elephants die, they have this compulsion to find hidden places covered with the bones of their ancestors. See, even though I'd never been south of Charlotte, I'm from Southern stock way back. The bones of my ancestors are all over Georgia."

"So you're planning to die here?" Eric lifted a skeptical eyebrow. "Somehow, I think you're going to get bored first and head back north."

"No, I think some sort of radioactive slime creature is going to ooze out of the basement and kill me while I sleep. Call it a premonition."

"God, you're an optimist, aren't you?"

"No." She picked at a corner of the cardboard box. "That's the last word I'd use to describe me." She grinned in a reluctant way.

He held his beer bottle out to hers. They clinked the bottles together, and finished drinking in long swallows.

"What about you?" she asked. "Why are you here?"

"Me?" Eric set his bottle on the worn wood floor. "It's a good place to take photographs, you know."

"You're a photographer?"

"Sort of."

"What about the CD store?"

"Oh, well, it's kind of a long story. I bought my house a few years ago and came into town one day to find a CD I wanted, and the only place to look was Wal-Mart. Not much of a selection there unless you like Garth Brooks. So I thought what the hell, I have a little money put away, I need to earn a living, this town needs real music. It just all came together."

Lara studied him. Then she held up her empty bottle. "You want another? It's the last two."

"Yeah, if you're having one."

She strode into the kitchen where the halogen bulb crackled as she switched it on. It made him realize how dark the rest of the house had become. "Why do you keep it so dark in here?" he asked when she returned.

"I don't know. I just kind of like it. Besides, I haven't unpacked my lamps yet."

"You should get Sterling to help you unpack. He wouldn't mind." Eric paused. "He's got a hell of a crush on you, you know."

"At his age, he probably has a hell of a crush on everyone." She handed Eric the beer. "I wish I were like that again. Wish I had that kind of energy."

He held the dewy bottle and watched her flop down onto her box. "Really? Not me. Every time I'm around him, I thank the Lord I'm not seventeen any more. I don't think I could handle every little thing being such a big deal like it is to him." He took a gulp of beer and studied Lara. "So, why are you really here?"

"What, you don't buy the elephant graveyard?"

He shook his head.

"Would you buy a broken heart?"

"Do you have one for sale?" He grinned at his own joke. Lara didn't grin back. Eric cleared his throat. "So, what's the broken heart about?"

She shrugged as if it didn't really matter. "A guy."

"Dylan?"

She bit her lower lip, then nodded.

"Did he walk out on you or something?"

"In a way. He died."

"Geez. . . ." He'd asked the question so glibly. "I'm sorry."

"Car accident," she said. "Nine months ago. It seems like—I don't know, like I'm not getting over it. I moved away to try to get over it." She stared at her beer bottle.

"Why move here, though?"

"I just drove until the car broke down at six in the morning in the middle of nowhere. The closest mechanic was here."

"So why stay?"

"I don't know. The house. I liked this house. Also, I guess—" she bit her lip, "I don't have anything to go back to."

He watched her throat jerk as she swallowed. She looked at the ceiling.

"You want a hug or something?" he asked.

She nodded and he set his beer down beside the box and crawled the few feet to her, letting her wrap her arms around his neck, overwhelmed by the smell of lilac-scented shampoo. He hugged her tight for almost a full minute.

"Thanks," she said when he sat back on his heels. "Sorry about you being an almost-stranger and everything."

"Sometimes almost-strangers are best, huh?"

She nodded and pressed her eyes with the back of her hand.

He returned to his box and looked around the shadowy living room, at the scuffed wooden floors and the dark gaping fireplace. "If you stay, you've got yourself a hell of a house. It was in the Bishop family for eighty years, you know. They were pretty social in their day. Had lots of parties here. At least, that's what I've heard." A faint glow from a street light down the block bathed the flaking walls. "Anyway, I can't wait to see what you do with the place."

"Yeah," she wiped her nose. "Well, I've got Sterling painting the kitchen now." She paused and frowned. "You know, he doesn't look like he belongs here—in this town, I mean. Give him some creepy black clothes and he could be doing performance art in a subway tunnel in New York City."

"Exactly!" Eric laughed. "That's exactly it, like some weird rhythmic poetry in a southern accent."

"In German, with a southern accent."

"Yeah, beating on a tambourine. I could really see that."

"Me too."

A car passed, its headlight beams tracing across the wall and onto the ceiling.

"It's getting late. Guess I'd better go," he said.

"You don't want another drink? I've got wine."

"No, I have to be up early."

"Are you all right to drive? I don't mind you waiting to sober up if you need to."

"I expect I'll sweat out most of the alcohol the second I'm outside."

She followed him to the door. "Sorry I broke down."

"Don't be. Hey, I appreciate the beer. I'll have you over to swim soon if you want. Or maybe you can come with me on Sunday when I take pictures. Maybe getting out of this house would do you some good."

"That'd be nice."

"We'll do it, then," said Eric. He experienced a moment of awkwardness. He wanted to hug her again but realized he didn't know her that well. Instead he lifted a hand. "Night," he said.

"Night."

As he walked to his car, he was keenly aware of her standing in the open doorway watching him.

October 12

"How'd you feel about her?" Captain Edgars thought Eric seemed dazed and upset.

"About Lara?" Eric shifted and fixed his eyes on the tabletop. "I liked Lara."

"She was a pretty nice person?"

"Yeah. Nice. Impulsive. It was kind of funny, she'd always go out of her way to keep you around. She'd always offer you one more drink."

"Why's that?"

"I don't know. It was such a big spooky house. Guess she didn't like being there by herself. She was lonely, you know. Sad. The guy she'd been with in Washington, they'd been together a long time, and she wasn't over him dying."

The captain straightened. "Dying?"

"A car accident. She was pretty torn up by it. That's why she came down here, to get away."

Edgars wrote the words *Death linked to boyfriend?* "Did she say anything about it? What did the guy do for a living?"

"He was a professor. American University, I think, or maybe Georgetown, I don't remember. Some kind of environmentalist, she said."

Edgars wrote down *Enemies?* "And you said it was a car accident? Are you sure?"

"That's what she told me. Said he had this sports car he liked to drive too fast."

The captain frowned. He watched Eric for a moment. "Were you all. . . ." the captain rolled his hand around in the air, searching for an inoffensive word.

"What? Involved?"

"Involved," Edgars echoed.

"No. Just friends."

"You ever fight with her?"

Eric smiled. "Oh yeah. Yeah, we fought all the time."

"About what?"

"Everything. We had different world philosophies."

"When's the last fight you had with her?"

"A few weeks, maybe a month ago. When I found out she was leaving."

"You were mad?"

"Not at first. I went over there to visit, and she was drinking too much, and—" Eric stopped and glanced at the captain.

"And?"

"And she was drunk. I got mad because every time she got upset she'd drink too much. I called her on it."

Edgars got the sense that Eric was covering up. "What was she upset about?"

Eric swallowed and returned his gaze to the tabletop. Edgars could tell he was struggling to keep his expression neutral. "Things just weren't going well for her down here. She was lonely, and she wasn't getting the house fixed up the way she'd planned. She was homesick."

"I thought she hired Sterling O'Connor to work on the house."

"That house needed more work than Sterling could handle. He could hardly tear up the floors or redo the wiring." Eric finally let his gaze stray from the table to the captain's face. "You know, that night we fought, that was the last time I saw her."

"How'd you leave her?"

"Aw, we worked it out. We said some ugly things to each other and then apologized."

Edgars leaned back and crossed his arms over his chest. "Nothing else I should know about?"

Eric shook his head while the captain studied his down-turned eyes. "Let me ask you this," Edgars said. "Do you know if she kept a diary?"

"Lara?"

Edgars nodded.

"I don't know. I mean, I remember seeing stuff that had been written on. But I don't know what any of it said."

Edgars slid an envelope out of the file that sat on the desk in front of him. "Will you look at this and tell me who you think she's talking about?"

Eric reached for the envelope. Bill Hanks had found it at the house and brought it over only an hour earlier. It was a short note. It said:

London Calling. Fate again? My favorite record in high school. He reminds me of normal things like brewing coffee in the morning and dozing in front of the television.

Eric gaped at the envelope. Edgars thought he slumped forward in the chair. "I think it's me." He pushed the envelope back across the table. "I think she's talking about me."

"Okay," Edgars said.

Eric leaned his forehead into his hands.

"Where were you last night?"

Eric looked up, startled. "Me?"

"Yeah. I have to ask."

"I was at home."

"Did anyone see you there?"

Eric gaped at Edgars. "No."

"Do you own a gun?"

"No."

"Ever shot a gun?"

"No."

"Ever seen Sterling O'Connor with a gun?"

"No."

"Ever been in Sterling's house?"

"Oh," Eric glanced away from the captain's face. "Yeah."

"A lot of times?"

"Once or twice."

"You ever seen a gun in his house?"

Eric shook his head. "No."

"Were Sterling and Lara Walton romantically involved?"

A long silence. Eric's eyes fixed on the table in front of him. "I don't know."

"If you had to guess. . . ."

"Don't think I could."

Edgars waited a moment before going on. "One more thing," He cleared his throat and shifted in his chair. "I need to know about Sterling O'Connor, about your relationship with him."

Eric winced.

"It's just that there's been rumors."

Eric sighed. He pressed the heels of his hands to his eyes. "Goddamned kid has no father. I've been trying to help him out, and look where it gets me."

"It'd be confidential, anything you told me," Edgars said.

"There's nothing to tell that I didn't just say. Those rumors aren't true. My girlfriend, Julie Knox, is in Italy."

Edgars nodded. "Okay. Just had to ask."

AFTER he left the police station, Eric debated whether or not to open the store. Finally, he went home. He moved around his house on bare feet, making coffee, feeling hollow and confused. For a moment, he couldn't remember where the coffee filters were.

He figured Sterling must know about Lara because his mother worked at the Quickie Mart, and all the cops went in there for coffee first thing in the morning. That made the decision for Eric. He'd open up in case Sterling came in.

Sterling came at noon, dragging in from outside, his rain-filmed hair glistening and spiked. He and Eric stared at each other. "Hey," Eric said.

"Hey."

"You heard?"

Sterling nodded and wandered over to stand behind the counter, beside Eric.

Eric lifted a hand, intending to place it on the boy's shoulder, but changed his mind and let it drop again. "You okay?"

Sterling didn't answer.

"The police talked to me this morning," Eric continued. He thought about Lara, about the things he'd said and done in the last week, and a sickening wave of guilt hit him.

"They ask about me?" Sterling said.

"Yeah."

"What'd you tell them?"

"What could I tell them? Nothing."

"I was with her last night. Pam Grier saw me leave."

"I know."

"So ain't you gonna ask me if I did it?"

Eric shook his head. "No."

"'Cause the police sure think I did it. Got me out of bed at four in the morning and took me to the station and asked me questions like I did it. They took a piece of my hair and ran this Q-Tip inside my mouth, and they scraped under my nails like they were gonna find something there. And they sprayed my hands with this stuff."

"Gunpowder residue. DNA. They did the same thing to me. If you didn't do it, then they won't find any evidence."

Sterling raked his fingers through his hair, brushing off beads of water that fell to the counter top. He wiped at the drops with his jacket sleeve, then took a deep breath. "I guess I better get to work, huh?"

"No. It's okay."

Sterling continued wiping the counter top, smearing the water around with his wet jacket sleeve. "Hell, the whole neighborhood probably saw her throwing stuff at me."

"You don't know that. Who knows, maybe she was being robbed, or maybe—" He stopped, and Sterling cringed. "She should have thought to lock the door, or thought . . . people don't kill people for no reason around here."

"Lara didn't think about anything," Sterling said. "She just did stuff." He pulled off his jacket, hung it on the peg by the door, and walked into the office.

"You've grown up a lot in the last few months, you know," Eric said as he followed him.

"Well, I sure as hell feel old, if that's what you mean."

"No, what you just said about Lara, about her not thinking, you're right."

Sterling slumped into the desk chair and stared straight ahead. "I went over to her place after the cops finished with me. It's like I thought she was still alive or something. I thought she'd be there and I'd tell her how mixed up everybody is for thinking she's dead. I thought she'd get a kick out of it."

"Hey," Eric said. "You don't have to stay. Go home. I'll pay you anyway."

"I don't want to go home," Sterling said. "I been home all morning thinking about her. Can't do that no more. Come on, man, give me some work. Something."

Eric perched on the edge of the desk, trying to get his thoughts together. "See, the thing is, I can't even think of what to tell you to do. I know there's all this stuff that needs doing, but I can't think of what." He picked up a stack of papers and shuffled through them. Outside, the rain fell heavier and louder, roaring through the gutters. "Guess we won't have many folks coming in today. What with the rain and all."

Sterling leaned forward, the chair squeaking. "What I wonder is where they're gonna bury her. I mean, will they send her back up north? Will her folks come down here? I'd like to see her again. They said I couldn't see her."

"I don't know," Eric shook his head, his throat tightening. "I can't imagine Lara buried. Cremated, maybe. It's like she wouldn't be able to take being buried."

"Yeah, she'd fight it," Sterling said. "Her ghost'd have to get out and walk around."

chapter seven

July 6

P AM Grier turned into her driveway as Lara was pulling her mail out of the mailbox.

"Hey." Pam waved.

"Hi." Lara flicked through a stack of credit card offers.

"I've seen that O'Connor boy around your place."

"I hired him to do some painting for me."

"Yeah, he's a real worker. My husband's sister taught him in school, you know."

"No, I didn't know."

"You don't listen to all those things about him, now."

Lara glanced up from the mail to see Pam's look of exaggerated innocence. "What things?"

"Oh," Pam placed a hand over her mouth as if she had accidentally let something slip. She walked closer to Lara, saying "You don't know?"

"Know what?"

"All that stuff about him not being his daddy's son. You see, his daddy's got red hair, and his mama's got blonde hair, and Sterling, well, he's got that dark brown hair, only you can't tell it any more from how he frosts it blond like that, which is pretty peculiar if you ask me. Now, if it were an older man going gray, I could see him maybe dyeing it back to its natural color, but to frost it like that, like a woman does, it's odd if you ask me."

She paused for a breath, but so quickly that Lara, stunned by the sudden deluge of words, didn't have time to interject something about hearing her phone ringing.

"Anyway, Sterling doesn't look like either Parker or Sandy, that's his daddy and mama, but he kind of looks like a boy Sandy knew way back before she got married. And that's why his daddy left them. But what I'm saying is, don't listen to that kind of gossip." Pam leaned closer, and Lara noticed her black eye disguised under a slathering of skin-toned base. "From everything I know, he's a good boy except for the skateboarding, but I guess that doesn't really hurt anyone, does it?"

Lara frowned. "Are you all right?"

"What?" Pam stopped in midbreath.

"Your eye. Is it okay?"

"Oh." A sudden, uncomfortable silence. Pam lifted a hand and gingerly touched the flesh near her eye. "I had a cash drawer spring back open on me at the bank."

"Does it hurt?"

"Not much any more. It looks worse than it feels."

"Well, if you need anything. . . . Are you sure it was a drawer?"

"What?" Pam backed away. "Of course I'm sure."

"Because, I mean if you need to talk or anything, or if you ever need help. . . ."

"I have to go let Daisy out," Pam muttered. Then she turned and ran up her porch steps and into her house.

"Do you remember the Arlington Metro Station?" Dylan asked Lara in her mind. "Do you remember that spot where you'd stand so you could be first on the train?"

Lara could picture the spot, three yards to the left of the escalator, just to the right of a stone bench. Every weekday she had stood in this spot at seven-thirty-eight A.M.

"Remember how, if someone else was standing there, you'd move so close to them they had to step aside?"

Lara wondered why Dylan was bothering her with this memory. How could the subway platform be relevant to anything?

"That spot put me on the train car whose door opened at the foot of the Smithsonian escalator," she told Dylan. "When I was first onto the train, I could be first off, and first up the escalator."

"I remember," he said. "You always loved being first up the escalator."

"Why does any of that matter?" she asked.

"You tell me," he said.

He was just jealous, Lara thought, jealous and trying to distract her because Sterling was on the stepladder again painting her kitchen. Just before Dylan interrupted, Lara had been debating which part of Sterling's body was the most sexually compelling. She'd spent minutes contemplating the strip of flesh below his navel and above the waist of his jeans, a flat, hard-looking line of skin striped with dark hair below his "outie" belly button. Lara determined that this bit of flesh was the most astonishing, perfect sexual thing she'd ever seen.

Earlier, Sterling had told her about how one of the kids at Dairy Queen heard chocolate was good on acne and smeared hot fudge all over his face one evening when he was cleaning up and how his face looked even worse the next day. Now he whistled tunelessly as he dabbed at the wall.

"You're ogling again," Dylan said.

Lara turned her eyes from Sterling and stared at her hands.

Finally, she stood and wandered among her boxes until she found the one she wanted. She knelt, tore open its flaps, and rummaged inside until she came out with a photo album. Curling her legs underneath her, she sat on the living room floor and leafed through pictures of Dylan, stroked his flat cool image with the tip of her finger.

"It's not like I'd ever touch Sterling," she said to Dylan.

She imagined that Dylan shook his head and said "You're falling apart."

chapter eight

October 12

CAPTAIN Edgars sat at his desk with his head in his hands. The investigation was starting badly, not that he'd expected any different. After he'd finished with Eric, he'd spent the rest of the day talking to Lara's neighbors. Most of them were decent folks who wanted to help, but all they could report about Lara Walton were rumors and snippets of their brief conversations with her. As a group, they'd looked upon her as an outsider, a curiosity.

Many of her neighbors had seen Sterling O'Connor at Lara's. A few thought he spent the night there sometimes. "So you're sure he stayed all night?" the captain asked Jared Nichols, who lived across the street. "You saw him leave in the morning?"

"Didn't see him leave at all. He could have left, but it would have been after midnight. I go to bed around then." Jared laughed. "From what I've heard, Sterling O'Connor's been through every girl in the high school. Guess he had to conquer some new territory."

A number of people Edgars talked to would stare at their feet as if ashamed, and say "Now, I did hear the Walton woman was trying to turn Sterling O'Connor into a communist."

Edgars understood that even though folks knew how ridiculous the story sounded, everybody hoped it was true. It would be just a little bit of excitement in the quiet town. It was a rumor that had Pam Grier written all over it: Lara Walton as an evil communist Yankee who seduced young boys to lure them into a life of socialist thinking.

Pam had a God-given ability to take small details of everyday life and lace them with traces of seediness and intrigue so that even decent folks found themselves drawn in. Even though the Berlin wall had been down for years and communism wasn't much of a going concern any more, Edgars knew there would be a small kernel of truth in Pam's story. The question was where.

From what the neighbors said, Lara hadn't made much of an effort to fit in. Edgars could tell by the edge in some people's voices that she'd offended them.

"I went over there to meet her and was worried because she didn't have any furniture. I said I didn't know how she was managing without furniture and offered her some chairs, but she didn't want them," Diane Fowler said.

Bernice Montague across the street offered the captain lemonade, then said "I invited Miss Walton to one of my Mary Kay parties to meet some people from the neighborhood. But she was rude about Mary Kay. She said she didn't wear makeup."

"I invited her to the social at Main Street Baptist," Edie Myers said. "Miss Walton said she didn't care to come, and that she preferred not to discuss religion with strangers."

"Sometimes she walked outside first thing in the morning wearing only her nightshirt." Jared Nichols ignored his wife's glare.

After a frustrating afternoon, Edgars decided to talk to Ellen McEachern. Ellen lived down the block from Lara Walton. She was observant and practical, and Edgars knew she would be honest with him. Ellen had just retired from the town's biweekly paper, *The Barton Herald*. Twenty years earlier, through sheer force of personality, Ellen had talked the editors into letting her write real news rather than the social column.

As they sat at her kitchen table, sipping iced tea, Ellen seemed to read the captain's thoughts, and her mouth formed into a grim line. "I didn't know Miss Walton," she said. "I'm sorry now that I didn't introduce myself. If even half of the gossip I heard about her was true, she was a girl I would have liked."

The captain smiled.

"There are a lot of rumors about Sterling O'Connor and Miss Walton. I was hoping you might be able to help me with them."

Ellen rolled her eyes. "I heard them myself, but I'll tell you right now, I didn't see anything to confirm them. He was over there a lot, yes. Late at night sometimes. But he was working for her. I saw him out mowing her yard. I saw him fixing the screen door. The poor boy has two other jobs. When was he *supposed* to work for her?"

Edgars ran his hand across his head. "How do you think the rumors got started, then?"

"Pam Grier," Ellen stated matter-of-factly.

"Pam Grier." Edgars sighed.

"There was a rumor that she gave Pam feminist literature to read," Ellen continued. "And I heard something about her converting Sterling to communism." Ellen snorted. "Ridiculous."

Edgars set his arms on the table and leaned forward. "I want to ask you a question, and I'd appreciate it if you wouldn't tell anybody I asked it."

Ellen studied him for a moment, then nodded.

"I'm asking you because I think you have a good eye for what's going on in this town." Edgars paused and took a breath. "What do you think went on at Lara Walton's house? What kind of a person do you think she was?"

Ellen frowned and took a sip of her tea. When she set her glass down she looked directly at Edgars. "I don't know why she came down here, but she never was a part of this neighborhood. She never tried to be. I think she spent a lot of time alone. And Sterling . . . honestly, I think he liked being over there instead of at home. We all know what's going on with Sandy. I think Miss Walton paid him well. I think that's all there was to it."

Edgars sighed and nodded. "I'm still hoping that it wasn't anybody in town. Maybe she brought the trouble with her."

*   *   *

Back in his car, Edgars lit a cigarette. The bullets that killed Lara Walton had been fired from a .38 caliber pistol. Edgars thought Sterling's father had owned guns. He'd seen Parker with a deer in the bed of his pickup truck; but whether Parker had owned a pistol, he didn't know. The coroner had put the time of death at around two in the morning, about the time Pam Grier thought she'd heard gunshots. If Sterling was to be believed, he'd been at home asleep at that time.

Could Eric Teague have a gun the captain didn't know about? Neither Eric nor Sterling had tested positive for gunpowder residue. But the killer could have worn gloves.

Edgars knew he'd have to call Sandy O'Connor in. He dreaded it. The poor woman had been through enough.

Sandy O'Connor was one of those people Edgars couldn't remember meeting. When he first moved from Atlanta eight years ago, he'd begun stopping by the Quickie Mart for early morning coffee and donuts, and Sandy was there. He didn't remember introducing himself or being introduced to her. He just got to know her over dozens of mornings of handing her crumpled bills and asking if the coffee was fresh.

Sandy was what happened in small southern towns when men deserted their women. Four years ago, right before Parker abandoned her, Sandy was pretty and quick to laugh. She had natural blond hair, long, parted down the middle and feathered back on the sides, an out-of-style look, but on her it was becoming. She liked to wear pink, and always said "Howdy, neighbor" when Edgars walked in.

The O'Connors weren't rich even when Parker was around, but they were middle-class with a small neat house in town and a swing set outside for the kids. After Parker left, his family had to move to a tiny rental house, not much more than a shack, on the outskirts of town. Sandy aged years in a month. The skin around her lips creased and withered like a dried apple. She stopped feathering her hair, so it hung in limp strings around her face. She had always smoked, but went up to two packs a day. Her teeth yellowed, her fingertips became stained, and her skin took on a dry, leathery look.

After Parker left, Sterling started getting into the Barton County equivalent of trouble. He hung out in the Wal-Mart parking lot with a wild group of high-school boys and girls. He drank poorly concealed bottles of Black Label by the loading docks. He got into fistfights at school. Edgars had seen the boy often enough, a bright-eyed, good-looking kid with an easy laugh like his Mama. Sterling's dark hair had been the talk of the town since the boy was about five. Parker's hair had been red, and some people said that Sterling was starting to look a lot like a guy Sandy used to date right before she got married. A few cops at the station talked about Sandy not being able to handle a spirited boy like that, how the kid needed a man's hand, and how a Sunday at church wouldn't hurt the family either. The talk made Edgars mad. "That boy's not getting into real trouble. His daddy disappeared and he's acting out. Go to Atlanta if you want to see real trouble."

As he prepared to question Sandy, Edgars pictured Sterling's face when he'd walked out of the interrogation room a few hours earlier. The boy looked like *he* was the one that had been shot.

"Sorry to have to bring you in from work, Sandy." Edgars stepped aside so Sandy O'Connor could enter the interrogation room. "I'll make it quick."

"I don't have time for this, you know." She sat down, reached in her bag for a Newport and pressed it between her pale lips. Then she took the cigarette out of her mouth and held it toward the captain. "They don't pay me for the hours I'm gone. Do you have a light?"

Edgars dug the lighter out of his pocket and held the flame to her cigarette. Her hand shook so hard that he had to grip her wrist to steady it. According to Officer Mason, Sandy had been swinging between anxiety and rage since he had picked her up at the Quickie Mart. Now she looked like a wreck.

Edgars waited while she inhaled deeply. She held the smoke in her lungs for a long time before letting it curl out of her nose.

"Just relax," Edgars tried to sound soothing. "I only need to make sure Sterling came home last night at around nine."

Sandy inhaled again, then nodded. She was wearing a stained pink sweatshirt with a smiling, large-eyed raccoon on the front. The contrast between the happy raccoon and Sandy's haggard face was striking. "Yes. Around nine."

"And he didn't leave after that?"

"No."

"If he'd left after you were asleep, would you have heard him?"

"Of course," she snapped. "Besides, I've never known him not to sleep real hard all night. Even when he tries to stay up, he always falls asleep. He's a teenager, you know." She took another long drag off her cigarette.

"Okay, that's what I needed to know."

Sandy began to push herself up from the chair.

"Oh, and just one more thing. Did you ever meet Lara Walton?"

"No, sir, I never did."

Edgars sighed and leaned back. "That's too bad, because I'm having some trouble here. You know how people talk, and sometimes it's hard to tell what's real from what isn't? See, I've heard a couple of things about Miss Walton, and I was thinking maybe Sterling told you some stuff. Do you know if she was a communist?"

Sandy flinched as if she couldn't bear to hear the word *communist* associated with her son. "All I know is she gave Sterling a book about communism."

"Did you mind that she gave him this book?"

"Well, yessir, I did. He's a good boy, and I don't want him turning away from what's right."

"Did you ever talk to Miss Walton about it?"

"No."

Edgars got the picture. Sandy had just talked to everyone else in town. He drummed his fingers on the table and waited for her to take a few more puffs on the cigarette. "Were they involved?" he asked.

"What?"

"Sterling and Lara Walton. Were they lovers?"

She flushed. "No."

"You know for sure? Or he didn't tell you?"

"He didn't act like it. Don't know why he'd want to run around with an older woman. He ain't never had trouble getting girlfriends."

Edgars reached into his file and pulled out a sheet of paper. He already knew what it said, but he paused and took some time studying it for effect. "Now, I got something here that says Parker had two guns registered in his name, a rifle and a pistol. Is that correct?"

Sandy's face went gray. "Yes, sir. He had two guns."

"Are those guns at your place, or did Parker take them?"

"Parker took them."

Edgars nodded. "Okay." He placed his hands behind his head and stretched his elbows wide. His back was aching and he wondered why they couldn't get more comfortable chairs. "We ain't charging him with nothing, Sandy, but make sure he stays around in case we need to ask him anything else."

Sandy covered her mouth with her hand. "Thank the Lord."

He understood what she was thinking. The family couldn't survive without Sterling. "I guess that's all I got for you."

"Thank you." She stood. "Sterling, he behaved good for you this morning? He told you what you needed to know?"

"Oh, yes, ma'am. He done good."

She turned toward the door.

"Oh, and Sandy, save one of them hot donuts for me?"

She laughed. "You gotta get in there before everyone else if you want one hot. You know I can't save 'em."

*   *   *

"Captain, coroner's report just came in."

Edgars glanced up from the expanding mound of paperwork on his desk to see John Sims, one of the Sheriff's deputies, standing in the doorway. Holding out his hand toward John, he snapped his fingers. "Well, don't just stand there. Let's see it."

John took a step closer, and Edgars snatched the file and flipped it open. Gunpowder residue on Lara Walton's body indicated she'd been shot at close range. Her stomach contents. Spaghetti with tomato sauce, eggplant. Red wine. Blood alcohol .09. Maybe a little more than tipsy. He traced down the line of information with an index finger, then stopped. No sign of struggle, no foreign tissue or hair under the fingernails. Coroner concludes she was killed by the first gunshot wound to the back of the head. Entry wound indicated a right-handed killer standing above her.

As tired as he was, the information swam in Edgars's mind. Nothing. The coroner's report gave him nothing new to go on. Edgars became aware that Sims was watching him. "Is there something else?" he growled.

"Just thought you might want to hear the latest from the house."

Edgars cringed. He'd forgotten to ask. "Did they find a point of entry?"

"No, the front door was locked from the inside. The killer must have gone out the back door, but he probably didn't get in that way. But there's a big hole in the foundation. Somebody could have slipped through it. The basement is flooded. They found water on the stairway and on the floor in her bedroom."

Edgars tried to sound confident. "See if you can collect a sample of water from the bedroom to compare with one from the basement. What about prints?"

"They found three different sets, hers and Sterling O'Connor's. The third are probably Eric Teague's. We're checking on that now," Sims said.

"Tell Bill to look down in the basement again. Maybe we'll find a piece of clothing or a footprint or something. And tell him to hurry before this rain they're forecasting washes the evidence away."

"You got it."

After Deputy Sims ducked out the door, Edgars closed it. He rested his head in his hands. "Basement," he mused. "Maybe it wasn't someone you knew after all, Miss Lara. Else why wouldn't you open the door for them?"

July 7

E RIC opened the shop door and stepped inside. From across the counter he met Sterling's cold glare.

"So what'd you do last night?" Sterling picked viciously at a loose edge on the vinyl countertop.

"Why's that any of your business?" Eric hadn't been able to put a quick end to his hangover with aspirin, and his temples throbbed with each beat of his pulse.

"'Cause you stole her from me, is why."

"I could only steal her from you if you were dating, which you aren't."

"Yeah, but maybe I was getting somewhere with her."

"Listen, do you know why she came down here?" Eric asked. "You never bothered to find out, did you? Her boyfriend just died. She's grieving. So let me give you the benefit of an older, wiser, more experienced perspective. Women like that need space. They're vulnerable. They're dangerous." Eric opened the cash register and brought out a roll of antacids that he kept in the penny slot.

"So what about you?" Sterling demanded. "It don't seem like you're scared of her."

"That's because I'm not going to date her." He tore open the antacid roll and pried out a chalky white tablet with his thumb.

"That ain't what you said yesterday."

"I changed my mind."

Sterling grinned. "Good, that means she's available."

"You don't listen to a damned thing I say, do you?"

Sterling's grin faded. "Her boyfriend died, huh?"

"Yeah," Eric said.

"So is she, like, okay?"

Eric shrugged. "I don't know."

T wo days later, as Eric pulled into Lara's driveway, he recalled his conversation with Sterling. For a moment, Eric entertained the idea that he was just following his own advice. After all, Lara needed company. He was only hanging out with her. It wasn't a date.

Eric studied his reflection in the rearview mirror, his freshly trimmed beard. His short light-brown hair, combed before he left home. Then he noticed his too-big eyes and his Adam's apple, which seemed obtrusive and jerked in an alarming way when he swallowed.

Lara's door flew open. Eric smoothed a hand over his beard.

She rushed out of the house, her dark hair flying, her legs stretching to leap down the porch steps. In an instant she pulled open the passenger door.

"Hi." She leaped in beside him, breathless. "Air conditioning!" She held her palms to the vent. "I almost forgot what cool air feels like. So where are we going?"

"I'm going to show you a couple of places that I think sum up Barton County," he said. "Since you're officially a resident now."

What Eric didn't confess was that the places they were going felt haunted and sacred to him. They embodied the quiet decay of small rural towns in the South and the decline of their people. Eric was trying to capture the slow death of Barton County on film because Atlanta and Athens would soon swallow it up, change it into a bedroom community with chain video shops and grocery stores, and huge new houses built on old pastureland.

Eric didn't tell Lara any of this. These thoughts, the passion he had for the sad old town, these things were personal, and right now Eric was just trying to keep her entertained.

"Why'd you tell me to wear bug spray and long sleeves?" she asked.

"Poison ivy. Mosquitoes. Some of the places I'm taking you are kind of overgrown." Eric cast a sidelong glance at her as he backed out of the driveway. He wondered how much she'd seen of Barton County or places like it. The bitter medicinal smell of bug repellent hung in the air around her. The too-long cuffs of her huge white shirt covered her hands, and he thought she looked like a child playing in grown-up clothing.

They drove through downtown, passing First Baptist on the corner of Main and Elm, its parking lot a checkerboard of rusted pickup trucks and '70s model sedans. As they pulled to a stop at the City Hall traffic light, Eric saw Mike Owens in a damp white dress shirt, standing in the gazebo that marked the center of town.

"There's a colorful local for you," he said.

"What's he doing?"

"Can't you tell?" Eric got a brief glimpse of Mike's red, dripping face and heard him yell "The great day of vengeance has come, and who will be able to stand?"

"Wow, a Bible thumper." Lara frowned. "That's dedication. I mean, if *I* thought the world was coming to an end, I wouldn't be spending my weekends broiling outside in heat like this just to save the unconverted."

"What would you be doing?" Eric asked.

"Something involving nudity and chocolate ice cream."

Eric tried to squelch a sudden very sexy image. His eyes lingered on Lara's heart-shaped mouth, which seemed permanently puckered to kiss. Finally, he forced himself to focus on the traffic light as it changed from yellow to red to green with no cars coming or going. A sultry breeze blew from the direction of the concrete block factory, dusting the town with a chalky film that frosted the shop windows white.

"So, what do you take pictures of?" she asked.

"Oh, lots of things. The South. Right now I'm working on a collection of photos of front-porch furniture. See, there's one I shot last week." As they drove by a row of dilapidated one-story houses, he pointed out a sagging orange sofa hunched beside the door. Its matted upholstery was stained dark. "That one's got personality, don't you think?"

Lara's head swiveled as they passed. "I guess you don't have a shortage of subjects here."

"No, I admit that's never been a problem."

"Have you had any photos published?"

"No," he said. "Guess I've never really tried to do anything like that."

"You should. I bet your pictures are good. Maybe you could take them to Atlanta."

"Shooting them is the part I like," he said. "I've never really tried to sell any. Too much work."

CALLIE Hill's place sat in a shady hollow amid a garden of junk. The house under the rusting tin roof was painted an eye-stinging lime green. There were many houses in town that had junk in the front yard, but Miss Callie's place went well beyond the usual collection of sofas, tires, and discarded lawn furniture. The old woman never threw *anything* away. Hills of junk clumped around the house like prehistoric burial mounds. On that overgrown lawn, Eric could feel the presence of lives lived, of tragedies, joys, and the endless minutiae of everyday work and survival.

As he pulled into the driveway, he gazed up at two giant oaks bordering the scene on either side. Draped with heavy curtains of kudzu, they framed the house, the yard, the junk. "This place always reminds me of some organic theater," he said to Lara.

She looked around as if the scenery was new and wonderful. "It's lush, there's no doubt about that."

He stopped the car in the pot-holed dirt drive and sat for a moment, looking. It *was* lush, the forest reclaiming the land, the house gradually decaying into fertile soil. As Eric opened the door, a rush of damp air swept into the car. He eyed Miss Callie's door. A dark form shifted behind the screen.

"Stay in the car," he whispered to Lara. "And don't make any sudden moves."

"What? Why?"

He didn't answer. Instead he focused on the shadow behind the door and climbed slowly from the car. Then he took a few steps forward.

The door creaked open and Callie Hill, who was seventy-two, fat, and insane, stepped onto the porch and pointed a shotgun at Eric's belly. She didn't have her teeth in, so her face, wrinkled like a brown walnut, collapsed inward at her mouth. Every few seconds, her gray tongue darted out and licked her lips.

"Hey, Miss Callie." Eric moved toward her, placing his feet carefully first on the dirt walk, then on the porch steps. "It's Eric Teague. I talked to you last week, remember?" He eased his hand into his pocket, "I brought you something." He offered her a tiny snow globe on his flattened palm as one might offer a sugar cube to a mean horse.

Miss Callie lumbered closer, eyes fixed on the globe. She was dressed in layers, a tattered skirt, an old housecoat, a pale yellow parka, all the faded colors swimming together as she moved. She reached out a thick arm and her fat fingers closed around the snow globe. The shotgun lowered until the barrel hung down at her side.

She accepted the offering, then glanced at the car. "She look like Miss Stacey Wendell what got caught under that bus in Atlanta and had her scalp pulled off." Miss Callie thrust her chin toward Lara, then turned, pulled open her screen door and disappeared inside.

Eric let out his breath. The hard part was over. Now he could take pictures of Miss Callie's junk.

Spindly rusting lawn chairs crouched in the long grass like giant spiders. The yard was a maze of decaying newspaper stacks and old frying pans, headless dolls and glass soda bottles; but Eric didn't see the piles as junk. He saw them instead as geometric forms, each with a unique shape and hue. He motioned to Lara; and while she climbed out of the car, he set up his tripod and began studying his shots.

"Is it safe to come out now?"

He squinted into the lens. "Once you give Miss Callie a present, she won't bother you."

Lara leaned against the hood of the car and crossed her arms over her chest. "Do you come here a lot?"

"All the time."

"And she doesn't remember you?"

"No, I think she does."

"How do you know?"

"She ain't shot me yet." He grinned, then turned back to the scene through the lens. While she watched, his shutter clicked quietly.

Eric became conscious of his body, the way he turned his head to the side, the minute movements of his fingers as he adjusted the focus. He pictured what he must look like to Lara, crouching, squinting, contorting his neck. It made each gesture seem important, with her watching.

When he was through, Eric felt breathless and dazed. He looked at Lara perched on the hood of his car. For an instant he saw her not as a person but as line and color, her blue-jean–clad legs crooked against the bug-spattered fender, the curve of her neck as she tilted her head sideways and peered at him. He took her picture.

In the car, Eric grappled the stick shift into reverse and backed out of Miss Callie's driveway.

"You said you were taking pictures of the real Barton County?" Lara asked.

"That's right."

"Tell me how she fits in."

"Miss Callie?" Eric wondered what to say. Could he explain how Miss Callie's place made him feel? Did he want to try?

Eric was keenly aware of how much time he spent alone, think-ing his thoughts to himself. Moving to Barton County had distanced him from his friends in Athens, and he was lonely sometimes. Seeing Lara staring at him expectantly, her lower lip pinched between her teeth, Eric realized the absurdity of holding himself back. Talking about things that were important to him didn't mean they were dating.

"I don't know if I can explain how she fits in. I take pictures based on emotion rather than logic. It's not intellectual, not something I can put into words. She reminds me of the South that's disappearing, you know, the way she keeps her old stuff hoarded around her, how she's scared and suspicious of anything new. Maybe her house used to be nice. Maybe she used to be sane. It reminds me of people in small towns around here and how they're going to seed."

"Going to seed. . . ." Lara muttered. "Maybe that's why I'm here. I'm preparing to go to seed." Her head fell back against the headrest and she seemed perplexed. "Hey, can I ask you something?" she said. "You know my next door neighbor, Pam?"

He nodded.

"Well, I saw her at the mailbox the other day, and she had a black eye. Does her husband beat her?"

It was common knowledge that Dave beat Pam, but Eric didn't want to spread gossip. He muttered, "Probably."

"Has anyone tried to prosecute him?"

"Dave's the DA. He'd hardly prosecute himself. Besides, Pam has never filed a complaint against him."

"That's kind of a cop-out, isn't it?"

"It's just the way things are."

Lara rolled her eyes and muttered, "I guess that's to be expected in the South."

Eric bristled. "Ugly things happen in Washington, D.C. too, you know. Only here you don't have a buffer of politically correct Yankee elitist college-educated intellectuals to shelter you from reality."

Lara gaped at him. "At least us politically correct elitist intellectuals are willing to get involved. We're willing to try and change things." She bit her lip and fell silent.

What Eric found ironic was the probability that at that very moment Pam was spreading malicious gossip about Lara all over town.

"Getting involved around here isn't like in Washington," Eric said. "Except for a few local churches, there aren't any organizations to help. Folks here are pretty much on their own. I've seen a few people pull themselves up and make something of their lives, but it isn't easy, and if people don't want to change, there's nothing you or I or anyone else can do to make them." He glanced at Lara, at her pouting mouth, her body almost engulfed by the huge white shirt, and he thought *she's lived a sheltered life.*

Feeling suddenly protective, he smiled and patted her clenched fist where it rested on her leg. "Damn, it's nice to re-draw the Civil War battle lines. Or should I call it the War of Northern Aggression?"

She smiled. Her fist relaxed and her hand opened.

"Well, I'm going to do something," she said. "I feel like I need to do something. I can't just see her with a black eye and do nothing."

Eric shrugged. "Good luck."

They drove in silence for a minute.

"Do you ever take pictures of people?" she asked.

"Sometimes. Not much."

"How can you show the South without pictures of people?"

"Because I think in this part of the South, people are invisible. They're poor, their way of life is disappearing. Heck, if folks here stand still long enough, the kudzu'll get 'em. But wait, I'll take a picture of you."

She stuck out her tongue as he reached for his camera and snapped the photo with one hand.

"Let's get something cold to drink. Want to?" he asked.

"Yes, I'm about to melt. I don't think I've stopped sweating since I got here."

"Well, it becomes you."

"You lie."

"A word of advice: check for ticks when you get home."

"Great." Lara's fingers strayed to her scalp.

Underneath the quips and the forced gaiety, Eric could sense the sadness in her. As they drove, he cast covert looks as she sat twisting a strand of her hair, eyes fixed on the view out the side window.

"So, do you want to talk about him?" Eric tried to sound casual as he maneuvered the car down the road.

"Who?"

"That guy in Washington. You know, Mr. Broken Heart."

"He's not Mr. Broken Heart, *I'm* Ms. Broken Heart. He's Mr. Drive Like an Insane Idiot in His Stupid Car."

"Ahhh, I stand corrected." He guessed it made sense for her to be angry. "What did he do for a living?"

"He was an assistant professor at American University. Toyed with the notion of being a communist for a while, but that didn't pay as well as a tenure track position."

"Where'd you meet him?"

"College. He taught a course I was in."

"No shit? A lot older than you?"

"Nine years. He'd just finished his Ph.D. in marine biology."

"Marine biology?"

"Mollusks. That was his specialty. He used mollusks as a way to measure levels of toxins being dumped into rivers and oceans. Fascinating, huh?"

Eric tried to picture Lara with a dreary, bespectacled science geek. "So what did you see in him?"

Lara grinned. "Oh, he scared my parents. He was kind of dark and dangerous."

"A mollusk man, dark and dangerous?" The science geek in his imagination suddenly wore black and had gaunt, sunken cheeks.

"It was the communism thing, that and he actually *was* an environmental terrorist in college. He spiked trees."

A sunken-cheeked science geek in hiking boots, wearing black hemp clothing. "So you're attracted to dangerous men?"

"Aren't all women?"

"Yeah, I guess they probably are." Eric became aware of his own lack of dangerousness. "How long were you guys together?"

A sudden catch in her voice. "Ten years."

The pastures blew by, the outlines of fence rows and cattle blurring with speed and the afternoon heat. Ahead, the dark pavement shimmered. "So, what do your folks think about your leaving Washington and coming down here?"

Lara shrugged. "They think I've lost my mind." She paused. "So stop asking about my life. Tell me something about you."

"What do you want to know?"

"I don't know. Just something. Whatever is important to you."

Eric considered how to answer. "I love to take pictures."

"I noticed that."

"Look," Eric changed the subject. "That's where we're headed."

On a rise ahead stood George MacKnight's gas station, its antique pumps rusting under a sagging overhang. Eric pulled the car off the road and parked out front.

"Want to come in?" he asked.

Lara nodded.

The screen door hung loose on its hinges and creaked as Eric pulled it open. He stepped aside so Lara could precede him into the musty store. The grimy, yellow windows muted the sunlight from outside. An ancient cooler hummed against the far wall. Eric strode over to it. "What you want, Miss Lara?"

"Beer."

"Nope. Sunday. Blue laws."

"Damn. Diet Coke."

"You got it." When he opened the cooler, the glass fogged and a welcome burst of cold air rushed around his face. He pulled out a Diet Coke for Lara and a regular one for himself, then took them to the register where George MacKnight was propped against the counter, smoking a cigarette. A neon Bud Light sign glowed on the wall behind him. "What say, George?"

"Can't complain." With his slow-motion reach, the old man took the Cokes and studied them, turning them over, looking for a price sticker even though Eric was pretty sure he knew exactly how much they cost. Then, just as slowly, George punched the amount into the register.

"Hot enough for you?" Eric asked.

"Reckon so." George eased the Cokes across the counter, took the bill Eric handed him, studied it for a few seconds, then handed Eric back change.

"Well, have a good 'un," Eric said.

George barely lifted his hand in acknowledgment.

Outside, Eric gave Lara her Diet Coke. She collapsed against Eric's car and brought the sweating bottle to her forehead. "So, do you know everybody around here?"

"Oh, yeah, pretty much." Eric leaned against the car beside her. "Ain't that many people to know. They all think I'm a little crazy."

Lara peeked over her shoulder at the store and sidled closer, whispering, "That guy was missing a few teeth."

"Hey, don't give him a hard time. He can't help it." Eric felt a prickle of resentment. He thought of the things he could show her; naked children playing in dirt yards, a Vietnam vet who spent the days pumping up and down the side of the road in his wheelchair because he had no place to live. Things no one in Washington, D.C. ever thought of or gave a damn about. He wanted to pop Lara's naive northern liberal bubble. He even knew the perfect way to do it.

He twisted the top off of his bottle and took a few long swallows. "We're close to Sterling's house. Want to see where he lives?"

She smiled, "Yeah. Maybe we'll surprise him."

"No, he's working today at Dairy Queen. They're open on Sundays now, so he works seven days a week."

"Is his house close?"

"About a mile."

They climbed into the car. "Hey, don't tell him about this, okay?" he said.

"Why?"

"Just don't."

After a few minutes of driving, they came to Sterling's house. Eric knew he could pass by it and not say a word. That would be the best thing to do. But instead he pulled off to the side of the road.

"What, lost?" she asked.

"No, that's his house there."

Even though he was used to the house and had seen it many times, looking at it always made Eric sick. There were hundreds of houses like this along narrow back roads, houses with decaying siding and plastic covering the windows. Houses with collapsing chimneys and rotten front stoops. But this one was Sterling's, and that made it worse.

"He lives here with his mother and twin little sisters," Eric said. "His father disappeared, and his mama fell apart. She doesn't try to do anything to get the family out of the mess they're in. Just keeps working at the Quickie Mart."

Lara lifted her hand and reached out until her fingertips touched the window. She pressed her palm against the glass. Eric looked at three bumper stickers on the back of the rusted truck in the driveway. Two read I'M THE PROUD PARENT OF A BARTON HIGH HONOR STUDENT. One had a picture of the Confederate flag and said, I AIN'T COMING DOWN.

"His father disappeared?" Lara said. "Like how? Is he dead?"

"He's out hustling women somewhere, I imagine." He studied her stricken face. "Hey, I'm sorry. Maybe I shouldn't have brought you here."

She didn't reply.

He watched her for a moment more. Shit, he thought, I shouldn't have done this. He wrenched the wheel around and soon they were speeding back down the road the way they'd come.

When Eric pulled into her driveway, Lara eyed her huge house, which could hold three of Sterling's family. She hung her head.

"Come in with me?" she murmured. "Please? Stay a while."

He felt horrible. "Yeah, sure. Just, Lara, just promise you won't tell Sterling I showed you his house."

*   *   *

ERIC and Lara lay upstairs on her futon eating chocolate ice cream out of the carton with one spoon. They'd wandered to the bedroom because that's where the fan was, and it rattled in the window, blowing hot air over them.

For an hour, Eric had waited for Lara to say something about Sterling, but instead she'd been distant and quiet. The waiting had given him time to reflect on what he'd done, and guilt was eating at the pit of his belly. Why couldn't he control himself better when he got those mean urges?

He wondered what she was thinking, whether she was upset with him. But something in the intensity of her silence kept him from asking. He watched as she dug a chunk of ice cream up with the slightly bent spoon and held it out to him. He opened his mouth so she could stick the spoon inside, then he shook his head.

"Geez. Cold, cold."

She skimmed a thin mushy film off the top and slipped it between her lips, then sucked on the spoon. The sunlight streaming through the old glass windows caught dust motes, and as Lara moved, the rush of air sent them spinning crazily around her, so that for a moment she seemed to be the center of a shimmering energy.

"I want to know how to help Sterling," she said.

"I didn't know if you were still speaking to me."

"I am. I guess in a way I'm glad you showed me. It helps me understand him better." She paused. "So what can I do to help him?"

"I give him stuff," he said. "But you have to be pretty subtle about it. I used to buy him clothes and tell him they were mine and I didn't want them. I had to put them through the washer and dryer a couple of times so he'd believe me. Problem is, now he's bigger than me so I can't use the hand-me-downs excuse any more."

"So you *do* get involved?"

The question puzzled him. "What do you mean?"

"I mean earlier in the car, you sounded like you didn't want to get involved in other people's business."

"I get involved." Eric became defensive. "I'm just not fooling myself into believing I can change things. I give him clothes, a little money sometimes. That's about all I can do."

"What about college, Eric? He seems bright."

"He has responsibilities here."

Lara grimaced. "Other people's responsibilities, you mean."

Eric frowned. "Listen, you can't get emotionally involved with this. You can help a little here and there, but if you get emotionally involved, it'll kill you. Help him if you want, but be careful about it. That's all I can say."

"But I don't understand how you *can't* get emotionally involved." She fell silent before finally brandishing the spoon at him. "Do you believe in reincarnation?"

"No. Why?"

"So what do you think happens to us when we die?"

Eric shifted uncomfortably. "You really want to know?"

"Yes."

"I think we rot."

Lara cringed and bit her lip. She set the ice cream on the floor. It was turning soupy around the edges. "You see, I do believe in reincarnation. I think you're an old soul."

"What's that?"

"Someone who's been floating around in the world for a long time, who's pretty wise, but still can't quite get it right enough to reach Nirvana."

Eric rolled onto his back and stared up at the white ornate molding around the light fixture. A dark water stain blistered the ceiling beside it. "So why am I not getting it right?"

"I don't know. That's your problem." She smiled.

"So, what about you? Are you an old soul?"

"I think I'm a new one. I think in my previous life I was a cockroach or something. I don't have a clue."

He grinned. She rolled onto her back too, and they both stared at the light fixture, listening to the rattle of the fan.

"Jesus Christ! When does fall come around here?"

"October, if you're lucky," he said. "You could always buy an air conditioner."

"They're bad for the environment." She sighed. "October. I'm going to melt by October. Melt, or turn into fire."

He liked the image, her blazing up in a pillar of flame. "Better eat some more ice cream before that happens."

"I'm full." She reached for the carton and rested it on her chest below her chin. Eric watched droplets of water roll off the cardboard and goosepimple her flesh, then slide down to disappear under the edge of her white shirt. He caught the next drop with his finger, wiping it off the carton, then holding it up so he could see the water reform and elongate. They both waited for it to drip and when it did, Eric wiped his finger dry.

"So what about you, Grover? You got a girlfriend?"

"Grover?" he grinned. "What's Grover?"

"You know. The blue guy on Sesame Street. You look like him."

"Blue? That's a new one."

"Girlfriend?" she insisted.

"Italy," he said.

"Italy? How long?"

Eric sighed. "Well, that's the funny part. See, Julie went to Italy on this art student exchange thing two years ago."

"What's funny about that?"

"She was only supposed to be gone for six months."

Lara bit her lower lip.

"It's funny, 'cause part of me is still waiting for her to come back. The least she could have done is sent me a 'Dear John' letter or something."

Lara patted his hand. "Well, maybe the Italian stud she hooked up with has got her barefoot and pregnant in his hovel in a vineyard; and when she's not having babies, she's too busy pulling grapes off vines with her bleeding fingers to write."

Eric laughed. He rolled onto his side too so they were facing each other with only the ice cream between them.

"So, did you move here before or after she left?"

"Three years before she left," he said. "Guess I thought I was going to show her I had my own stuff to do—you know, the front porch sofa photograph collection."

"But you haven't finished it yet."

He shook his head, then studied Lara's face. Her bright eyes held his and she sucked on the spoon until he grinned. Flipping the spoon out of her mouth, she rapped his nose with it.

"Hey, it's finally dark," she said. He glanced at the window, now a black square at the far end of the room. "Let's go outside. It'll be cooler."

They walked around the block. The violet light of dusk filtered through the arch of black, heavy leaves overhead. Fireflies pulsed above the lawns, and all around them the earth exhaled warmth and moisture. The sweet scent of honeysuckle perfumed the air. Occasional white flashes of heat lightning illuminated the sky, and bats flitted after insects on silent, leathery wings. They didn't talk, and it felt okay not to.

Back on her darkened porch, Eric watched Lara grope in the huge handbag for her keys. "You didn't need to lock the door," he said. "Or bring your purse."

"Old habits," she replied.

Minutes passed, and he started to grin. "You need a miniature St. Bernard with a miniature keg of brandy to go in there and dig your keys out."

"Shut up." In the faint glow of the street lamp he could tell she was smiling. "I just can't see anything." She stopped the search and shook her purse violently. They both heard the keys jingle. She brought the bag closer to her face, shoved her hand inside, and groped around. Finally, with a triumphant "Aha!" Lara brought the keys out and stood squinting at the door. "I can't even see the keyhole."

"Here, wait a second." Eric jogged to his car and turned on its headlights so the front porch was lit by a sudden burst of white light. Lara found the keyhole, unlocked the door, then turned toward Eric, shielding her eyes against the bright glare. As he stood, wondering if he should leave, Lara sauntered down the porch steps. He watched her hips sway as she clasped her hands behind her back and moved toward him.

"Guess you've got to get going?" she asked.

"Guess so, maybe."

"Can I come visit you at your store?"

"Of course."

She stopped in front of him, her eyes level with his nose. "Well, thanks for the day and all."

"I hope it wasn't too boring."

"No. It was the best day I've had in a long time." Lara rose up on her toes and kissed him, a quick dry brush of her lips against his. "Really, thank you." Then she turned, flitted back to the porch and waved over her shoulder. She disappeared into the darkened house.

He slid reluctantly into the car, started it, put it in reverse, and cast one last glance at the old Bishop place. The house was a hulking black shadow. Lara had not turned on a light.

chapter ten

October 13

"SUSAN Lyons called last night." Mary Edgars stood in the kitchen, her back to Jimmy. Her shoulders worked as she whisked four eggs in a metal bowl. "She wanted to say she was sorry that the FBI was taking over the case."

Edgars watched his wife pour the foaming eggs into the frying pan.

"The FBI isn't taking over the case," he growled. "*We* ain't even had the case but twenty-four hours."

Edgars had known this was coming the second he laid eyes on Lara Walton's body. He picked up his fork and began rapping it on the tabletop. "Hell, no one in the town thinks I know what I'm doing. Maybe it's been eight years since I investigated a murder, but I spent twenty-eight years on the Atlanta force and I've seen plenty. One of the local officers threw up at the scene yesterday. He'd never seen a dead body before, much less someone's brains all over the wall."

Mary slid the skillet off the stove and approached the table. She watched him rapping the table with the fork and cut him a cross look, which made him stop.

"Everyone's saying Sterling O'Connor did it. Susan said he and the Walton woman were having an affair." Mary dished out the eggs with such ferocity that they splattered in thick yellow chunks across her husband's plate. Edgars held up a hand to keep egg bits from flying into his eye.

"I'm sorry," Mary said. "It's just that the idea of people saying Sterling O'Connor killed someone upsets me. I told Susan she didn't know what she was talking about. I taught him in two classes. He's a good kid. He isn't capable of killing anyone, and even if he was, he's too smart to just go home afterwards and wait for the police." Mary circled the table and lowered herself into her chair. "I mean, what kind of trouble has Sterling ever really gotten into? None, is what kind. Everybody is just against him because of that stuff about him being illegitimate, and the fact that they don't go to church."

"His haircut and those earrings," Edgars said. "He looks like a freak, and he skateboards all over the place. That's enough to scare the folks around here half to death." He picked up the fork again and dug into his eggs. "Anyway, I don't think it's him. I think she was involved with something in Washington, D.C. Her boyfriend there died not too long ago. A car accident, they said. He was some kind of environmentalist. I'm having the autopsy report on his death faxed down here this morning." He brought the fork to his mouth. The eggs were warm and soft and buttery. They slid down his throat. "I just can't imagine someone here did it. It's got to be people from outside."

An hour later, Edgars stood on the front porch of Lara Walton's house. It was the first time he'd been by since driving past it on his way home last night. He didn't find it any less eerie in the gray damp daylight. The rain had continued all night and into the morning, and the captain's hair dripped into his eyes. He cursed himself for forgetting his umbrella.

"We gave her a citation, you know?" said Bill Hanks, who stood shivering in a thin overcoat on the porch beside him. Bill was a youngster, thirty years old, with a round boyish face and an eager expression. Edgars liked him. He was smart and picked up on things, and Edgars had decided to groom him to take over his job when he retired.

"We did? What for?"

"Disturbing the peace. Grier called it in. She and Sterling O'Connor were out front on the sidewalk messing around on his skateboard. She paid up the day after we wrote the ticket."

"Grier," Edgars rolled his eyes.

"I think he's enjoying this," Bill said.

Edgars didn't want to think about Dave Grier. He rubbed his hands together against the cold. "So, where are we?"

"I think we'll be able to take the tape down this afternoon." Bill pulled out a small notebook. "We got a shoe print outside that hole in the foundation; woman's size seven."

"What size did Lara Walton wear?"

"Give you three guesses."

"Well, that's worth shit then. Anything else?" Edgars asked.

"Whoever it was must've come through the basement. There was water all over the stairs, but no shoe prints we could make out."

"Any fibers?"

"Yeah, on the bricks around the basement opening. We're sending those off to the crime lab. The fingerprints all match people we know were in the house before. Sterling O'Connor, Eric Teague, and that fourth set belonged to Betsy Bates over at the realty company."

"Damn," the captain sighed. Why couldn't he get just one break? Something positive to tell the newspaper, something that would show the town he knew what he was doing.

"When we picked that futon up to ship it to the crime lab, we found a half-empty box of condoms underneath. We couldn't get any good prints off of it 'cause of the blood, but we're sending it to the lab, too. Maybe they can pick something up."

"So was she sleeping with someone, or were the condoms there just in case?" Edgars mused. "And if she was sleeping with someone, who was it?"

Bill shrugged. "Good question."

"She wasn't pregnant, was she?"

Bill flipped through his notebook, then paused to read. "The coroner says no."

Edgars had been through the coroner's report and his own crime scene report so many times in the last day that he'd almost memorized them. He began to recite the details out loud. "No sign of struggle. Her back was to the shooter. No blood trail either. Nothing was stolen, at least we don't think so. No sign of a sexual assault." He paused and looked at Bill. "Shooting someone five times when you killed 'em on the first shot. Wouldn't you call that a crime of passion?"

"I would," Bill said. "Everything we've got now points to this being something personal."

"Without her being raped or beaten? It's kind of cold and distant for personal. It's more like an execution."

"So why five shots?"

"To make sure she's dead," Edgars said.

"We didn't find any drugs in the house, and the coroner says she was clean. Why would someone execute her?" Bill asked.

"I don't know. Why did she come here? Maybe she was running from something or someone, and they found her."

"But if it was a professional hit, they'd have used a silencer, and there's nothing in her background that suggests she'd be a target for a professional hit."

"I'm not saying it was a professional hit, but whoever did it didn't have a point to make. They didn't want to confront her or humiliate her or fight with her. They just wanted her dead."

Edgars stood chewing his lip, then he sighed. "I sure hope that autopsy on her boyfriend Dylan Montgomery shows us something." He shoved his hands deep in his coat pockets. "I think I'm going to take one more look around inside, now that it's daytime."

Dark print powder smudged the knob, and when Edgars turned it, the front door creaked open onto silence. He stepped into the entrance hall and smelled the metallic scent of blood. To his left, he saw the stain on the parlor ceiling. It was about two feet in diameter now and turning black, along with the smaller stain on the floor below. A chill prickled down his spine. "Ain't you coming?"

"Oh. Yeah." Bill followed him inside, closing the door behind him and coming to stand next to Edgars with his arms crossed over his chest. Edgars could tell that the house unnerved Bill too.

They walked through the living room, each step playing a new creak in the old wood floors. The room was still filled with her boxes, empty since most of their contents had been spilled out and searched by the police. Lara's possessions carpeted the floor. Edgars stooped and looked at some of them: an empty picture frame, silverware, fuzzy red bedroom slippers. Nothing that could tell him what had happened.

"Her folks'll be here tomorrow," Edgars said. "See if we can't get somebody to get rid of that blood. No one should have to see that, least of all family."

Edgars thought he'd seen Lara once, an unfamiliar face at the grocery store. Then again, maybe he'd never seen her and was just making up a picture, motivating himself to keep going with this ugliness. He went into the kitchen and opened the empty cabinets. If she'd left a day earlier, maybe she'd still be alive. Already, the kitchen counters were accumulating a thin film of dust. Everything looked old, beat up. Only the walls were freshly painted.

Edgars went to the basement door, which was almost black with print powder. The door groaned when he pulled it open. He felt a rush of damp air from below. Sterling O'Connor's prints were on everything down there, the banister, the walls. Edgars closed the door.

He climbed the stairs to the second floor and walked to her bedroom where the bloody futon and the condoms had been removed. "I don't know," he said to Bill. "Can't do a damned thing until we get those forensics results back." He stared at the blackened stain on the floor, the wide shallow pool of blood now caked and dried. "What's worse is I'm going to have to question Dave Grier."

"That's one job you can have," Bill said.

"Miss Lara Walton. . . ." Edgars muttered. He couldn't get a clue about her from this place. It was as if she'd never lived here. He'd seen her picture, a pretty young woman with green eyes, but nothing exceptional, nothing extraordinary.

On his way back to the staircase, he noticed a blacked-out window he didn't remember seeing the night before. He wondered why someone would paint over it. The upstairs hallway could use the light. Edgars went to the window and opened it. Instead of looking outside, it opened into a small dusty room illuminated by a French door on the opposite wall.

"Bill," he said, "did y'all see this?"

"What?" Bill came to stand beside him. "Well, I'll be. There's a room back there. I thought it was a window to the outside."

The dust on the floor had been disturbed by footprints that cut a path between the blacked-out window and the French door. In the middle of the room stood a gleaming telescope.

"Look at that," Bill said. "I wonder how long it's been here."

"Not too long. See, there's no dust on it, and you can tell where someone's been walking in there. Let's get prints off of it."

"Sure thing."

Edgars stepped back and looked around the hallway. Water stains darkened the ceiling, and the paint was flaking. The wood floors were dull, the banister chipped. A thought that had been half forming in his mind for hours suddenly blossomed.

"I'm going to go walk around outside a minute," he said.

In the back yard, he noticed the same sort of thing. Old paint, general disrepair. Even her fence needed work.

"What I want to know," he said when Bill came up behind him, "is why it looks like Mr. O'Connor did almost no work on this house. Not three months' worth of work, at least."

"I was thinking that same thing myself," Bill said.

Edgars shook his head. "Could the coroner tell if she was having intercourse with anyone at all?"

"His report says there were no signs of recent sexual activity." Bill glanced at the captain. "Did you ask Eric Teague?"

"He said they were just friends."

"Well, there's that other theory," Bill said. "You know, that maybe he was jealous of how the O'Connor boy felt about Miss Walton."

Edgars gave Bill a perplexed look. "Surely you don't think Eric Teague could kill a woman. Hell, last time I was at his store he was trying to catch a cricket and put it outside."

Bill shrugged. "From what I've heard, Eric Teague is hiding his true personality."

Edgars dismissed Bill's idea with a wave of his hand. "The only ideas I've got right now are someone from D.C. coming down here to kill her, or else it was Sterling O'Connor, and I still don't feel like that boy did it. He seemed too shocked when I told him she was dead."

"You know, I read somewhere how people can get torn up inside and commit murder, then forget they've done it," Bill said. "I've read case studies on it. She was leaving, right? What if Sterling had a thing for her and couldn't admit to it? What if he went nuts 'cause she was leaving? That might explain why there was no assault. He was crazy and just wanted her dead."

Edgars frowned. "I think the boy would remember doing something like that. Let's wait and see what the crime lab says. Maybe that will help point us in the right direction."

DYLAN Montgomery's autopsy report lay on Edgars's desk. His eyes ached and his vision blurred around the edges from having stared at the damned thing for so long. Cause of death, blunt force trauma to the head. From the pictures of the car, Edgars was amazed they found enough of a body in it to do an autopsy. The metal was twisted and wrinkled into an unrecognizable shape.

The police report said Mr. Montgomery was at fault. He'd cut in too close in front of an SUV, hit it, flipped over five times and landed in the path of oncoming traffic, where he was hit again. He wasn't drunk or drugged. Everything pointed to a plain old car accident, a bad one. But Edgars couldn't let go of the notion that there was more going on. He'd asked the D.C. police to look into the possibility of a homicide, as a professional courtesy. The officer he spoke with seemed to stifle a groan, but agreed to do a cursory and, he emphasized, quick investigation. Edgars hoped they'd turn something up. Otherwise Sterling O'Connor was going to be looking more and more like his only suspect.

A few years ago, George MacKnight's health had begun failing along with his faith in America, so he sold his dairy farm, bought a small gas station on the edge of town, and began stockpiling guns, canned food, and propane. Edgars knew him as a man of few words and even fewer gestures. When George recognized the captain driving by him on the road, he'd barely lift his index finger in greeting. George considered speech a thing for women, and was known to sit through church potluck suppers without saying anything to anyone. Now, according to Mary, who was friends with George's wife, he had a house full of kids and grandkids. George was so annoyed by all the noise and goings-on that he was sleeping in a hammock in his garage at night. During the day, he had to haul in water because the kids took too many showers and the cistern dried up.

Captain Edgars pulled up to George's gas station, expecting him to be there because it was a refuge from his family. The station was on the route Sterling took home from Lara Walton's place. George stayed open late. Maybe he'd seen something, but Edgars knew that getting the information from George would be like squeezing blood from a turnip.

"Howdy," the captain said. George stood behind the cash register chewing a toothpick. "Sorry to bother you here, George, but I need to ask you some questions 'bout the night before last. Any chance you saw that O'Connor boy?"

George blinked at the captain, his hard, pale blue eyes shining.

"You know Sterling O'Connor? Sandy's son? Good-looking kid with that wild hair-do and them earrings? From what I figure, he walks by this place a couple of times a day. I just wondered if you saw him night before last."

"Maybe," George said.

"So you did see him?"

"Seen him walking home 'fore it got dark."

"What time did you close up that night?"

George shifted the toothpick to the other side of his mouth and chewed on it for a minute or two before he said, "'Bout eleven."

"So you saw him walking home, but didn't see him walking back toward town?"

George nodded. He gripped the toothpick and began digging around in his teeth, and from the way he did it, Edgars thought that George wasn't finished with his story. "'Course, I did see the O'Connors' truck."

"What?"

"That truck he drives sometimes. Seen it 'round eleven when I was locking up."

"You remember which way it was headed?"

George pointed toward town.

"You sure it was their truck?"

George turned all his attention to scratching a scaly spot on the back of his hand. Edgars shifted impatiently. Finally, George looked up and said, "Looked like it."

"What makes you say that?"

More scratching, followed by a close inspection of his cash register tape. "Headlight was out."

Edgars nodded. "Thanks George, that's what I needed to know." Damn, he thought. Could Bill have been right about Sterling going crazy?

Back in the car, Edgars wondered what might have sent Sterling over the edge. Lara leaving? Did he have a thing for her? Everything

Edgars had heard about Sterling told him the boy wasn't unstable like that. Still, he was starting to wonder if the rumors about Sterling and Lara were at least part true. And, if so, how did Eric Teague really feel about it?

It was three o'clock when the captain pulled up to the Dairy Queen. Sterling would be at Eric's store. When Edgars stepped through the door, the three kids lounging behind the counter gaped. Bob Waits, the manager, appeared from the kitchen, wiping his hands on a dishtowel.

"Howdy, Captain," he said. "What can I do you for?"

"I need a quick word with you, Bob. Outside, maybe?"

"Sure thing." Bob tossed the towel on the counter and followed Edgars into the muggy afternoon.

Bob reached into his back pocket and pulled out a pack of Camels. He glanced over his shoulder through the glass door as he shook out a cigarette. His hair was slicked back, and, unlike the kids inside, he wore a button-down short-sleeved shirt and a tie, which had a big chocolate stain on its tip. He was twenty-two years old, and had a keen business sense. He was already the manager of the only restaurant in town open on Sunday. Bob had taken a lot of flak for that decision, and a few local churches now boycotted the Dairy Queen.

"Guess you know why I'm here," Edgars said.

"Guess so." Bob cupped his hand over the Camel to light it, blew smoke and shook out his match.

"Did you hear Sterling say anything?"

Bob flicked the match into the parking lot. "All's I can say is he ain't been himself for the last month. I had to move him back to the kitchen 'cause he was making mistakes on the register, which he ain't never done before. He's just been real distracted and quiet like. Ain't normal for Sterling."

"Any ideas as to why?"

"Well, I thought it was trouble at home. I heard him and Sandy got into a big flap a few weeks ago, but you know the way people talk around here. No telling what really happened."

"You think he was involved with the Walton woman?"

Bob shrugged and took a pull on his cigarette. "That's what I heard, but Sterling never talked about it, and it ain't like him not to brag. You should ask Jaylee and Chip inside. They know what's going on with Sterling better'n me. He's been pissed about me moving him back to the kitchen and ain't hardly said a word to me for two weeks."

The captain nodded. "Sorry to have to bother you with all of this. It'd be best if you didn't talk about it until we can start putting some things together."

"Sure thing." A cloud of smoke obscured Bob's face.

"Is it all right if I go talk to those kids?" Edgars asked.

"Go ahead. It ain't like we got a big rush on."

Back in the air conditioning, Edgars went to the counter. The two boys had disappeared, but he could hear them whispering in the kitchen. The girl stood with her hands resting on either side of her register.

Edgars called to the boys. "Y'all come out here for a second. I need to ask you some stuff."

Chip Milton and Harry Pierce popped around the corner. Chip was a defensive tackle on the Barton High football team. He was a big kid with small eyes set too close together and a wide flat nose that looked like it had been broken a few times. Harry was in the marching band and had bad acne and hair that shone with oil. The girl, Jaylee Culpepper, had been one of Mary's students. He remembered Mary saying she was boy-crazy. She looked like a child who'd gotten into her mother's makeup. Lips painted bright red. Blue eyes rimmed with thick black liner.

"I'm sorry to bother y'all," the captain began. "And I'd appreciate it if you wouldn't go around talking about me being here, but I just need to know if you all ever heard Sterling say anything about Lara Walton."

"He said she was hot." Jaylee snapped her gum, and Edgars got the sense that she was exacting revenge. "The first time he saw her in here, he said she was hot."

"So you saw them together?"

All three kids nodded. The boys had moved up to flank Jaylee, both with saucer-eyed stares, except that Chip's stare wasn't so wide because his eyes were so small and near-set.

"Did he say if there was something going on between them?"

The kids glanced at each other and began shifting their feet, looking down.

"I ain't out to get Sterling or nothing," the captain said. "I've just heard a lot of rumors and I thought you all might be able to straighten me out on what's true and what's not."

"She ain't been in here but a few times," Chip said. "But I seen 'em Sunday out in the warehouse parking lot." He picked at a zit and stared at his feet.

"Did you talk to them?"

Chip snorted. "Hardly."

"What were they doing?"

The kids tried to stifle grins. "Kissing," said Chip.

"Like a small kiss on the cheek, or. . . ." Edgars waved a hand in the air.

"Like his tongue down her throat," Chip blurted, while Harry giggled and went bright red.

"You sure it was them?"

"Yeah, I honked at 'em, but old Sterling didn't notice."

"And you're sure it was Sunday? This last Sunday?"

Chip nodded.

"Did Sterling say anything else about her, other than about her being hot?" Edgars asked.

"Only that he hoped she wanted more than just his help fixing up her house." Chip couldn't stifle his grin any longer.

"So he had a thing for her?"

"No, he didn't," Jaylee protested. "He always goes on like that."

"Sterling ain't never had trouble getting girls." Chip spoke with obvious admiration. "But when he asked her to go out with him, she laughed like he was a retard and said he was too young."

"Did that make him angry?"

Chip shook his head. "Naw. I think he kind of liked someone telling him no for a change."

Edgars wondered if Lara Walton ever stopped saying no. "But you don't know if they ever dated," Edgars asked.

"Naw," said Chip. "We thought he struck out with her. At least I did 'til I seen 'em Sunday." He grinned wider, shook his head and muttered, "Man."

Edgars left the kids whispering and drove back to the station. Now at least he had something solid to go on. He began thinking of a new series of questions to ask Sterling.

chapter eleven

July 8

L ARA stood in the parlor and watched Eric pull out of the driveway, the yellow glare of his headlights tracing along the bare
walls. Once he'd turned and disappeared around a corner, she locked
her door.

Dylan. Today she'd gone for hours without thinking of him. And
then there was Sterling and Eric and poor Pam Grier and Miss Callie
and the old guy at the gas station with three teeth, all these lives
going on, all these people moving through their own worlds. *I'd forgotten the world actually exists,* Lara thought.

She felt her way to the hall, reluctantly switched on a light, and
meandered into the kitchen where she opened a bottle of merlot and
poured herself a large glass. Then, taking the bottle and glass both,
she went onto the back stoop and sat in the dark and watched fireflies flicker over the lawn.

Hours without thinking about Dylan. She gulped the wine. Could
she really have loved him if she could go an afternoon without thinking of him? She ran a finger around the lip of her wineglass. The
crystal vibrated and hummed.

Lara leaned against the wall of her house and smelled the damp
green smell of things growing. She remembered the strange verdant
places Eric had taken her today, could see the jungle swallowing the
pathetic local attempts at civilization.

Then with a sudden stab of pain, the image of the subway insinuated itself once again into Lara's thoughts. She remembered darkness in the concrete tunnels, the glare of white lights, the regularity of smooth manmade arches. The surreal subterranean world. Sterile. Artificial.

In a rush she realized that she loved this town. She loved the way kudzu twined its way across lawn chairs left out too long and infiltrated old outbuildings and draped electric poles in green curtains. She loved the almost deafening noise of crickets, the barrage of moths at her windows in the evenings. Here humankind couldn't overcome the earth. Despite all of her involvement with the environment, working to protect it, thinking about it, using equations to calculate what might happen to it, Lara realized that in Washington she'd been removed from it. Today, walking through those lush hushed places, she'd felt as if she were waking up after a long sleep.

She poured herself a second glass of wine and drank it quickly. Half the bottle was gone already. Her head was beginning to fuzz, the sleepiness descending like a dark curtain over her thoughts. She wanted to be numb.

"Corporations own the world." She remembered Dylan as he stretched out on a picnic blanket beside the Tidal Basin, back around the time they first met. The Jefferson monument, a few tourists milling around it, rose behind him gleaming white in the sunshine. "Corporations own politicians. They own their workers. And all they care about is money. They don't give a damn about what's happening to the environment. They don't give a damn that their employees don't have time to spend with their kids." He'd fixed Lara with his flashing brown eyes. "It's a sick world we're living in. A sick world."

Listening to him, seeing the fervor in his eyes, Lara had been swept away. How could she not be? It had been so exciting to hear someone speak contemptuously about everything her parents held sacred. Her face had grown hot with shame as she confessed, "Daddy's a defense industry lobbyist, a retired colonel. He's a Republican. He wanted me to go to West Point. To be in the military."

Dylan grimaced. "Guess it's good you're a free thinker, then." His hard expression softened, and he brushed a stray hair from her face; the first romantic gesture he'd ever made. "How did that happen, huh? How did a kid with your background become a free thinker at age twenty?"

Sitting at her kitchen table now in Barton County, Lara wondered if she'd ever truly been a free thinker. Or had she simply traded one older man's ideals for another's? Dylan may have been an activist in his youth, but when Lara knew him, all he did was talk. He never took her to protest rallies. They never lobbied their representatives. They did nothing but work each other into impotent fits of self-righteous indignation.

She took another swallow of wine and suddenly found herself choking on it. A bitter red stream spurted from between her lips and ran down the corners of her mouth. *Oh shit.* She began to sob. She pounded the porch floor once with her fist. The subway. The measured, even mundaneness of their lives. If only she'd known what was going to happen, she wouldn't have worried about her damned spot on the subway platform. She would have kept him in bed in the mornings, would have made love to him until long after they were both late for work. She wouldn't have stayed at the office until eight o'clock every night. Wouldn't have spent weekends at the computer. They would have gone to the beach and watched waves roll in to shore. They would have hiked in the Blue Ridge Mountains. Or sat on their balcony staring at the D.C. skyline and getting drunk on expensive cabernet.

But they'd missed their chance.

And on top of this thought came the image of the shack where Sterling lived, superimposed ghost-like on the image of the subway station.

Lara found herself trying to stand. She was lightheaded, and white spots bubbled before her eyes. The door to the house whirled and swam for a moment before she managed to grip the handle. She staggered inside to the kitchen, leafed violently through the tiny town phone book and found Eric's number.

"Eric?" she slurred when he answered.

"Lara?"

"I just, I wanted to know. Sterling. Does he have a life?"

"Are you drunk?"

"Because, I mean, he works at your place and at Dairy Queen and here. Does he have a life? Does he ever have any fun?"

There was a brief silence at the other end of the line. "I'm sorry for showing you his house."

"It's not that. I just want to know if he has a life. Does he get enough to eat? He looks thin. Does he go to parties?"

Another pause. "He's okay, Lara. You don't have to worry about him. I shouldn't have shown you his house."

Lara felt a frustration bordering on rage. Eric didn't understand. Eric stood at a distance and took his pictures and watched the lives of others go by as if they were no more than an artistic backdrop.

"He's seventeen," she said by way of explanation. "How long ago did you say his father left?"

"Sterling's okay," Eric said. "It just seems worse than it is because you're drunk. Sleep it off and call me tomorrow."

"Will you see him tomorrow?"

"I see him every day except Sunday."

"Then remind him to come by here, would you? He said he'd come by."

"Okay," Eric said. "Get some sleep. Take care of yourself."

She picked up the glass and wine bottle, went into the living room, and sat in front of her computer, watching animated fish swim across the screen. Her mind strayed from Sterling to Pam Grier's black eye. She logged on to a search engine and typed "Domestic violence shelters, Georgia," then printed out the information, stuffed it into an envelope, and wrote Pam's name on it in a scrawling, uneven script. *God, I'm drunk,* she thought. *Must sleep.* Gripping the envelope, she rolled out of the chair and lay down on the floor.

July 9

L ARA slept too late to catch Pam leaving for work. She awoke at ten, groggy, her mouth tasting like Styrofoam. She dragged into the kitchen and forced herself to eat and to drink cup after cup of strong black coffee. She had things to do today. She couldn't just lie around any more.

B Y eight o'clock that evening, Pam still hadn't returned, and Lara, feeling relieved, gave up on confronting her until tomorrow. Instead, she turned her attention to cooking spinach lasagna. Spinach for iron and vitamin C and folic acid. Cheese for protein. Pasta for carbohydrates.

When the lasagna was done, she ate some, along with salad and bread, leaving the rest scattered on the table like accidental leftovers. When Sterling knocked, she dashed to the door to let him in.

"Hey." He grinned at her. When she saw how crooked his teeth were, she fought the urge to fling her arms around his neck.

"How about dinner?" she blurted, before he'd even stepped inside. "I made too much for myself, so I have all these leftovers. I don't know if you've eaten, but if you're hungry, there's plenty." She grabbed his hand and pulled him toward the kitchen. "See," she pointed at the food and watched his face. He swallowed hard when he saw the lasagna. "Go ahead, you'd be doing me a favor. I'll get you some iced tea."

Sterling sat down and gazed at the melted cheese on the fragrant lasagna. His mouth went all wet, and his stomach growled. He picked up a fork and dug in, thinking no dried-out hot dogs for him tonight. Lara sat across the table holding a crystal glass half full of red wine. She looked wild, cheeks flushed, hair falling across her eyes. He didn't think she looked like someone who was sad. He wondered if what Eric had said was true, about her boyfriend dying. If it was true, Sterling guessed he should feel kind of bad for her.

"Is it good?" she asked.

"Best meal I've had in ages. I get tired of Dairy Queen hamburgers."

"Do they let you eat for free?"

"Naw, charge me half price."

Lara shook her head. "You'd think the least they could do is let you eat for nothing. I get so pissed off at the dismal conditions of service industry workers."

He cocked an eyebrow at her but didn't stop eating.

"You all need a union or something. You need to get rid of management, control the means of production."

He took another bite, eyed the lasagna in the pan and wondered if she'd let him have more.

"I mean, it makes me appreciate communism to see stuff like this going on."

He choked and gaped at her. "What?"

"Communism. It makes me appreciate it when I see how poorly some workers are treated."

"Communism?" He knew his mouth was hanging open, but he couldn't manage to close it.

"Dairy Queen could use a good dose of Marx."

He felt uncomfortable. He'd never been around anyone who'd said anything good about communism before. "Communism ain't right."

"Why? Why isn't it right?"

"Ain't got no—you don't have any freedom under a communist system."

"You're thinking of a Stalinist version of communism. You see, what I'm talking about is Marxism."

"Well, way I see it, all Russians are the same."

"Marx wasn't Russian, he was German. I bet you don't know anything about communism."

For the first time, he thought she seemed mean. Sterling didn't give a damn about communism, really. He just wanted more lasagna, so he shrugged. "I know it isn't right."

Lara saw him looking at the food. She grabbed a spoon and served him another mound of lasagna, even though he wasn't finished with what he had.

"Well, I'll tell you something about communism then." She smacked a pile of salad onto his plate as if she were angry at it. "See, right now, you work for the corporate millionaires who own Dairy Queen, and their wealthy stockholders. They pay you minimum wage and don't give you benefits because the less they pay you, the more money they make." She tore off four pieces of garlic bread and dropped them beside the lasagna on his plate. "And to add insult to injury, you can't eat what you're selling, you have to buy it, which gives them even more money."

She slid the plate back to him.

"Now, if you and the other people working at Dairy Queen owned it yourselves, all the money you made would go to you, not to the rich corporate heads. Think about how much you'd make."

"I guess I'd make a lot," he said.

"Exactly. That's all Marx was saying. He wanted to empower the workers and get rid of the millionaire executives."

"You're trying to convert me." Sterling grinned.

"I just wanted you to know the difference. Most of the ideals behind communism are good. It just wasn't put into practice well."

"Yeah, that happens a lot once people get hold of good ideas, huh?" He turned all of his attention to eating, and in a few minutes was wiping his plate clean with a piece of bread. Then he leaned back, placed a hand on his belly, and breathed deeply. "You can cook supper for me any time."

Lara smiled. "You ate fast enough. You'll get indigestion."

"Naw, I think I'm digesting just fine."

"Well, there's still some left. Tell you what, I'll put it in Tupperware and you can take it home."

He shrugged. "'Kay."

He watched her walk around the kitchen searching the cupboards, her bare legs brown against the white cabinets. Sterling covered his mouth and belched quietly. He felt bad that her boyfriend was dead. But he was glad she was here letting him eat her supper.

She finally found a Tupperware container, and, after spooning the rest of the lasagna into it, she set it in the fridge. "Don't forget to take it with you." She paused and leaned against the counter, facing him. "I don't know what to have you do for me tonight. Now that you're through painting the kitchen, I hadn't thought of anything else."

Sterling looked at the torn linoleum in the corner by the refrigerator and at the loose cabinet handles, and thought he could work here full-time and never get close to fixing everything that needed fixing. "Close your eyes and point and there'll be something I can work on."

She tilted her head and frowned. "Are you tired?"

"What?"

"Tired. How many hours have you worked today?"

"I don't know." The food was settling into his belly, and if she didn't have him up and moving soon, he thought he might nod off. "I'm not too tired to do some work for you. Especially after that good supper."

"How about on the computer? Would you look up some things for me on the computer?"

Sterling didn't tell her he hardly considered that work. He just shrugged and said "If you want."

She led him into the living room, and he sat down in front of the screen.

"I need mailing addresses for these five agencies. They should be listed on the web."

"'Kay."

He touched the mouse and the screen saver vanished. Lara stood behind him while he checked the first name on her list and started typing, wishing he could do it better because he could only use two fingers. He heard the floor creak as she returned to the kitchen and started washing dishes.

Friends from school had talked about how hard it was to figure out computers, but Sterling thought it was easy. Within ten minutes, he'd found all five addresses.

He glanced over his shoulder. Lara was drying dishes in the kitchen. He turned back to the screen and stared at the white box marked SEARCH. He typed in "Hubble Space Telescope," and waited.

The computer came up with a long list of sites, but he went to the official one. A set of pictures appeared. Sterling's heart began to pound. He couldn't believe how many pictures there were. Bright red and gold explosions of gas and matter against the black universe. One explosion looked like the atomic energy sign. It was massive, neon-red with a small bright spot in the middle. He clicked on it.

"NGC 6543, nicknamed The Cat's Eye," the caption read. "Hubble reveals surprisingly intricate structures including concentric gas shells, jets of high-speed gas, and unusual shock-induced knots of gas. Estimated to be 1,000 years old, the nebula is a visual 'fossil record' of the dynamics and late evolution of a dying star."

A dying star. Sterling stared at the nebula and wished he could find out where in the sky it was. At least he could look in its direction one night, even if he didn't see it.

"Hubble, huh?"

He jumped up.

"I'm sorry," Lara laid a hand on his shoulder. "I didn't mean to startle you. Sit down."

"I got them addresses for you," he stammered.

"You're a space buff, huh? I mean, what with this and the Pathfinder the other night. Go on, sit back down."

His hands were shaking. "I'm sorry I was messing around. I—"

"Did you ever take an astronomy course?" she interrupted.

"What?"

"Did you ever get the chance to take astronomy?"

It took a moment for him to grasp what she was asking. "No, but I've read about it. Miz McEachern gave me some books, and one of the science teachers helped me learn some equations and stuff for extra credit."

"Did you like it?"

He nodded.

"What about school? Did you like school?"

"Some of it, I guess." He sat down and stared at the Web site, wondering if he should close it.

"Have you ever thought about going to college?"

He felt cornered with her standing over him. "Here's your addresses." He handed her the sheet of paper. She put it down on the desk.

"You could take lots of astronomy courses in college, right?"

He looked at the Hubble pictures glowing on the computer screen. She leaned against the table, facing him, so that one half of her was dark, the other half blue from the computer screen light. He thought again about that nebula, that bright explosion, the shock waves, and he wanted to tell her how hungry he was to sit in front of her computer all night and read about it. He wanted to tell her how his mouth watered at the thought of college and studying the red shift, Einstein's Theory of Relativity, and stellar class.

But he couldn't say it. She'd just tell him to stay at the computer when he had to get home soon. She'd tell him to apply to college, and he'd have to explain how his family didn't have much money.

"I gotta get home," he said. "I need to see my sisters before they go to bed."

She crossed her arms over her chest and studied him. "How many sisters do you have?"

"Two," he said.

"How old are they?"

"Six. They're twins."

"Do they look like you?"

"I got a picture."

"Can I see?"

He leaned forward and pulled out his wallet, unhooking it from its chain while Lara leaned in close. He could almost see down the front of her shirt. He flipped to the picture and held it in front of the computer screen's light. Lara squinted, then smiled. "They're adorable. What are their names?"

"Dayla and Darlene."

"I bet they're a handful."

"Yeah, Mama and me's always threatening to turn them in for quieter models." Sterling shoved the wallet into his pocket.

Lara reached toward his face, touching one of his earrings. Her fingers brushed the side of his cheek. "Why did you pierce your ears?"

He stared at her throat, her bare shoulders, her breasts. She smelled like red wine and he thought about touching her. "I saw some guy on TV had it done and thought it looked pretty cool. Went ahead and did it myself. Like to given Ma a heart attack." He fingered the gold loops in each lobe. "Didn't do it too good, though. They ain't even."

"I like those earrings. Did you get them around here?"

"Some girl gave 'em to me."

"Your girlfriend?"

"Naw, just some girl." He wanted to sound casual. "Haven't had a girlfriend since I got done with school. Ain't got time."

"You can't tell me that there's not some old high-school girlfriend still hanging around."

He looked around the darkened living room. "What you need to do is get you some lamps in here."

"He changes the subject." Lara pushed away from the desk and went to run a finger along the mantel as if checking for dust.

When he'd been younger, Sterling thought the girls around here were okay. Sex was easy to get. Now that he was seventeen, the sex was still great, but a lot of times he wanted to be able to talk to them, too. Most of them didn't even get his jokes.

He watched Lara examine her finger. "I gotta get going." He stood up, casting a longing glance at the Hubble images on the computer.

"I need to pay you."

"You paid me a few days ago." He followed her into the hall where she groped in her huge purse and came out with some bills.

"No, I didn't." She handed him three twenties.

"Yeah, you did. I'm the one getting paid, right? I'd be the one to remember."

"I know I didn't pay you."

"Well, I know you did." He forced the wadded bills back into her hand.

She glared down at them, then dropped them back into her purse. "When's your next day off?" she asked. "Because I want you to go to Atlanta with me. I need you to help me carry some stuff."

"What, you finally buy some furniture or something?"

"No, it's just some stuff I need carried."

"Well, I don't have to work for Eric on Sundays, but I work at Dairy Queen. Guess I could get a day off from there if I asked for it."

"Good, let me know when." She began tracing lines in the wood-grain trim around the door.

"Guess I'd better be gettin' on home, then."

"Hey, don't forget the leftovers. Do you need a ride?"

He shook his head. "It ain't far, a couple of blocks."

"I'll give you a ride. Really, it'll give me the chance to get out of the house." She dashed to the kitchen, returning a moment later with the Tupperware and her car keys.

"I don't need a ride," He took the container from her.

"You can stay and play on the computer if you want."

"Naw, I gotta go."

"I don't mind if you want to stay."

He smiled thinking it was cute how bad she wanted him around. "I gotta get home. I'll call you about going to Atlanta."

As he turned to go, he cast one last look at her over his shoulder. He thought she seemed sad.

Later, at home, Sterling leaned against the kitchen doorframe, watching his mother doze in front of the television.

"Hey, Mama," he said.

She started awake and turned around. "Hey there." With a groan, she pushed herself off the sofa. The twins were curled up together asleep in a mound of curly hair and pajamas. "It's late. Biscuits'll be dried out."

"I ain't hungry," he said. "I'll eat 'em for breakfast."

"You sure?" She brushed by him and flicked on the kitchen light.

"Yeah. I ate a lot at Dairy Queen."

"I don't know why she's got to keep you so late." His mother turned off the oven, then took out the biscuits.

"She didn't keep me. She's got this computer. I was messing around on it some."

His mother frowned. "Tara Wells was telling me the other day how she seen this thing on Oprah about a boy who got hooked up with some homosexual over the computer and ended up killing hisself."

Sterling laughed. "I ain't talking to nobody on the computer. I'm looking up stuff about the space telescope."

"Well, you never know who might be out there."

"Whatever." She'd never finished high school and sometimes he got frustrated with how dumb she could be.

"I know she pays you good money." His mother opened a drawer and pulled out a plastic freezer bag. "But we don't really know nothing about her. I mean, the way she's got you crawling around under her house. What do you know about fixing a hole in someone's foundation? It don't seem right, her asking you to do that." She dropped the leftover biscuits into the freezer bag and put it on the counter.

"She's okay," he said. "I promise I ain't gonna talk with no queers over the computer."

She sighed. "You sure you don't want something to eat?"

"Naw, I ain't hungry. Think I'll turn in. 'Night, Mama," he said.

"'Night, darlin'."

The floor squeaked as he headed to his room. Once inside, he closed the door and turned on the light beside his bed. He brought out the rest of the lasagna, ate it all with his fingers, then wiped them on his T-shirt. Afterwards, he pulled off the T-shirt and tossed it onto a pile of dirty clothes in the corner. He picked up the book he'd been trying to read, *The Right Stuff,* about the first astronauts; but, instead of reading, he stretched out on his back, the book open on his chest.

Evenings were hard on him lately. In years past, it used to be he could think about the end of summer, about going back to school and the people he'd see, the stuff he'd do, the girls he wanted to go out with. Now he was starting to realize that, come fall, he wasn't going back to school. Instead, he'd keep working. Tomorrow would be like today. Every day would be like today, forever.

Sterling thought about how old his mama looked and realized he'd probably look that way when he was her age. He switched out the light and lay on his back staring at the stick-on glow in the dark constellations on his painted-black ceiling. Cassiopeia, Gemini, Virgo. He imagined floating out there with all those stars, far away from home. Floating, with nothing to do but look around the universe.

❦ chapter twelve ❦

July 14

WHEN Sterling was eleven, his daddy had taken him along on a haul up to Kentucky. Sterling remembered how new the world had seemed on that trip. Even the sky didn't look like the same old sky when he was sitting beside his daddy in the rumbling, rough-riding cab. As he looked down at the cars humming by like insects, he realized that the world was bigger and more amazing than he'd imagined, and it made him feel excited and a little scared.

Whenever they stopped at a truck stop, he put on a hard tough act for all the other drivers because inside he felt shaky. But he felt different too, his stomach dancing with the sight of the mountains and how high up they seemed.

That's the way he felt around Lara. Different, and sort of shaky.

Sterling got a day off from Dairy Queen and at eleven o'clock Sunday morning found himself sitting beside Lara in her car, his eyes stinging from the wind blasting through the open windows. She looked pretty in a pale blue sundress. He liked how when she pulled her hair up, he could see soft brown fuzz on the back of her neck.

"Haven't been to Atlanta since I went to a Braves game for my birthday a couple of years ago," he said, then paused. "Hey, my birthday's next month. You think you'd go out with me if I was eighteen?"

She laughed. "You don't give up, do you?"

"I could enlist in the army when I'm eighteen. Least you could do is go out with me."

She flashed him a smile. Her teeth were so perfect, so straight, even, and white. They almost glowed. He wanted to tell her how beautiful her mouth was. How he fixated on it sometimes—well, most of the time.

THE interstate cut an asphalt ribbon through forests draped with kudzu, and Lara's little car wove among a moving tractor-trailer maze. Exit signs advertised gas stations and fast food franchises, but all Lara could see were softly mounded trees and the rest of the traffic. Sitting in the car beside Sterling, she thought about how good it was to get him out of Barton County.

She remembered leaving her own home at twenty to move in with Dylan.

"You're wasting your life," her father had said as she boxed up books in her room. "Environmental Consultant. Why do you want to be an environmental consultant? There's no money in it. Everyone in Washington sees those types as freaks. You're ruining your chances at a real career."

Lara had continued to shove books into the box, determined to ignore her father who'd already lectured her on this subject a dozen times.

"It's that Dylan's fault."

"His name isn't 'That Dylan,' Dad."

"You're twenty years old," her father said as if it explained why he hated Dylan. "You're not even old enough to drink, and you're following him around like a puppy. He's ten years older than you."

"Nine," Lara protested.

"Too old for you," her father insisted. "You know how I feel about this." He jutted his chin toward the boxes. "You're not married. You shouldn't be living together. You're too young." Lara folded the flaps of one box , set it on the floor, then picked up an empty one. "You're being impetuous."

"No, Dad, I'm following my heart."

"Following your heart? Ha!"

Lara's face burned with shame and anger. She stopped packing and glared at her father. "You just don't want my job and my relationship with Dylan to embarrass you. You live in this narrow, selfish world where you don't care about anyone or anything but yourself and the money you make and who your precious friends on The Hill are."

She braced herself for a barrage, but instead was met by silence. Her father's face turned pale, his jaw clenched. With an abrupt about-face, he wheeled and strode out of her bedroom, slamming the door behind him.

That night, Dylan met her at his apartment and she cried in his arms until long after midnight.

"You're an adult," Dylan kept repeating. "You don't need his permission. You're old enough to make your own decisions."

LARA glanced at Sterling, who had a foot propped in the open window. His shoe was dirty and torn. His head lolled against the headrest as he watched the passing cars. Staring at his shoe and then his handsome profile, Lara thought she might love him in the way she imagined girls used to love soldiers bound for the front: a passion born of pity.

Lara wanted to say something nice, to build Sterling up and make him feel good about himself. "I'm impressed by how much you like astronomy. I always thought it was a difficult subject."

He rolled his head toward her and his eyes fixed on her face. His mouth straightened into a serious line before he turned back to the window. She didn't understand his expression. Was it anger? Regret? It froze her into silence.

She began reading license plates: Georgia, South Carolina, Florida, Pennsylvania. She thought about how many cities were connected by this highway, how if she turned north and drove for ten hours, she'd end up back home. Maybe she should do that, should take Sterling with her. There were other places she thought of taking him too. The King Memorial, the High Museum, Fernbank.

Streams of cars spurted onto the interstate. The highway widened to eight lanes. Her heart raced. This landscape was familiar. No more trees and kudzu, but parking lots, strip malls, car dealerships, everything surrounded by steaming asphalt, as if humanity could no longer endure nature and overcompensated with blacktop. Crowded highways like the ones around Washington. Like the one that had killed Dylan.

"That's our exit," Lara saw it coming up fast on the right. She began maneuvering into the exit lane, cutting off cars so that Sterling gripped the dashboard and gave an Indian war whoop.

"This is great," he breathed. "Man, I wish I had a car. I'd be out of Barton County in a second."

"What's wrong with Barton County?" She feigned innocence as she jerked the car into the exit lane.

"You want that list in alphabetical order?"

"A whole list? Is that a good way to talk about your home?"

"There ain't anything to do in Barton County that I haven't done a hundred times," Sterling muttered. "I want to go someplace big where nobody knows me."

"I was thinking," she began, then faltered, cleared her throat and started again, "I was thinking about going to see Martin Luther King's memorial."

Something in her tone of voice made Sterling uneasy. That and the way she gave him a sidelong look, as if trying to see his reaction without him noticing. Then all of a sudden he understood. After the communism thing, she was trying to see how ignorant and redneck he really was. Sterling felt sick and hated himself and her both. He thought about how to get back at her, and had an idea.

"No way," he said. "Man, I ain't going to that place."

He watched Lara's face lose its color. "Why? What's wrong with it?"

"Well, you know my mama's in the Klan." He tried to pull out the drawl in his voice so he sounded even more redneck. "Some day I's gonna be in the Klan too, and they won't let you in the Klan if you ever been to that Martin Luther King place."

Lara's mouth hung open for a second. Then she pressed her lips together until they turned white.

"And I wouldn't want to miss my Klan initiation 'cause they have this big picnic, and you know what's best about that?" He waited for her to answer, but all she did was make a little choked sound in the back of her throat. "The best thing about that-there picnic is the food they serve. Dead possum scraped right off the road."

He couldn't be mad any more when he saw the look on her face. It was like kids in the Elks' haunted house who stuck their hand into a bowl of Jell-O and got told it was mashed eyeballs. The kids stood for a second imagining those mashed eyeballs and feeling squeamish until they realized it was just Jell-O. Lara's mouth began turning up at the corners like she understood what he'd said was Jell-O. Sterling couldn't help but grin.

"Creep!" She breathed, her face flushing. Then she punched his arm. "You shouldn't joke about that. It's not right to joke about it."

"Yeah, well, it isn't right to assume stuff about folks either." His temper rose again. "I've been to Dr. King's memorial three times. And if you want to know why some country white guy took the trouble to go there, it's 'cause Dr. King accepted the responsibility God gave him. He took the burden on himself and didn't expect anyone else to do it for him." Lara was quiet. She stared straight ahead of her. "So you see, I might not know much about communism, but there's some stuff I do know about."

"You don't understand," she murmured. "That's not what I meant."

They sat silently as the car crept along in traffic. He felt bad for snapping at her, but then decided he had the right. He was sick of people acting like they knew everything about him when they didn't. And he hated that she thought he was some dumb redneck.

When Lara turned toward a brick warehouse surrounded by cars, he couldn't resist getting in one last jab. "So we aren't going to the King memorial?"

"Maybe another day," she said.

Thin, sickly trees with papery ash-colored leaves separated the rows of parked cars. A few huge shopping carts stood abandoned in the lot. "What'd you have to come all this way to buy, anyways?"

"Groceries." Lara pulled the car into an empty parking space. "I thought you wanted the chance to carry grocery bags for me."

He remembered how she wouldn't let him carry her bags at Ingles's. "Man, I been living to carry your groceries." He grinned and she smiled back.

As she got out of the car, a breeze caught Lara's blue skirt and swayed it around her legs. *All this way for groceries,* he thought. *Lord, she's two bricks shy of a load and counting.*

The inside of the farmer's market was a vegetable maze. The ceiling was too far up to notice, and the lights glared bright like full sunshine. Sterling found himself surrounded by wet, dewy piles of peppers, broccoli, squash, eggplant, sprouts. Every kind of vegetable he'd ever laid eyes on, and some he'd never seen before, towered around him.

He watched Lara push a giant shopping cart through the crowd the way she'd driven her car on the highway, fast and wild, so that people veered out of her path and shot angry looks over their shoulders. When she stopped suddenly to stare at a basket full of mushrooms that looked like dried pig ears, two people almost ran into her from behind.

An Indian woman stood nearby holding a round-faced baby. Sterling gaped at her dark skin, a shining dot painted between her eyes. The place was crowded with men and women like her. They looked so beautiful and so different from what he was used to.

Lara moved forward again and he followed, turning sideways to slide between other shopping carts. People brushed against him. So many people. His heart pounded like it had at the truck stops when he was a kid, and he liked it, the feeling of not knowing what was going on, of being lost someplace strange. Hurrying in front of Lara, he jumped onto the end of the shopping cart opposite her, his feet resting on the metal tube above the wheels. The cart tilted toward him.

"Careful," she warned. "I don't want this to turn into some bizarre episode of *Rescue 911*."

He tried to sound like William Shatner. "It started out as an ordinary shopping trip."

Lara cast him a grin, then paused to pick up a long, thin reed that looked like something you'd find growing in a pond.

"You know, most of this stuff looks like what you feed cattle," he said.

"This is lemon grass. For Thai cooking." She slid the reed into a clear plastic bag.

"Tie?" He pronounced it tah, and she smiled.

"Thai. You know Thailand, right?"

He didn't know Thailand. He felt that same angry prickling he had earlier, along with a wave of shame. Was she *trying* to make him feel like an idiot? He jumped off the cart and scuffed his feet along the floor.

"Jesus, what did they teach you at school?" Lara demanded. "Look, I'll make you Thai food when we get home. It's spicy. You'll like it, and Thailand is in Asia, near Cambodia. Please tell me you've heard of Cambodia."

He hadn't heard of anything. He shot her a bitter glare and with quick strides plunged into the crowd.

All at once, he was out of vegetables and into fruits, the green giving way to yellows and oranges. He turned around, but couldn't see Lara. *Good*, he thought. *On my own*. He let his gaze roam down the aisle. He'd never seen so much fruit in one place. He noticed the waffled texture of cantaloupe rinds, the fuzz on peaches, fat blueberries filmed with moisture. *Fruit is beautiful*, he thought.

He rounded a corner to see a pile of strawberries burying a long table in a bright red mound. Sterling couldn't remember the last time he'd eaten a strawberry. His mouth watered, and the idea of tasting strawberries held him paralyzed. He thought about stealing a few.

"Hey, Sterling," Lara came up beside him, startling him. She touched the back of his hand with cool fingers. "I'm sorry."

He didn't answer, just stared at the strawberries, then at his feet, at his dirty tennis shoes.

"Let me make it up to you," she continued. "I'll buy you anything you want. Pick something."

He was strongly tempted. His face twisted as his eyes lingered on the strawberries. The air smelled like honey. Then he shook his head. "Naw, you don't have to buy me anything."

"I'm really sorry," she said again.

He walked to a pile of peaches and picked one up, testing its ripeness. Lara walked over and took a peach too, holding it out to him and asking "Does this look like a good one?"

He shrugged. He took the peach from her hand, squeezed it, and said "Yeah, it looks okay."

She carefully placed it in the cart and they continued on.

The food in the next aisle looked like science fiction fruit. It was so strange that for a second it made Sterling forget about being angry. He walked around gaping, then seized a long, thick, bristling root. "What the hell?" Cocking it behind his shoulder like a baseball bat, he took a few practice swings.

"Jamaican breadfruit," Lara said. "I've never had it."

He put the breadfruit back. "Look at how tiny them oranges are."

"Quince," Lara said.

Sterling grabbed three of the quince and juggled them, the fruit sailing in circles around his head while Lara laughed. When he stopped, Lara applauded. Some other folks did too. He took a bow.

By this time, Lara's cart had become so full that she was disappearing behind the groceries. Sterling felt a reckless delight at the way she picked up things without looking at the price, without standing for minutes trying to calculate if she had enough money.

"I'm wondering when the cart is gonna start breaking apart under all this weight," he said.

"Shut up." She seized a box of chocolates and threw them at him. He caught them and tossed them back.

They waited in line at the register for a long time. When it was their turn, Lara began unloading her food onto the conveyer belt. One item after another went across the scanner and was placed in plastic shopping bags by a pretty foreign girl.

Lara dug in her purse. The girl clicked the total key and said "$128.42." Sterling watched Lara's expression to see how she'd react. He wondered for a second what she'd put back. Then she brought out her checkbook and he realized she was going to buy it all. $128.42. All for groceries for one person. He gaped at the green lighted numbers on the cash register, then made himself look away.

"Time to get to work." Lara smiled.

The illuminated green $128.42 still floated in Sterling's vision as he took hold of the loaded shopping cart and maneuvered it outside. After the cold store, the air was heavy and oppressive. He didn't want to be pushing her cart, didn't want to be lifting her groceries into the back seat like a stupid bag boy. The $128.42 grew larger in his mind and projected onto the side of her white car like a movie onto a screen. He finished loading and slammed the door shut. Lara stood a few feet away shielding her eyes, looking at the sky. Thunderheads were rolling in, and to the west the sky had turned slate gray.

"I think it's going to rain," she said.

LARA stared at her hands as they rested on the steering wheel. Sterling had become quiet and sullen. She didn't understand. He'd seemed over his anger a minute ago. What had happened to make him this way again? She felt miserable. Nothing had gone the way she'd wanted it to. She'd insulted him twice, and hadn't found a way to take him to the movies or the mall or anyplace a teenager might want to go.

What am I doing? Lara thought. *I don't really understand what he's going through, or how to help him. I've never needed money, don't know what it's like to need it.* She looked at Sterling, who was sitting the way he always sat, leaned back, legs falling apart, that great adolescent look like he had no interest in the world because it was all too boring.

Lara slid the key into the ignition. "We should have done something else first," she said. "Now we have to get the groceries back to the fridge. I'm sorry, Sterling. I'm really sorry."

He gave her a distant look, and didn't respond.

On the highway, thick drops began to spatter the windshield. The silence in the car was oppressive, and Lara wondered if she should apologize to Sterling again. A flash of lightning illuminated the sky, followed by a crack of thunder. Lara rolled up her window. As the storm broke, the windscreen began to fog over. Lara switched on the defroster, which blew warm air. Traffic was heavy and slow. She held the wheel tightly as a gust of wind blasted the car and it veered sideways. Ahead of her, the other cars were obscured by rain, the outlines of the road melting away with the water.

"I can't see anything. I'm going to pull over."

She maneuvered the car off the highway, finally coming to an abrupt stop at the side of the road. Outside the passenger window, a wall of pine trees bent and swayed in the wind. As the warm rattling defroster blew in her face, she heard the endless stream of traffic spraying past and the drumming of rain on the roof. The world dissolved into a blurred, hazy green. She turned off the defroster and cracked her window open to ease the heat, then glanced at Sterling who was staring outside. She looked at her watch. It was noon. He must be hungry. She studied his flat belly for a moment and urgently felt the need to feed him. *Wait,* a stern voice in her head began, but she ignored it. After all, she had to do something to make him feel better.

STERLING watched the rain hit the asphalt. He couldn't stop thinking about Lara's groceries.

"Are you hungry?" Lara asked. "It's lunch time." Not waiting for him to answer, she reached into a grocery bag in the back seat. She brought out a pint of strawberries, popped open their plastic lid, and picked out a big one. "Makeshift lunch," she declared. Rolling down her window farther, she dangled the strawberry outside to rinse it in the rain. When she brought it in again, the strawberry glistened with moisture, and a single elongated drop of water hung from its bright red tip.

"Here." He watched the strawberry as it came closer to his mouth, its green stem pinched between her fingers. She wagged it a little, tempting him. "Have one."

He opened his mouth, feeling the cool tip of the fruit touch his tongue. He dug his teeth into the flesh and took the berry out of her hand, his lips brushing her fingertips. Then he bit down, catching the stem in his hand.

Sterling was stunned by the strawberry's sweetness, by the way its juices exploded in his mouth. He let his head fall back. She offered him another and he sucked it right out of her fingers, her nails against his teeth. It was weird, he thought, how one second he was ashamed around Lara, and the next he was turned on.

Somewhere between the sixth and seventh strawberry, the storm ended, but it took him a while to notice. He looked away from Lara's fingers to see the world lying quiet and dripping beyond the window. As the sun broke, the steaming pavement gleamed and water droplets sparkled on the windshield.

"It's like a whole new place," Lara said, then paused. "I'm sorry I didn't take you to the King Memorial. I'm sorry we didn't do anything but grocery shopping."

Sterling thought she looked unhappy. "You don't want to go back, do you?"

She shook her head.

"Me neither." For a few seconds they were both silent. "How 'bout we drive to the desert?"

"The desert? Out West?"

"Yeah. At night we'll pull off the road and sit on the hood so we can see all the stars real bright. You know, the light coming off of those stars had to travel for so many years that the stars are dead now."

"That's sad," she said. "But going to the desert sounds nice."

"It ain't like we don't have enough food to keep us."

She smiled. He lifted his left arm and with forced casualness draped it over the back of her seat so he had his arm around her even though they weren't touching. "You ever been to the desert before?" he asked in a low voice.

"No, I never have."

"I bet you've been a lot of places, though."

She nodded. "Yes, I guess."

"Where's the wildest place you've ever been?"

"Define 'wildest'."

"You know, some place where you didn't have any idea what was going on."

"That's easy, your home town."

He laughed. "Yeah, I guess you might feel kind of strange if you weren't born there. Hell, I feel strange, and I lived there all my life."

She looked at him, and her eyes seemed very big. "Maybe that's because you don't belong there."

"Yeah?" He leaned closer to her, lowering his voice. "Where do I belong?"

"I don't know. I guess that's for you to find out."

He stared at her intently. "I really like you a lot."

Her face flushed red down to the neck. "I like you a lot too, kiddo." She sounded too cheerful. He stared at the soft hair under her ponytail and wanted to touch it but thought he'd better stop. He'd come pretty far already today and didn't want to spook her.

He pulled his arm back to his side and looked out the window. "I guess we gotta be getting that food to your fridge 'fore it goes bad, and I told my sisters I'd hang their swing for 'em."

"No," she said. "Let's go somewhere, really. You choose. I don't give a damn about the groceries."

"Naw, I gotta get home. I gotta fix that swing."

"Oh." She hung her head for a moment, then looked up. "We have to have dessert." Lara reached into a bag and brought out a chocolate bar. Pulling away the foil wrapper, she exposed the dark flat slab. She broke off a piece and handed it to Sterling, who turned the chocolate over, studying it, feeling it cool and hard against his fingers. He put it in his mouth, let it dissolve and run down his throat, rich and dark, so that it took his breath for a second. "Damn," he muttered.

"Good, huh?"

He nodded, dropped his head back, and closed his eyes.

When she pulled back onto the highway, Sterling rested his head against the rim of the open window. The air had the hot metallic smell of wet asphalt. He felt changed by the day, like he was going home a different person. He looked over at Lara and thought about how mad he'd been earlier. Only now he wasn't mad at all. Now he kind of loved her. He wondered what it would be like to kiss her. How her lips would taste. Right now, like strawberries and chocolate. "I can't believe you went all the way to Atlanta for groceries," he said.

"I guess it was pretty stupid."

"It was great. I never played baseball with a breadfruit before."

"Let me make you dinner?"

"It's not even close to dinner time."

"Well, you could stay until then."

"I gotta fix my sisters' swing."

"Can't you do it after dinner? It'll still be light."

"You know, for someone who won't go out with me, you seem mighty anxious to have me around." He gave her a long hard look. Her ears turned red.

"You're seventeen," she said as if it explained everything, which, he thought, it didn't.

BACK in town, he helped her unload groceries, and she made him dinner. Now it was late and dark and raining again. He knew he'd be in trouble for not hanging the swing. "I best be getting on," he said.

"I'm sorry. I never meant to keep you so long. Let me give you some money."

"For what? I didn't do anything."

"You carried groceries."

"That was nothing. 'Sides, you made me dinner."

"But you helped."

"Listen, I ain't taking your money."

They stood frowning at each other for a second. Then Lara turned and went to get her purse in the living room. "Well if you won't take money, at least let me drive you home." She started searching in the purse for her keys.

"Naw, it ain't far."

"But it's pouring."

"I don't mind."

She gave him a hard look. "I'm driving you. That's all there is to it."

He didn't know what to say. He couldn't argue. He'd get soaked if he walked, so he shrugged. "Okay."

They ran to the car, hunched against the rain. Inside, they slammed the doors and sat gasping for a few seconds. The windshield began fogging. "Just tell me where to go," she breathed. Water rolled from her hair onto her cheeks.

He thought fast and came up with a plan. As they drove he gave her directions, careful directions to a house in town that wasn't his any more. Not a big or fancy house, but a neat little clean house with a picket fence, azalea bushes, and a nice flower garden out front. He felt pretty smug for coming up with the idea. So smug he didn't think he'd mind getting wet when he walked two miles home in the rain.

"Here," he pointed.

"What?" For a moment, Lara looked like she'd drive right by.

"Here, right here," Sterling insisted. "Pull over."

Lara pulled over and sat gaping at the small white house. "That's where you live?" she asked.

"That's it."

Lightning flared, and he saw her face lit by the glare. Her eyes seemed huge. "This is it?" Her voice quavered.

"Yeah."

"But—"

"What?"

Another flash of lightning and she clutched the steering wheel. Her chin trembled.

Sterling squinted at her in the dark. "What's going on?" She didn't say anything. He bent closer and peered at her face. "I'll see you tomorrow, you know," he said. "I'll come by after work and fix that screen door."

She nodded. Sterling put his fingers on the door handle.

"No, wait. It's raining."

"It's only a little ways."

"Just wait until the rain stops."

He shrugged. "Okay."

Lara put the car in neutral and pulled on the parking brake. He peered at her, not understanding why she seemed so unhappy. "You're . . ." he started, then faltered. "I mean, if you're feeling real low or something, I'll go back to your house and hang out 'til the storm's through. I could walk from there. It isn't a big deal." Lara remained silent. "Is it that guy?" he asked awkwardly. "That guy from Washington?"

She didn't speak, didn't move, just sat with her chin trembling, gripping the wheel. The headlights' beams caught falling streaks of water. Sterling felt waves of emotion coming off Lara like heat off asphalt. He could almost see them ripple around her in the dark.

"You want to go to the desert and watch stars?" she asked.

"Yeah."

"Let's do it then. Right now."

For a second he hoped she was talking about sex, but then realized she meant leaving town for real.

He felt the cold suddenly, understood he was shivering, knew his muscles ached and that he was bone-tired and that his stomach felt funny from all the strange food he'd eaten today. He knew his mama would be waiting to give him hell, and the girls would be in their pajamas, looking out the window for him.

"I can't." The words sunk him. "I gotta get home, Lara."

"I know," she said. "I was just pretending."

He stared out at the rain, thinking about how wet he was going to get, and how cold, and maybe even hit by lightning. He gripped the door handle. "It's been a real nice day."

"Can't you wait until the rain stops?"

He shook his head. "Naw. It might go on all night."

She touched his arm and said, "Good night," and when he turned to say good night too, she kissed him on the mouth, a light little kiss like the feel of a feather. He sat for a second, breathing hard.

"You want to come back over here and do that again?" he asked.

She shook her head.

He waited a second to see if she meant it. She didn't move. "I guess I'm going." He opened the door and slid into the rain.

He ran to the tidy white house like it was his own, ducked around back, and waited until the car motor started up. Then waited some more. The rain pattered on his head and soaked into his T-shirt. His jeans stuck to the flesh of his legs, and still she didn't leave. He stood there dripping in the rain, begging her in his mind to drive away.

Finally, the headlights' beams flared across the wall of the house next door, then arced down the street, leaving him in darkness. He came around the corner and crossed the front yard to the sidewalk, turned east, and began the long walk home.

chapter thirteen

E RIC had just turned off the TV when the phone rang.

"It's Lara." She sounded upset.

"You shouldn't be calling. There's lightning."

"I'm sorry. Hey, I needed to ask you: that house you showed me, Sterling's house? It really was his, right? You weren't just joking?"

"Yeah, it was his."

"Jesus, Eric, I just gave him a ride home, only the place he told me to go to wasn't the one you showed me. I left him there. I didn't know what else to do. It's a long way from his real house, and he's walking in the storm. Do you think you could find him and give him a ride?"

Eric reached for his jacket, frustrated by the absurdity of the situation. "If it'll make you feel better, I'll try. The dumb kid should just be honest with you. Tell me where you dropped him."

Lara described the house and its location.

"That's his old house," Eric said. "The one he lived in before his dad left."

S TERLING was already home by the time Eric made it into town. He stood dripping on the worn linoleum in the kitchen, feeling warm and good inside even though he was shivering. He'd thought about Lara all the way home: that wave of heat coming off of her, the way she kissed him.

In the living room, the sofa was pulled out into bed form and his sisters huddled under the blankets, eyes round from the thunder and lightning. He lunged toward them, fingers clawed to tickle. They shrieked and curled into tight protective balls.

"No!" his mother called from the kitchen. "Don't you go getting them all worked up. It took me two hours to get 'em calm enough to lie down after you not showing up all day."

He leaped onto the sofa bed, grabbing Darlene, who screamed and writhed.

"Sterling!" His mother sounded fierce. "I mean it now. Stop fooling with your sisters and go dry off. I don't see why that woman couldn't give you a ride home."

"I wouldn't let her, Ma. Ain't her fault. She asked. I just wanted to walk."

"Well, she shouldn't have let you, way it's raining out."

As he walked toward his room, he saw a flash of lightning.

"Sterling!" His mama stopped him short at his bedroom door. "Come on in here." He knew he was in for it and dragged into the kitchen, head hanging. "I know she pays you good money, baby," his mother whispered so the girls couldn't hear. "But you told them you'd fix that swing and spend the afternoon with them."

"I know, Mama, I'm sorry. The weather just kept us in Atlanta longer'n I thought."

She nodded. "Okay, but next time make sure she gets you back earlier. It's been a hard day for them girls." His mother stared at him for a few seconds. She did that sometimes, as if she couldn't believe she'd had a brown-haired baby and wondered if he'd been switched at birth. She reached out and touched Sterling's hair. "It's getting long again. You want me to cut it for you?"

"Naw, not yet."

"The color's growing out."

"I know."

She touched his cheek, then let her hand fall to her side. "Promise me you'll put that swing up tomorrow."

"Yeah," said Sterling, "I gotta go over to Lara's, but I won't stay long."

"Them girls has already had one daddy leave 'em."

"I know," he said. "I had one daddy leave me too."

July 16

A s he watched Sterling roll across the parking lot on his skate-board, Eric understood that showing Lara his house was going to have far-reaching consequences. Things were getting messy, and he resented it.

Sterling bounded up the stoop, burst through the door, and strode into the shop whistling. *Damned kid,* Eric thought, *he's never tired. He walked home in the worst storm of the summer, and from the way he's strutting around you'd think he'd spent the night at a Bermuda resort.*

"What's up?" Eric asked as Sterling dropped his skateboard in the office, then hunkered down behind the counter and loaded a CD into the store's sound system.

"What's up is I'm about to get me a date with Lara." He straight-ened and grinned as Garbage's "Stupid Girl" started playing.

"What's your evidence?"

Sterling's head began bobbing to the music. "She kissed me good night last night."

For an instant, Eric experienced a rush of envy, then he thought *wait, she kissed me good night, too.* "A light little kiss on the mouth?"

Sterling nodded.

"Sorry, Romeo, but she kissed me that way too. I see how you could mistake it for meaning something, but some people kiss hello and goodbye, and I think Lara's one of those people."

Sterling seemed nonplussed. "Naw, it was more than that." He passed behind Eric, clapping him amiably on the back. "Hey, you got one of them books that has all the maps of the world?"

"What, an atlas?"

"Yeah, that's it. Can I borrow it?"

"Sure. Why?"

"Just want to. And I want to borrow some other books too."

"Like what?"

"I don't know. Like books to read, you know."

"That's generally what you do with books."

"I mean good books, like literature and stuff."

"If you'd done your English homework, you'd have already read a lot of literature."

Sterling leaned against the counter. "I swear that kiss wasn't just nothing, Eric. She seemed pretty worked up, if you know what I mean."

A Labrador retriever, Eric thought. That's what the kid reminded him of. The kind of dog that, even when you stopped throwing the ball, would hang around with the sure belief that you'd throw it again if he only stared at you hard enough. It made Eric resentful. He wished he could be like that—young and self-confident and full of arrogance. He wanted to deflate the boy's ridiculous sense of triumph.

"Yeah, she was worked up. She was trying to figure out why the hell you asked her to drop you at someone else's house."

Sterling stared at Eric blankly at first. Then his expression darkened.

"You should have let her drive you home. She knows where you live."

"What do you mean, she knows where I live?"

"I pointed it out to her."

Sterling's face twisted. "You showed her my house?" Eric sensed the boy's body coiling, his hands balling into fists. For a moment, he thought Sterling would hit him, but instead he whirled and stomped into the office.

Eric followed him. Sterling collapsed in the office chair, muttering "And here I was feeling all good about last night. Turns out she just felt sorry for me 'cause I'm so poor and pitiful." Sterling folded his arms on the desk and laid his head on them. "Man, and dinner, and all that fruit and stuff in the car, and paying me for doing nothing. Shit."

Eric regretted that he'd said it.

"And when the fuck did you show her my house? You said you weren't going out with her again, but you must have, to show her my house."

"I—"

"Leave me alone," Sterling growled. "Just leave me alone."

A T eight o'clock when Eric and Sterling stepped out of the air-conditioned store and into the parking lot, the sun was beginning to set. The sky overhead flushed pale pink and the heat from the pavement washed around Eric's ankles like warm water. Sterling hadn't spoken to him all day.

Eric unlocked his car. "So are you going to forgive me long enough to let me give you a ride home?"

Sterling dropped his skateboard to the pavement and prodded at it with the toe of his tennis shoe, then shielded his eyes and stared across the street in sullen silence.

"Come on," Eric urged. "You don't have to talk to me or anything. Hell, be as pissed as you want." He held open the passenger door. "Hop in."

Sterling looked as if for once in his life he was too tired to argue. He grabbed the skateboard, slouched toward the car, and slumped into the seat, pulling the door shut behind him. Eric jumped in and started the engine. After backing out of the lot, he turned right onto the deserted street. They drove in silence.

"I'm sorry about showing her your house," Eric said. "But you're too proud. You're making this a bigger deal than it is."

"So what, I ain't supposed to be proud no more?" Sterling muttered.

"No, I meant she doesn't care where you live."

Sterling fell silent again. Crossing his arms over his chest, he bit his lower lip with an ugly scowl like he hated the world and everything in it.

Eric remembered a day nearly four years ago when Sterling, then just a stringy fourteen-year-old, had come into work scowling like that. It was just a few months since his daddy had disappeared.

"Hey, Eric," he'd said, pressing his fist under his nose. "Could you teach me how to fight?"

Eric studied the boy's bruised cheek and scraped arms. "What happened?"

"Aw, some guys at school was givin' me shit."

"'Bout what?"

Sterling fell silent. He hung his head and his eyes shone. Eric realized the boy was about to cry. Sterling let his fist fall and Eric saw a trickle of blood under his nose. He hurried to the office, brought back some Kleenex and handed it to the boy.

"I know the guy who owns the karate school. I'll see if he can give you a few pointers."

Sterling blinked back tears. "Thanks, man."

Eric gripped the boy's shoulder and shook it a couple of times. "Don't let it get to you. I've seen half of those kids' daddies passed out behind the liquor store on Sunday mornings."

Sterling had always been a fighter, Eric thought, but not in a mean-spirited way. He didn't go hunting for disagreements; he just couldn't turn down a challenge. Eric remembered how, at thirteen, Sterling took on the responsibility of earning money for his family with grim seriousness. He remembered the boy standing beside him, brow furrowed with concentration while Eric taught him how to work the register and fill out order forms.

In the months after Sterling took the job, Eric had watched as the boy's body, face, and demeanor seemed to grow to match that adult gravity. He grew seven inches between his fifteenth and sixteenth birthdays, and by seventeen was six feet tall. His scrawny form filled out, his facial features hardened from those of a scared kid to those of a young man. It was as if Sterling bypassed the worst of adolescence, the long gangly limbs and bad skin, and went straight into adulthood.

Except for a streak of rebellion. The day Sterling turned sixteen, he'd strutted into the store and stopped in front of Eric, turning his head left, then right, waiting to be noticed. Eric glanced up and did a double-take.

Sterling's dark brown hair was gone. In its place gleamed a platinum buzz cut. His mangled ear lobes were swollen red and bristling with tiny gold-loop earrings.

"What in God's name did you do to yourself?" Eric demanded.

"Dyed my hair."

"What did your mother say?"

"She ain't seen it yet." Sterling gave a sheepish grin. "Somebody'll tell her about it 'fore she sees it, so I'm thinking maybe she'll have a chance to get over being angry by the time I get home."

"No, trust me, she'll be plenty angry. What the hell were you thinking?"

Sterling stuck his chin out. "I was thinking if everybody in this goddamned town is gonna look at me and whisper about me all the time, I might as well give them something to look at."

"You're going to get the crap beat out of you," Eric said. "If your mama doesn't do it, the guys at school will."

"I ain't afraid of them."

"What about girls?" Eric demanded. "You'll never get a date looking like that. In Athens, maybe, but not with the country–western girls around here."

Sterling's grin widened. "Shoot, I can get any girl I want."

Eric had lifted a skeptical eyebrow and thought *geez, the kid has self-confidence.*

A few weeks later, Sterling came into the shop breathless, and, springing onto the counter, sat swinging his legs and watching Eric.

"What's up?" Eric knew from experience that Sterling needed only a small nudge to start talking.

"I did it," Sterling announced.

"Did what?"

"*It.*" Sterling insisted. "You know."

Eric stopped filing new CDs and gaped at Sterling who grinned. "You had sex?"

Sterling bit his lip, which was what he always did to keep from smiling too wide.

"With who?"

"Mandy Jennings."

"That little blonde girl? I thought she had a boyfriend."

Sterling stopped trying to disguise his grin, and it burst across his face so brightly that Eric had to smile too. "She does. Brad Richter."

"So what are you doing having sex with her?"

"Brad called me a queer. Guess I proved him wrong."

"Having some guy call you queer isn't a reason to be doing his girlfriend," Eric protested.

"Sure it is," Sterling said.

"Tell me you used a condom at least."

"'Course. You scared the shit out of me with that AIDS stuff."

"I'm glad something sank in." Eric turned back to the CD rack and continued filing for a moment. How had he gotten into this position, he wondered? This wasn't his kid. Still, in some strange way he felt proud and delighted. Sixteen years old. What he wouldn't have given to do it at sixteen. He looked at Sterling and grinned. "So, how was it?"

In a way, Eric guessed he lived vicariously through Sterling. His own adolescence had been a long acne-filled nightmare spent preoccupied with yearbook, band, and how to look like he weighed more than 115. During high school, Eric watched boys like Sterling from a distance as they flirted and grinned and charmed their way through life. He envied the hell out of them. Now, at age thirty, through some twist of fate, Eric found himself sort of raising a boy like that. Problem was, he hadn't quite gotten rid of the envy.

A few yards from Sterling's house, Eric looked at the dejected boy and tried to think of the right thing to say. A way to apologize for letting adolescent jealousy get the better of him. "Listen, you're an adult," he said. "I can't tell you what to do, but what I'd do is I'd go and talk to Lara. Let her know how you feel."

Sterling spread his fingers and looked at his dirty nails. "Naw, I been workin' all day. I ain't clean."

"You look fine," Eric insisted. "You go over there dirty all the time anyway. Listen, she was worried about you last night. When women get worried like that, you can use it to your advantage."

Sterling examined Eric's face. "What about you? Don't you want to go out with her?"

Eric debated what to say. "Yeah, but I think I want to go out with her for the wrong reasons, so I'm going to back off."

"What reasons?" Sterling asked.

"'Cause she's pretty and I haven't had a date in a while."

"Sounds like a good enough reason to me," Sterling said.

"That's 'cause you're seventeen. When you're older, you'll know what I mean. And anyway, I'm sorry for showing her your house."

Sterling frowned and stared at his nails.

"Come on," Eric urged. "We both know you want to see her."

chapter fourteen

July 16, 8:00 P.M.

LARA sat on the front porch, arms wrapped around her knees. As she ignored the occasional mosquito sting and waited, she thought about last night, about lying in the dark while lightning struck so close to the house that the air sizzled for an instant before thunder shook the walls. She had been unable to sleep from thinking of Dylan and from knowing that Sterling was walking home under the pouring, electric sky. What if something had happened to him? He could have fallen and hurt himself. He could have been hit by a car.

The storm had rolled on, the thunder growing softer, the lightning fading. Murky night had enveloped the house and seeped into her bedroom. Crickets began creeling. She couldn't shake the ache that had been with her since Sterling left the car. She touched her mouth where she'd kissed him. What if he was dead? It would be her fault for not driving him home.

That morning, Lara had come across the domestic violence shelter information lying on the kitchen counter. Desperate for something positive to do, she grabbed the envelope and sat on her front porch, watching for Pam Grier. When Pam bustled out of her front door wearing a pressed flowered dress and clutching her purse, Lara jumped up and dashed across the small swatch of lawn that separated their houses.

"Pam!" She waved the envelope as she ran. Pam turned and stared. "I have something for you." Lara stopped short in front of Pam, panting. "I hope I'm not out of line, and if I am, I'm sorry, but just read this and talk to me if you need to." She couldn't look Pam in the face as she shoved the envelope into her limp hand. Then overcome by a sudden panic, Lara turned and fled back across the lawn, up her porch steps and through the front door. She continued running all the way up the two flights of stairs and into her bedroom, where she fell onto her futon, burying her face in her pillow. She half expected an enraged roar to come floating up from the Griers' driveway. But the roar never came; and when Lara went downstairs and peeked outside, Pam had disappeared.

Now, waiting for Sterling, Lara noticed Pam's sedan in the driveway and wondered if she should talk to her. Just then, Eric's car turned the corner. Lara's heart lurched. Was Sterling with him?

Eric pulled into the driveway and Sterling jumped out. Lara didn't even notice Eric's wave. Instead, she watched Sterling stand on the curb, hands shoved deep in his blue-jean pockets. *Thank God he got home okay,* she thought. *He doesn't seem any the worse for wear.*

He strolled toward her, looking first over his shoulder as Eric drove away, then at the sky, then at the neighbors' windows, as if everything around was a lot more interesting than Lara. At the foot of the steps, he glanced up as if just noticing her. "Hey."

Lara held open her arms.

He took a step back. "What?"

"I want to hug you," she said.

"No." His eyes darted to Pam Grier's window. He climbed the steps and brushed by Lara into the house.

She followed him. "Why not?"

"Everybody could see."

"So we're inside now." She moved toward him, but he shrank away. Lara let her arms drop.

Sterling stared at the floor. "See," he started, then cleared his throat. "See. . . ." he faltered. "Eric told me that you know where I live and all."

"Oh." Lara sank to the steps. Sterling fingered a peeling paint scale by the door. For a moment she was angry with Eric. He had begged her not to talk about Sterling's house, and then had turned around and done it himself.

"I don't care where you live," she said. "I just didn't want you walking home in the rain."

"I just . . . I get kinda tired of people thinking I'm pitiful, is all," he murmured. "I get tired of them feeling sorry for me."

"I don't think you're pitiful," she said.

He picked violently at the paint scale. "So why've you been giving me food and letting me mess around on your computer?"

"Because I thought you might like it. Didn't you like it?"

"Yeah, but I don't want you doing stuff for me out of pity."

"What about gratitude?" she asked. "What if I want to do things out of gratitude?"

"I ain't—haven't done anything for you to be grateful about."

"What do you mean? You've gone into my basement. Do you have any idea how scared I am of going down there? That alone is worth years of dinners."

"Yeah, well, you paid me for that."

She ran her fingers through her hair. What should she say? She'd had something special planned for the evening, something she knew he would like. Now it seemed ridiculous, like putting a Band-Aid on a bullet wound.

Sterling decided he wasn't going to let her get away with some lame-ass excuse about being grateful. They both knew she felt sorry for him. He tried to remember if he'd ever felt so low.

"There's a box in the living room that I want you to help me unpack," she said. "Something I want you to help me put together."

He was relieved. If he could just do some work and get paid for it, like before, he'd feel better. "Which one?" He stepped into the mass of boxes.

"It's over by the computer. The dusty one. Hey, do you want something to eat?"

"They're all dusty."

"There by the computer. How about spaghetti?"

She was trying to trick him into eating. "I don't want you feeding me no more."

"Why not?"

"I'm not so low that I gotta take charity."

"Did you ever think maybe it's *me* who needs charity?"

He studied her face, determined not to fall for whatever game she was playing.

"I mean, maybe I ask you to eat with me because I'm lonely. I hate eating by myself."

She stood in the hallway, large-eyed and pouty-mouthed, with the kitchen light shining behind her. Sterling's resolve weakened, and he cursed under his breath.

"Please." She drew out the word. "I haven't eaten yet and I always feel depressed when I have to eat alone. Do the gentlemanly thing and let me make you dinner."

She played him just right, and he hated her. "You fix things so I can't even say no."

"So you'll let me make spaghetti for you?"

"Yeah, yeah," he huffed.

"The box," she insisted as she walked to the kitchen. "That beat-up one by the computer."

"Okay, okay." He saw the box in the light from the monitor and went to it. The flaps on the top bulged out. The cardboard was shredded like some dog had chewed on it. Kneeling beside it, Sterling pried the flaps open. It was too dark to see what was inside, so he just reached, his hand closing around something cool and smooth. Metal. Glass. Small enough to hold in his palm. Pulling it out, he lifted it to the light and turned it over.

"What is this?"

"Keep unpacking. You'll figure it out. At least I hope you will, because I have no idea how to put the thing together."

Again he reached, again metal, a thick tube, like a pipe, and heavy. He gripped it underneath with his other hand, bringing the object out of the box and putting it on the floor. Then he sat back. With a rush that made his face hot, he realized what it was. "How long have you had this?"

"Years. Since high school. I haven't used it in ages."

He stroked the rounded sides of the telescope, sensing another trick but wanting to let her win this time. The telescope lens was about eight inches across, and he was dying to see how well it magnified. "So you just all of a sudden got the urge to look through it?" he asked.

"Exactly," she said brightly. "After we eat."

An hour later, his belly was warm and pooched out like a milk-fed puppy's. He and Lara sat on the kitchen floor picking through the pieces of the telescope. Her hair wasn't tied back, and it fell across her face in waves, hiding her eyes.

She handed him a bolt. "Try that on the eyepiece. I should never have taken this apart. What if we can't get it back together?"

"We will." He watched her fingers flit through the pile of nuts, bolts and screws. They reminded him of hummingbirds darting between flowers. She grabbed another bolt and brought it close to her face to study.

Sterling cleared his throat. "So, see, what I figured is that if Eric showed you my house, he told you about my daddy."

Her fingers continued to roam through the pile. "Does that piss you off?"

He wanted to answer, but when he opened his mouth nothing came out, so he just shrugged like nothing ever made him mad.

"Do you want to tell me about your father?" she asked.

"Yeah, well . . . I'll tell you this, if I ever see him again I'm gonna beat the crap outta him."

Sterling fell silent. He figured that about summed up what he thought of his daddy.

When they finished assembling the telescope, they hauled it upstairs, Lara pulling from the front, Sterling lifting from behind. At the top of the landing, Lara unlatched a window, which opened into a dark secret room. On the wall opposite, moonlight streamed through a pair of double doors.

"Do you think we can get it in there?" she asked.

"Don't know."

They set it down, and Sterling climbed through the window into the musty room. The floor was carpeted with a thick layer of dust so that his footsteps stirred up clouds, and his eyes watered.

"See if you can push it," Sterling said.

Lara heaved the telescope toward him through the window. He managed to pull it the rest of the way. She climbed in after him, and together they hoisted the telescope through the French doors and onto the balcony.

"See, it's better here. The house shields us from the street light," she said.

Sterling set up the tripod, placing its legs on the pulpy wood of the balcony's floor. Then he looked for the moon.

"There," she said as if reading his mind. He swiveled the lens, leaned over and looked into the eyepiece. "What do you see?" She pressed against him.

The light hit his pupil with such brilliance that he squinted, and in an instant he saw the moon. It filled the lens so he couldn't see anything else. It was covered with hills and valleys and mountains, all of them stark and clear. "Man, you can see everything!"

"Let me look."

He moved out of the way and watched her bend over, the image of the moon still swimming as a bright spot across his right eye.

When their eyes were strained and tired, Sterling and Lara stood side by side on the balcony, looking over Lara's back yard at the dark oak tree with its heavy leaves. Their arms were touching. Sterling felt the exact spot where Lara's arm touched his and forgot all the other parts of his body. Beyond Lara's yard, a spattering of lights came from the neighborhood—houses, street lamps, the occasional car head-lights—but these little earth lights didn't seem like anything after looking at the moon.

"Do you miss your dad?" Lara asked.

He thought about the guy in Washington who'd died, and won-dered if Lara was over it yet. Then Sterling thought of his daddy and realized there were some things you couldn't get over. "You sure ask personal stuff."

"You don't have to answer."

He shifted and looked at the stars, now small watery points of light. "I kind of missed him when he first went away. I mean, when he was around he was a sonofabitch, but we did stuff together some-times like throw the baseball and stuff. Now I don't know. Guess I don't miss him so much as the idea of him. Hell, he probably ain't my daddy anyway."

"Oh."

Sterling was glad he couldn't see Lara's expression in the dark. "Least that's what most folks around here think."

"What do you think?"

"My mama says the reason I don't look like either of them is 'cause I look like her granddaddy. He had dark hair like mine, and we kinda have the same face and all. Folks 'round here just ain't got anything better to talk about than other folks' lives."

"Sounds like you've got a pretty mature attitude about it."

"Ain't no use getting worked up about stuff you can't do anything about."

"Maybe. I can't help getting worked up sometimes, though."

Sterling ran his hand down the telescope. "Yeah, me either." He stroked the warm metal and thought that since he'd told her this much, he might as well keep talking. "He took off on a haul, my daddy did. He was supposed to be gone a week, and a week came and he didn't get back. My mama started calling the police and the hospitals. Then she called the company and found out he quit. Mama was trying to get money from him, but she couldn't ever find him." Sterling paused. "I just wish I knew why he left, is all. Whether it was another woman or something. Can't understand why he left."

Lara's hand slid around his, her fingers damp and warm. He held hands with her and swung their arms back and forth while she said "Sometimes people just do things. Like Dylan driving too fast. People mostly don't make sense, I've decided."

"Yeah, well, I'm glad you decided that, 'cause you don't make sense at all. You leave a great place to come here. You don't unpack." And you hold my hand, he wanted to say. You tell me I'm too young, then you hold my hand and you kiss me in the car like it's nothing. Maybe it *is* nothing to you.

Lara was looking at the moon. "I can't unpack," she said. "I can't look at his stuff." She lapsed into silence for a moment. "I feel like I'm going insane from missing him. Do you know what that's like?"

Sterling didn't know what to say. The air felt charged. Part of him hated the dead guy because Lara missed him, but part of him understood how it felt to have someone around and then disappear.

"Yeah," he said. "I guess I know what that's like."

"The thing is, seeing you, and talking to you and Eric, are the only things I look forward to. Honestly, if you stopped eating dinner with me, I don't know what I'd do."

He swung her hand a few more times. She let go, walked to the edge of the balcony, and looked down at her back yard. He wanted to say something funny because the whole conversation had brought him down. "Guess I have to keep letting you cook me dinner then, huh?"

"I guess so," she agreed. He felt sorry for her and liked it better than feeling pitiful himself.

"I guess we both got left," he said.

"I guess we both did."

She went to the door and paused with her back to him. "Well, it's getting late. I've kept you too long, as usual."

He got up the nerve to lay his hand on her arm. "I had fun. Besides, us left-behinds gotta stick together."

Downstairs, he stood by the front door, slapping at the dust on his jeans.

"Don't be too mad at Eric," she said. "He didn't mean any harm."

"I know." Sterling nodded. "I was pissed as hell earlier, but you can't stay mad at Eric for long. He's too much of a good old guy."

Lara smiled. "He's like your big brother."

"He won't let me do anything without thinking it out, that's for damned sure."

"I'll drive you," she said.

"Naw, I like to walk."

"You should let me drive you. It's a long way."

"I like to walk it," he insisted. "It's quiet. It's the only peace I get."

"Are you sure?"

"Yeah," he laughed. "Now stop asking."

"Hey, I've got something for you."

He rolled his eyes. "You gotta stop doing this."

She darted into her kitchen and was back again in an instant, handing him a book. He turned the cover so he could see it in the hall light. *The Communist Manifesto.*

"Just in case you're curious."

"You're trying to get me killed," he said.

"Just take it, you noble proletariat worker."

"All right, comrade." He lifted his hand. "'Bye."

W HEN he reached his house, Sterling hung on the tire swing that he'd put up that morning. The TV blared from behind the thin walls. The girls shrieked, and Mama scolded them. Sterling looked at the moon, now so pale and far away. He felt like his insides were bigger, big and warm, like they'd pop out of his skin, his heart beating bare and open to the air.

A good night. Nice, goofing around, having fun. Walking home, he'd had one of those moments, like the kind he used to get as a little kid; a moment where he was a part of everything, of the sky and the grass and the trees, a moment where his life seemed perfect just the way it was.

When he finally went inside, his mama spotted the book right away. "What's that?"

He flashed the cover at her while she squinted, moving her mouth as she read. The warm feeling left him. "*The Communist Manifesto,* Mama," he said.

"The communist what?"

"By Karl Marx."

"That woman has no business giving you nothing about communism."

"It was just a joke." He slumped into the kitchen chair and braced himself for biscuits and whatever. "She didn't mean nothing by it."

"Maybe that's just what she wants you to think, Sterling. Maybe that's the way they start off converting people."

He laughed. "She's not like that. She's just educated."

"Well, them educated folks is the ones causing all the problems, causing this country to move away from family values—"

"Mama," he interrupted. "Them's just lines the politicians feed you off the television. Easy for them to talk about family values from their fancy houses in Washington. Ain't none of them ever had to work for a living. They just put everything in such a way that folks without no sense eat it up."

She yanked a blackened pan out of the oven, her mouth a hard line. She flicked two biscuits onto his plate.

"What?" He could tell he'd said something wrong.

Setting the pan down with a bang, she gripped a saucepan on the stove and violently spooned out a slimy red mound, the consistency of gravy. Stewed tomatoes. "What, Mama?"

"Now I ain't got sense."

"That ain't what I meant."

"This woman, I ain't even met her, and now you start coming home with communist books and mouthing at me about politics and looking at me like I'm some kind of idiot. Well, I'm sorry I never had the chance for an education. I was too busy raising you and taking care of your no-good daddy."

"Sterling!" The twins were getting impatient for him to notice them.

"Hey, both of you get back into that living room 'fore I take a belt to you," their mother snapped.

"I'll come and kiss you good night when I'm done eating," Sterling said. "Me and Mama was talking."

"'Bout what?"

"Grownup stuff." He watched them shuffle off in their little nightgowns. "I was thinking about the food stamps," he said as the girls climbed onto the sofa together.

"We ain't going on food stamps," she spat. "We ain't sunk that low."

"Yeah, but Mama, we gotta get those girls more to eat. Both of them look thin to me."

"Well, I'm sorry I ain't as good a provider as your daddy. Maybe he wouldn't have left if you'd've had red hair like his."

This was her favorite battle tactic: blame Sterling for everything, blame his dark hair. As he put the warm tomatoes into his mouth, a part of him knew he couldn't pretend he hadn't already eaten a much better supper. One swallow and he dropped the spoon and shoved the plate away from him.

"Hell, I can't eat this shit." It was the worst insult he could give her, but he didn't care. He was sick of her and this house. He was sick of being a father to two little girls when he was really only their brother. Maybe only their half-brother.

His mother stood by the stove, arms folded across her chest, lips quivering.

"I'm going to bed," he stood up.

"You do that," she snapped after him. "You just do that."

He went into the living room to kiss the girls good night. They looked up at him with frightened eyes. "Hey, it's okay," he said. "Mama and me's just tired. We'll be over it in the morning." He kissed each little girl on her forehead and then went to his room carrying *The Communist Manifesto*. He locked the door behind him.

chapter fifteen

July 22

O N Sunday, Eric invited Lara to his house for a swim. She arrived dressed in a yellow tank top and a light, almost translucent white cotton skirt dotted with yellow stars. She stood at his front door, wiping sweat out of her eyes with the back of one hand and clutching a towel and suntan lotion in the other. Eric blocked the doorway, so busy looking at her that he forgot to invite her inside.

"Can I come in?" she finally asked, arching an eyebrow.

"Yeah, sure." Eric took a step back and watched her cross the threshold.

"This is nice." She took in his narrow living room, the worn blue sofa, the old TV set, the torn recliner. He wanted to apologize for the run-down condition of his possessions. Then he thought of Lara's house and its dearth of furniture. At least he *had* furniture. "How long have you lived here?" she asked.

"I bought it from this bigwig Atlanta lawyer about five years ago. He owned a hundred acres including this house. He was going to tear it down. I think two bedrooms wasn't quite big enough for him." Eric grinned.

"So you have a hundred acres?"

"Oh, no." Eric said. "I have two. He subdivided the land. He was bankrupt or something and sold it off in parcels to pay his debts. At least that was the rumor. He gave me a great deal on the house. He'd already put in the pool. A really nice pool. Twelve feet deep. I thought it was strange, putting in a pool before you even build the house. The contractor said he thought the guy was planning to drown his wife in it for the insurance money."

"I guess you haven't unearthed any bodies yet," Lara said.

"Not yet," Eric agreed. "Maybe one day, if I'm lucky."

She smiled, slung her towel over the back of a chair, and strolled toward the wall behind the sofa where his pictures hung. He felt anxious about what she might say.

Hands clasped behind her back, she stared at the photographs. She pointed to a shot of pallets with sunlight streaming through them. "I recognize this from that day we took pictures. It looks great."

"Yeah, I was pretty pleased with how it turned out myself."

She peered at a black and white closeup of a bare chest. "Is that Sterling?"

"Yeah."

"He let you take that picture?"

"He was asleep by the pool. It's funny, he still hasn't recognized himself."

"Kind of homoerotic, don't you think? Taking pictures of the bare chests of boys while they bask in the sun."

He shrugged uneasily. "What can I say? I'll shoot any good bare body part that comes my way. Besides, it didn't take you long to recognize whose chest it was."

"Touché." Lara grinned. She studied the other pictures on the wall, and Eric became uncomfortable when he realized how many of them were of Sterling's body parts—the boy's bare foot, his hand, the back of his head.

"You should try to sell some of these. Really. They're good." She wandered to the window and perched on the wide sill, the summer sun flooding in behind her, blazing her hair. Outside, a breeze caught Eric's wind chimes and they tinkled and clanged. Lara kicked off her sandals. Her feet were white with powder. She tried to force a stray strand of hair back into her ponytail.

"So, when do we swim, Grover?"

"Can I take some pictures of you?"

"Pictures?"

"Yeah, you know. Photographer. Pictures."

She shrugged and twisted the strand of hair. "Sure, I guess. As long as you're not talking about bare body parts."

"I'm not." He rushed to get his camera, afraid that the moment of shadow and light, of Lara's hair glowing in the sun, would be gone before he could get back. But it wasn't, and as he knelt to shoot her, she covered her face, peeking out between spread fingers, the moment crystallized forever in his memory.

He took ten pictures, all that was left on the roll. When he was through, he sprawled on the floor looking up at her.

She smiled. "Can we swim now?"

He motioned toward the sliding glass door that led out back. "After you."

Outside, Lara stripped off her skirt and tank top while Eric tried not to stare. Underneath, she wore a yellow bathing suit.

"The water looks great." She flashed him a smile. After walking to the edge of the pool, she tested it with her toe. "Warm," she said.

"It's been getting warmer all summer. Some day I expect to see it boiling." He settled into a plastic lounge chair while Lara climbed onto the diving board and marched to the end. As Eric shielded his eyes to see better, Lara lifted up on her toes, balancing for a moment, arms spread wide. The cross shape of her body in the yellow suit stood out against the green trees behind her. She jumped twice, the board propelling her upward with a hum. In the air, she whipped one arm around, clenching it close to her side so she spun like a top before slicing into the pool, barely leaving a ripple.

There was a moment of stillness before she broke the surface, gasping and shaking water out of her hair. "God, this feels great."

"That was a pretty dive. I'd give it a 9.8."

"I used to be on the diving team in college," she said. "But I'm kind of rusty these days." Hands on the lip of the pool, she pushed herself out of the water and came over to drip on Eric.

"Hey," he protested, covering his head.

"Aren't you swimming?"

"In a minute. I want to get good and hot first. The kid said he might come over after work." Eric had decided that sharing Lara would be good penance, especially since Sterling would get to see her in a bathing suit. "I guess you guys worked it out?"

She rolled her eyes. "There wasn't that much to work out. He's sensitive as hell, you know."

"He just wants to impress you."

"He's already done that."

"Yeah, you and every fifteen-year-old girl in the county." Eric was gratified to see Lara grimace.

Lara studied him for a moment. "You mean a lot to him. You have a lot of influence with him."

"You don't know what you're talking about. He doesn't listen to anything I say."

"But he does. You just don't want to admit it, because then you'd have to feel more responsible for him." Lara bent over and mussed his beard with wet fingers. "You're pretty damned adorable, even if you're in denial," she said. "I'm going back in."

The wetness from her fingers lingered in Eric's beard. He considered the word *denial* and watched Lara climb onto the board and dive once more.

Eric recalled a day about two years ago when the mailman, Lester Maxwell, had come into the shop on his daily rounds. Lester was a good-old-guy type, friendly, but kind of a gossip. He also was a great customer and bought every Johnny Cash CD Eric could manage to order. As Lester had breezed through the door, he'd caught sight of Sterling in the office.

Dropping a pile of mail on the counter, he'd leaned toward Eric, muttering "Hey, I don't want you to think I'm saying anything about it, cause I ain't, but there's someone in this town, a couple of people, saying you got an unnatural interest in that boy."

Eric remembered the sensation he'd experienced, a crawling along his scalp, a sick surge in his stomach. He was terrified that anything he said to Lester, any expression on his face might be misinterpreted as guilt, so he just stood gaping, searching his memory for anything he'd done to cause this rumor. All he could come up with was the fact that he'd let Sterling stay overnight to watch movies on the VCR.

"Just thought you should know," Lester said. "Don't mean I put any stock in it."

In a panic, Eric had called his girlfriend, Julie. It was a month before she left for Italy. Once she got to his house, he drove her into town, bought her a Coca Cola at the gas station on the corner, and then made out with her in the gazebo for half an hour until she demanded that they go back to his place. The Sunday following the make-out session, Mike Owens had given a ferocious sermon about sins of the flesh while standing in the same gazebo, and Eric had heard no more of the rumor.

In the days that followed, Eric had become ashamed of how he'd handled the situation. He realized that his response had dignified the town's homophobia. He felt weak and swore that from now on he would do what he wanted without deference to public opinion, but he found it hard to live up to his vow. There were days when Sterling was unhappy, and Eric found himself lifting a hand, intending to give the boy a friendly clap on the shoulder, only to experience a sudden profound discomfort which made him drop his hand to his side again. Since he'd heard the rumor, he had not touched Sterling.

As Lara pushed herself out of the pool, the water flowed away from her in a sheet. She walked around to the diving board again, her feet slapping on the concrete, leaving a trail of wet footprints. Eric watched her and experienced a sense of urgency. He wanted a girl-friend. Needed one. It had been too damned long since he'd felt a woman underneath him.

A long, silent afternoon. Even the bugs seemed too hot to make noise. Eric lay on his lounge chair, drinking beer and watching Lara dive. The only sound was the reverberation of the board. Finally, she collapsed onto a towel beside him, grabbing the beer he handed her and taking a few long gulps before rolling onto her stomach, arms pressed to her sides. "I think I could sleep right now."

"Go ahead. I'll wake you up before you burn." Wake you up before you burn. As if she might ignite there by his pool. He could picture her igniting like that.

"Are you looking at me?"

He started. "What?"

"I feel like you're looking at me."

"Yes, I am."

"Do I have excessive cellulite on my thighs or something?"

"No, you're beautiful."

Eric waited for her to say something, to take the compliment or reject it, but she just sighed, dark lashes closing over her eyes, and soon he thought she was asleep.

STERLING arrived at Eric's house, sticky with sweat and with the sweet white residue from the ice cream machine. He didn't bother to knock. They wouldn't hear him from the pool anyway. Instead, he twisted open the doorknob, his fingers gumming the metal with gooey prints.

He found them out back, Lara on her stomach in a yellow bathing suit, both of them asleep. He stood and stared at Lara's ass for a while before stripping off his shirt and proclaiming, "Damn, I hope I don't get lazy like y'all when I get old."

With a whoop he tore toward the water, legs and arms churning. At the lip of the pool he hurled himself into the air, tucking into a cannon ball that stung his skin when he hit and sprayed Eric and Lara with a shower of drops.

They sprang up, gasping.

"Wake up, old folks," he mocked them. "Time to put your teeth back in. *Matlock*'ll be on in a coupla minutes!"

"Creep!" Lara dashed to the edge of the pool and kicked water at him. He swam furiously to make a grab for her ankle. With a yell of triumph he caught it. He tried to pull her in.

"Come on!" he called to Eric. "Help me out here!"

"Sorry, you're on your own!"

Lara twisted herself free and sank to her knees, panting.

"Aw!" Sterling hit the water so it arced over Lara, splattering her. "Y'all are no fun."

"You know," Eric came to stand by the edge of the pool beside Lara, hands on his hips, "You can borrow a pair of my swim trunks. I don't see how you can stay afloat in those jeans."

Sterling shot out of the pool. The jeans made a squishing sound as he ambled toward the house. "When I get back, I want to see you two in the damned water!"

He heard Lara laugh.

After Sterling changed, he came out back and charged the pool. Launching himself, he stretched his arms to dive, but missed, his belly skidding painfully across the surface of the water.

"Are you all right?" Lara asked when he came up for breath.

His eyes were tearing from the bellyflop, but he tried to laugh it off. "Come on in, Lara. It's great."

She slid in and treaded water a few feet from him. "Okay, I'm in."

With a lunge, Sterling grabbed her.

"Whoa!" she said as he pulled her close, gripping her waist and hoisting her into the air. "Sterling!"

He threw her away from him and watched as she splashed down and submerged. Under the water, he could see the dark flash of her body, like a fish. She snaked toward him, shooting up with a rush. She pressed her palm on the top of his head to force him under, but she wasn't strong enough.

He dove beneath her, then stood so that for a moment she was riding his shoulders, her wet thighs against his neck. The game went from screaming to silence. The rolling sound of his own bubbles. A rush in his ears as he gulped air at the surface. A shriek from Lara.

Their wet flesh squeaking together. Muted splashes as he submerged again.

"Careful," he heard Eric call.

Sterling wrapped his arms around Lara's waist and pulled her under. Then he rose into the hot afternoon light, holding her tightly. Her body, slick and weightless, pressed against him. He didn't want to let go.

"Stop," she panted into his ear so that it raised goose bumps on his skin. "I can't breathe. You're killing me."

Reluctantly, he let her loose and watched her swim to the pool's edge, drag herself out, and lie gasping on her back on the concrete. Springing out behind her, he flicked water at her face so that she flinched.

"Hey, play nice," Eric scolded. "She ain't one of your little sisters."

Sterling went to where Eric lay in his lounge chair.

"Can I get a drink?"

"Coke in the fridge."

A s Sterling walked away, Eric watched Lara. Her eyes followed the boy's bare back like cat eyes on a fish-bowl guppy.

"What are you doing?"

"What?" She whirled toward Eric, startled, as if she'd forgotten he was there.

"He's seventeen years old. You shouldn't look at him like that."

Lara pushed herself up, crawled over, and stationed herself on her beach towel beside him. "But he's sexy as hell."

"And he knows it. Don't you think he notices you looking? His head is swelled up big enough without you encouraging it. You'll give him ideas."

She stared at the sliding glass door through which Sterling had disappeared, then down at her hands. "You get worked up too easily, Grover. I was only joking."

* * *

F LOATING.

Clouds tinged pink by sunset. Water lapping at her ears. Her body, suspended, turned slowly so that the clouds rotated above her. Lara watched the sky ripen from pale blue to orange.

All afternoon she'd tried to banish visions of Dylan's dark, unkempt hair, his endearing but infrequent smile, the way he frowned over the newspaper on Sunday mornings as if working out how to cope with more bad news. *How can you let someone go?* She wondered. *How can you do it and still love them?* Now, floating in Eric's pool, she saw Dylan's shape in the clouds, his knobby shoulders. She remembered how they jutted up under his skin.

Sterling's shoulders did not jut. Earlier, when they'd played in the pool, Sterling's body felt composed of clean smooth lines. Rather than swim, he fought the water like an enemy, thrashing and clawing his way through to come up under Lara, so she could ride for a moment on his dripping shoulders. For that moment, she'd felt like part of the world again.

Lara watched the clouds darken and shift, thin out into tendrils. The image of Dylan's shoulders blew away. Lara wished it could be as easy to let him go. *I want to be held,* she thought. *How much longer can I go without being touched?* Then she realized that Dylan would never be touched again. He'd go forever without being held.

She tucked her knees up, and her body sank. With strong strokes she swam to the edge of the pool. Eric and Sterling were dozing in their lounge chairs. Lara, trying not to look at Sterling, looked at Eric instead. When he was awake, Eric's eyes were very round and seemed open too wide, so that he always looked surprised in a happy way. He lay with his long thin legs stretched out, his eyes closed. His bare feet seemed too big and turned out at strange angles while he slept. He looked vulnerable.

Beside him, dozing with his mouth hanging open, Sterling looked vulnerable too, his skin brown and warm. Lara's own skin felt thick and rubbery, as if it could be poked with a needle and she'd still feel nothing. For the first time ever, she wished she could let Dylan go. She was taking on too many of his dead characteristics. *If I could just touch someone . . . like with Sterling in the pool, if I could just feel the skin of someone who's alive. . . .*

STERLING woke feeling dizzy. As the sun set, he lay splay-legged in the beach chair and watched Lara float. Eric was awake and watching Lara float, too. "You about ready to eat?" Eric asked. "It's getting dark."

"Yeah."

"I guess I'm going to barbecue some stuff. Come on and help me?"

Sterling didn't want to. He wanted Eric to go away so he could watch Lara float by himself, but since Eric was the one supplying the grub he said "Okay." With a sigh he heaved himself up, his legs heavy, his eyes burning from the chlorine.

Inside, Eric turned on the lights, and the pool lit up from the bottom so they could see Lara's dark shadow floating on top. The patio lights cast a white glare onto the tree branches, making the leaves look stark and strange. Eric switched on the power to the bug zapper, which cast a lurid neon-purple circle onto the brick.

"Hamburgers okay?" Eric asked.

"Can you put that onion soup stuff in 'em?"

"Sure thing. The meat's in the fridge. Why don't you get it out?"

Sterling decided there was something sexy about shaping raw meat and onion soup mix into hamburger patties while looking out the window, watching Lara float in her bathing suit. By the time she stopped floating and started swimming laps, Eric had come up beside him, and they both watched her. With her body lit from beneath, her movements cut dark ripples on the surface.

When she climbed out of the pool and looked toward the kitchen, they both glanced down. She wrapped herself in a towel and walked to the house, slid open the glass door and stepped inside.

"I'm going to take a shower." She sounded breathless. "Gosh, it's cold in here."

"Go ahead. Dinner'll be a little while. How many hamburgers do you want?"

"I'm a vegetarian," she said. "Grill me up some of that corn and I'll just make a cheese sandwich or something."

"You got it," Eric said. Then he turned to Sterling and whispered. "You and I are going to have to eat a lot of meat—unless you're going to be a vegetarian, too, now."

AFTER dinner, while Sterling took his turn in the shower, Eric watched as Lara wandered out by the pool and stood looking over the lighted water, sipping a glass of wine. He went to stand with her. There was a soft breeze and it lifted her skirt.

"It's a nice night," she said. They stood side by side. "Crazy" started playing on the stereo, and Lara swayed to the music. "I like this one. Dance with me?"

The request took Eric by surprise. "Sure."

She set her glass on the ground out of the way, and he took hold of her awkwardly, one hand on the small of her back, the other stretched out to receive her fingers. He rocked back and forth, feeling like he was dancing in a grade-school social. The bug zapper popped and sizzled.

"You can get closer than that, you know." Lara took her hand from his and slipped both arms around his neck so he had to hold her, enfolding her waist, stooping so his chin rested on her shoulder and he could smell the floral aroma of her hair.

"Much better," he said.

They barely danced, just swayed slightly, more like a protracted embrace. He wondered what it all meant. Should he kiss her when the song stopped? Or was she just lonely? The music faded and she pulled back, saying "I've had a really nice day." Hugging herself, she walked to the edge of the pool.

"Me too." He followed her. "I've got to take the kid home, but I don't know, do you want to hang out for a while, wait for me to get back?" He laid a hand on her shoulder.

She shook her head. "I'd better not."

"Oh, okay."

From inside came a loud slam. Sterling walked through the lighted living room. Eric waited a moment, then wrapped his arms around Lara's waist in a possessive way. He heard the glass door slide open. Eric looked at Sterling. The boy stood watching them, his mouth hanging open.

Lara pulled away and walked along the pool until she was out of arm's reach. She ran her fingers through her hair. "I'd better get going."

Eric studied her back, the stoop to her shoulders. If only she'd stay, he thought. "Yeah, I guess I'd better get going too," he said. "You don't want to know what this town was saying about me last time he stayed the night here."

October 16

C APTAIN Edgars hung up the phone. He leaned forward and rested his forehead in his hands. The cops in Washington, D.C. had given him nothing.

"Death due to blunt trauma to the head caused by a motor vehicle accident. And the car is a metal cube at a junkyard, so we can't see if it was tampered with." The officer had sounded bored.

They didn't take Edgars's case seriously, these big-city cops. They didn't understand what it was like to think that someone in your town, someone you probably knew, had killed a young woman in cold blood.

But Edgars still held out hope. Maybe it wasn't someone in his town. Maybe it had been someone passing through. Or perhaps the cops in D.C. were wrong.

E DGARS felt a twinge of pity as he lowered himself into the seat opposite Sterling O'Connor. The boy sat hunched in his chair, staring at the table, his eyes sunken and dull-looking like a sick dog's.

"I need to ask you a few more questions and make sure I got all this straight," the captain began, opening the case file in front of him and picking up his pen. "Now, you said you went home about ten the night she died."

"I went home at eight-thirty or nine." Sterling's voice sounded flat.

"And you never went out again, not until the officer woke you up the next morning?"

"That's right."

"Hmmm." Edgars steepled his fingers and placed them under his chin. "Did you find Lara Walton attractive?" He thought the boy flinched, but Sterling made no attempt to answer. "Did you hear the question?"

Sterling shrugged. "Yeah, I guess she was kind of pretty."

"Did any boyfriends come to her house that you know of?"

"Don't know," he mumbled.

"See, Lara Walton's neighbors are saying that you might have been her boyfriend. Might have kissed her out by the old warehouse on Green Street the other day."

"Who said that?"

"Lots of folks."

"The same folks who say I ain't my daddy's son?" Sterling glared. "The same folks that gossip about everybody in this town all the time and even said some ugly things about you not being able to do this investigation?"

Edgars's face grew hot. He took a deep breath. He must have hit a nerve. He adopted a philosophical expression and spread his hands wide. "You understand I gotta ask these questions. It's my job." He placed his hands back on the table. "You know anything about forensics?"

Sterling shook his head.

"Then let me tell you a little bit about how we investigate a murder scene. First we dust for fingerprints. Another thing we do is vacuum up stuff. When we vacuum, we sometimes find hair or fiber from clothes or carpets to tell us who's been where in the house. There's a crime lab in Atlanta. We send things there to be examined. Take Ms. Walton's futon, say. It's amazing what they can find on something like that. Hair, semen, dead skin, even fingerprints."

"Yeah, well, I've been all over that house. My fingerprints are probably on everything, and maybe some of my hair too."

"That's another thing I meant to ask you," Edgars continued. "If you worked so hard on that place, how come there's hardly anything been done? I mean, the place doesn't look like it's been fixed up."

"I painted the kitchen and I did some work on her basement and in her yard."

"Did you ever go into her bedroom?"

Sterling paused. "Yeah. She had me carry stuff around for her, move boxes, unpack stuff."

"And you never left your house again that night after you went home?"

"No! I told you that a thousand times!" Sterling raked his fingers through his hair.

"So if somebody saw your truck on the road at eleven, it wouldn't have been you driving it?"

"If somebody saw *our* truck, it was probably Mama going out to buy cigarettes. She gets those cravings in the middle of the night."

"And she doesn't wake you up to tell you she's going?"

"Naw. She ain't gone that long. Why? Did somebody see our truck?"

Edgars shrugged. "Maybe." Then he paused.

"Is that it?" Sterling asked.

"You ever fight with your mama?"

Sterling cocked an eyebrow as if the question surprised him. "Sometimes."

"You ever fight with your mama about Lara Walton?"

"Yeah."

"Why'd you and your mama fight about her?"

There was a long silence. Although Sterling's face remained stony, his expression neutral, Edgars got the idea that the boy was figuring how best to answer.

Finally, Sterling took a deep breath and said "She didn't like that I was spending a lot of time over there. I mean, I told her it was earning us extra money, but she thought I should be at home more to look out for my sisters."

"So things have been kind of rough at home lately?"

Sterling hung his head. "I guess you could say that."

"You ever kiss Lara Walton?"

The boy's mouth twisted into a grimace. "What do you mean?"

"Kiss her. Your lips on her lips. You ever do that?"

Sterling turned away abruptly, and Edgars studied his profile. His jaw was clenched so hard that the captain could see a vein pulsing in his neck.

"That ain't none of your business."

"It *is* my business. She's dead."

"Yeah, well, I didn't kill her!" Sterling slammed the table with his fist. "Damn it, I told you all this stuff already!"

Edgars made his voice soothing. "Listen, I believe you didn't kill her, but you gotta be honest with me, or you start looking suspicious. That futon. Hair, skin, semen. You sure you ain't got nothing to tell me before I see those forensic test results?"

"Okay, yeah, outside the warehouse that day I kissed her 'cause she was leaving and I wasn't ever gonna to see her again." Sterling met Captain Edgars's eyes. "You can call me when you get those tests back if you need to ask anything else. I ain't going nowhere."

AFTER the interview, Sterling hurried to a pay phone outside Dan's Quick Stop and called Eric.

"What'd they ask?" Eric said.

"Man, I can't take this no more," Sterling breathed into the receiver. "All this stuff that ain't none of their business, Eric. All this stuff about Lara and me they ain't got no right to ask. It's like they're trying to ruin my memory of her, and I ain't got nothing else, and they're . . . they're trying to mess it all up and get inside it 'til it's ruint."

"What did you tell them?"

"Nothing."

"Did they ask anything about me?"

"Naw. But he was telling me about how they investigate. I started thinking about all the stuff in that house, and I don't know if she packed up some of it or not, and if they found it, they're gonna ask me more questions, and they're gonna think I did it." A mechanical voice interrupted, demanding thirty-five cents. "I gotta go," Sterling said. "Ain't got no more change."

"You want to come by the house tonight?" Eric asked. "You can swim."

"I can't swim in that pool," Sterling said, then hung up.

W HEN he got home, Sterling barely had the energy to slouch into his room. He'd almost gone to Lara's just from habit, but had to stop himself and point his feet in the right direction. Home. Nothing now but home.

When his mother called him for dinner, he couldn't eat. He went to bed early, fell asleep, and dreamed about Lara. Dreamed she was right there in the room with him. The dream started Sterling awake. He lay in bed gasping, his heart pounding. His room was so dark he couldn't see anything, and he groped for the lamp. His hand froze on the switch as he fought his imagination for a few moments before working up the courage to flick on the light. Lara wasn't there.

"Hell," he breathed as he struggled to stand. He pulled the blanket from his bed and, slinging it around his shoulders, staggered into the living room where his mother and sisters had fallen asleep with the TV on. If there'd been space, he'd have climbed onto the sofa–bed too, but instead he wrapped himself in the blanket and curled up on the floor beside them, leaving the TV on so the room would be lit. He didn't sleep the rest of the night.

October 17

C APTAIN Edgars walked through the Quickie Mart door and headed straight for the coffee pot on the counter. Two customers were at the register paying for gas, even though the Quickie Mart had pumps that accepted credit cards outside. Edgars knew that the whole town was suspicious of those new pumps. They all figured it was fine way to get your credit card number stolen.

Edgars poured coffee into a small Styrofoam cup, then leaned against the counter blowing on it while Sandy finished with the last customer and eyed the captain nervously. When the door had swung shut and they were alone, he turned to her.

"So, you said Sterling didn't go out again that night?"

She glanced over her shoulder as if someone might be watching. "Yeah, I'm sure. He went to bed and didn't get up."

"And did you go anywhere?"

"No."

"'Cause someone saw your truck out about eleven."

"Eleven? Oh." Sandy's eyes roamed the room. "Oh yeah, I was out at eleven."

"Thought you said you didn't go out."

"I thought you meant late. I went out at eleven for some cough syrup. One of the girls was having trouble sleeping. Darlene, you know she's got them lung problems, and there's that cough syrup I get for her, so I drove over to the all-night Eckerd's. But it was only for five minutes. Sterling didn't leave."

"Are you sure about that? Did you check his bed when you got back?"

"Yeah, I checked it." She fixed her eyes on a point behind Edgars.

"He's eighteen years old, and you check his bed at night?"

She looked down, her lower lip trembling.

"Listen, Sandy, I don't want it to seem like I think he done it, but I gotta know the truth, or it'll be worse for him in the long run."

"You know who I think done it is Dave Grier," Sandy said. "He was always running Lara Walton down, always saying bad things about her. Sterling'd have no reason to do it. He liked her. He just worked for her. She was paying him. Why'd he want to kill someone who paid him good money?"

"I ain't saying he killed her. I'm just asking questions, so tell me the truth. Did you go out in the truck?"

She looked at her hands. "Yeah, about eleven like I said, for cough medicine."

"How long were you gone for?"

"I don't know, maybe fifteen minutes."

"And you didn't check his bed when you got back?"

"No. But he was there at five when Officer Daniels came by."

"I know. And you say you got that cough medicine at Eckerd's?"

"Yessir. I bought it from Mike Owens down there."

"Okay," Edgars took another sip of coffee. He liked the way the coffee here was always fresh. "That's all I needed to know."

Sandy's lips quivered as if she might cry.

"Don't worry. I don't think Sterling did it. We'll get to the bottom of it, all right?"

She nodded, and he patted her hand.

EDGARS pulled his car into the Eckerd's parking lot, thinking about Sandy going out in the truck. Had she really bought cough syrup, or had she gone to Lara Walton's house and killed her? Could she have murdered Lara Walton? He didn't think it was likely. Besides, her motive for murdering Lara would be that Sterling spent too much time over there. If Lara was moving away, Sandy's problem was solved.

Edgars opened his car door and stepped into the gray afternoon. It was around one, and Mike Owens would be on his lunch break in the tiny employee break room behind the pharmacy.

"Howdy there, Colonel." Mike lifted a fleshy hand as Edgars poked his head around the corner. "You been working on that murder, I hear."

"Must say I have. Can I sit down?"

"Help yourself." Mike indicated the chair across from him.

Edgars lowered himself onto the chair, which felt shaky, as if its legs weren't screwed on right. He thought it was an awful lot to ask of any chair to bear Mike's weight day after day.

"Listen, I need to ask you a question about that night the Walton woman was murdered."

"You're asking *me?*" Mike leaned forward. "You're making *me* a part of the investigation?"

"I'm afraid I've got to. I need to know if Sandy O'Connor came in here that night."

"Sandy O'Connor? You think it was the O'Connor boy that did it?"

"I didn't say that."

Mike shook his head like he hated to go on but was resigned to it. "Them O'Connors are a bad lot. They ain't been out to church since Sandy's folks passed. That's the reason they've had such bad stuff happen to them. They ain't right with the Lord." Mike was a deacon at Calvary Baptist on Broad Street, and he sometimes stood in the gazebo downtown on Sunday mornings yelling Bible verses at passing cars.

"Do you remember seeing Sandy that night?"

"I don't know," Mike screwed his face up so his eyes disappeared in folds of flesh. "It's kind of hard to remember any particular night. I know she was in late some time around then."

"You remember what she bought?"

"Cigarettes. That's part of their trouble, her smoking. The good Lord says we shouldn't put nothing foreign like that in our bodies."

Edgars raked his hand through his hair. Why couldn't people just answer his questions? "Anything else?"

"I believe she bought some cough syrup for her girls. One of them little ones has lung problems. Probably from all that smoking. So you gonna arrest that O'Connor boy?"

"I can't talk about that, Mike. You know that." The captain tried to keep the edge out of his voice.

"He used to cause all kinds of trouble skateboarding in the parking lot and messing around with some of them girls. The way these children act today. . . ." He paused. "I tell you, Captain, there's a change coming in this world. The Bible predicts it, a change, and we'd better all be ready."

Edgars almost knocked the chair over in his haste to stand. "Thanks for your help, Mike." He gathered his notebook thinking that for someone so Christian, Mike hadn't lifted a finger to help Sandy or her kids.

"Any time," Mike said. "Glad to do it."

Edgars walked through the parking lot. A group of folks standing by the pay phone studied him. Everywhere he went now, Edgars felt people's eyes on him, saw how they leaned together and whispered as he passed.

Edgars opened the car door and slid onto the driver's seat. For a moment he stared at his hands as they rested on the wheel. It had been his experience that the obvious solution to a case was usually the correct one. But there was no obvious solution to this crime. There was no obvious motive. He wondered again whether Bill could have been right. Could Sterling have gone temporarily insane?

Edgars slipped the key into the ignition and started the car. The kid was smart. The dull service jobs he worked didn't offer much to interest him. Girls around Barton County were easy for him to get. Lara Walton had been different. She'd refused to date him. She'd given him a copy of *The Communist Manifesto*. So how would Sterling feel if the one person in town who challenged him, who gave him something to aspire toward, just decided to up and leave?

chapter seventeen

July 23

LARA wrote: *Last night when I danced with Eric, I felt his attraction to me. But the whole time we danced I kept thinking of his photographs, pictures of life from a distance, a way to remain connected without getting involved. We are two people who spend more time thinking about life as an abstract concept than actually living it. At first I'd wanted to be touched, but by the end of the dance I wanted to run from him. For a moment I was scared he'd kiss me.*

LARA had lost the heart to make Sterling do any work. The only real excuse to have him at her house was if he worked. But she couldn't bear the thought of his wasting time on drudgery. So the house, as before, lay around her in disrepair. The house hated her. She'd made it so many promises, yet after a month only the kitchen had been painted.

That evening, a Monday, she decided to plant some flowers out front as a sort of sacrifice to the house, a peace offering since she'd been neglecting it and letting it remain dusty and rundown.

Lara knelt outside, knees pressed into the gritty soil. Digging with a trowel, she unearthed first anemic topsoil, then gravel, finally hard red clay. She wondered if anything would grow there. Still, trying to cultivate flowers was the first positive thing she'd done in a while. If she blended in the clay-buster and fertilizer they'd recommended at the nursery with the less-than-promising earth and watered the flowers religiously, maybe they would give her blossoms. A simple relationship where she didn't have to worry about hurting the flowers' feelings or causing them to walk miles in thunderstorms out of pride.

She set the first flowers into the dry red hole. To her left, across the bushes that divided her house from the Griers', she heard the squeak of a screen door, then a slam as it shut. She began filling in the hole, alternating clay-buster, red soil, and water from a Tupperware container. Lara patted the soil into place and sat back on her heels, examining her work.

A cough came from the porch next door. Wiping her dirty hands on her jeans, she looked up to see a small, thick man leaning against the porch rail, arms crossed over his belly. Lara was surprised by him, by his mass of short silver hair, his almost delicate facial features and fine straight nose. Until now, she'd only seen him from a distance. He was very short, his build block-like. He didn't look like a wife-beater.

Dave Grier stared at Lara in a bold, unconcerned way, his eyes taking her in, looking her up and down as if her whole worth and soul could be surmised from her appearance. Lara found the look disconcerting in its lack of subtlety, and began searching for something snide to say when she saw the pistol clutched in his right hand.

Her heart began to pound. *A bully. Don't let him bother you.* But then she remembered Pam. Was Pam okay? Had Dave found out about the domestic violence information? *No, he's probably just standing out there with his gun because that's what redneck DA's do on weekday evenings.* Trying to be cool and ignore him, she turned her attention back to the flowers. A snap, and out of the corner of her eye, Lara saw him level the gun at her. Before she could dive for cover, he aimed and then jerked the barrel back as if firing. He mouthed the word "pow."

Lara sprang up and charged to the clump of shrubs that separated their lawns. "Excuse me," she said. "I happened to notice that you were pointing a gun at me just now. I'd appreciate it if you'd do your little pretend target practice on something else. Not only is it dangerous, it's not neighborly."

With a jerk of his hand, Dave flicked out the revolver chamber and stared into it. Lara could see light through the hollow rounded tubes and understood that it was empty. He blew into the chamber, then flicked the gun closed again and leveled it at her head, smiling.

Lara glared at him. "Goddamned prick." She wheeled, suppressing the urge to flee into her house.

"Well, now, that ain't very ladylike," he called after her.

She flipped him a bird over her shoulder.

She stomped back to her flowers, knelt in the dirt, and finished planting while Grier took a few more imaginary shots. Only when she was through and had patted the earth around the delicate roots did she stand and walk to her porch, up the steps, and into her house.

Later, over dinner, she tried not to wish that Sterling were there, and instead felt proud of herself for her bravery. She was even prouder at the computer when she e-mailed Alexei to tell him what had happened and to jokingly give him Dave's name and address in case she ended up missing or dead. Over a glass of wine on her balcony, Lara felt strong as she watched another evening's thunderheads roll in. Later, in bed, listening to the rain pelt the roof, she thought *I'm probably the only woman who's ever stood up to him. I hope it taught him a lesson.*

Then the power flickered off. Outside, the intensifying storm shook the trees and sent pellets of hail clattering against the side of the house. Branches beat against the windows. Flashes of lightning illuminated the bedroom's dark corners with stark white light. Lara began to think about the basement.

A strange noise, at first a small scratching, like mice behind the walls. Lara held her breath and listened. The noise grew quicker, louder, more abrasive. What was it? It sounded like denim pant legs

rubbing together as someone walked. A creak, the wood floors shifting, another creak, louder. Fear prickled her scalp.

She sprang up and felt her way frantically to the door, thinking
someone else is up here. Peeking into the hall, she could see nothing
until another lightning flash lit the empty landing. Lara stumbled
forward, pausing at the top of the steps, the creaking suddenly
behind her. A flash and a shadow. Long legs. Thin. A girl? She
whirled just as the hallway went dark. The image of the lightning
glare swam across her eyes. In a panic, she turned and groped her
way downstairs and into the kitchen where she tried to calm her
breathing so she could listen. A bump upstairs, a creak. Someone
was in the house.

Fumbling along the counter for the phone, she prayed that the
lines weren't out. Finally, her hand closed around the plastic receiver
and she lifted it to her ear. A dial tone. *Focus. Be calm. Dial.* As she
heard the ring at the other end, she crept to the drawer where she
kept the cutlery and opened it. She felt as quietly as she could for her
carving knife.

"Hello?"

"Eric," she whispered.

"Lara?"

"Could you come over?"

"What's wrong?"

"I think there's someone in the house. Please hurry."

"I'll be right there. Call the police."

But she didn't call the police. Instead, she pressed her back against
the wall, a door to the hall on her right, the kitchen and its opening
to the living room on her left. She had two avenues of escape. She
crouched there, starting at every noise. *Breathe,* she told herself. *Stay
calm.* Her fingers ached from clutching the knife. She knew it would
take Eric ten minutes at least, even if he drove fast. The floor
squeaked overhead. Her heartbeat pounded in her ears. Should she
make a run for it? But Lara found she couldn't move.

*   *   *

WHEN Eric reached Lara's house, the lights were still out. He crept up the porch steps and felt for the door handle. It was unlocked, and he opened it slowly, bracing himself for whatever he might find inside. He didn't know where Lara was, or if she was okay, but he was afraid to call out to her. He stood for a moment, trying to pick up any unusual noises, but the rain was so loud on the roof, and against the windows, that he heard nothing but its thrumming roar.

He stepped into the hall, switched on his flashlight, then turned right and walked through the living room. A flare of lightning. He spied Lara in the kitchen, huddled in the corner. Another burst and he saw the knife clutched in her right hand.

He approached her, saying "Lara, hey. What's going on?" She shrank away from him. "It's just me," he whispered. "Your door wasn't locked so I walked right in."

She pushed herself out of the corner and fell into his arms. "God, I'm glad you're here. I thought I locked the door. Someone must have broken in."

"Come on. Let's check out the whole house. Where did you think the person was?"

"Upstairs. I thought I saw a girl up there."

"A girl?"

"A teenager. But I'm not sure."

"Let's look down here first."

They crept through the kitchen, the high-powered beam of Eric's flashlight illuminating wide swaths of floor, counter, and wall. Lara followed him, clutching his hand. They checked the pantry, the living room, the wide entrance hall, the parlor across from the living room, the walled-in area off the back porch, the huge closet beside it. Shadows danced on the walls. The rooms downstairs were all empty.

In front of the door to the basement, Lara paused.

"Down there too?" Eric asked.

"I hate that place. God, sometimes I think if that place didn't exist, I'd be a lot happier."

"I'll check it out for you."

He opened the door, smelled the mildewy air, and fumbled along the wall for the light switch before he remembered that the power was out. Eric had to acknowledge the prickle along the back of his neck as he inched his way down the rickety staircase, his flashlight reflecting off the water below. At the bottom, as far down as he could go without getting his feet wet, he circled the beam along the earthen walls. The basement was dripping and empty. "There's nothing down here."

He rejoined Lara, and together they climbed the stairs to the second floor, pausing on the landing to check a hidden nook in the wall. Once upstairs, they moved more slowly. Despite the rain, the noise of their footsteps seemed deafening, amplifying as it echoed through the empty space. One by one they blasted the flashlight beam into deserted rooms. Each time they approached another one, Eric's gut clenched as he braced for what they might find, but each time there was nothing. By the fifth room, he was beginning to feel more relaxed. They checked the bathroom and the long thin closet that ran the length of the house, and, finally, Lara's bedroom and balcony. The rooms were bare and dusty, no people, no footprints, nothing out of place.

"I feel like an idiot," she breathed. "I'm so sorry to have dragged you out here for nothing."

"I don't mind." He slid an arm around her shoulders. "These old houses can make some pretty awful noises during storms. Come on. Sit down. You're shaking."

"For a minute, I thought it was my next-door neighbor."

"Dave Grier?"

"Yeah."

They sat cross-legged on her futon while she told him about Grier, the gun, and the battered women's support information.

"Geez, Lara, you've got to be careful. This isn't Washington, D.C. You don't have any anonymity here. Everything you do is going to come back to you."

She fell into a brooding silence.

"Are you going to be okay?"

"I just wish the power would come back on."

"Do you have candles?"

"In one of my boxes."

Downstairs, under the glare from the flashlight, Lara locked the front door. Then they dug through box after box, spilling the contents onto the floor. Eric saw the bits and pieces of her life, books on global warming, Sierra Club and Greenpeace calendars, a pair of hiking boots that looked like they'd never been worn.

"Why don't you unpack?" he asked. "You've been here a while. It'll be fall in a couple of months. Unpack and admit you're staying."

"Here." She held up four red candles with white wax snowmen on the sides.

She found matches in a kitchen drawer, and Eric melted the wax on the bottom of each candle and then stuck them into the mouths of four empty wine bottles he spied on the counter.

"There. That's better." He switched the flashlight off, and the room around them faded. In the flickering circle of light, Lara looked pale, her eyes huge. "You want me to stay?"

"Would you?"

"Of course." She brushed a strand of hair out of her eyes.

"You never answered my question," he said.

"What question?"

"About unpacking."

"Oh, I don't know. I just don't want to."

"Come on, there's got to be more to it than that."

"It's stuff from my past, you know. Stuff Dylan bought me. Stuff we had together."

"So get new stuff."

"I can't. Not yet."

The candle flame shivered. "You need to go on with your life."

"What life?" She asked.

T HEY sat on her futon playing gin by candlelight. Lightning flared, but the muted thunder that followed sounded far away. Eric thought the storm gave the scene an ominous air, as if they were playing gin for their very lives. They had been playing for an hour now, and he caught her yawning.

"Want to sleep after this hand?"

She nodded. "I thought I'd never get calmed down again." She took another swallow of red wine. A flash of lightning. In that stark glare, her wine-stained lips looked black. She beat him again, calling "gin," and triumphantly flicking her cards onto the futon. "I win, five games to two."

"Geez, you're not competitive or anything."

"Of course not." She smiled. Eric couldn't stop looking at her mouth, at the shadowed crease between her lips. She gathered up the cards, turned them and tapped them until they were aligned, then slid them into their cardboard box. The white nightshirt tightened around her breasts as she stretched to place the cards on the bedside table. "Should I try the radio to see what they're saying about the weather?" she asked.

"What's the use if you won't go down in the basement? You know, if there's ever a tornado, you need to go down there."

"I'd rather be swept away," she said. "Maybe over the rainbow like Dorothy."

She was so close, Lara and her stained lips. Without thinking, he leaned over and kissed her mouth, reached out and touched her side, his thumb brushing underneath her breast. Behind the scent of candle smoke and hot wax, he could smell her hair and the wine on her breath. She made a strangled noise and shrank away.

"I'm sorry," he said. A heavy silence ensued, and he knew he had to say something else fast. "I don't know what I was thinking. I mean, I know you're still grieving. I just. . . ."

She pulled her knees into her chest, a protective gesture, and began to smooth the sheet around her legs.

"It's just, the other night when we danced by the pool, I thought there might be something going on."

Lara continued to smooth the sheet.

"I guess I wanted there to be something," he said.

She stopped smoothing and stared at her knees. "Eric . . . I'm sorry."

Eric swallowed, his stomach in his feet, his heart in his stomach. "So what was that stuff at the pool about? Was it my imagination?"

She shook her head. "No. I don't know what it was. I don't know what I'm doing."

Eric understood that she acted on momentary needs with no thought of consequences, and that these needs changed suddenly and, sometimes, with no good reason. He'd known this since their first conversation, but he became angry anyway. "Well, I wish you'd figured that out before you started screwing with my mind."

She hunched on the futon, looking guilty and miserable.

Eric swallowed. He rubbed his hands hard against his thighs then clapped them together. "Guess I'd better get going." He knew it was cruel to leave her alone with no power after her scare, but he wanted to be cruel.

He could tell from the way her voice choked that she was crying. "I'm sorry, Eric. I'm a bad person."

He wasn't going to make it easy for her and say she wasn't. "Good night."

"Okay." She wiped at her eyes. "Take a candle." So he did, picking one up and shielding it with a cupped hand. He looked at her huddled in bed, and it almost broke his heart except that he was hurt. As he left her room, his shadow spread huge and wavy onto the walls and ceiling. It followed him as he wound his way down the stairs to the kitchen, where he picked up his flashlight. At the front door, he looked back the way he'd come for any sign of candlelight from her bedroom. He saw none. The house creaked and groaned in the wind. He blew out the candle and set it down, then twisted open the knob. As he stepped onto the porch, the wind pulled the door shut behind him with a click. He tested the knob. It was locked.

❦ chapter eighteen ❦

July 24

THE weather worsened as Eric drove home. Once in bed, he lay awake, tormented by self-recriminating voices as the storm raged outside. *I shouldn't have left her,* he thought. *Even if I was hurt, it was ungentlemanly to leave her.* Long after midnight, the voices gave way to an aching self-pity. *Why should Lara be different from any of the other women I've liked? Why should I hope, even for a second, that I won't be lonely forever?*

He finally got to sleep around three, hours after the storm had passed. He slept too long the next morning, and got to the store late.

A few minutes after Eric arrived, Sterling burst in. "Man, Eric, you should have seen it," he exclaimed. "Jaylee was making this malt, and she didn't get the cup in the machine right. It was like a god-damned snowstorm in there. I still got malt in my hair."

"Well, go brush it out then. The last thing I need is fucking malt sticking to everything."

Sterling squinted at Eric. "You look like you got rode hard and put up wet."

"Storm kept me up."

"The girls too. Had both of 'em in bed with me 'fore it was over."

And he still had all this energy. Eric wanted to scream.

* * *

Sterling wished the day would hurry up and be over. He wanted to see Lara, hoped they'd look through the telescope and maybe hold hands again. The hours crawled by and, to make the time go quicker, he began inventing conversations that might happen between Lara and himself. But it didn't help.

By eight, he thought he'd go crazy from wanting to leave, and when Eric finally locked up, he was already on his skateboard, pumping hard toward Lara's.

He rolled through the streets until he reached her cracked and weedy driveway. He flipped the board into his hands with a stomp, ran up her porch steps, and rang the bell. He saw her, dressed in white, moving toward him from the darkness like a ghost. Like a ghost when she opened the door, pale and sick-looking, hair all rumpled, eyes red. She wore a huge white T-shirt and sagging white socks.

"Hey," he peered at her. "You okay?"

Her chin puckered and her face twisted as if she was trying to smile except her mouth wouldn't work. A tear squeezed out of one eye and rolled down her cheek.

"Hey, hey, what's wrong?" He set his skateboard down and faced her, uncomfortable, not sure what to do.

She blurted out the whole story, Grier with the gun, Eric in her bedroom, how he'd left her alone in the storm. Sterling got angry. "I'm gonna kill that dickhead next-door neighbor of yours," he said. "I'm going over there right now and give him a piece of my mind."

Lara gripped his arm. "No. I don't want you to get in any trouble. I'm fine."

But he broke loose and, face hot, ran down the steps and across the yard to the Griers' house, where he pounded on the door. Pam answered.

"I need to speak to your husband, ma'am," Sterling said as politely as he could. He waited by the open door, fuming, clenching his hands into fists and testing their weight until Dave Grier rounded the hallway corner and approached him.

"What you want, son?"

"You lay a hand on her, you even talk to her again, and I'll kill you. You understand that?"

He didn't wait for Grier to say anything but whirled and marched off, part of him scared to look back.

"I'm calling your mama, boy!" Grier yelled.

Sterling tried hard not to think about what he'd just done.

Lara stood in the hallway where he'd left her, arms hanging limp at her sides. "You don't have to worry about him any more," Sterling declared.

She sank onto the stairs, wiping her eyes with the back of a hand and sniffling. Then suddenly she laughed. "I guess chivalry isn't dead after all. I mean, with Eric. . . ."

"Eric's a fucking wuss. He should have gone and told off Grier last night."

"The thing about Eric is that he just accepts everything the way it is," she said. "It's like his photographs. He takes these pretty pictures of things exactly the way the are. He makes piles of trash in some old woman's yard look nice."

"Yeah, well, I think he's just a wuss. And he shouldn't have left you. I wouldn't have left you."

"I wasn't fair to him. He was right to be upset. I hurt his feelings."

"It's his own fault. You want me to go tell him so?"

"No, no." She shook her head. "It's all right. I'll talk to him later." She stood and walked into the kitchen, pulled off a paper towel, and blew her nose. "I'm sorry," she said. "You must think I'm falling apart. Let me go put on some clothes."

"Eric's lower than a nit on a worm!" he called after her.

In a few minutes, Lara returned wearing shorts and a different T-shirt. Her eyes were still puffy. She gave him a pathetic half-smile. "I've always had an overactive imagination. If I'd just kept it under control last night, none of this would have happened."

"Some of those real bad storms scare me too," he said.

She lifted an eyebrow like she knew he was lying.

"What do you need for me to do tonight?"

"I don't know." Her eyes wandered the entranceway and came to rest on his skateboard. "I don't see how anyone can stay on those things."

"It's easy. Want me to show you? We gotta go outside and show Dave Grier we ain't scared of him anyway."

"I don't know."

"Come on. You been in this old house too long. That's part of your problem."

They went outside and Sterling hopped onto the skateboard in her driveway. He pumped the board along the ground and did a couple of ollies to show off, flipping the board in the air and landing on it again. Then he turned to see her reaction. She was clasping her hands together. He hopped back on the board and rolled over to her.

"Wow," she said. "I'm amazed you're still alive."

"Come on, try it. Get on."

"I don't think so. I'm too old for that kind of thing."

"Come on," he insisted and held out his hand.

She took it, her fingers curling around his. She stepped onto the board like she thought it might take off. It rolled a little and she crunched his fingers, trying to keep her balance.

"It's okay. Loosen up. You gotta keep your knees relaxed or you'll fall."

He pulled her slowly down the sidewalk, looking out for broken pavement. "You're doing good." The wheels hummed. He stopped and they turned around and headed in the other direction.

"I'm doing it," she breathed. "I'm letting go." Releasing his hand, Lara spread her arms wide and crouched like a bird about to take off.

"You ain't going too fast there." He gave her a little shove and she shrieked. She wobbled along for a few seconds, arms flailing. Then she fell. Sterling lunged forward and caught her just in time. When he looked up from her face, from her hair all fallen in his eyes, from the damp, salty smell of her skin, he saw the prick next door on his porch watching them. Sterling waved at Dave Grier, and when Lara saw, she waved too.

"You ain't supposed to be skateboarding on the sidewalks!" Dave Grier called. "I phoned the police."

Lara shot Sterling a look, then pointed toward her door. "You want to make a run for it?" she whispered.

He picked up his skateboard and nodded. They dashed into the house. Lara slammed the door shut and locked it. Then they tore upstairs and crouched breathless and giggling on the landing. Lara covered Sterling's mouth to muffle his laughter.

It was only a minute before they heard a knock and clutched at each other, wide-eyed and grinning, holding their breaths. Another knock, and someone yelled for Lara to open the door before she got into trouble. Sterling shook his head urgently and they continued to huddle beside each other, stifling laughter. More knocking, more yelling, then a conference in low voices. Finally, silence. Sterling crept on hands and knees into Lara's bedroom and peeked out the window.

"They're gone," he called.

A citation for disturbing the peace lay on the floor in front of the mail slot. Lara laughed. "I'll pay it," she said. "It was more than worth it."

T HEY sat beside each other at the kitchen table while Lara ate chocolate ice cream straight from the carton. Sterling liked the way she turned the spoon upside down in her mouth and sucked on it.

"Want some ice cream?" she asked.

He grimaced and held his hand up. "Can't stand the stuff."

"You have to look at it all day, huh?"

"Yeah."

She leaned toward him conspiratorially. "I wonder what the neighbors thought about the skateboard lesson."

He grinned.

"When's your eighteenth birthday again?" She gave him the kind of look that made him know his heart was beating.

"Three weeks."

"How are you going to celebrate?"

"Aw, I don't know. Mama'll bake me a cake."

"Eighteen is a pretty big birthday."

"No, it ain't. Used to be you could drink when you were eighteen. Now the only thing you can do is smoke, like I'd want to do that."

"You don't smoke?"

"Never saw the sense in doing something that expensive that just kills you in the end. Eric told me about how much them cigarette companies have covered up over the years."

"You know, land that's used to grow tobacco could be used to grow food instead."

"Commie." He made a poke at her ribs. "No red-blooded American'd talk about getting rid of tobacco to grow food. That's commie talk."

"What about R-rated movies? You can see those now, right?"

"You see any movie theaters around here? Hell, I've seen X-rated movies anyway."

She frowned and sucked on the spoon. "So what do you want for your birthday?"

"From you?"

She nodded.

He flashed her a grin.

"Within reason."

He grinned wider.

"Forget it." She laughed. "Goddamned flirt."

THEY set up the telescope and he looked at the Orion nebula and explained to Lara that on a really clear night, you could see it with the naked eye. He told her it was the remains of a supernova, and that he wished he could see it up close. They took turns looking until eleven, when she offered him a ride home and he accepted, thinking there was nothing to hide from her any more. In the car, he watched her drive, her face silhouetted against the moonglow.

"Do you think the next weekday you've got off, you'd go to Athens with me? Maybe you could check out the university," she said.

She sounded just like Eric, and Sterling was sick of it. Neither of them understood what his life was like, and they just made him feel worse by bringing up college all the time. "I'm not going to college."

"Why not?"

He didn't answer.

Lara drummed her fingers against the steering wheel. "Why not?" She sounded irritated, and he could tell she wasn't going to let it go.

"I don't have the money."

"You can get around that," Lara said. "There are scholarships and federal grants and loans. . . ." She paused. "I think you're just scared."

"Yeah, scared that my mama and my sisters'll starve."

"No, I mean scared for yourself. I know exactly what you're thinking. You're thinking what if you go to college and you're dumber than everyone else, and the girls don't like you because you don't have the coolest clothes, and the guys make fun of you? What if you don't have any friends? What if your education at that backwater high school hasn't done you any good, and you fail all your classes? What if you screw up?"

Sterling sat silent beside her, feeling naked. As the engine hummed, and the sound of crickets and tree frogs came through the open windows, he crossed his arms over his lap.

"Do you know why I gave you that copy of *The Communist Manifesto*?" she asked.

"Because you want everyone to be a commie like you?" he said.

"No, it's because I knew you'd read it. You'd think it was boring and hard to understand, but you'd read it, and you'd get something out of it. Right? You've started to read it, haven't you?"

"Yeah."

"And is it boring and hard to understand?"

"Yeah."

"But you're getting something out of it? You'll finish it anyway?"

"Probably, yeah."

"Well, most of the guys I knew when I was an undergraduate, most of the guys who had expensive prep-school educations, wouldn't have read it at all. They'd have tossed it in some corner while they went out and got trashed. You see, I think you're smarter and more mature than most of the guys I've known, seventeen and older. That's why I gave you *The Communist Manifesto.*"

Sterling's throat went tight like he might cry. "Yeah?"

"Yeah. You could go a long way, kid, on persistence alone, not to mention smarts."

His stomach tightened. He stared at Lara, trying to see her in the dark. Was she serious? He knew she was serious, but he couldn't quite believe it. All this time, he'd been wrong about her. She didn't think he was stupid at all. She actually understood him. The urge to confess every personal thought or idea he'd ever had rushed over him like a wave. But for now he said nothing because speaking would ruin the moment. So he stared at her, the car rumbling underneath him, the smell of drying hay coming through the open window, and the thick night air weighing on him. He heard the crickets chirping, the dull soft thumping of bugs against the windshield.

They turned to travel the last mile to his house.

"I'd have to leave home to go to college."

As they turned on to his gravel driveway, the headlights caught the dingy siding, the flaking window frames, the sagging roof.

"You could leave. They'd manage."

He nodded, the teary sensation bubbling again in his throat, trembling across his chin. She pulled the car to a stop, shifted in her seat and leaned closer. "Listen to me." She took his hand and he felt a surge of electricity through his arm. "Don't wait until it's too late to live your life. If you wait too long, you might never get the chance. Believe me, I know. And don't stay here because you're afraid of not being as good as anyone else. That would be a stupid reason. Promise me you won't stay because of that."

He couldn't find his voice to answer.

"Come on, promise me."

"Okay," he choked.

"Good." She patted his hand twice, then let go. "Sorry to keep you out so late. Sorry for being such an emotional wreck."

"You just had a rough night, is all. I've had those myself."

She was silent for a moment. "Thanks. You always cheer me up. You always make me feel better."

"You too," he said. "I mean, you always make me feel better too." He looked again at her darkened face, waiting for something he knew wouldn't happen.

"'Night," she said.

"'Night." He heaved open the door and slid out, then stood in the driveway and watched as Lara turned the car around and drove off.

His mother sat in the kitchen. Behind her, in the living room, the girls slept on the pull-out couch, their faces bathed red by TV screen light.

"She's feeding you, ain't she?" His mother said.

The way his mama looked in her shabby housecoat with her stringy hair and stained teeth, it disgusted him. Why couldn't she even try to keep herself up?

"I waited supper on you. Then I got to worrying that something was wrong 'cause it was almost ten, and you wasn't home."

"I would've called, but we ain't got a phone. Couldn't pay the bill, remember?" She wasn't old, he thought, only six years older than Lara, and still she looked so rundown. He strode to the refrigerator, opened the door, and pulled out the water jug. He unscrewed the metal top and brought the jug to his mouth.

"You pour that in a glass," his mama warned.

He glared at her, then drank from the jug.

With a sudden lunge, she seized it from him and cuffed his cheek. "What'd I just tell you?" A murmur came from the sofa bed, and she lowered her voice. "I'm starting to wonder what you're doing spending all your time over there. Pam Grier called me at work and told me you talked ugly to Dave and that you and the Walton woman was out front playing around on your skateboard. That don't sound like working to me."

His cheek stung from where she'd hit him, and he started to lift his hand to touch the spot, but made himself stop.

"There's ways to earn money that ain't right," his mama hissed. "I don't want you going back there no more." She shoved the water jug into the fridge, then felt around in the pocket of her housecoat for a cigarette.

"If you'd quit smoking, maybe I wouldn't have to work extra hours to keep you in cigarettes," he countered.

"Maybe smoking is the one pleasure I got left. Maybe after years of raising you and them girls my looks is gone, and my money's gone, and I ain't got nothing else to enjoy." Her voice took on the high, strained tone it usually did right before she cried. Sterling pressed his hands to his ears so he didn't have to hear any more. He wheeled and stalked away from his mother down the hall to his bedroom.

"I ain't finished with you yet," she spat after him. He shut the door. As her footsteps followed him down the passage, he turned the lock so she couldn't come in. She stopped right outside. He waited, but nothing happened. Then he heard her walk away. He let out his breath, thinking maybe come morning she wouldn't be so angry.

After stripping down to his boxers, he stretched out on the bed and picked up *The Communist Manifesto*. He could only read it with the help of a dictionary Eric had given him a few years back. Every word Sterling didn't understand, he looked up and wrote down in a notebook to learn and practice. It seemed like he spent more time reading the dictionary than the *Manifesto* itself. It had taken him almost a week, at four pages a night, to reach page twenty-four. He opened the book to that page now and read:

The bourgeois claptrap about the family and education, about the hallowed co-relation of parent and child, becomes all the more disgusting, the more, by the action of modern industry, all family ties among the proletarians are torn asunder and their children transformed into simple articles of commerce and instruments of labor.

It was one of the few paragraphs he'd been able to read all the way through without looking up a word. He read it again, stunned. This communist guy was talking about him. What the hell kind of family did he have? He was just an "instrument of labor," slaving all day to help his sisters who he never saw, and who he was starting to resent. He, Sterling, was an article of commerce and an instrument of labor, a machine they paid just enough to keep running and no more.

"Damn," he muttered. He picked up the atlas Eric had loaned him and looked up Russia and thought about communism. If this book was saying what communists really thought, then what had gone wrong? Because what this book was saying sounded pretty good and pretty fair to him.

chapter nineteen

July 25

H IS mother started in on him again at breakfast.

"I don't want you going over to that woman's house today."

"Well, that's too bad, 'cause I'm going." Dayla padded in on slippered feet and slid into Sterling's lap. "She hired me to work for her, she pays good, and I'm going. Don't bother waiting supper on me."

"Maybe you should think twice about coming home at all then, if you ain't gonna be a part of this family and eat supper with us. Maybe you should think about just leaving like your daddy done."

"Hey, darlin', hop up now," he said to Dayla. "I gotta get going." He helped the little girl off his lap, then stood and stomped out the door without looking at his mother and without eating the breakfast she'd made for him.

Outside, the sky was hazy, the grass damp and glistening with dew. He started walking. A good quiet half-hour walk would be better than five minutes in the truck with his mother. He imagined how he'd get to Dairy Queen, and instead of going in, he'd keep walking. The sun would rise higher and beat on his head. He'd start to sweat, but he wouldn't stop walking. He'd just keep walking out of this town, out of this state, all the way to the Pacific if he could. Imagining that made him feel better.

* * *

WHEN Lara saw Dave Grier drive off in his white Cadillac, she dashed across the yard and up the steps of the Griers' brick ranch. Pam opened the door and, just as Lara caught sight of her swollen nose, shielded it with her hand.

"Well, hey there." There was a menacing quality to Pam's cheerfulness.

"Hi. I just wanted to drop by to, you know—" Lara faltered, "to see how you are. Did you read the information I left?"

Pam wore a pink bathrobe. Her huge hair was pulled back with two flowered barrettes. She smiled, but her eyes glittered coldly.

"Did you read them?" Lara insisted.

Pam leaned closer. She reeked of perfume and hair spray. "That O'Connor boy is seventeen years old."

"Yes, I know that."

"Do you?" Pam asked. Then she said. "I'm sorry, darling, I got to get ready for work. I'm going to be late." The door swung forward and slammed in Lara's face.

"Shit." Lara raked her fingers through her hair, and taking a deep breath, rang the bell again. She waited and rang, waited and rang.

"Screw it," she muttered as she trudged back to her house. "I hate this town."

THAT afternoon, when he stepped into Eric's store, Sterling began to think about how Eric had treated Lara. It made him mad, but also kind of sorry for Eric, so he didn't know how to act. As the door swung shut behind Sterling, Eric looked up from where he stood behind the counter.

"Hey," Sterling said.

"Hey."

Sterling was just about to mention Lara, but Eric nodded his head toward a girl flipping through the CDs. "She's been here half an hour."

It was Alicia Hopkins. She was wearing high heels and a hot pink tube top. Sterling used to like it when she dressed like that. Now he thought she looked cheap.

Alicia gave him a sly look. Sterling turned his back on her. "I'm going into the office," he muttered to Eric. "Tell me when she's gone."

But it was too late. She had come over to the counter. He could smell her flowery perfume.

"Hey, Sterling."

He kept his back turned. He didn't want to talk to her. She was a kid. Why wouldn't she leave him alone? "I gotta work, Alicia," he said.

"You've been hanging out with that woman who bought the Bishop house."

"Yeah," said Sterling. "So what?"

"So, don't you think she's kind of old?"

He turned around and met Alicia's mascaraed, glittering eyes. "Hey, women like her know a lot more than girls like you." He gave her a vicious smile and watched her face go red.

"Come on, Sterling." Eric butted in. "You've got a lot to do today. Alicia, you'll have to excuse him. He's got work to do."

After Alicia had stomped out, Sterling leaned back against the counter. "Man, she's starting to creep me out."

Eric shrugged. "I imagine she'll come to her senses soon enough and go find another boy to bother. Just ignore her."

Sterling thought again about how Eric had treated Lara. "Thanks for the advice, bourgeois pig."

"Christ, she really gave you *The Communist Manifesto,* and you're really reading it."

"Yessir, capitalist swine."

"Watch it, I'm a petty bourgeois capitalist swine, on the brink of becoming a proletarian myself. I'm going to loan you *Animal Farm.* Ever heard of it?"

Sterling shook his head.

"Just consider it a companion book."

"Yeah, well, I'm tired of being an instrument of labor. I'm going to start a union at Dairy Queen."

"That sounds like a damned fine way to lose your job. Besides, Lara's the bourgeois one. Hell, she's more bourgeois than anyone in this town, as much money as she's got."

Sterling grinned. "Guess I'm willing to overlook that 'cause she's pretty."

"Ah. Sounds like you really have the revolutionary fervor going."

"It pisses me off plenty that Dairy Queen ain't fair to its workers," Sterling protested.

"Yeah, well, Dairy Queen's about the only option you got in this town unless you want to break your back at the concrete factory or spend the day with your hand shoved up a dead chicken's ass down at the poultry plant." Eric paused. "You shouldn't take Lara seriously anyway."

Sterling fell into the desk chair. He didn't like it that Eric was trying to run Lara down. "Just cause she blew you off the other night doesn't mean she ain't smart."

Eric looked startled, then mumbled "Well, it was fucking considerate of her to tell you."

"I thought you were gonna back off. I thought you said women like her are dangerous."

Eric rolled his eyes. "Hey, I'm not the only one she's been leading on."

"Yeah, well, she can lead me anywhere she wants." Sterling shot Eric a wicked grin.

Eric shook his head. "She's going to get you in trouble if you're not careful."

"That's what I'm hoping," Sterling said.

As the afternoon wore on, Eric's anger toward Lara grew. What right did she have to tell Sterling what had happened between them?

What right did she have to act like the injured one? *He* was the one who'd been used. He wasn't going to just let her get away with it.

As casually as he could, he offered to give Sterling a lift to Lara's that evening, then with equal casualness he followed the boy up the steps and stood shifting from foot to foot on the porch.

When Lara opened the door, her eyes fixed on Eric. She backed away, retreating into the hall. Eric gritted his teeth and forced himself to pursue her until she was pressed against a wall and could go no further. "Hey, will you come outside for a second?" he mumbled.

"Why?" She eyed him.

"I want to talk to you."

She glanced over his shoulder. Sterling had moved into the living room and stood there, looking with forced interest at one of Lara's boxes. "Get yourself something to drink, kiddo," she called. "You know where it is." She turned back to Eric, muttering "Come on, then."

They stepped onto the porch and shut the door. Facing Lara, he noticed how her hair was different today, piled on top of her head, wisps framing her face. His mind seized on her hair, and for a moment he could think of nothing else.

"Eric, what do you want?"

The sharp tone of her voice brought everything back to him. "Thanks a whole hell of a lot for telling Sterling about the other night."

"Well, you told him about Dylan."

"That's different."

"And you showed me his house without his permission."

That was a low blow, Eric thought. "I wanted you to understand that he's had a hard life and doesn't need you fucking with his mind."

"What?" she demanded.

"You're doing the same thing to him that you did to me."

"And what did I do to you?"

"You used me. You flirted with me and made me think there was more going on than there really was, just so you could feel a little better."

She fell silent. Eric waited for her to argue. He steeled himself and began preparing a vicious retort. But instead of arguing, Lara hung her head and, with her sandal, prodded the torn green artificial grass covering the porch. Then she said "You're right."

He was surprised. His angry words died on his tongue. Part of him had hoped she would deny it. Lara bit her lower lip. Eric crossed his arms over his chest. It would have been easier if she'd denied it. Easier not to have his worst fears confirmed. He cast a longing glance toward his car. Couldn't he just make a run for it?

"So now I guess you won't hang out with me any more," Lara murmured. "I'm really sorry, Eric. I think you're a great guy. I treated you badly."

His anger was fading. After all, he'd known from the beginning why she flirted, but had nonetheless talked himself into believing that deeper feelings were involved. The notion of abandoning her just because he wasn't going to get her into bed seemed suddenly pathetic and adolescent, because, when it came right down to it, he enjoyed her company. Still, he tried to land one last blow. "Yeah, well, just stop it with Sterling. He doesn't understand."

He waited for her to reply. She just stared at her feet.

Inside, Sterling began to whistle. Eric and Lara's eyes met, and they smiled at the same time.

"I don't want you to be mad," Lara said. "I want to be friends. It was something important to me. Especially in this town. *London Calling* and all."

Sterling began singing loudly and off-key.

"We were listening to Nine Inch Nails in the store today."

Lara rolled her eyes. "Terrific. Now I have to hear Sterling O'Connor imitating Nine Inch Nails all night."

Eric grinned. "Incidentally, I'd have you know that thanks to your subversive influence, I was called a bourgeois swine today by my only employee."

Lara's face broke into a delighted smile. "Good for him. That's a major step."

"Becoming a hostile laborer?"

"No, quoting the *Manifesto*. Besides, if the bourgeois swine shoe fits. . . ."

"Hey, I pointed out that you're more bourgeois than I am."

"What did he say?"

"He said it didn't matter because you're cute."

Lara sighed. "Clearly, I need to continue his indoctrination."

"If you expect a seventeen-year-old boy to think with anything other than his dick, that's your error in judgment."

She laughed and he felt good. "At least we still have our kid in common," he said. It was like it had been before, the two of them joking around. Was it going to be this easy to pretend nothing bad had happened between them?

S TERLING stood near the front window and strained to hear what Eric and Lara were saying, but he couldn't. Part of him hoped they worked it out, but another part was scared they might work it out too well, that Lara might change her mind and start dating Eric. Sterling felt like he wasn't a very good friend, wanting Eric's heart to be broken. But since last night, Sterling realized he couldn't stand the thought of someone else dating Lara, or touching her, or even look-ing at her.

Outside the window, Lara laughed, and Sterling panicked. *They're working it out. Lara's falling for Eric, and I won't be able to take it.* He began pacing the living room. Should he go outside? Should he try to stop them from talking? He had to do something. But before he could make up his mind, he heard the front door open.

Rushing into the hall, he almost collided with Lara. Eric wasn't with her. "What happened?" he demanded. "Are you guys going out now?"

"No. Why do you keep asking that? We just talked." She shut the front door and took his hand. He felt a thrill as she meshed her fin-gers with his and led him toward the staircase. "Come on. I need you to help me with something."

"You sure you're not going out with Eric?"

"I'm sure," she insisted and smiled at him. "Stop worrying, little boy."

He felt weak-kneed with relief and looked at their interlaced fingers, Lara's long and thin and brown, his thicker and rougher. Hell, he thought, our hands don't even look right together. It made him start worrying again. But the worrying slipped away as she led him through her bedroom door.

Everything was low to the ground and white. Her futon, covered by a white sheet, stood on the floor with a white lamp beside it. Long white curtains hung over the double glass doors that led onto the balcony, their bottoms crumpled and spread out on the floor like the train on a bride's dress. There were no pictures, no knick-knacks. The white walls were bare. Sterling decided that there was something pure about her room, something clean and perfect.

Lara let go of his hand to grab a bag lying beside the door. She pulled out sheet after sheet of adhesive glow-in-the-dark stars. "I'm going to put them on the ceiling. Will you help?"

"I got those in my room. My room's painted black so it looks like space."

"Brilliant minds think alike," she said.

Sterling walked to the center of the room and tilted his head back, surveying the ceiling. "What sky do you want?"

"What do you mean?"

"What constellations? What month of the year?"

"Oh, that's easy. I'd like right now. This month. That way when I look up, I'll think of today, and of you helping me."

She circled him, wide circles that got tighter, and as they did, his insides twisted tighter so that by the time she stood beside him, it hurt to have her so close. "I've got October in my room," he said.

"You like October?"

"I like the fall of the year. Cooler weather, you know." He felt a pang. "And I always liked school starting. But July is good. Today's good." Sterling hoped she'd always remember this summer like he would. "We'll have to get a sky chart for July. It might take some time. I got mine outta the library."

"Forget the chart," she said. "Just give it your best guess."

His best guess. He started worrying right away that he'd mess it up. As he went downstairs to find the stepladder, he tried to picture the constellations in his mind. July. He imagined the black background of a sky chart, the bright orb of Polaris. He dragged the ladder upstairs to Lara's room realizing there was no way he'd remember everything. She didn't have that many stars anyway. He'd have to pick a few constellations, good ones like Pegasus and Cygnus.

"This will be great," she said when he struggled into her bedroom with the ladder. "I think this house needs a little piece of the universe inside it."

"It needs some paint and some pictures, is what it needs." He was hot and sweating, even though the window was open and the fan was running. "Air conditioning, too." Sterling pulled off his shirt, used it to wipe the sweat from his face, then tossed it onto the floor. *There,* he thought, *might as well give her something to look at while I work.*

As he set up the stepladder, he mentally listed the names of the stars in the July sky: Enif, Deneb, Sadr. He thought of his own name, Sterling. A stupid name. He remembered his mother saying his name made her think of silver, of something valuable and pure. He wondered if she'd named him after something pure because he really wasn't, because she hadn't been.

When the ladder was ready, he climbed almost to the top. The air near the ceiling was still and sweltering. He reached down and snapped his fingers for Lara to hand him some stars.

As Sterling stuck the stars one by one on Lara's ceiling, he said their names reverently out loud. "Enif, Beham, Homam, Markab, Scheat, Matar." He hoped that by speaking those names, he'd be able to recreate the constellations exactly, because he wanted Lara's ceiling to be perfect.

"It sound like you're chanting a spell," she said.

"It's the stars' names. Pay attention, 'cause there's gonna be a quiz when I'm done."

After a while, his neck and back began to ache. He was aware of her watching him. He wondered what she was thinking, but was glad she was quiet. The stars took concentration.

When he was through, he leaped off the ladder, slapping his hands on his jeans.

"It looks great," she said, her neck craned back to see. "I can't wait until it gets dark so I can watch them glow."

Her shoulder brushed his arm. Her hair smelled good, like coconuts, and her skin felt soft and damp against his. "Your hair's real pretty that way," he said.

She didn't respond, but instead collapsed onto the futon. She stretched her arms and legs out. "I'm just going to lie here and wait until it gets dark and the stars start to glow. Why don't you put the ladder up, then come back and we can pretend we're in the desert."

He folded the ladder and carried it downstairs. On the way back, he stopped at the fridge and pulled out two Diet Cokes. The cans were cool and swollen with carbonation.

He lowered himself onto the floor next to the futon and handed her a Coke.

She propped herself sideways on her elbow and studied him. "I got those stars in Athens, by the way, and while I was there, I swung past the university and picked you up an application and some financial aid information."

"You did, huh?"

"It's downstairs."

He hooked a finger under the tab and jerked it up. The can exhaled with a loud hiss as foam spurted through the opening and he sucked it off the rim. It tasted like metal. He took a swallow and coughed, the carbonation stinging his nose. Then he looked into Lara's pretty face and thought *why would I want to be in Athens while you're here?*

"Did you ever take the SATs?" Lara asked.

He nodded. "Miz McEachern made me."

"Good, so do you want to look at the application?"

"I'll take it home with me." Sterling didn't want her to watch while he read the information promising some new and different life, didn't want her to see the hungry look on his face, because then she'd feel sorry for him. He'd liked the way she was last night better, giving him a hard time, saying "You could go a long way, kid, on persistence alone, not to mention smarts." Just thinking about it made him warm. Plus she was so pretty lying there. Sterling thought his heart might melt. "Thanks, Lara," he said.

"You're welcome." She rolled onto her back again, arms thrown over her head so her breasts rose under the blue tank top. He could see the outline of her bra. He thought her arms looked nice, so brown and smooth. "You know, I'm kind of tired tonight," she said. "I don't know why. I didn't do that much today."

Slowly, he reached out and ran his fingertips down the side of her arm, saw her flesh goosepimple with the contact. She lay very still, and he kept stroking her arm so gently he could barely feel her skin. Outside, the evening was alive with noises of crickets and tree frogs, laughing children and traffic, but the old house muffled those sounds and made them seem unreal, like it all came from a different dimension, a place where he and Lara had never lived. He caressed her warm brown arm while she stared at the ceiling, the house big and silent around them.

His heart pounded. Lifting his hand, he brushed a fine strand of dark hair away from her face, touched her soft ear, then ran the back of his fingers along her cheek.

Suddenly, she launched herself up. It startled him. She hugged her knees into her chest. "It's late," she breathed. "Let me drive you home."

It took him a moment to recover. Then he said, "What about the desert? I want to see the stars."

"I'm really tired. You have to go so I can sleep." She crawled to his shirt and tossed it to him. "Come on."

She was halfway downstairs before he could say anything. He

stood, his dick stiff in his pants, his knees shaking, and followed her. She was waiting for him by the front door. "Lara—" he started toward her.

"Here's the application." She shoved a folder into his hands. "You'll read it?"

He felt dizzy and weak from wanting her.

"Promise me you'll read it."

"Ain't I already said I would about eighty times?" He tried to meet her eyes, but she wouldn't look him in the face. "Come on, Lara, let me stay and see the stars."

"No." She opened her door and disappeared into the night.

He followed her. While Lara climbed into her car, Sterling caught sight of two shadowy figures running off down the street. He heard laughter and the click of high heels on the sidewalk. Alicia Hopkins, he thought. Shaking his head, he walked to the rickety car and climbed in while Lara turned the key and gunned the engine. Then she squealed out of the driveway and sped down the street.

They drove in silence. The sky was black up top, but faded into purple and red just above the horizon. Around them, the trees were blurred gray shapes against the sky. Round haybales lay hunched and dark in the pastures. Lara turned on her headlights and rolled down the window. He strained to see the wind lifting her hair, blowing it out of its pins.

She didn't talk until they stopped in his driveway, and then she said, with forced casualness, "Thanks for helping me with the stars." Her hair floated wildly around her face.

Again, he touched her arm, his fingers traveling from her shoulder to her elbow, then back again. Pausing at the top, near her neck, he traced a circle while she sat motionless, staring hard out the window, her hands gripping the wheel.

"Lara?"

"You're seventeen years old," she said as if wanting to remind herself that it was true.

"I don't care," he said.

Silence.

"Do you?" he asked.

She didn't answer.

"I know you miss him, that guy," Sterling stammered. "But you gotta move on some time."

Sudden light. Himself trapped in the glare with his fingers on her shoulder. He shielded his eyes against the porch light from his own house, feeling panicked all of a sudden. "My mama. I gotta go. I'll see you tomorrow." He jumped out of the car before she could reply. As he headed to the door, kicking at a rock in his path, the bright gleam of Lara's headlights caught his back, the glare from the porch light illuminated his front, and Sterling felt exposed from both sides.

chapter twenty

October 19

EDGARS had been putting it off for too long. He had to question Dave Grier.

According to both Sterling and Eric, Dave had pointed a gun at Lara, but neither could tell him the exact circumstances because neither had been present. Just recounting the story had made Sterling so upset that the captain had to get a signed guarantee that he would stay away from the D.A.

Now the captain settled into the driver's seat of the Ford sedan, and, as he turned the ignition, eyed the flat slate-gray sky, thinking a cold soaking rain would be the perfect capper to what promised to be a dismal day.

Edgars had worked with Dave Grier for eight years, and, although he never said so, he hated the man. The D.A. was physically small and wielded his power like someone who'd been picked on as a child and was out for revenge. Edgars made it a professional mission to avoid Grier whenever he could. This time he couldn't.

DAVE Grier's office was designed to intimidate. Everything in it was dark and heavy. Wood-paneled walls enclosed plush burgundy carpeting and an expanse of desk that covered half the room. Oil portraits of past D.A.s frowned from the walls.

"Come on in and have a seat, Jimmy." Dave slapped him on the shoulder.

With a groan, Edgars lowered himself into the burgundy leather armchair across from Grier's desk. Edgars noticed how neat the desk was, how clean, almost devoid of paperwork, and he pictured the forest of files rising from his own desk and thought *hell, I went into the wrong profession.*

Outside, rain pattered on the window, but in this muffled expanse of wood and carpet no other sound penetrated. "Great weather we're having," Edgars tried to start with a joke.

Grier folded his meaty hands on the desk. "What can I do for you, Jimmy?"

"Well, sir, I guess I need to ask you some more questions about your neighbor."

"Okay." Grier's voice had an unpleasant edge.

Edgars felt small in the huge office. "I want you to understand, sir, I'm just doing my job."

"Well sure, Jimmy," Grier rewarded the captain with a tobacco-stained smile. "'Course it's your job. Shoot."

"You lived next door to her and all."

"And I saw the O'Connor boy and her fighting. That kid has hung himself by the balls for sure."

"Well, actually," Edgars cleared his throat and studied a hangnail he just now noticed on his right index finger, "kid says you pointed a gun at Lara Walton. So does Eric Teague."

Captain Edgars watched the color rise from Grier's neck into his cheeks. He imagined steam exploding from the D.A.'s ears.

"Now wait just one second." Grier pointed a thick finger at Edgars. "What exactly are you suggesting?"

"I'm not suggesting anything, sir. I just needed to ask you about why you pointed a gun at Lara Walton."

"I didn't point a gun at that woman, and anyone who says I did is lying. If you want to ask questions, ask that O'Connor boy what he and she were doing all alone in that big house at night."

"So you didn't point a gun at her?"

"Ain't that what I just said?"

"Yeah, yeah, it is." Edgars cleared his throat. The hangnail started to throb and his back felt clammy with sweat. "Just one more thing. Do you know if Lara Walton ever gave your wife any pamphlets or anything?"

"Any what?"

Edgars cleared his throat again. His windpipe felt like it wanted to close up. "Pamphlets. You called her a femi-Nazi the other day, and I just wanted to know why you said that, if she'd been giving feminist stuff to Pam or anything."

"Well, you just had to look at the woman to tell. She didn't look like a regular woman, if you get my meaning. She didn't fix herself up."

"So she never gave Pam any sort of pamphlets?"

Grier glared. "Now, Jimmy, how would I know anything about that?"

"Just asking." Edgars paused. "So just to sum up, you never pointed a gun at Lara Walton, and you and Pam didn't like her, and you don't know if she ever gave Pam anything."

"I never said we didn't like her."

"Yes, you did, at your house the other day."

"Oh," Grier finally smiled. "Guess you caught me there, Jimmy. That's why you're the detective and I'm only the D.A., huh?"

"So you didn't like her?"

"No, I must admit we didn't."

"And Sterling O'Connor and Eric Teague were both lying about you pointing a gun at her?"

"That's what I said."

"Any idea why they would lie about something like that?" Edgars gripped the chair arms to brace for the blast he knew was coming, but Grier was eerily quiet and gave him a half-smile.

"Now, how am I supposed to know that, Jimmy? You're the detective, not me. Hope I don't need to see about replacing you." Grier paused to give his words time to impact. "Could be that Lara Walton made up that story to get them feeling protective of her. Some women like to use men that way."

Edgars wanted to ask a question, but had to take a deep breath before he managed to blurt it out. "Did you find Lara Walton attractive?"

"What?" Grier half rose out of his chair. "You're going too far there, Jimmy."

"I was just wondering. I heard Ms. Walton would walk around outside in her nightshirt. I've seen pictures of her. She wasn't hard on the eyes, so I just wondered if you found her attractive."

"No," Dave said. "I never noticed how she looked. Now, do you have anything relevant to ask me, or is this conversation over?"

Edgars had a suspicion he couldn't quite place. "That's about all I came to ask, sir, unless there's anything else you can tell me."

"You go back and talk to Sterling O'Connor. Ask him what the two of them did up on her balcony every night. Sandy needs to learn to control that boy. But, hey, maybe it's too late for that. Prison'll control him just fine."

"Thank you, sir." Edgars stood, turned, and walked from the room. He felt Dave Grier's scowl boring into his back.

Outside, he pulled on his slicker and stood in the rain, the sound of water beating on his plastic hood. *Hell, what a week,* he thought. The crime lab was moving slowly and he didn't know when he'd get those forensic results about the fibers and water samples, and about the futon and condoms. He just hoped they'd tell him something, anything, because, as a whole, this town wasn't talking. Either people were lying to protect Sterling, or they were exaggerating the truth to make him look guilty. He wanted to stop relying on people and start seeing some good hard evidence. What was worse was that Edgars had to talk to Pam Grier again. He hoped to God the conversation wouldn't get back to Dave.

T HAT afternoon, Edgars took his paycheck to Pam's window at the bank. She sat talking to another teller and twirling a dark curl around a red-nailed finger.

"Hey, Mrs. Grier. You getting along okay after the other night?"

She gave him a tortured smile and nodded. Edgars knew he'd have to act fast as she took his deposit slip and began keying the amount into her computer. "Say, what exactly did Lara Walton do to upset Dave so much?"

Pam leaned over the counter toward Edgars, close enough that he could see a fading bruise on her cheek. "It was that envelope with that information."

"And Dave saw it?"

"No, I threw it away, but I mentioned it to him. He was mighty angry."

"What sort of information was it?"

She rolled her eyes to the ceiling as the hand holding Edgars's deposit slip hovered over the receipt machine's slot. "Feminist things. Very extremist. It scared me a little."

"So he pointed a gun at her?"

"Oh, he didn't mean to," Pam said. "He was just fooling around."

"And how did she react?"

Pam's voice dropped to a conspiratorial whisper. "She came right up to the porch and cursed him to his face."

"Do you remember what she called him?"

"Oh, yes, sir, but I couldn't repeat it in polite company."

"That bad, huh?" Edgars stifled a grin.

"It was awful."

"What did Dave do?"

"Oh, nothing. I think he was sort of surprised. She went right back to working on her yard, too. Didn't even act ashamed or go inside after she said those things."

Good for her, thought Edgars.

Pam ran his deposit slip through the machine and handed him the receipt.

"Thanks, Pam," he said. "And do something for me: Don't mention this to Dave. He was pretty mad at me for having to ask him questions in the first place. It's just my job, you see, and I wouldn't want him to get upset with you."

Pam's mouth hung open, and Edgars watched her go through the

process of realizing that she had just told him something her husband hadn't.

"You have a nice day now," she said in that way Southern women
have of saying something pleasant-seeming and meaning *drop dead.*

Edgars headed his car back toward the station and thought about
Lara. He wished he could have been there to see her giving Dave
Grier hell. Edgars considered Grier. He'd lied about the gun and the
feminist information, but that didn't mean he'd killed Lara Walton.
If she'd been moving away, why would Dave bother to kill her? Then
there was Pam. The woman was under all kinds of stress. Could the
information Lara gave her have pushed her over the edge? She had
access to Dave's gun, after all. Edgars wanted to check Dave's gun
against the bullets found in Lara Walton's bedroom, but he knew
Dave wouldn't give it up without a legal battle. And Edgars didn't
have enough evidence to take the gun in the first place.

Looking at his watch, he noticed the date, October nineteenth. It
was a good time to talk to Sterling O'Connor again and see if his story
had changed. He radioed ahead and asked Mason to bring the boy in.

"Sorry to have to call you back out here, son."

"I'm not your son," Sterling said.

Edgars paused to take a sip of coffee "How's your mama and them
little girls doing?"

"Why am I here?"

"I need to ask you a couple more questions."

"So ask."

"You said Dave Grier pointed a gun at her?"

"Yeah."

"Did you see him point a gun at her?"

"Nossir, I told you already, I got over there and she was upset and
she told me Dave Grier had pointed a gun at her."

"How do you mean *upset?*"

"You know, upset. Crying."

"Was that why she was moving back to Washington?"

"What, 'cause she was afraid of Dave Grier?" Sterling snorted. "Naw, Lara wasn't afraid of nobody."

"So why was she crying?"

Sterling paused and Edgars could tell he was choosing his words. "Her power went out the night before, and she couldn't sleep and got to worrying about Dave, so she was pretty tired and kind of shaky when I saw her the next day."

"Why was she going back to Washington?"

Sterling chewed at his lower lip. Edgars wondered what he was trying to hide.

"Would you stay here if you could be in Washington?" Sterling said.

Edgars found himself stifling a smile. "And you weren't upset about her going?"

"I'd miss what she paid me and all, but no, I wasn't *upset*. I told you that already."

Edgars leaned back and frowned at Sterling, who would not meet his gaze. The boy was covering up, but damned if Edgars knew how to get at the truth. Sterling had an excellent memory for what he'd already told the captain and, so far, hadn't said anything inconsistent with his original story.

"You ever stay the night over there?"

Edgars watched the kid take a sudden fierce interest in his own fingers. "You asked me that already."

"No, I asked if you were involved with her. What I want to know is if you ever stayed the night over there." Sterling's mouth hung open. "I'm going to find out anyway," Edgars continued.

"So why ask me?"

"Because if you tell me the truth, it'll seem less like you've got something to hide."

"Yeah, and what if I think it ain't right to ask folks personal questions like that? What if I'm morally against that question and won't answer?"

"That's your right, of course. I just wish you'd start thinking about your family and about yourself. If you cooperate with us, things'll go easier on you, no matter what we find out."

"How am I not cooperating? I come in here every damned time you ask me!"

"You said you kissed her out by the warehouse that day. Did she kiss you back?"

"What?"

"If you kissed her, on the mouth, right, did she kiss you back?"

Sterling squirmed. "Hell, I don't know."

"Sure you do," Edgars prodded. "I know she ain't the first girl you've kissed."

"It was just a kind of quick kiss," Sterling said. "I was just saying goodbye to her is all. It wasn't nothing romantic."

"But you kissed her on the mouth?"

"Yeah, but it wasn't a big deal."

"So if people saw you kissing her in, well, in a romantic way. . . ."

"They'd be exaggerating," Sterling cut in. "But I guess no one in this town ever tells fish stories."

Edgars paused. The corners of his mouth twitched. "I wouldn't say that."

The boy grinned, and the captain found himself grinning back. It was the first time Edgars had seen Sterling smile. The kid had a bright, contagious smile that lit up his whole face.

"What kind of work did you do for Lara Walton, again?"

Sterling's grin vanished. "I don't know. Painting and stuff."

"And what'd you do outside on her back balcony?"

Sterling raked his fingers through his hair, then started to tug on one of the many earrings in his pierced left lobe. "She had a telescope she used to let me look through. I'm into astronomy."

"So why didn't you just say you stayed late to use the telescope?"

"'Cause that ain't usually what I stayed late for. I stayed late 'cause I was working."

"Like the time you two went skateboarding on the sidewalk. Were you working then?"

"That was *one time*," Sterling said. "We were bored."

"You know, Mr. O'Connor, like I said last time, I been into that house. It don't look like it's had much work done on it. I have a hard time believing it when you say you were over there night after night working on it."

"Well, that's what I was doing."

"Why don't we go over there. You can show me what you did."

Sterling paled.

"It'll just take a minute."

"I can't."

"Why not?"

"I just can't." Sterling bit his lower lip until it turned white.

The captain frowned. "You know what I think? I think you were in love with her."

Sterling's eyes reddened and his mouth trembled, but the glare he shot Edgars was stony.

Edgars sighed. He'd hit a nerve, but did he have the heart to push the issue? He found himself backing off. "Tell you what. I'll give you some paper and a pencil, and you make me a list of everything you did at that house."

Sterling's shoulders sagged, and he nodded dumbly. Edgars watched the boy write a list, and, when he was through, slide it across the table.

"Can I go now?" Sterling demanded.

"Hang on." Edgars read the list. *Scraped kitchen walls. Painted kitchen walls. Moved boxes. Mowed the lawn. Scraped fence out back. Put stars up on ceiling. Carried telescope around. Looked up addresses on the computer. Fixed kitchen cabinet handles. Looked for problems in the basement.*

"This ain't much of a list," Edgars said.

"Well, it was a hell of a lot of work and it took a long time." Sterling's jaw was set, and Edgars realized he wouldn't get anything else out of the boy. Not today, at least.

So what had Sterling been doing all that time? Edgars was sure about one thing. Sterling's feelings for Lara had gone well beyond an adolescent crush. Whether Lara Walton had reciprocated these feelings was another question. But now she was dead and the boy was suffering. Edgars could see it in his eyes.

"The day before she died, you kissed her outside the warehouse. What were you doing out there?"

"Walking home," Sterling mumbled. "I ran into her. She had the U-Haul on her car and was driving back to her house, so she stopped to say goodbye."

"So, how did you end up at her house?"

"We got to talking, and I offered to help carry boxes."

"So you helped load boxes, and then said goodbye and went home?"

"Yeah."

"Did you kiss her again?"

Sterling gave the captain a withering, hate-filled look. "I kissed her hand."

"And then you left?"

"Then I left."

Edgars nodded. "Okay. Get out of here."

Sterling shot out of the chair, threw open the door, and fled down the corridor.

Edgars pictured the boy taking Lara Walton's hand in his own and bringing it to his mouth. It was a strange, noble kind of gesture, but he had no trouble imagining it. It seemed like something Sterling O'Connor might do.

chapter twenty-one

July 26

E RIC realized that bad things might happen when people stopped asking him about Lara, and started telling him about her. Now, instead of "who is she?" and "what church does she go to?" he heard other things: "You know, somebody said that Lara Walton's got something going on with that O'Connor boy." Eric would reply: "Sterling's helping Lara fix up the house. He needs the money." "Yeah, well, from what I've heard that ain't what she's paying him for." Or: "My mama said she don't go to church and that she don't believe in God, even." Or: "I heard she came down here to escape the law."

If Lara had wanted to be a member of the community, this talk would have devastated her chances, but luckily, Eric thought, Lara had no interest in being a part of this town. It seemed as if she cared only about helping Sterling, and maybe Pam Grier, who was probably the source of most of the rumors to begin with. None of this gossip reached Lara in her old house, and Eric doubted that she'd notice or care if people stared at her at the grocery store and whispered. He just hoped the rumors wouldn't spin out of control, causing the townspeople to act against Lara. He hoped they wouldn't make Sterling feel worse about himself than he already did. Then things might get ugly.

* * *

D ID she want to move on? Could she move on? Lara pushed her gimpy-wheeled cart around Ingles's lime-green linoleum floor, past a flock of teenaged girls huddled around the pay phone by the door. They giggled, passed around a poorly concealed cigarette, and followed Lara with their eyes. As she turned the corner into the produce section, two of the girls whispered to each other, then separated from the group and pursued her.

Lara didn't notice. She was preoccupied with the feel of her body. She thought of Sterling's fingers, how they'd felt as he'd stroked her cheek the night before. At the thought, an erotic tremor tingled through her chest and down her hips. After she'd dropped him off, she'd returned home and lay looking at the glow-in-the-dark stars on her ceiling, unable to sleep. This morning, she couldn't eat. How could she be doing this? Letting herself be touched? What would Dylan think? *But he's dead, Dylan's dead.*

Part of her wanted to seduce Sterling, to lure him to her bedroom and rip off her clothes and then his, and kiss him and touch him and be as hot and wild as she could be, to show Dylan that she didn't care. He could watch from whatever spirit realm he now inhabited, and Lara didn't care if he was jealous or angry. He should have thought of that before he drove so fast on I-95.

She criss-crossed the aisles, forgetting to pick up vegetables, spaghetti, aspirin, and all the other things she'd come to the grocery store for. She floated in a kind of sensual daze, overcome by images of what might have happened if she hadn't made Sterling leave. She brought to life again their small flirtations, the brush of her fingers against his earlobe, the feel of his thrashing, wet body in the swimming pool.

Lara looked up and found that she had traversed the entire length of the store. She now stood in the milk section with an empty cart and a vague sense of uneasiness. She paused by the cheese and stared at it, confused, not sure what she had wanted to buy. A bright flash of color a few feet away caught her attention and she noticed two girls casting sidelong glances at her. Lara grabbed a pack of shredded mozzarella and dropped it into the cart, feeling better for having selected at least one item for purchase.

Her thoughts went to the circles Sterling had traced on her shoulder. *Stop thinking about it.* But she wanted to think about it, to play it over in her mind, to recreate the pleasure of it.

Lara wheeled her cart away from the cheese and turned down the bread aisle. In front of her, the two girls peeked around the corner, then ducked away. A dim curiosity filtered through the haze of Lara's thoughts, and she wondered what the girls were doing. After picking out a loaf of bread, she resisted drifting back into her dreaming, and instead wheeled the cart around the corner to the next aisle, where the girls stood waiting. This time Lara made eye contact with one, who, instead of fleeing, stood her ground. She twisted a platinum blond curl around her finger as Lara approached.

"You bought the old Bishop house on Church Street, didn't you?" the girl with the platinum hair asked.

"That's right," Lara said.

"Sterling O'Connor works for you."

"Yes." Lara flushed at the mention of Sterling's name.

The girl slit her eyes and gave Lara a cold up-and-down look. "I'm his girlfriend."

The tile floor went soft beneath her feet. Lara focused on the girl, on her pale, glowing skin, her shining hair curled and sprayed to hold a perfect shape. Short-shorts exposed her long beautiful legs, and below them, little red toenails peeked out from high-heeled sandals. The girl wore a tight red shirt, and clutched a red leather handbag. A small gold cross hung on a delicate chain above her "Wonderbra" cleavage. A strange kind of innocence, Lara thought. Would Jesus approve? Then, with a sinking in her stomach, Lara added all the parts together and came to the conclusion that the girl was lovely: thin and slight and young.

"Sterling seems like a nice kid." Lara tried to keep the tremor from her voice.

The girl lifted an eyebrow, as if not fooled for a moment by Lara's pathetic show of polite indifference. Underneath her mascara and eye shadow and lipstick, she had the face of a beautiful child, but there was an adolescent cruelty about her expression that made Lara uneasy.

"Did you just graduate from high school too?" Lara asked.

The girl nodded. With a subtle movement, she slid a hand into the red handbag. Something about the gesture alarmed Lara. The girl seemed to sense Lara's fear, and gave a wicked smile as she pulled out a tube of lip gloss.

"Well, it was nice meeting you." Desperate to escape, Lara pushed her cart forward, the gimpy wheels dragging with maddening slowness. The checkout counter seemed miles away. Her knees felt like jelly and she had to steady herself, so she gripped the cart handle, her fingers aching. She arrived breathless at the register, where she tossed her purchases onto the belt. A loaf of bread and some cheese. Hadn't she come to the store for more than that?

She paid for the groceries numbly, then fled. She wasn't aware of driving home, or of wandering up the porch steps; but when she unlocked her front door and stepped inside, the house's stillness appalled her. She dropped the grocery bag in the foyer, crumpled onto the stairs and said, out loud, "Stop it!" Her words echoed off the walls, coming back faintly to her from the living room.

"Do you really think he likes me?" she'd asked her friend Beth Adams as they slipped out of Dylan's classroom at American University after a lecture.

"Look at the note!" Beth poked the returned term paper emphatically with her finger.

"It just says 'See me.'"

"But it's the way he's written it. See how big the handwriting is? Anyway, he spent the entire class looking at you. You *have* to ask him out. This is the perfect chance."

"I bet he couldn't go out with me if he wanted to. I bet there are rules."

"Rules, shmules. He doesn't have tenure. He's nothing more than a glorified grad student. And yesterday was, what, the third time in two weeks you've accidentally bumped into him and had coffee and talked for six hours?" Beth rolled her eyes.

"But what if it's my imagination? What if he really does want to talk about my term paper? I'll feel like an idiot."

"Then just pretend you really love mollusks. He'll never know."

"I don't think I can pretend to love mollusks," Lara said. Beth laughed, and Lara did too.

"Okay," Lara took a breath. "I'm going right now." Without waiting for Beth to reply, she whirled around and headed back to the classroom.

Dylan was still at the podium, handing back papers. Lara leaned against the door frame and when she caught his eye, he flushed red down to his neck.

When the other students were finally gone, Lara approached him, brandishing the paper. "It says 'see me.'" Her heart fluttered in her chest.

"Yeah." Dylan shifted and cast a glance at the empty classroom. "I was wondering if you'd be willing to switch to Rhonda Hoffman's section."

For a moment, Lara was stunned. Was her paper that bad? But then Dylan's gaze caught hers and held it. "You see," he cleared his throat. "You see, it'd be best if someone else taught you this course, because I think I'm falling in love with you."

GRIPPING the banister in her silent house on Church Street, Lara hauled herself up and walked into the kitchen to call Eric. *Always leaning on Eric,* she thought.

"You'll never guess what just happened to me." She tried to sound lighthearted when Eric answered. "I just ran into Sterling's girlfriend at Ingles's."

"His girlfriend? I didn't think he had one right now." Eric paused. "It must be a hanger-on. He's got these ex-girlfriends who won't leave him alone even though he never calls them. What did she look like?"

"She was beautiful."

"They're all beautiful," Eric said as if Lara should know. "What color was her hair?"

"Blond. Platinum, and I think it was natural."

"Ahhh, Alicia Hopkins. She's one of the hangers-on. Kind of a creepy one, actually. I'll have to tell Sterling she thinks they're still together. That'll freak him out."

"So she's not his girlfriend?"

"He went out with her right before school let out. Sterling said he'd rather spend an evening listening to an old screech-owl squawking."

Lara gulped air.

"He's been out with half the girls in the school," Eric continued.

"I know. He's a flirt, isn't he?" She forced a weak laugh.

"He's an expert. He's got this way of making them feel like they matter to him. If I could bottle it and sell it, I'd be a rich man."

"Is he there?" Lara choked.

"Yeah, you want to talk to him?"

"No. Just tell him something's come up and I have to run to Atlanta, so I won't be home tonight."

"Sure thing," Eric said.

She hung up the phone and climbed the stairs to her bedroom, where she curled in a tight ball on her futon. She stayed that way for the rest of the day and long into the night.

"Was that Lara?" Sterling popped his head into the office.

"Yeah," Eric said. "She has to go to Atlanta this afternoon, so she doesn't need you to come by." Sterling looked crestfallen. "You really like going over there with the telescope and all, huh? Call her back and see if you could go anyway. I bet she wouldn't mind."

Sterling shook his head. "Naw, Mama's been after me to spend more time at home."

"Hey, guess who Lara met up with at the grocery store. Alicia. She told Lara she was your girlfriend."

Sterling frowned. "What?"

"Lara got a kick out of it. She was laughing about how you have all these girls hanging around you."

"She thought it was funny?"

"Yeah." Eric peered at Sterling's face, and for the first time got the sense that something unusual was going on. "Hey, is something wrong?"

Sterling shook his head, "Naw. Alicia's just psycho, is all. I think she was hanging around outside Lara's house the other night."

"Maybe you need to talk with Alicia and explain to her that you don't have any interest."

"I already did that. She just won't leave me alone."

"Remember that time she came in here and you hid under the counter?" Eric chuckled. "I should have told Lara about that."

"Man, it ain't funny," Sterling said.

"I wouldn't worry about it. Girls Alicia's age get strange crushes. It'll pass."

chapter twenty-two

July 27

STERLING hurried to Lara's right after work the next day. His heart was beating hard, and he knocked on Lara's door, feeling like he'd been eating sweet white icing off a cake, his stomach cramping, his body all wired from the sugar.

She called out "Come in."

He found her at the computer, staring hard at the screen.

"Whatcha doing?" He went to look over her head as she typed in a column of numbers.

"Working," she said.

Being so close to her overwhelmed him, and he couldn't help putting a hand on her shoulder and stroking his thumb up and down the side of her neck. As he rubbed, her muscles knotted under his fingers. She shrugged his hand off and stood abruptly.

"I need you to mow the lawn out back. I'm sorry. I know it's hot, but I just need it done." She rushed away from him through the kitchen, calling "Come on, I'll show you where the mower is."

The rusting mower sat in the middle of her back yard. Sterling looked across the yard and felt sick.

I fucked up, he thought.

He walked to the mower. It became a sudden emblem of his yard-boy status and he kicked it. Then he started it up.

Clouds of dust billowed from underneath the mower and made

him gag. As he crossed along her fence under the old oak tree, he cursed Lara and Alicia and women in general. The only thing he'd been thinking about all day was seeing Lara, and now here he was eating dust, about to melt from the heat, and Lara was inside so he couldn't even look at her.

When he was done, sweat covered him like an extra layer of skin. He left the old lawnmower near the back stoop, kicking it again for good measure. By the side of the house, he turned on the hose. As the water spattered down, the freshly mowed dirt released sweet-smelling steam. He noticed the dark hole still gaping in the foundation and wondered why she hadn't had it fixed. It was just one more thing about Lara he didn't understand. She wouldn't go *on* with her life. It pissed him off.

Pressing his thumb against the nozzle, he sent showers of drops over the cracked ground. He watched the drops pockmark the earth, then stooped to drink.

When he dragged into the kitchen, wiping his face with his balled-up shirt, there was a place set at the kitchen table: plate, fork, knife, spoon, a glass filled with iced tea. One place. He strode into the living room where Lara hunched over her keyboard. She didn't turn around, just said "Your dinner's in the oven."

"Why aren't you gonna to eat with me?"

"I'm busy."

"She isn't my girlfriend," he blurted. "I haven't seen Alicia in ages."

Lara's fingers hung motionless above the keyboard for an instant, then she said "I know. I just need to get that yard looking decent. And I'm really busy. I've got a big project due soon. Why don't you go ahead and eat?" She smiled at him briefly before turning back to the computer.

"Ain't hungry." He stared at her back.

"Then I'll take you home."

"What about the telescope? We haven't looked through it in a while."

"I don't have time." She stood.

"Lara—"

She smiled indulgently. "I'll just bore you tonight."

"You can't bore me."

"Come on," she said. She reached for her purse.

In the car, she started talking about nothing, about the weather and how her computer wasn't working right, and she rambled on until they reached his house.

He paused before opening the car door, wondering if he should touch her arm again, but she sent off waves that made him scared to try. He thought about apologizing, but didn't know what to apologize for. "Lara, just . . . whatever is going on, I mean—"

"Good night." She patted his arm. "I'll see you tomorrow."

"Lara—"

"Sterling." Her voice had a hard edge. "I need to get back."

He slid from the car, slammed the door hard behind him, and scuffed to the house, hearing the crunch of gravel as she wheeled the car around.

After supper, he lay in bed, trying to read *The Communist Manifesto* but giving up. He wondered what had caused the change in Lara. What had Alicia said? Or did it not have anything to do with Alicia? Was Lara still missing the dead guy in Washington?

Sterling rolled onto his stomach and pressed his face into the pillow. He prayed to God. *Whatever I did, please make Lara forgive me. Or at least make her tell me what it is.* His one comfort was that she'd said she'd see him tomorrow.

July 28

S HE sat at her computer again the next day. From the rigid line of her back and the way she refused to acknowledge him, Sterling knew things weren't going to be any better than yesterday.

"There's a scraper on the kitchen table," she said as she tapped at the numbers on her keypad. "I need you to scrape the back fence."

Sterling felt his insides sink. He didn't know if he could take another day of this. He walked over and stopped beside her desk so she had to see him. He rested his hands on his hips and said "Just tell me what I did wrong."

She gave him an innocent look. "What do you mean?"

"You're blowing me off. What'd I do?"

Her mouth widened into a patronizing smile, as if he were some kid she had to be patient with. "I'm not blowing you off, sweetie. I'm stressed. I have a lot of work. Please, just take care of that fence for me. I'd really appreciate it."

"Fine." He stomped into the kitchen, seized the scraper, and burst through the back door. As he eyed the sagging fence, he suppressed the urge to kick its boards to splinters. Only a few thin lines of white paint streaked the gray weathered surface. "What the hell am I doing?" he muttered as he leaped off the stoop and crossed the mowed red dust.

He stopped two feet away from the fence. Termites had honeycombed the boards, making the wood porous and rotten. He swore under his breath, found a small patch of paint near the bottom, then, bending, forced the blade violently down the pulpy two-by-eight. The paint curled away and dissolved like ash. Dusty white flakes floated to his nose.

As sweat began to run off his forehead into his eyes, he thought *I went too far, stopped acting like the goddamned hired help and started getting too comfortable with her, and now she's reminding me of my position.* With a fierce thrust, he forced the scraper down again.

A sudden searing pain startled him as a splinter drove under his thumbnail. "Ahhh, shit!" He hurled the scraper to the ground and shoved his hand between his legs.

As the sting ebbed to a dull throb, he marched across the yard, sucking on his thumb, thinking Lara could get any damned person in the world to scrape that fence. He wasn't going to be her yardboy any more.

When he slammed through the back door, he found Lara leaning over the stove. The way she whirled around, her hand at her throat, scattered his anger. He brushed by her on his way to the sink where he turned on the cold water and held his aching thumb underneath it.

"What happened?" Lara came up beside him. "Did you cut it?"

"Splinter," he muttered.

"Here. Let me see."

When she took hold of his hand, it made him want her so much he thought he'd die. He looked at her pink cheeks, her pretty mouth.

"It's bleeding," she murmured. "We've got to get that splinter out. God only knows how much lead is in that old paint." She let go and began rummaging through her boxes, finally coming up with a needle.

"Aw, no." He drew his hand to his chest.

She lit a match and held it to the needle for an instant, then came toward him. Reluctantly, he let Lara grip his thumb while he squinted and turned away. "Big baby," she laughed. "Hold still."

He squeezed his eyes shut, felt pressure, then a quick sting.

"There. All done."

"That's it?" He peeked at her.

"That's it." She brought his thumb to her mouth and kissed it. He thought this sympathy stuff was great and wondered how else he could hurt himself.

She tried to let his hand go, but he held on. He ran his thumb along her knuckles.

"Sterling." She pulled away and began wiping the needle off with a paper towel.

"You aren't dead, you know," he said.

She glanced up.

"I was just thinking about how you told me to live my life while I had the chance. The way you said it, it sounded like your life was over already, but it isn't."

She bowed her head and went back to wiping the needle.

"You're alone all the time, and you won't buy an air conditioner, and you live out of boxes like some damned hermit."

She stiffened. "You don't know anything about my life."

"I know you ain't got a life right now, so I'm just gonna say this. You going around all sad forever is plain stupid."

She dropped the needle onto the table and stared at it. He felt bad all of a sudden and leaned toward her, touched her wrist with his fingers.

"Go home," she said.

Sterling didn't move.

"Go home. That fence is too much work. I'll get someone with a sander to do it."

He swallowed, his thumb still shot through with the soft feel of her lips, his head fuzzy and spinning. He kept trying to look her in the eyes but she wouldn't look back. *I'm still the fucking yardboy,* he thought. Keeping his eyes fixed on her face, he stood. "I'm sorry I'm not good enough for you, Lara."

She didn't say anything, didn't look up.

He whirled around. His chair got between him and the door, so he kicked it over on his way out.

❧ chapter twenty-three ❧

August 9

STERLING stood in front of his bedroom mirror, hating his clothes. Nothing fit him right. Here he was going to dinner and a movie in Atlanta, and he looked like a twelve-year-old dressed in too-short jeans and an old black T-shirt. Even his tennis shoes were dirty.

He collapsed on his bed.

There was a knock on the door and his mother stuck her head around the corner.

"There's my birthday boy." Once again he felt a stab of resentment toward her. Maybe if she hadn't driven his daddy away, he'd have some decent-looking clothes. Then he felt guilty. His daddy was a sonofabitch. It wasn't Mama's fault.

"I know you don't get to go out a lot like your friends, so you just take your time. The girls got to finish their present for you anyway."

He propped himself on his elbow. "Maybe I should get the girls' present tomorrow, Mama. That'll be the easiest thing, so you don't have to keep 'em up waiting on me. I don't know where Eric's gonna take me."

"It won't be your birthday tomorrow," his mother said. "We'll wait up if we got to."

After she left, Sterling rolled onto his back and stared at the stars on his ceiling. Eighteen, he thought. What the hell difference did it make?

It wasn't like he had any plans for his adult life. He dragged himself off the bed, refusing to look in the mirror again, and went outside to sit on the tire swing in the shade and wait for Eric. The thick rope holding the swing wound and unwound, turning him in slow circles.

For almost two weeks now, he'd been trying not to think about Lara, but it wasn't working. He was hungry for the sight of her. It seemed like he couldn't get through an hour of the day without playing back everything that had ever happened between them, looking for some answer to what had gone wrong. Some hard part of himself kept coming to the same conclusion: he wasn't good enough for her and she knew it. Still, deep inside, in a dark, secret place, he held on to a hope that the hard voice was wrong.

He sifted through details of their conversations and tried to find things to feed that tiny little hope and keep it alive: the quick pulse-beat in her neck when he touched her, all the nice things she'd said to him, the way she watched him when he had his shirt off. But then the hard voice broke in, saying *Even if all those things did happen, they still don't mean she thinks you're good enough for her. Anyway, she's not coming. It's been almost two weeks and she hasn't even tried to see you. Why do you think she'd come today?*

He heard the sound of a car but kept his back to the road and gazed over the pasture that bordered his house. A herd of cattle stood in the middle of the field, so still they looked painted. The sound of the motor got louder, gravel grated beneath tires, and still Sterling couldn't bring himself to look. He wished he could be like those cows, peaceful and unconcerned. The car stopped, the motor idled. A door creaked open. In the pasture, a cow flicked its tail.

"Sterling?"

It was Lara's voice. He whirled to see her standing by the open car door, shielding her eyes, looking beautiful, fresh, and clean.

Who the hell did she think she was, ignoring him for two weeks and then showing up like nothing had happened? He wasn't going to let her get away with treating him like that.

*　　*　　*

ERIC watched Lara open the car door and slide out of the front seat. There was something strange and eager in the way she did it, but she'd been acting strange all afternoon. He remembered standing in Lara's kitchen as she set Sterling's birthday cake on the table.

"I made it from scratch," she murmured.

He surveyed the ugly, amorphous lump drizzled with watery chocolate frosting that had run off the sides and pooled on the plate.

"It looks like something you'd find in a cow pasture." She sounded like she might cry.

"No, it doesn't," he lied. "Besides, it's how it tastes that's important, right?"

"I guess. I just wanted it to be great."

"He'll love it," Eric said.

She smiled wanly.

The pale blue tank top she wore hugged her body and scooped low in the front, showing cleavage. Her straight print skirt was darker and dotted with light blue flowers. She'd piled her hair on her head, and Eric could see the freckles scattered across her nose and the flush of her sunburned skin. She looked beautiful. More beautiful than she should for a trip to a pizza joint and a strip-mall movie theater.

Now in Sterling's driveway, Eric watched as Lara rubbed her hands down her skirt like her palms were sweating, then licked her lips and lifted a hand to Sterling, calling his name.

For a moment the kid swayed on the tire swing, eyeing Lara. Then he slipped off and sauntered past her without a glance, as if not noticing she was there, never mind how good she looked.

"You take the front seat," she said when he reached the car.

Sterling shot Lara a glare that surprised Eric, then said "Can't believe you're here. Thought you'd be too busy to make it." As he slid in beside Eric, his tone lightened. "Hey, bourgeois parasite."

"Listen, if you don't want to partake in the evil capitalist system, we'll just leave you here and go by ourselves."

"No need to get a burr up your butt. I was just joking with ya."

"Are you excited?" Lara asked as she climbed in back.

Sterling shrugged and drummed his fingers on the dashboard. A sudden palpable tension filled the car. Eric wondered what the hell was going on. As they turned onto the road, the tension continued to build. The air in the car seemed heavy and barely breathable. Eric turned up the air conditioning and tried to break the silence by joking: "Hey kid, we decided to forget the pizza and take you out for a real gourmet meal: sushi."

"Ha, ha," Sterling said. They lapsed back into silence.

Things didn't get better at the pizza place. The hostess showed them to a booth, and Eric sat on one side with Sterling slipping in across from him. Lara stood by the table and looked from one man to the other. "Which one of us gets lucky?" Eric asked. She smiled, then slid in beside Sterling.

"Aw, damn," Eric protested.

"He's the birthday boy."

Sterling muttered "Guess I ain't so bad you can't sit next to me."

Lara's smile faded. She cast a glance at Eric.

He didn't know what to do. The undercurrent of adolescent bile was making him wish he were somewhere else. "What's going on?"

"How big are their salads?" Lara perused the menu as if it was a holy text.

Eric met Sterling's gaze and gave him a questioning look, but the boy only scowled.

"What's going on?" Eric repeated. Sterling still didn't answer.

"Maybe I'll just have a salad," Lara said. "I guess that's what I'll do."

The leaden silence fell again. Sterling creased and uncreased the corner of his napkin while Lara's eyes remained fixed on her menu. *Hell,* Eric thought, *I'm not going to carry the conversation all night.* He stared out the window and watched cars roll in and out of the parking lot.

When he looked back to the table, Sterling was wadding his napkin into a tight ball. Lara cast a covert glance at the boy, and Eric braced himself. She was going to do something, but, from the set of Sterling's jaw, Eric knew that whatever she did would be rejected. He stifled the urge to stop her. Instead, he watched as she set her purse on the table.

"I've got a present for you, Sterling."

Sterling began picking his napkin into tiny paper snowflakes. Lara brought out an envelope and placed it on the table in front of him. He seemed too absorbed with shredding the napkin to notice. A whole minute went by. Eric gripped the edge of the table. Lara looked like she might cry. "Come on, Sterling," he snapped. "Open it already."

With a resentful look Sterling dropped the napkin and picked up the envelope. The card he pulled out was bright and big. Sterling's gaze traveled across it with disinterest.

"Can I see?" Eric asked.

Lara watched Sterling with huge eyes. "There's something inside," she murmured.

"Come on," Eric urged.

Sterling flipped open the card. A piece of paper twirled out of its interior.

"It's a gift certificate," Lara said, her chin trembling. "For clothes from Old Navy for your birthday."

Sterling leaned back and folded his arms across his chest. The gift certificate lay untouched on the table in front of him. "I guess what I'm wearing is pretty crappy, huh? I guess you're ashamed to be seen with me."

Lara sat frozen for a moment. Then she rose, holding on to the table as if to steady herself.

"I'm not hungry," she said to Eric "I'm going to, I don't know, I guess I'm going to wander around the stores for a while. I'll meet you at the car after the movie."

"Lara—" Eric protested, but she lifted a hand to silence him and, after one last plaintive glance at Sterling, turned and walked away.

Eric whirled on the boy. "What are you doing? That's a hell of a nice gift. Why are you acting this way?"

Sterling eyed the door. "Only reason she gave it to me is 'cause she's sorry for me."

"Haven't we been through this before?"

"She thinks she's too good for me."

"The way you're acting, maybe she's right."

Sterling picked up Lara's abandoned napkin and began to shred it too. "Man, you don't know nothing."

"Why don't you tell me, then? What's going on?"

Sterling glowered. "She ain't let me in her house for two weeks, and then she just shows up tonight and acts all happy."

"What did you do?"

"What do you mean?"

"I mean what did you do? Why hasn't she let you in her house?"

"I didn't do anything."

"Yes, you did. What was it?"

Sterling slumped low in the booth. "Man, it was nothing," he muttered. "I just, like, touched her arm."

"You touched her arm? What do you mean, touched her arm?"

"She was laying down, and I just touched her arm, just with my fingers." He looked at Eric with wide innocent eyes. "Next day she wouldn't hardly talk to me. She made me mow damned dirt in her back yard, and the day after that she told me she didn't want my help on the house no more." Sterling started nudging the pile of napkin snowflakes, arranging them to form a square.

"She's not going to be your girlfriend, you know." Eric said.

Sterling became still.

"That's what this is about, isn't it? You think you deserve to go over there any time you want. You think you deserve to flirt and to touch her so you can feel like there's something going on between you two."

Sterling didn't reply.

"She doesn't think she's too good for you. She's grieving. She's not ready to move on with her life yet; and even if she was, she's too old for you. That's a very different thing from her thinking you're not good enough. And you're being a dick."

"Why are you sticking up for her? I thought you said she was leading us on."

"I'm sticking up for her because I don't think she's a bad person. She's just really lonely and sad, Sterling, and I've already told you, you have to watch out for women like that. I just wasn't smart enough to take my own advice. Be friends with her, but don't let the way she flirts make you think its more than friendship, because it isn't. It's just her being lonely. It has nothing to do with you."

"So you're saying she doesn't like me at all."

"I'm saying she likes you a *lot,* but she's not going to be your girlfriend. She just gave you a hell of a nice birthday present, for someone who doesn't like you at all."

Clutching the gift certificate, Sterling crossed the parking lot thinking about how Lara had used him all this time, and how he'd fallen for it. Well, he was going to use her now. Use her three hundred dollars to buy some new clothes so he could pick up some girl at the movie theater and maybe even get laid. It'd been way too long since he'd gotten laid.

"You go ahead and find Lara," he'd told Eric after they were through eating. "I'm gonna buy me some clothes."

It was a long walk across the parking lot. Sterling slipped between cars, paused and waited for traffic, fuming the whole time, thinking Eric was right as usual. Lara would never date him. She'd never really kiss him or touch him back. She just wanted attention.

Finally, he reached the Old Navy store. Hell, he thought, at least I'll get something out of it for myself. Inside, he went straight to the bargain rack. He could make that three hundred dollars stretch if he was careful what he bought.

*   *   *

ERIC found Lara in the Target store in the mall. He saw her from a distance as she stood amid gift baskets of jewel-colored soaps and examined jars of perfumed bath crystals. When he walked over to stand beside her, she looked up at him and smiled feebly. He fingered a price tag on one of the baskets.

"You have to realize that you have this kind of aura."

She raised an eyebrow. "What kind of aura?"

"The kind of aura that says 'comfort me and take care of me.' You're doing this thing." He extended one hand toward her with his palm facing out like a cop stopping traffic, and with his other hand he beckoned for her to come to him. "It's confusing. Hell, it confused me, and I'm thinking with my brain as opposed to other parts of my anatomy like Sterling is."

"I never asked to be taken care of." Lara glanced around the aisles at the other shoppers and lowered her voice.

"Maybe not out loud, but you asked all the same."

"Why do guys always do this? I mean, how do you get from 'I want to comfort you' to 'Let's go to bed'? I don't understand."

"Seventeen-year-old boys translate everything into sexual terms."

"I'm not talking about Sterling."

"Well, I am. You cry on his shoulder. You get him to protect you from Dave Grier. That's more than just casual for him. And then he comes on to you, and you realize it's gone a little too far, so you stop. Don't you know how that makes him feel?"

Lara raked a hand through her hair. "I didn't ask him to say anything to Dave Grier. In fact, I tried to stop him. Anyway, why am I always the bad one?"

"Because you're the adult. You're old enough to know that how you act has an effect on him."

"You don't understand."

"Then explain it to me, Lara, 'cause I sure as hell can't figure it out."

She paused and frowned. "You think he wants to take care of

me? Well, I think he doesn't want to take care of anyone." She walked away, letting her fingertips drag across the gift baskets as she went. "His family puts too much pressure on him. It doesn't have anything to do with me." She stopped and picked up a bottle of bubble bath.

"It's got *everything* to do with you. He doesn't understand that you're just friends. He's got it bad for you."

Lara froze with the bottle held under her nose. Eric saw her swallow, then set the bottle down.

"What movie are you guys seeing?" she asked.

"Shit," Eric raked his fingers though his hair, not wanting to let her change the subject.

"The movie?" Lara insisted.

"Some action thing. Are you going to come?"

"Do you think that's a good idea? After all, Sterling might take it as I sign that I want his body."

"I guess you could spend the next two hours in here." He encompassed the gift baskets and the boys' clothing across the aisle with a sweep of his arm. "That sounds like a good time."

"Sterling doesn't want me around. I think he made that pretty clear."

"Come anyway. It'll give you a chance to talk to him. To explain that you're just friends. He isn't sophisticated enough to understand the idea of friendship with a woman."

She gave a wry smile and shook her head. "Oh, no, he's plenty sophisticated, Eric. Seventeen years old, and he's a master at manipulation. He knows exactly what he's doing."

"What are you talking about?"

She gave a frustrated huff. "Nothing. It's nothing."

"He took that gift certificate and went to buy clothes," he offered.

"Really?"

"Yeah. We're supposed to meet him at the theater. I told him I'd bring you. So please just think about what I said. Think about what I said and come to the movie with us. For me."

He didn't know if that would be an incentive, but she smiled. She walked over and took his hand.

"Okay, Grover. You win. But I'm going under duress."

"Duly noted," he said.

STERLING waited for them in new clothes. Dressed in baggy jeans and a dark blue pullover jersey with a white collar, he looked good and knew it. Leaning casually against the side of the movie theater near the ticket booth, he cast long disinterested glances at pretty girls walking by. After a few minutes, he spotted Eric coming across the parking lot. Lara was with him. Eric waved, and Sterling lifted a hand in response.

"Great shirt," Eric said when they reached him.

"I put some bags in your car." Sterling didn't look at Lara.

"Go get your ticket," Eric said. "We're right behind you."

At the ticket window sat a girl with red curly hair, and, even though she wasn't that pretty, Sterling leaned against the counter and grinned at her. She glanced around at the other cashiers, then turned back to him and smiled.

"*Hard Nights,*" Sterling said. Then, resting his elbows on the counter, he asked. "So, is it a good movie or what?"

"Huh?" The girl's face went red.

"Is it good, the movie?"

"I haven't seen it yet."

"What's your name?"

"Stacey Mae."

"I got an aunt named Stacey. What time you get off work?"

"Eight." She fidgeted with her keyboard.

"Eight, huh?"

"Yeah." The girl gave him a shy smile; then, with a start, seemed to notice the line forming behind him and the manager hovering in the background. "That'll be four-fifty."

"Oh." He motioned to Eric and Lara behind him. "My folks are paying."

Eric stepped up to the window. "That's right. Us old folks are paying."

"So, maybe I'll see you later," Sterling said as Stacey Mae handed him a ticket.

She lowered long lashes over her eyes. "Maybe."

Sterling winked at her, then headed toward the theater door, not waiting for Lara or Eric. He stopped a few feet away from the concession stand, staring at the menu board until they came up beside him.

"Man, these prices are high," he said.

"And we just ate, which is why we're not buying anything."

Sterling's eyes strayed after a group of girls. "Bet I could get some girl to buy me popcorn if I acted pitiful enough." He gave Lara a sharp look. "Maybe Lara'll buy me some."

"You know, Eric and I can see the movie alone if you want to flirt with that ticket girl some more," she shot back.

Sterling glanced over his shoulder at the ticket booth. "Naw, she seemed kinda young. Besides, there's other girls around." His eyes latched on to one in a short skirt who walked by with a huge tub of popcorn and gave him a quick glance out of the corner of her eye.

"I mean, we don't want to cramp your style," Lara said.

"Let's go get some seats before all the decent ones are gone," Eric said.

"You guys go on," Sterling watched another girl walk by. "There's more interesting stuff to see out here, if you know what I mean."

"So you're not even going to the movie?" Lara demanded. "Why the hell did we bother to come if you're not going to the movie? There are things I'd rather have seen than *Hard Nights.*"

"It's his birthday," Eric said. "If he wants to watch girls, let him watch girls. We'll sneak into one of the other theaters and see something else, if you want."

"Fine." Lara slit her eyes at Sterling. "Have a great time."

When they'd gone, Sterling went to the pinball machine, fished a quarter out of his pocket, and started playing. He mashed the buttons until his fingers hurt. When the game was over, he checked with the guy taking tickets and found out when Eric and Lara's movie would get out. Then he went to look for the girl in the short skirt with the big tub of popcorn.

Lara and Eric came out of the theater ninety-eight minutes later. Sterling had timed it just right and stood talking with the pretty girl in the short skirt who was letting him eat the rest of her popcorn. He cast a casual glance toward Lara and Eric, like he didn't know them. Eric frowned and motioned for him to come on. Lara turned away. Sterling smiled.

"My folks are here," he said to the girl whose name he'd already forgotten. "How 'bout you give me your phone number?"

She set the tub of popcorn down on a bench, pulled a pen out of her small handbag, and took Sterling's hand. Turning it over, she wrote her phone number on his palm. Sterling hoped Lara was watching.

"So call me?" She clipped the lid back on the pen and gave Sterling a very hot look.

"Yeah." The number had an Atlanta area code. He gave her a quick kiss, then backed off and lifted his hand. "Later."

Shoving his hands in his pockets, he strode by Lara and Eric, whistling. He paused by the ticket window and made a point of smiling at the poor redhead, who turned almost the color of her hair. "Gotta go," he called. "But, hey, maybe I'll see you around."

He imagined the look on Lara's face and grinned.

chapter twenty-four

August 9

D USK. Lara leaned her head against the window and watched the countryside roll by. They'd left the cars and lights of Atlanta behind and now traveled a narrow two-lane back road. The sun hung low on the horizon, and above it the sky glowed a pale iridescent violet. The smudged gray shapes of trees framed fields of wheat-colored grass. Dark silhouettes of cattle lined the fences, and dandelion puffs hovered along the side of the road.

Eric had turned on the radio and the music blared, drums, electric guitars. The glass was hard and warm against the side of Lara's head as she watched the sun set. She felt as if she and Sterling and Eric were in a lifeboat, passing through this sea of trees and grass, the silent kudzu tendrils, the dark, damp forests. The headlight beams caught hovering insects, so many that it seemed as if it was snowing bugs. They splatted on the windshield. Lara, sitting in the front seat this time, started every time a big one hit.

She thought about how, soon, she'd be alone in her house in that silence with this world stretching out around her. Could she stand it? An aching began deep in the pit of her stomach. She told herself *I have never felt so lonely,* and wondered *Do I deserve the loneliness?* The top of Sterling's head cast a hazy reflection in the glass. She slid her hand around the side of the seat closest to her door until she felt the denim cuff of his jeans. Her fingers closed around the stiff new fabric. She wasn't sure he even noticed. Part of her hoped he didn't.

"So, did you have a good birthday?" Eric broke the silence, and Lara loved the sound of his voice, so even and reassuring.

"Yeah." Sterling sounded strange and subdued. "I'm eighteen."

"That you are. You want me to drop you off somewhere so you can buy a pack of cigarettes?"

"Hell, if I wanted smokes I could get 'em from Mama."

Sterling hadn't moved, and Lara continued to finger the small fold of denim. She thought of the earrings in his ears and wanted to finger those, to tug at one gently.

The music played. Eric and Sterling talked about baseball, and Lara watched the sky darken, watched the trees and pastures disappear until only the treetops were visible, black mounds against the strange purple sky. She saw fireflies, listened to the bugs smacking into the windshield, and felt inside as if she'd been abandoned on the side of the road, not knowing where she was or what to do, waiting for nightfall. She heard Eric and Sterling's voices as if from a distance, and gripped harder at the denim thinking *please, please, please.*

"You're quiet." Eric glanced at her, and she slid her hand back around the front seat and placed it in her lap. "You okay?"

"I feel mournful," she said. "Do you ever feel mournful?"

"*I* do," said Sterling. "Sometimes. This time of day, you know, with the sun going down."

The sun going down. The moment between day and night. A time of transition. Didn't monks and nuns pray at dusk and at dawn?

Lara lapsed into silence, feeling frozen in the past.

At some point she'd have to choose: stay in the past, or move on. Sterling was right. She was alive, and she'd already wasted too much time on the Metro.

The pastures and the trees faded, and the car hummed forward into darkness.

*   *   *

I n the back seat, Sterling stared at Lara's fingers as they gripped the hem of his jeans. What should he do? Touch her? Then she might let go, and he didn't want that. What was she doing? She was so quiet and still up there, in that way that made him ache for her. He felt awful for how he'd treated her. Then Eric started talking about baseball, but Sterling kept his eyes on Lara's fingers; and when they let go and her hand disappeared, he felt disappointed and wished he could figure her out.

It was totally dark by the time they reached Lara's house. As they pulled into the driveway, Sterling thought about trying to get Lara alone to talk. But she invited Eric in too. They climbed the creaking porch stairs. He and Eric exchanged grins as Lara dug in her huge bag for the keys. They waited and waited, shifting from one foot to the other, stifling laughter. Finally, she found the keys and unlocked the door.

"Wait here." Lara flicked on the hall light. Sterling watched her weave among boxes toward the kitchen, then squinted against the harsh fluorescent glare of the kitchen bulb. He heard her rummaging through drawers, opening the fridge, the sharp sound of a cabinet being shut. Then she called out "Okay."

The cake sat in the center of the table. Sterling tried not to smile. It looked so sad. She'd stuck one huge red candle right in the middle and lit it, the kind of candle you'd set on a table, not in a birthday cake, and it leaned sideways like it would fall over. She'd set out a bottle of champagne that dripped rounded beads of water beside three champagne flutes.

"I hope it tastes better than it looks," she said.

"Guess it'd have to." Sterling grinned.

"Creep. Go on, make a wish and blow."

He wished for getting out of town and for his sisters to be okay. He wished for Lara to get over being mad. He blew the flame out.

"Go ahead and cut it. I'll open the champagne."

She wrapped a towel around the neck of the bottle, twisting and pulling until they heard a pop. Sterling cut three big slices from the cake, thinking his mama would have a cake for him at home that would probably look just as bad because the girls would have iced it.

"You know he's underage for alcohol," Eric said to Lara.

"I'll break the law in my own house if I want to. You want a drink, Sterling?"

"Sure as hell do."

"Good."

E RIC wandered into the living room thinking *Fine, if she wants to give an underage kid alcohol, let her. It's no skin off my back.* In front of the stereo, he found her CD collection and, kneeling, began to thumb through it. All sorts of stuff. Classical, jazz, reggae, punk, R&B, rock. He picked out a Cat Stevens CD and put it in the player. The music filled the room. Sterling came in with cake and champagne and handed them to Eric. After turning out the kitchen bulb, Lara followed with candles in holders and set them around the room. Eric remembered the night of the thunderstorm. "There's such a thing called lamps, you know."

"But this is nicer, don't you think?"

He did think, but the candlelight made him unhappy. He took a gulp of champagne.

Sterling stretched out on the floor, using a box as a table, and Lara sank down near him, while Eric stood by the CD player. "Sit," Lara ordered him. "And pretend that cake is good even if it isn't."

"It's good," Sterling said through a mouthful. "Best damned cake I ever ate."

"But don't go overboard, or I might not believe you."

Eric sat in the open space by the CD player and ate his cake, which did taste better than it looked, although it would be hard for it to taste worse. Lara took a swig of champagne straight from the bottle, then handed it to Sterling who did the same. Cat Stevens sang "Wild World."

Eric put down his plate. "Lara, dance?"

She looked surprised, then smiled. He went to her, held out his hand and pulled her up. He spread his fingers across the small of her back, while she placed a hand on his shoulder. They swayed to the music, her skirt swishing around his legs as they moved.

"Hey, when do I get to dance?" Sterling asked.

"You young folks don't know how to dance," Eric said.

"Y'all don't seem to have much of an idea either. Reckon I could do as good as you. Besides, you can't dance to this old hippie music anyway."

"This is Cat Stevens," Eric said. "He's one of the greatest song-writers that ever lived."

"This guy? If he thought the world was so wild in the sixties, I don't imagine he'd able to handle it now."

Lara laughed. "He has a point."

Eric moved her back and forth across the room while Sterling made derisive comments. Finally, after a dismal attempt at a spin, both Eric and Lara slumped to the floor in a silent and mutual agreement to quit while they were ahead.

"How about different music?" Lara asked.

"Okay, what?"

"*Rite of Spring.* Stravinsky. It's in there somewhere."

"*Rite of Spring?*" It seemed like a strange choice to Eric.

"What's *Rite of Spring?*" Sterling asked.

"It's a ballet about a sacrificial rite," Lara said. "The first time it was played, there was almost a riot. It was so different from the music people were used to that it disturbed them to the point of violence."

"Cool, let's hear it." Sterling rubbed his hands together. So Eric put the CD on the player while Lara crawled back to her place beside Sterling and leaned against the boxes.

THE music started, a high mournful whistle reverberating off the bare walls, echoing into the parlor, up the stairs into all the hidden silent spaces of the house. It made Sterling think about the house all at once, about how, as they sat here, all those empty rooms waited overhead, gathering dust. He watched Lara tilt her head back and close her eyes. Then he turned to Eric, who was watching Lara too, and said "You want some more to drink?"

"Shhh," Lara scolded. "You have to listen to this. It's not background music."

Sterling grabbed the champagne bottle and took another swig. He felt dizzy and a little drunk.

The high whistle changed into vague grumblings, like the instruments couldn't quite get themselves together to play something that made sense, and one after another blurted out loud startling sounds. Sterling pulled his knees under his chin and wrapped his arms around his legs to listen. He listened and watched Lara with her head thrown back like she was surrendering to something.

The music made no sense to him. There was no beat or melody he could follow. He thought about how disagreeable he'd been to Lara, and it bothered him. He remembered what she'd said about the riot, and pictured all those folks dressed up to hear some nice music and getting this thing instead. No wonder it upset them. It made him squirm now. The music began an awful banging. He covered his ears. "Man, turn it off. It's scaring me."

"You have to listen to the whole thing," said Lara.

"What, are you trying to torture me?"

"Just listen," she insisted. "Listen to this. It's my favorite part." The loud banging faded, and in its place came a whistle playing a sad melody, then underneath it, a pulse, like a heartbeat.

The beat echoed off the walls. It seemed to Sterling like the house was stirring, breathing in and out, coming slowly alive around them. The pulse continued, joined by a low note, and then above it came a frail tune, the saddest, most beautiful thing he'd ever heard.

It made him think about dying. He shifted and stared at the floor.

When he looked at Lara, she was looking at him. He understood suddenly how important the music was to her and how much she wanted him to like it. He felt something coming from her, like heat.

"The first time I heard it played live, I cried," she said.

"Why?" Sterling asked, keeping his voice low, linked with her again in the same quiet, tense way they were linked in the car when she touched his jeans.

"It gave me this overwhelmed feeling. I guess you think that's pretty stupid, huh?"

Sterling shook his head and pictured her in some dark concert hall crying. He cast a glance at Eric, who was finishing his last bite of cake. Lara had that sad faraway look she got sometimes, the one that broke his heart and made him sure he'd do anything she wanted if she'd just ask. "I'm sorry about today," he said. He stretched out a hand, and she took it, her fingers sticky from the champagne foam and the cake. He wondered if they'd taste sweet, and curled his fingers around them. She tugged at his hand, pulling him closer. He balled up beside her like a kid, letting his head fall onto her lap, her fingers in his hair, spread wide, combing up and away from his scalp. Underneath his cheek, the flesh of her leg felt warm through the thin skirt. She smelled like wet roses. He wrapped an arm around her legs and hugged her close.

She leaned over him, her breasts brushing his head, her voice low in his ear. "I'm sorry too. I don't know what I'm doing. You've got me all confused."

E RIC watched Sterling and Lara with a forkful of cake frozen in front of his mouth. The photographer part of his mind wished he had his camera. They looked perfect, Lara on the floor, legs stretched out, bending over Sterling, who curled beside her with his head in her lap, letting her stroke his hair. They were beautiful together. Like a strange, sexual Pietà. Still, Eric knew that this wasn't right. It was a hell of an intense way to make up after fighting.

He sprang to his feet, clapping his hands. "Okay. That's enough of that." He pushed the power button on the CD player so the music stopped. Lara and Sterling sat up blinking.

"Come on, Sterling. Let's get going. Your ma'll be worrying about you."

"No." Sterling was looking Lara hard in the face.

"Come on, it's late."

"I don't care," said Sterling. "I'm gonna stay. I want to hear the end of the CD."

"Trust me, you don't. You need to see your sisters before it's their bedtime."

Sterling gave up staring at Lara long enough to fix Eric with a sharp look. "Man, I ain't a kid. You can't tell me what to do all the time."

"I'll take him home," Lara interjected.

"You're drunk," Eric said.

"I'm not."

"Hey, I'm drunk too. I don't want Mama to see it. I'll walk. That'll give me time to get sober."

"But—"

"Jesus, he wants to walk, Eric. Let him walk. Here, I'll make you some coffee before you go." Lara sprang up, and Sterling did too, following close on her heels into the kitchen.

"So are you leaving or not, Sterling?" Eric trailed behind them.

"I'm drinking coffee with Lara."

"Fine, I'll drink coffee with Lara too."

Sterling shot him another look, but Eric didn't flinch. "Do you want help, Lara?"

"No." Her voice was dry and pinched. She began spooning coffee into a filter.

Eric tossed Sterling the keys to his car. "Go out and fetch your bags if you have to walk."

Sterling cast a lingering glance at Lara, then went out. As soon as he heard the front door close, Eric muttered "What the hell are you doing?"

"Making coffee." Lara slid the filter into the coffeemaker. Eric heard it snap into place.

"You know what I'm talking about."

"No, I don't. Jesus Christ, you can be weird sometimes."

"He's seventeen years old!"

"Eighteen. You have this really annoying tendency to recite peoples' ages. If you want an obsession, maybe you should take up compulsive handwashing or something."

"What were we just talking about today?" he insisted. "About you leading him on and confusing him. What the hell do you think you're doing now?"

"What?" She faced him, hands on hips, green eyes wide. "What, for Christ's sake? If you're going to bitch at me, at least have the courtesy to tell me what I'm doing that's so wrong."

"He's going to think you're trying to seduce him."

"I'd hardly have to seduce him, Eric. Seduction involves at least some ambivalence on the part of one of the participants, doesn't it?"

"This isn't funny. You're acting like you're going to give him something you're not. It's going to hurt him."

"What the hell business is it of yours, anyway? We're both above the age of consent."

"He's just barely above the age of consent."

"Which is more than you can say for the girls he's already fucked."

The front door slammed. With a rustle of plastic shopping bags, Sterling came into the living room. "Coffee in a minute." Lara called. "Eric was just leaving."

When Sterling came into the kitchen, they both stared at him. "Are you guys fighting?"

"No," Eric said, just as Lara said "Yes."

"What about?"

"Nothing." Eric glared at Lara as if daring her to speak.

"Were you guys fighting about who gets to drive me home? Guess I'll put y'all out of your misery and just get going right now."

"But the coffee," Lara protested.

"Hell, it's hot as the devil's dick out there. I don't want coffee. Eric, maybe you could give me a lift as far as Hog Mountain Road since you're going that way."

"Sure."

"Guess I need to take the bags back out to your car."

"No, I'll get them. You thank Lara for the cake." Eric picked up the bags, gave Lara a significant look, and then strode through the living room into the hall.

Sterling waited until Eric shut the door behind him before turning to Lara.

She stood by the sink with her back to him, wiping furiously at the counter with a dish towel. He approached her from the side, dragging his fingers along the lip of the countertop until she got in his way. Then, lifting his fingers from the vinyl, he ran them along the small of her back. "Hey," he said low into her ear, "I'm coming back." Standing right behind her, his fingers resting on her hip, he waited for her to say no, but instead she leaned against him. So he wrapped both arms around her waist and squeezed her and kissed her hair. "Twenty minutes," he whispered.

"Okay," she said.

chapter twenty-five

August 10

E RIC had just gotten off the phone when Sterling slouched into the office and collapsed into the desk chair, resting his head on his arms. "Hung over?" Eric asked.

"Yeah, hung over," Sterling mumbled into his hands.

"Was your mama mad?"

"My mama?"

"About you being drunk."

"Oh, no."

"So, did you have a good time?"

"What?" Sterling turned his head sideways so he was looking at Eric with one bloodshot eye.

"Yesterday. Was it a good birthday?"

Eric thought the boy stifled a grin. "Yeah."

"Good. So how about it, you want to fill out an order form?"

Sterling groaned and pushed himself upright. "Guess that's what you pay me for, huh?"

"Guess it is." Eric opened a drawer and took out some blank forms. He dropped them on the desk in front of Sterling. "Take it easy with the bottle next time, and you won't feel so bad."

"Okay, Dad."

Eric stepped out of the office, and Sterling tried to turn his attention to the call numbers on the order form, but in a few minutes he was asleep with his head on the desk.

Last night, when he arrived back at Lara's, he stood for a minute at the foot of the porch wondering how he was going to play this one. Casual? Joking? Want to go look at the moon through the telescope? But would that make her think he didn't want more?

He climbed the porch steps. He'd carried his shopping bags all the way from Hog Mountain Road, and the plastic handles had cut into his palms so they burned.

She'd left the porch light on. He saw his own image in the glass door, vaporous and superimposed over Lara, who sat waiting inside on the steps. She was barefoot, and her little toes curled and uncurled around the lip of the riser. As he reached to knock, she sprang up, dashed over, and threw open the door.

"Hi." She'd taken down her hair, and it fell in messy waves across her face.

He set the bags on the floor. "Sorry it took so long. Eric drove."

She kissed him. It wasn't one of those little feather kisses like last time, either. It was a kiss where he could taste what she'd been drinking.

T HE phone rang three times, and Eric waited for Sterling to pick up. On the fourth ring, Eric burst through the office door and reached over the sleeping Sterling to answer the phone. "Hello?"

"Eric, it's Sandy."

"Oh, hey, Sandy. How'd the cake go over last night?"

A stony silence. "Is he there?"

"Yeah, hang on. I'll get him for you."

Eric put a hand over the receiver and nudged Sterling with his knee. "Hey, Sterling, wake up." The boy didn't stir. "Sterling." Eric poked him harder until his eyes blinked open and he sat up. "Your mama's on the phone."

"What?"

"Your mother. She's on the phone for you."

"Oh." Sterling rubbed his eyes and took a deep breath before grabbing the receiver. "Hey," he said into the mouthpiece.

Eric heard the shrill sound of Sandy's voice. Even though he couldn't understand what she said, he could tell she was mad.

"I'm sorry," Sterling muttered. A long silence followed while the kid listened. Eric went to a file drawer and pretended to rummage around for some sales records.

"I said I was sorry. What the hell else do you want me to do?" A higher and louder pitch from the other end of the line. "You know that ain't true." Sterling paused to listen. "I said I would, didn't I? Tell 'em to hang on to it and I'll see 'em tonight." Sterling slammed the receiver down.

"Everything okay?" Eric asked. "Did you hang up on her?"

"Aw, she's pissed 'cause I got home so late last night, and 'cause I was drunk. The girls were already asleep and didn't get to give me my birthday present. I told her to wait 'til tonight, but she didn't listen to me. She doesn't ever listen to me." He rubbed his eyes.

Eric lifted a hand to set it on the boy's shoulder, but then stopped himself. "You need a good night's sleep. Want to get off a little early? I don't need you here. You could run the deposit to the bank for me and then head home."

"Oh, man, that'd be great. Really?"

"Yeah. Let me get the deposit slip added up so you can go."

"Thanks, Eric. I appreciate it. I ain't been good for nothing today."

He hadn't been. Earlier, at Dairy Queen, he'd felt like he was living two lives, one where he took orders and punched in numbers on the cash register, and another that was hot, soft, blurred around the edges, and too damned good to be real. All morning he'd tried to focus on his work, then he'd get a flash of last night.

"And an order of fries." Sterling would snap back to Dairy Queen and have to ask to hear the order again. Then, instead of handing the order to the kitchen, he'd call it over his shoulder because his dick had gotten hard, and if he moved away from the counter someone might see.

Last night, he'd laid with his head resting against the small of Lara's back, a wedge of moonlight bright against her skin. With his head resting there, the illuminated curves and shadows of her back looked like some smooth lunar landscape. He kissed the small of her back and she shifted underneath him, a noise like a purr coming from her throat.

All this morning it had gone like that, from wiping down the plastic countertop to his skin slipping against Lara's, himself sliding in and out of her. He was already tired; but, with his mind going back and forth, by the time he got to Eric's he was exhausted.

He'd barely slept, lying there with her, his leg half off the futon, his head against the small of her back. The unfamiliar bed made it hard to sleep, and when he'd finally doze, she'd shift and he'd start awake, expecting one of the twins with a nightmare or needing a glass of water. Then there was the fact that he didn't want to sleep because it meant he wouldn't be feeling her, or seeing the way she looked without her clothes, or smelling the way she smelled. Finally, he lifted his head from her back and scooted up beside her so that he could see her face, the shadow between her lips. He touched her mouth and she half smiled even though her eyes were closed. He lay and watched her sleep with that half-smile curving her lips.

When her clock-radio read 5:30, he rolled over and sat up. She sighed and squirmed and sat up too. In the light from the street lamp outside, he could see her rubbing her eyes. "I gotta get up," he said. "Can I use your shower?"

"Sure." She watched him stand in that hungry way she'd always watched him. "Will you come back tonight?" Her voice sounded small in the dark room.

He grinned as he grabbed his clothes. "I can't believe you just asked me that. How could you've asked that?"

BLEARY-EYED, Sterling dropped the deposit at the bank. Pam Grier eyed him from behind the customer service counter while Mrs. Hanks took the deposit slip and counted the money. "How's your mama and sisters gettin' along? They doing okay?"

"Yes, ma'am."

"How old are those little girls now?"

"Six."

"Six. Well, they're the two cutest things I ever saw, with all those red curls. Look just like. . . ." She stopped.

Everyone within hearing distance suddenly got busy. It had been this way ever since his daddy left. He knew not all of them meant to be ugly, but they made him feel bad just the same.

"Yeah, they look like Daddy," he said. He wanted to go on, *And I don't, and I know what you all have been saying behind my back. I can't believe you've got nothing better to do. Even if he wasn't my daddy, I can't help it.*

"Here you go." Mrs. Hanks handed him the receipt, which he stuck in his wallet to give to Eric. Then he brought out his last two dollars.

"Can I get change, please?"

"You sure can. Quarters okay?"

Sterling nodded and held his palm out to receive the eight quarters. This was it for his money until Friday. He left the bank and strolled across the street to the corner gas station restroom. As he turned the door handle and was greeted by the sour smell of stale urine, he thought *At least I have something good to spend my last eight quarters on.* Sterling locked the door and began feeding the quarters into the condom machine. As he turned the knob and watched the small square packet drop onto the metal tray, he felt bad for a second. He should go see his sisters. They'd be with Cousin Paula since Mama was at work. He could take them home and get their present.

But he didn't want to go home. He wanted to see Lara. In fact, he was pretty sure he'd explode into some sort of quick-burning fire if he didn't get to see her soon. Besides, he was so damned tired of having to take care of Mama and the girls. For once he wanted to do something that *he* wanted to do. So he turned in the direction of Lara's house and began walking.

*   *   *

THE night before, as the tension had left Sterling's body and he sagged into her, Lara leaned against the living room wall, bracing herself for the wave of guilt and regret she knew was coming. The sex had been fast, aggressive, so consuming that, for the few minutes it lasted, her mind had seized only on feeling it. Now, Sterling stood before her, stunned and silent, breath coming in quick rasps, forehead pressed to the wall above her shoulder. She stroked the back of his neck. It was covered with a fine film of sweat. She kissed his chest. It tasted salty. Sterling's legs crumpled underneath him and he sank to the floor, pressing his face into Lara's stomach, his labored breath warm.

Instead of self-recrimination, Lara was overwhelmed with tenderness. *It's okay,* she told herself. *It's fine. Fine.* She stroked Sterling's hair while he pressed harder against her. Sliding down the wall, she sat as he turned his face away.

"What?" She touched his cheek. "Since when are you shy?"

But he wouldn't look at her.

"Kiss me?" she asked.

He kissed her hotly and for a long time, then moved to sit beside her and sling an arm around her shoulders.

"Maybe we should have kissed more first," she said. "Maybe we should have taken it slower."

He looked at her with the familiar glint of humor in his eyes. "Naw, I don't think so."

Smiling, she dropped her head to his shoulder. They sat in silence, and she dozed, exhausted from the strain of the day and the previous weeks, warm and sleepy from giving in. For the moment, she felt content to exist without thinking. A tickling drop of sweat ran down between her breasts. In the kitchen, the refrigerator hummed.

She didn't know how long they sat before Sterling shifted, then stood and offered his hand. "Come on."

He led her upstairs. She leaned against him, letting him support her weight with his body. At the bathroom door he stopped. She pressed her face against his neck, smelled his damp, salty smell, ran her fingers up his spine, thinking of how his back muscles flexed and relaxed. How perfect he was. "Are you staying?" she murmured.

"Yeah. I'll be there in a second." He sent her toward the bedroom with a gentle shove.

Her clothing felt damp and strange, as if she'd been caught in a violent storm and everything was out of place and wet, her bra around her waist, her skirt turned backwards, her panties still downstairs. She began undressing. As she pulled her tank top over her head, she noticed that it was ripped. She held it in her hand and stared, thinking *my God, he ripped it.* Dylan had never ripped anything.

The bathroom floor creaked as Sterling moved around. She peeled off her wrinkled skirt and crawled under the white sheet, pulling it to her shoulders. Now that she was lying down, her legs felt shaky and the overwhelming exhaustion returned.

The bathroom door clunked open and she followed the sound of Sterling's footsteps as they moved down the hall toward her bedroom. She saw his denim-clad legs stop beside the bed. He still had his tennis shoes on. Dylan had never kept his shoes on.

"You awake down there?"

"Yes." She kept her eyes fixed on his legs, heard him unzip and watched his pants fall to his ankles. Then he pried off his shoes, stepped out of the pants, and walked around to the other side of her futon. She felt him climb in behind her, his hot skin, his cotton boxers against her butt.

"No, take off everything," she said.

He slid his boxers off underneath the sheet, then pulled her against him. His arms around her, his breath and warmth.

G UILT didn't attack her the next day either. Instead, the warm, safe, sleepy feeling lingered. She dozed on the floor beside her computer, ran a hand along the curve of her hip, wondering how it felt to Sterling to touch her. She watched the minutes tick off her computer's clock. As the afternoon progressed and the sun turned deep gold on the horizon, she didn't suffer a moment of regret. Instead, she felt languid, open and relaxed, ready for Sterling to return.

He startled her with the suddenness of his arrival, bursting through the door, charging toward her, declaring "I been thinking about you all day."

She managed to stand just in time for him to hook his arms under her butt and pick her up.

"Hi." She wrapped her legs around his waist and kissed him as he staggered into the kitchen.

There, he set her on the counter, pushing at her skirt until it bunched up around her hips.

The sunlight caught the fine dark hairs on his arms as his hand slid under her shirt, and he caressed her breast. Lara closed her eyes. He yanked off her panties and was inside her before she could speak. She laughed, and said "So, how was work? How was your day?" while her head banged back into the cabinets until she braced herself, wrapped an arm around his neck, and held on.

Just as it was starting to feel good, he was through.

He sank to his knees on the tile floor, breathing hard and grinning. She didn't know what to do, wanting him still, panting. She stretched out a bare foot and rested her toes on his shoulder while he kissed her ankle. Looking down at him, she thought *He doesn't have a clue what he's doing. Ninety seconds of sex and he thinks he's a genius.*

He tugged her foot so she slid off the counter. He opened his arms, pulled her in, and she thought *Maybe I'll let him be a genius for a while.*

chapter twenty-six

October 26

EDGARS noticed Henry Jacobs from *The Barton Herald* striding toward him. He slipped back into his office in the hope that Jacobs wasn't looking for him. A few moments later a knock came. Jacobs cracked open the door and peeked inside.

"Howdy there, Captain. Got time for a quick interview?"

"Well, Henry, I'm really pretty—"

"Or we could schedule one. I myself would just as soon get it over with. The paper's riding my ass about this Walton murder. Besides, right now I only got a few minutes, so I can guarantee it'll be short and sweet."

Might as well do it, Edgars thought. "Fifteen minutes. That's all I got."

"Great." Jacobs sat down in the chair beside Edgars's desk without being asked and took a notebook out of his pocket.

"I guess what I need from you, sir, is the police angle on this thing. Any suspects? How long do you think it's gonna take? That sort of thing."

"You know I'm not wild about commenting on this."

"Is Sterling O'Connor a suspect?"

Edgars felt protective of the boy. "Right now we don't have any suspects. We're following up on leads and waiting for forensic results."

"Was she raped or robbed or anything?"

"Not that we know of. We're still waiting for conclusive tests on lots of things."

"How long's it been since you investigated a murder, again?"

Edgars stiffened. He could see where this was headed. He tried to sound relaxed. "About eight years, Henry. You know that."

"So, do you feel kind of rusty?"

"I've kept up on the literature. I've gone to seminars about new forensic techniques. I feel pretty comfortable that I know what I'm doing."

Jacobs set the notebook in his lap and peered at the captain through slit eyes. "And how are you feeling, sir, if you don't mind my asking? Is your health okay?"

"What?" The question startled Edgars. "Is someone saying my health is bad?"

"Well, I heard you had heart problems and that the stress of the investigation was making them worse."

Edgars fought the urge to curse. "I don't have heart problems, Henry, but even if I did, it wouldn't be anybody's business. Now, I have a meeting to get to." He stood and began gathering files.

"Just one more question?"

"Not today," Edgars said, and he hurried from the room.

chapter twenty-seven

August 12

S TERLING picked up the girls at Cousin Paula's. When they saw him, they yelled his name, flung their little arms open, and ran toward him. In an instant, they were clinging to his legs.

"Hey, Sterling," Paula stood in the doorway with her arms crossed over her chest.

He lifted his hand.

"You want to come in? I got some lemonade made."

He mussed the girls' hair. "Naw. I got to get these two home." He turned to his sisters. "Come on, let's get going."

"'Bye now!" Paula waved. "Y'all say hi to your mama for me."

Sterling herded the girls around Paula's house. In the back yard, he held up the barbed-wire fence so the girls could climb into George MacKnight's hayfield. He slipped through after them.

The sunset was bright and hot. The air smelled like scorched grass. The field had been mowed and was littered with mounds of yellowing hay. As they waded through it, grasshoppers jumped away from them, wings whizzing.

"Look!" Darlene pointed to a patch of blue flowers growing along the fence row. "Can we pick some, Sterling?"

He nodded and let go of their hands. They dashed to the flowers and bent over, their hair shining. Sterling wiped sweat out of his eyes and wished for a breeze while the girls picked handfuls of cornflowers, held them beneath their noses and sniffed. Bees and butterflies flitted by. He thought he should enjoy watching the twins pick flowers, but he was too hot and too tired and just wanted to get home.

"Come on," he said. "Let's go."

They tripped along beside him, and he slowed his pace so they could keep up. He remembered how little they'd been when his daddy left, just two years old, teetering around and getting into everything. Still, two sweet little girls weren't much responsibility. He didn't understand why his daddy couldn't handle that tiny bit of responsibility.

Sterling felt worse than ever for missing his birthday with them. Maybe Mama was right. Maybe he was like his daddy and didn't want the responsibility either. Maybe now, walking slowly so they could keep up even though he was hot and tired and wanted to get home, he felt kind of angry toward the twins, as if they were holding him back from living his life.

When they reached the edge of the field, they climbed through more barbed wire and turned right onto the road. Dayla broke away and ran ahead of them. "Hey," he called after her. "Come on back here!"

But she didn't listen. Their house was at the crest of the hill and she ran the whole way. Sterling picked up his pace, dragging Darlene behind him part of the way before hoisting her up and letting her ride piggyback until they reached the yard.

"Hey!" Dayla screamed. "I want to ride piggyback! I want to ride!"

"Not when you disobeyed and ran on the road like you just did. You come on in the house right now." He unlocked the door and held it open.

Dayla poked herself through the tire swing, her front hanging out one side and her butt hanging out the other. "Push me!" She called. "Push me!"

"Me too!" Darlene cried.

"Come here," Sterling ordered. "You all need to get your bath. I ain't got time to mess with you."

"Push me, Sterling!" Dayla insisted.

"I ain't gonna push you, now come on inside 'fore I get the belt."

Her little shoes scrabbled along the dusty ground and she pulled herself out of the tire, then dragged her feet and hung her head all the way to the house while he stood and held the door open for them.

Inside, the house was stuffy and hot. Sterling went around opening windows, watching a breeze lift the green curtains in the living room while the girls kicked off their shoes and danced around after him. "We got you a birthday present," Darlene said. "I'll get it."

"No, me, wait!"

"Un-uh," he interrupted. "You all take your bath first."

"But we have to give it to you now."

"Oh, yeah? How come?"

"'Cause we have to, Sterling. We gotta give it to you now."

"Well, I guess you'd better go on and get it, then."

They bustled to the sofa, stumbling over each other. Falling to their knees, they came out with a box wrapped in newspaper, which Dayla tucked under her arm.

"No!" Darlene protested. "Sterling, she won't let me have it."

"Bring it to me together, both of you, or I ain't gonna open it." So both girls took hold of the box and brought it toward him with outstretched arms. "That's a mighty pretty package." He took it from them. "Think it'd be okay if I unwrapped it?"

They nodded. He unwrapped it slowly to tantalize them, grinning at their half-open mouths, their wide eyes. By the time he got down to the shoebox, they were jumping up and down. He set a hand on the lid, then lifted it.

Inside lay a quilted stuffed animal. He could tell they had made it by the button eyes and the crazy way it was sewn together. He didn't know what kind of animal it was supposed to be. Its two pudgy arms poked forward. Stuffing bled out between awkward stitches. He recognized the fabric from one of their old dresses, blue with little hearts on it. He took the animal out of the box and hugged it.

"Oh, man, this is great. This is the best toy I ever seen. I'm gonna sleep with him every night." He kissed the mutant thing on its button nose and set it gently back in the box, afraid it might disintegrate if he held on to it for too long. "Thanks." He kissed both girls on their button noses. "That's the best present I ever got." He held them at arm's length, looking at how cute they were. His little sisters. "Now go on and get ready for your bath." He stood and walked into the bathroom, plugged the drain in the tub, and started running water. "You all throw them dirty clothes in the basket. I don't want to see that stuff on the floor when I come back in here."

In a few minutes, the girls were splashing in the bathtub and Sterling sat at the kitchen table, hands folded in front of him, waiting for his mother to come home.

At the sight of their truck pulling into the driveway, Sterling's insides curdled. His mama climbed out. Her hair looked oily and she wore a white T-shirt with a pink sequined bunny on the front. It was an old shirt, stained yellow around the neck and under the arms. He hated the sight of her, hated her completely and all at once.

She stopped just inside the kitchen door, her eyes latching onto him like a hawk's eyes on a rabbit. He wished he had a hole to crawl into. She smelled of cigarettes and sweat. Sterling thought of how good Lara always smelled.

"Girls are in their bath," he said before she could get a word out.

She dropped her handbag on the kitchen counter, went to the fridge and poured herself some water. Inside the fridge, he could see his birthday cake, lopsided, the white icing blotched with red and green, like the girls had finger-painted on it.

"Did they give you your present yet?" she asked.

"Yeah."

His mama took a swallow of her water, then set the glass on the counter. "I hope she's worth it, that woman you're sleeping with."

He stared at his hands.

"Older woman like her. Is she giving you money for it?"

Sterling sat still for a moment looking at his hands, at the way his fingers twisted together. Then he pushed himself up and strode from the kitchen to his bedroom. He opened his bureau and pulled out clean underwear, T-shirts, and socks. From the closet he got two pairs of jeans.

His mother followed and stood blocking the doorway. "I don't know why else you'd leave your family for some older woman unless she was giving you good money for it."

He slammed his closet door shut, fell to his knees and groped under the bed for his backpack. He shoved the clothes inside, then stood and faced her.

"What, are you going back tonight too?" She demanded. "Is she some kind of sex addict or something?"

"Shut up," he said.

"What'd you say to me?"

"Shut up!"

"So now she's got you talking back, too?"

"You don't have any idea what you're saying, so just shut the hell up!" The splashing in the bathroom stopped. He could picture the girls sitting in the tub holding on to each other like they always did when he and Mama fought.

His mother twisted her face and stuck her nose in the air. "*You don't have any idea.* Listen at you. You even sound stuck up. Well, you ain't gonna tell me to shut up, even if you say it fancy." She brushed by him, threw open the closet door, and came out with one of his belts.

"What? You gonna whip me? I'm eighteen years old. You can't whip me."

With a vicious snap of her arm, the belt shot forward. The leather stung the side of his face just below his eye. He stood frozen for a moment, then touched the burning spot on his cheek.

"I'll whip no matter how old you are, you smart-mouthed shit!" She took another swing. He felt a breeze as the belt whizzed and snapped close to his ear. She brought the belt back to her side and swung again. He punched out blindly, flailing his arms. The belt grazed his shoulder just as his fist connected with her chin, and his mother fell backwards, landing on the floor, her legs splayed out and a surprised look on her face.

The impact stung his knuckles. As she sat there blinking, he thought he might puke. He waited for her to say something, but she just gaped dully until he couldn't stand to see her any more. He seized his backpack and the shoebox with the girls' stuffed animal, then strode out of the room and into the hall. He cracked open the bathroom door, forcing his voice to be calm.

"I gotta go again, sweet-peas. You be good."

"Sterling!" One of them called, but he'd already shut the door and was headed through the kitchen.

By the time he made it to the road, he was crying, the tears burning the wound on his face. He touched it again, then held up his fingers. She'd drawn blood. He took a breath, wiped at his eyes, and walked faster.

The pink air shimmered as he walked by Jim Dobbs's cow pasture. The cows stood or lay, grazing, chewing their cud, big ears flapping as their jaws worked. That'd be the life, he thought, to be a cow, get milked twice a day and then just lie and eat and swat flies with your tail. He wanted an easy life like that.

When he reached Lara's house and saw the glow of her computer in the living room, his throat tightened again. When he knocked, Lara came to the door, her face breaking into a smile. He wanted to tell her how good it felt that she smiled at the sight of him. But when she saw the gash on his cheek, the smile faded. A little crease appeared above her nose.

"What happened?"

The question made his throat go tight. He turned sideways so she couldn't see his face. "Nothing."

"You're bleeding." She tried to touch the welt, but he flinched away. "Are you all right?"

"Yeah." His chin puckered and his eyes stung. He clenched his teeth to keep from crying and tried to think of something to say, but couldn't.

"Come on in. Come sit down. I'll get some ice."

He followed her into the kitchen and watched while she scooped ice cubes into a plastic freezer bag and handed it to him. He pressed it against his cheek, the cold stinging at first, but it numbed the soreness. Lara poured him some tea, then sat down across the table. "Are you sure. . . ." she began. He shot her a desperate look, and she stopped. They sat in silence while he waited for the weepiness to pass.

"Do you want to go to the emergency room?" she asked. "It might need stitches."

"No. I just want to sit here a minute, okay?" His voice sounded calmer than he thought it would. "Just let me sit here."

"Okay." She stood and walked around behind him. For a moment she rested a hand on his shoulder and kneaded his neck muscles with her fingers. "I'm going upstairs. Come up when you want."

He nodded.

She disappeared around the corner, and he heard the stairs creak. He inhaled, held his breath, then let it out, pressing the ice to his cheek, his fingers going numb from the cold.

Bugs whirred against the windowpanes. The light above him hummed and popped. He could see why Lara liked this old falling-down house. It was a good place to be sad. So he sat with the night noises, the tree frogs, the bugs' wings, the old refrigerator motor lumbering as it turned on, and he felt sad for a long time about everything.

It was late when he finally went upstairs, trying to walk softly. The steps groaned anyway. The hall was dark, but a light glowed from Lara's bedroom. He stopped in the doorway, looking down at Lara sleeping on her stomach. Her lips were parted, her eyes squeezed together in a way that made her cheeks puff out. Her back was bare and brown. Pale bathing-suit lines crossed her shoulders. She had left space for him on the right.

He felt like an actor playing some guy who came home to this woman, who slept in the same bed as her, some guy who didn't think twice about how strange and different it was to suddenly be undressing and climbing into bed beside her, like she was his wife and this was their home. Leaning down, he switched out the light. He crawled under the sheet, turning his back to Lara, not wanting to wake her. With a sigh, she rolled over and stretched herself against him. Their legs tangled. Her toes curled around his. His limbs went heavy, the muscles unwinding from how they had been, all coiled up tight. He fell into an exhausted sleep.

August 13

S TERLING woke at 4:00 but went back to sleep. At 5:15 he woke again and squinted at the numbers on Lara's clock-radio. He had to get up.

The room was cool. The fan rattled in the corner. The open French doors let in the damp morning air. Sterling groped for the sheet, which lay matted at their feet, and he pulled it up over them. Beside him, Lara looked like a watercolor painting in the misty gray light, her outlines all soft. After last night, he felt close to her, and it scared him, made him want to say all kinds of things about how he loved her and needed her. When he threw back the sheet and stood up, Lara shifted and opened her eyes.

"'Morning," he whispered.

"Is it morning?" Her voice was hoarse.

"Yeah, you looked so pretty sleeping last night, I didn't have the heart to wake you."

"Will you kiss me?" she asked.

He fell to his knees and kissed her. "I gotta go. I'm gonna be late to Dairy Queen."

"What time do you go to Eric's?

"It's Sunday. I don't work for him 'til tomorrow."

"Has Eric figured out what's going on?"

"No, and I'm not telling him. We'd both catch hell."

"It's not his business anyway," Lara said.

August 14

B Y the time Eric made it to work the next day, he'd heard three different stories about Sterling's fight with his mother. The boy was standing with his elbows propped on the counter by the cash register, cheek resting in his hand as he checked off new CDs on the order form. He was whistling like nothing had happened.

"Hey," said Eric.

"Hey," Sterling flashed him a grin. "You're late, bourgeois parasite."

"I'm confiscating that damned *Manifesto* if you don't cut that shit out." Eric shook his fist.

"You can't confiscate it. It's Lara's." He said Lara's name like she was a goddess who would visit some horrible plague on anyone who defied her.

"Yeah, well, she shouldn't have given you the thing to begin with. She had no idea what sort of trouble it would cause." Eric opened the register and began shoving the small bills he'd picked up at the bank into the drawer. Sterling went back to whistling. Eric cleared his throat. "Listen, I got to tell you, I heard from three different people that you and your mama had a fight."

Sterling stopped whistling but continued picking up CDs, examining them, then checking their names off the order form. "What people?"

"Well, there was your mama's cousin Paula, and Claire Nettles at the bank, and Ruth Kinsley at the post office."

Sterling moved his hand from his cheek, and Eric saw the scabbed-over welt. "Did she do that?"

Sterling nodded. "Yup. Belt."

"No one mentioned that."

The boy flashed a bitter smile. "Why don't that surprise me?"

"What happened?"

Sterling shrugged it off. "We fought, you know. Just fought like usual."

"About what?"

Sterling paused to check off another CD. "Thought everyone in town told you already."

"Everyone in town says Lara was trying to convert your family to communism."

Sterling laughed. "Shit."

"So what happened?"

Sterling straightened up and faced Eric. The welt on his face was haloed by a blue bruise. It made Eric angry. Whatever the boy had done, he didn't deserve that kind of beating. "Aw, Mama thinks I'm spending too much time at Lara's. She don't complain about the money I bring home, but I smarted off to her and she grabbed the belt and *smack!*" He fake-slapped himself across the face. "Thing is, I kind of lost it and I hit her back. I didn't mean to, but I just lost it."

"You hit her back?"

Sterling nodded.

"Christ."

Sterling was silent.

"Are you really all right?" Eric asked.

"Yeah, man, I'm fine. Just kind of tired of it, is all."

"Okay." Eric wanted to pat the boy on the shoulder. "Just don't hit your mother again. You shouldn't ever hit a woman, you know that, right?"

Sterling nodded.

"You can always take off from here early if you need to."

"Thanks," Sterling said. "I appreciate that."

Eric paused. "When's the last time you saw Lara?"

"Last night."

"When last night?"

The boy eyed Eric. "Why?"

Eric's insides went cold. He could read everything on Sterling's face. "Shit," he muttered.

"What?"

"Forget it. Nothing. Hey, go down to McDonald's and get me a coffee."

"Now?"

"Yeah, now."

Sterling huffed. "Okay."

Eric handed him two dollars and watched him walk out the door and across the parking lot. Then he reached for the phone and dialed the Quickie Mart. Sandy answered. Eric wasn't sure why he'd called, what he wanted to say. All he knew was that his insides felt like they were falling out. He hung up quickly, without speaking.

August 14

LARA found Sterling's backpack in the bathroom. It was full of clothing, as if he wasn't planning to go home for a while. She took it to her bedroom and began unpacking his things, hanging his pants in the closet, folding his boxers and putting them in a drawer. Finally, all that was left was a blue T-shirt. She sat on her futon and fingered a hole in the sleeve of the shirt.

She thought of how he kissed, holding her face between his hands. Deep, slow, aggressive kisses that turned her limbs to liquid, his hips thrust hard against hers. First base, second base, third base. She couldn't remember what the bases were any more. It was always the boys who cared about the bases anyway. Lara fingered the hole in Sterling's shirt and thought *So what now? Let him move in? Take him away? Maybe back to Washington?* She wished she could keep him forever, give him books to read, show him how to have sex properly instead of like some freight train, which once it got going took a mile to slow down and stop.

She thought about Dylan, about the first time they'd made love. It had been at his apartment, on the sofa, after a horrible Italian dinner that he'd cooked and she'd barely managed to choke down. He'd always been a lousy cook. A little too much red wine, candlelight, the TV on but muted. He'd taken half an hour to undress her, pausing in between buttons to talk about energy policy and the need to convert to solar power. Lara sat beside him burning, running a hand up and down his leg, too shy to touch him where she really wanted, hoping he'd take her hand and put it there.

"Not to mention the whole ethanol question," Dylan murmured into her neck, his fingers tracing circles precariously close to her bra strap.

"Shut up," she'd muttered.

"What?"

"Shut up. I don't care about energy policy right now."

And even then it took time. He was shy and thoughtful, considerate, deliberate. Being close to him comforted her, held her mind still for a while.

"Dylan," she said out loud now, testing his name in the silence. She braced herself for some sign that he was there, that he'd heard her. But there was nothing.

She said out loud: "You're gone."

Around her the silence stretched long and empty.

WHEN he got back from work, Sterling found Lara in the kitchen. "Eric invited us to swim Sunday." He wrapped his arms around her waist and nuzzled her neck. "I hope I can play it cool around you. It'll be hard, you know."

She gave him a slanted grin and he poked at her ribs. "That ain't what I meant. You got a dirty mind." He slid one hand inside the waist of her shorts, gripping her ass, and with the other hand he undid his fly.

Lara laughed. "Downstairs again? I'm starting to feel like some sort of drive-through depository. I've been having these bizarre muscle spasms in my legs from doing it standing up."

The words stung him.

"Come on," she was urging. "Let's go upstairs. Let's slow down. You've been doing it so fast I hardly get a chance to feel it."

A chill crept through him. He'd waited all day for this, and now all she could do was tell him she didn't like it? He shoved away from her and stood with his hands on his hips. "Man, that's great, Lara. I guess us country boys aren't up to your standards."

"That's not what I'm saying," she insisted.

But he didn't listen. Instead he looked around the room, not quite sure what to do, not understanding why he felt as if the breath was crushing out of his lungs. "I think I want some fresh air."

Outside, Sterling stalked the deserted streets, trying to decide where to go. But he couldn't think about anything except Lara.

The sun set, and a mosquito buzzed around him until he smashed it on his arm, smearing blood across his skin. His stomach growled and he thought about the food in Lara's refrigerator and wondered what time it was and where he should go. Home was out, and he didn't want to call Eric because then he'd have to explain things. He stopped walking and just stood on the sidewalk, hands on his hips, thinking *Might as well not walk. I'm heading nowhere.* A cop car drove by and he realized he'd better go someplace. The police had it in for him as it was, without him standing around downtown by himself in the dark. Maybe he'd go back to Lara's after all. Maybe he'd tell her he'd screwed lots of girls and she wasn't anywhere near the best.

When he walked through her front door, he found Lara sitting inside on the steps waiting for him, wearing a white nightgown. One strap hung off her shoulder.

"I'm not doing this any more," she said, as he stood frozen, looking up at her. "I have to be able to talk to you, and to be myself. If you're going to be so goddamned sensitive that I can't tell you what I want, then you'd better find someone else." She stood. The cotton nightgown was so thin that he could see the shape of her nipples and the dark triangle of her pubic hair. "If you decide you're secure enough to deal with me speaking my mind, then I hope you come to bed."

He watched her turn and climb the stairs. He wanted to yell something after her, but the way her hips rocked under the pale film of fabric distracted him. When she had disappeared from sight, he stomped to the kitchen and poured himself a glass of milk, then began eating corn chips out of a bag.

So she wanted it different? Was it his fault if she was weird and didn't like sex like she should? What the hell kind of woman was she, anyway? But then that annoying voice he had, that voice that made him read *The Communist Manifesto* and look up all those words in the dictionary, the voice that kept him hunting for articles on sunspots and solar wind, that voice said: *Why don't you just see what she wants? What she wants might be great.* He told the voice to shut up, that it had gotten him into this mess to begin with. Why did that part of him always have to be so curious? Sterling wished he could stop being curious.

An hour passed. He finished the entire bag of corn chips. His mouth felt dry and shriveled inside from all the salt. He drank three glasses of water thinking about Lara upstairs. If he didn't go up there, he'd wonder forever what he'd missed. But if he did go, he'd be giving in, letting her win. What kind of man let a woman tell him what to do? Even while he thought these things, he knew he'd go up, and hated himself for it. "You're fucking whipped," he muttered.

After he got the taste of salt out of his mouth, he climbed the stairs and walked down the hall to her bedroom. She sat on her futon reading, the book propped in her lap, her hair falling loose onto her shoulders. The yellow glow of the lamp cast long shadows across the walls. In the distance he heard thunder, and the white curtain over the French doors billowed into the room like a sail catching wind.

Seeing him, Lara set the book on the floor, wrapped her arms around her knees, and looked at his face.

"I think a storm's blowing up," he said.

The curtain expanded and curled into the room. Lara pushed herself up so she was kneeling and lifted the nightgown over her head. It surprised him. He stared at her naked body in the lamplight. He remembered what Eric had said about sex being a game. Only this didn't seem like a game to him. It felt serious.

Lara reached for him. He took a step toward her and she gripped the waist of his pants and pulled him closer.

"I feel like you think I'm an idiot or something," he choked. She unbuttoned his pants and unzipped his fly. She slid her hand inside his boxers, grabbed his cock and pulled it out. He was starting to feel dizzy.

"I don't think you're an idiot. I adore you."

Parting her lips, she took him into her warm mouth. No one had ever done this for him before. Not that he hadn't thought about it a lot in English class when it got boring, and at Dairy Queen, and at home in bed at night, and, well, pretty much all the time. But in his imagination, he never realized that it would feel this good. Sterling stopped worrying so much about what Lara thought, and started wondering, instead, how he'd lived so long without this. A second later, he stopped thinking. All his energy, all his blood, all his sensation focused in Lara's mouth. He braced his hand against the wall because he felt like he might pass out. Just then Lara sat back on her heels and grinned up at him.

"Hey, no," he protested.

She smiled.

He jumped her. Rolling his body onto hers, he pressed her down on the futon, pinning her hands over her head. "You're a tease, is what you are."

"Kiss me," she said. "The way you kiss, it melts me."

"I want to melt you," he said. "Show me how to melt you."

O VER the days that followed, she showed him some stuff, and he figured out other stuff on his own. At first, he was embarrassed, but soon the hot feeling of shame changed to a different kind of hot feeling, and he started hoping she'd ask for stuff in her breathless way.

Her fingertips. The soft skin inside her elbow, the flesh below her bellybutton, the place where her neck met her shoulder. Places on Lara he hadn't thought much about until he realized that kissing them, or dragging his tongue across them, or biting at them did something to her. Every muscle in her body tightened, but she was loose too, pliable so he could twist her, turn her, position her any way he wanted. Sometimes she'd press her mouth to his ear and whisper some pretty dirty things. They kissed a lot, even though it was hard to breathe and kiss, and he really needed to breathe and thought she did too. And one night, in the middle of all that, he knew she got off, just like Eric said he would. He knew for sure, surer than he'd ever known anything. And it was great.

August 17

"MAYBE you could write a letter of recommendation for me," he said one night when they were lying in bed listening to the rain. "You know, for college."

"You're applying?"

"Yeah."

"That's great, Sterling."

"So you'll write me a letter?"

"What kind of letter? Like that you worked for me?"

"Naw, I was thinking of something a little more exciting."

"You want an X-rated letter of recommendation?"

"I figured if I'm going to start fooling around with older women, it might as well help me get into college. I mean, there's gotta be some older women in the admissions department, right?"

She laughed.

chapter twenty-nine

August 20

ERIC and Lara floated like leaves, revolving slowly, eyes squinted shut against the white glare of the sky. At different ends of the pool they drifted, had been drifting for a while, as silent as the oppressive afternoon. Eric's face was beginning to feel raw and burned, but he didn't want to get out. The silence of floating was a refuge from conversation.

Sterling had gone to Lara for comfort, and she was giving Sterling a kind of comfort that Eric never could.

He heard a splash, felt a ripple, and stiffened so his body sank as Lara kicked to the side of the pool and finished her glass of iced tea. Then she tipped out an ice cube and ran it along her forehead and down the back of her neck.

Eric swam to the side too. He threw water on the hot asphalt to cool it before taking hold. "You want a beer?" He kept his distance from Lara, as she had kept hers from him all afternoon.

"No, I think I'll stick with tea."

"Really? That's the first time I've known you to turn down a drink." It felt good to be mean. Seeing her floating in the yellow bathing suit with her bare brown shoulders, looking like some cute unobtainable pool toy, pissed him off.

She glared at him, then pushed off the wall backward.

"Lara," he called after her.

"What?"

"Did you see Sterling last night?" He didn't even try to hide his accusing tone.

Lara was silent for a moment, then righted herself and began to tread water. "Yes, last night."

"What did you guys do?"

She frowned. "Nothing. Ate. Looked through the telescope."

"So is he or isn't he actually working for you any more?"

She fell silent.

Eric could sense her shutting him out. He kicked his legs to buoy himself higher. "How's his face looking?"

"Still bad. What the hell was that woman thinking?"

"Oh, probably wasn't thinking anything. Probably was just pissed off. Domestic violence is a cottage industry in this town."

"God, I hate it when you do that," she said. "Doesn't it even bother you a little?"

"Of course it bothers me. I'm just not living with the illusion that I can do a damned thing about it. I don't have the influence over him you do. Maybe if I had tits he'd listen to me."

She opened her mouth, then shut it again. He could see the blurred forms of her arms and legs treading the water just under the surface. The wrinkled sunlight on the pool flashed over her skin. They glared at each other for a moment. Then she stopped paddling and spread her arms. He watched as her legs rose to the surface and she began floating.

Eric floated too, and was almost asleep when a violent splash startled him. Spray flew into his open mouth and waves tipped him over. Sterling shot up from below the surface, pointing at Eric and laughing. "I swear, y'all don't do anything when I ain't around!"

"We enjoy peace and quiet, is what we do." Eric swam to the edge, hefted himself out, then padded to his chair, grabbing his towel. "I think that's a fitting end for me. I'm going to take a shower and then we'll barbecue something. Sound good? Lara, come start the salad."

Lara cast a quick glance at Sterling, then swam to the side of the pool. "Sure."

Half an hour later, Eric stood over the barbecue, turning his face away from the charcoal smoke, prodding the hamburgers with a spatula. Lara sat behind him drinking a gin-and-tonic while Sterling splashed in the pool, doing an awkward backstroke.

"I know what's going on," Eric said to Lara in a low voice. "The whole town knows. You're asking for trouble." As he flipped a burger, grease dripped, spitting, onto the coals.

She swirled her ice in the glass, then picked out the wedge of lime. "I like this gin."

"I'LL drive him home," Lara said. It was late, and she and Eric were by the pool gathering up paper plates and plastic cups. A cloud hung over the moon.

I bet you will, thought Eric bitterly, but he called out: "Hey kid, don't forget your stuff out here." He wanted to say something to scare Lara off, to make her unhappy the way he was unhappy.

He leaned toward her. "This town is like a perfect circle. Everything you do is going to come back to haunt you. I've already heard a bunch of stories about you. You're not thinking about Sterling. This is going to make his life hell, between Sandy and all the rumors. They already gossip about the poor kid enough, and now they'll talk more. You're being selfish. You're not even thinking about him."

She tried to give Eric an innocent look, one eyebrow arched as if she didn't have any idea what he meant. "I'm not going to be here forever," she said. "And neither is Sterling."

❦ *chapter thirty* ❦

IN the mornings when the alarm went off, Sterling would turn over in bed, making soft smacking noises with his mouth, and Lara would muster what energy she could and climb on top of him. She'd feel his hand touch the back of her head, his fingers tangling in her hair, and he'd say, in a hoarse, sticky voice, "Lara, get up. I gotta go to work."

But she wouldn't move.

He'd laugh, his chest and belly shaking underneath her. "Lara, baby, I gotta go."

"No," she'd croak.

"Yeah. Come on, gal." Gripping her waist, he'd push at her gently.

She'd wrap her arms around his neck and hold on, and he'd laugh even harder. "I'm gonna be late."

"You can't go in today."

"I gotta go in."

"I won't let you."

With one strong surge, he'd flip her over, and for a moment her body would lie pinned under his. She'd curl her arms around his neck, run her fingers across the soft hair at the back of his head. "It's not fair. I want you to stay."

"Yeah, well, I want to stay too, but I gotta work." He'd give her a lingering kiss, then stand while she'd make one final lunge for his leg, and he'd skip away laughing.

They repeated the scene every morning, a sort of ritual to ease parting. At least if he had to go to that horrible Dairy Queen, Lara thought she'd send him off smiling.

When he was gone, Lara fell asleep again, waking an hour or two later. Rolling onto her back, she stared at a water stain on the ceiling that Sterling said looked like the old fat Elvis. He'd joked about letting people come see it and charging admission. She imagined a line stretching round the block and Pam Grier frowning from her porch.

Lara looked at the clock and counted twelve more hours until she saw Sterling again. She pictured the moment he'd come through the door, moving toward her. At that moment, she always felt a little afraid, but wasn't sure why. Dylan had never come at her that way. So when Sterling rushed forward, already pulling off his shirt, she felt alarmed and off-balance and a little embarrassed, sure she didn't merit this aggressive desire.

As he grabbed for her, the situation seemed out of control. Everything: him, the sex, this relationship, it was all spinning fast and wild, and she couldn't slow it down or stop it. What if there came a time that she didn't want it any more? What then? Would he leave? Could he go from being like this to nothing? Then, as he kissed her, a different fear came. What if he left her? What if he looked at her one day and realized that she was too old, and decided that he wanted to go back to young girls with perky boobs. How could she stand not feeling so beautiful, so sexy, and so desperately needed?

September 9

THEY sat in the empty parlor, her favorite room because it still looked elegant. The stuffed animal Sterling's sisters had given him sat on the mantel, surveying the open space. They sprawled on the floor opposite a huge window that looked onto the porch. Lara sat between his legs, her back leaned against his chest. The two of them did this sometimes, just went into one of the empty rooms and sat, like they were trying to keep little sections of the house from getting lonely.

The rain roared on the roof and thick gray drops spattered against the windows. The parlor filled with a misty green light that didn't cast shadows. For a while now, Sterling had wanted to tell Lara how he felt, but it was hard. He was scared of what she might say. But lying here like this, feeling her breathing, looking at her bare brown legs, he felt stupid for being afraid. After some of the stuff he said while they were doing it, nothing should embarrass him anyway.

"I love you," he said.

She craned her neck around and smiled at him. "I love you too."

A rush of elation. Thunder sounded in the distance. He decided to go on. He cleared his throat. "So, you think you might want to marry me or something?"

"What?" She turned back to the window and let her head fall against his chest.

He cleared his throat again and struggled to get the question out. "You think you maybe might want to get married?"

She laughed like it was funny, the sound cutting into him.

Sterling felt his insides turn to stone. He understood in a flash that he meant nothing to her. "I wasn't joking," he said. He placed his hands on her shoulders, shoved her away, and sprang up.

She looked at him with an innocent expression. "Sterling." She rose. "Come on." She moved toward him with her arm stretched out. "Sterling, come on. Don't be stupid."

If there'd been something else in the room, a chair, a lamp, anything he could have kicked or thrown, it might have been okay, but there was nothing. Just Lara smiling at him like he was a dumb kid who didn't understand anything. "Don't call me stupid," he warned.

"Then stop acting stupid."

He grabbed her arm, jerked her forward and smacked her hard across the face with the open palm of his hand.

Lara reeled back and hunched over. She covered her cheek with her fingers and gaped at him.

The image froze in Sterling's mind like a still photograph.

"Bastard," she said.

"I'm not a bastard! Don't call me that!" He raised his hand to hit her again. She shrank away. For a second, he felt awful and wanted to tell her not to be scared, but before he could say anything, she seized the deformed stuffed animal from the mantel.

"Get out." She hurled the little creature at him. It hit the side of his head, then landed on the floor at his feet. "Get out! Get out!"

What should he do? Leave? Apologize? Hit her again? Leaning over, he picked up the stuffed animal and cradled it in the crook of his arm. When he looked at Lara, she was crying.

He couldn't stand to see her and whirled, strode through the hall, and slammed out the front door. On the porch, he paused. Where should he go? He decided it didn't matter. He just had to get away from here. He ran down the steps and began walking fast toward the street, cuddling the animal to his chest, both of them getting soaked by the storm. A sound behind him, and Lara's door flew open. His book bag, stuffed with clothes, came sailing over the lawn, shedding shirts and pants and underwear in its flight. Then the door slammed shut.

He felt another stab of rage. "Well, fuck you too, you bitch!" he yelled at the closed door. Then he began collecting his wet clothes in the rain.

E R I C was almost asleep in front of the TV when Sterling called. "Hey, man, can I come stay at your place for a while?"

"What happened?"

"Can I just . . . can I just come over? I need a ride."

As he pulled into the gas station parking lot, Eric saw Sterling huddled against the wall. His arms were wrapped around his waist and he was soaked, hair plastered to his forehead, T-shirt wet and transparent, clinging to his chest. Eric stopped the car, leaned across the passenger seat, and pushed open the door so Sterling could climb in.

"Sorry, man, I'm all wet." Sterling tossed his bedraggled pack into the back seat and settled up front with a squishing noise. The heat and humidity from his body began to fog the windshield, so Eric turned on the defroster.

"What happened?"

Sterling shrugged. "Nothing. Just got caught in the rain, is all."

The storm had created a mini-ocean in Eric's pool, the wind kicking up small foamy waves, the rain dimpling the surface. Eric stood in the kitchen looking at the pool while Sterling dropped his backpack on the floor.

"Hey, why don't you go take a hot shower?" Eric said. "The lightning's died down."

"Okay." Sterling hugged himself, shivering.

"Well, go on before you freeze."

Sterling nodded and headed to the bathroom. In a moment, Eric heard the shower start. He stood listening to the water running and to the rain on the roof and wondered if he should call Lara. Part of him felt almost happy. Maybe next time Sterling would listen to him. Maybe next time the kid wouldn't hide things from him. Then he felt bad. Sterling had already had his fair share of pain.

Eric went to his bedroom, fished out a clean T-shirt and some sweatpants, and tossed them into the bathroom.

Sterling emerged a few minutes later, wearing Eric's clothes. He collapsed onto the sofa and propped his bare feet on the coffee table.

"You want a Coke?" Eric asked.

Sterling shook his head and stared at the darkened TV screen.

"Hell of a storm," Eric said. "I had hail right before I came to get you. Did you get any?"

Sterling continued to stare at the TV.

"So, you want to tell me what happened?" Eric asked.

Sterling shook his head.

"I tell you, women are a pain in the ass," Eric said.

Sterling scowled and began to pick at a loose thread in the sofa fabric. Even now he wouldn't confess, and Eric was hurt. Sterling had always told him everything before.

He went to the kitchen, got himself a Coke, and leaned against the counter watching the boy. "I told you she'd tear your heart out and eat it for breakfast, but did you listen to me?"

Sterling shot him a bitter look. "If you're such an expert on women, how come your girlfriend ain't come back from Italy?"

Eric took a swallow of Coke, then said "Touché."

"I feel like killing her," Sterling muttered.

September 12

S TERLING moved back home three days later. After Eric dropped him off, he stood in the driveway, looking at the place where his family lived. It seemed more run-down than he remembered. He unlocked the kitchen door, glad his mama and the girls weren't home yet. It was good to be alone for a while. After he'd unpacked his sack, he collapsed onto his bed and made himself look at the stars on his ceiling and feel nothing.

When he heard his mother's truck in the driveway, he went to the kitchen door and watched her unload the girls and groceries. Dayla spied him, cried "Sterling!" and came running toward him, Darlene at her heels. He hunkered down to embrace the twins, then stood again so his mother could pass.

"Hey," he said to her as she climbed the steps. She remained silent. He took one of her grocery bags, and while the girls swarmed around his legs, he placed it on the kitchen counter and began unloading powdered milk, salt, butter. His mama set her own bag down, then stood with her arms crossed looking at him. He waited for her to say something about Lara, but she didn't.

chapter thirty-one

September 13

T HE day after Sterling returned to his family, Lara called the shop and asked Eric to come over. Dreary shadows lengthened across the road in the humid twilight as he drove into town. As always, after eight o'clock, the streets were almost deserted, the storefronts dark and empty. The pink-tinged street lamps cast lurid pools of light on the cracked sidewalks. It was a creepy place, Eric thought.

Lara's house was creepy too. In the twilight, the sky overhead gleamed deep violet. The moon, haloed by a murky gold aureole, perched on the crest of Lara's tin roof. All of the house's lights were off, and its hulking form blocked out the last rays of sunset. Eric climbed the front steps. He paused by the door, feeling for the bell in the dim light.

"Eric?" Lara's voice came from beside him, and he turned to see her sitting hunched against the porch railing.

"Hey." He walked over to her, straining to see her face in the dark.

She craned her neck to look over her shoulder at a lighted window in the Grier house. A shadow moved behind the Griers' lace curtain.

"She's always watching me," Lara said. "Her or one of Sterling's little girlfriends. Goddamned small towns. . . ."

Eric's foot knocked against an empty bottle, which toppled over and rolled with a hollow sound across the slanted porch.

"I gave up wine for bourbon."

He hunkered down beside her, barely able to make out her features. "Are you okay?" "Is Sterling at your place?" she blurted.

"No, he's back home."

"Great." She pushed herself onto all fours, crawled over to the empty bottle, and seized it. "I need another drink."

She struggled to rise, gripping the porch railing and pulling herself up. Once standing, she swayed unsteadily for a moment, then reeled to the front door.

Eric followed close on her heels, worried she might fall or bump into something. Lara opened the door and disappeared inside.

The house was black and silent. As he stepped in after her, Eric felt swallowed by it. He wondered why she did this to herself. Why this desolate house? Why the heavy drinking? Why the naive kid, when Eric would have loved her and taken care of her?

Lara staggered to the kitchen, not bothering to turn on the fluorescent bulb. He watched her walk to the refrigerator, the sudden wedge of light from the freezer cutting across her chest. The ice cubes clinked loudly as she dropped them into a glass. She got another bottle down from the cabinet and poured herself a generous shot.

"Lara, this is insane." He strode over, snatched the glass and dumped the bourbon down the sink. "Getting drunk is hardly a healthy way to deal."

He waited for her to argue, but instead she brushed by him and wove to the kitchen table, where she sank into a chair. He felt the weight of her misery and sensed the abandon with which she was hurling herself into oblivion. "It's hard to talk to someone in the dark like this," he said as he sat down opposite her. "What did you want to ask me about?"

There was a long pause. He heard her inhale, and she said "I'm leaving. In a month."

Eric was stunned. His first thought was *Good.* Then he considered Sterling. "It's going to kill the kid, you know."

She remained silent.

He realized he also wanted Lara to stay for himself. *She's running away*, he thought, *just like she ran away from Washington.* "I hope you plan to sober up before you drive," he said.

He heard a rustling sound, like paper crumpling, and realized she was sliding something across the table. "Take this," she said. "It's a check I made out to you for ten thousand dollars. Sterling's going to get into college. Promise me you'll make him go. He won't have any excuses with this money."

Eric was incredulous. He shoved the check back to Lara. "What are you doing?"

"I'm giving him money for college."

"What do you mean?" Eric demanded. "Jesus Christ, Lara, why didn't you just pay him up front for the sex? It would have been more honest."

There was a long silence from the other end of the table. The room had grown so dark that Eric could only see the shape of Lara's body across from him. In a low voice, she said "Fuck you."

"Yeah, well, better me than a goddamned teenager."

"You're just jealous."

Eric winced. It was partly true. "Listen, I've spent the last three years trying to turn Sterling into a decent man. And believe me, it hasn't been easy in this town. Here folks measure manhood by how many girls you knock up and how good you are at beating them to keep them in line. And just when he's starting to act like a mature adult, you come along and decide to use him to get over a dead man."

"Just give him the money," she said. "Stop lecturing me when you don't know what you're talking about, and take the goddamned check. Make it seem like it came from someplace other than me, if you want. Just give it to him."

The check sat in the middle of the table. Neither Eric nor Lara touched it.

"I know what's going on," she finally said. "You don't want him to leave. You'd rather have him here in this godforsaken place working that shitty job, dealing with his insane mother, than have him leave you."

The room went cold. "That's not true."

"Yes, it is. He listens to you. But that's exactly why you want him here, so you can feel important. So you can feel like you're doing something worthwhile with your life instead of just hanging around in the middle of nowhere taking pictures that you never try to publish and moping over some girlfriend who dumped you years ago. And when I said you were jealous just now, I didn't mean you were jealous of him, I meant you're jealous of me. You can't stand that Sterling spent time with me instead of you. Listened to me instead of you."

Eric reached out and folded his fingers around the check. "You're full of shit. You don't know what you're talking about." He crumpled the check into a ball. "All I've been trying to do is to keep him from getting used." He tossed the wadded-up check across the table, back to Lara. "Thanks so much, Lara, for giving him such a valuable learning experience about women. I'm sure it'll have great long-term impact on his self-esteem. And yeah, he *is* getting into college, but he'll make it through without your help."

A choking noise came from the back of her throat. She pushed herself up and stumbled into the front hall and out the door. Eric followed her, switching on the porch light so he could see her curled against the railing. Behind her, across the lawn, Pam Grier's lace curtain moved.

Eric swallowed and forced his voice to be calm. "I want to know why you did it, Lara. Did you just want to screw someone to make you feel better? Or maybe you're actually in love with him. Maybe it scares you that you're in love with someone so beneath you."

She took her hands away from her face. In the bright light, he saw the puffy blue bruise on her cheek and his insides went cold. It took a few moments for his confused thoughts to sort themselves out. He reached out to touch the bruise, to test its reality, but Lara flinched away and Eric dropped his hand. He took a deep breath and looked past her driveway to a house across the street. Light spilled from the windows and faint laughter drifted from an open door. "Jesus Christ," he murmured.

She sat silently, shielding the bruise with her fingers, then said "He asked me to marry him. I thought he was joking and laughed. It was insensitive, Eric. I can be such a bitch sometimes. But he's so fragile. He gets hurt at the smallest things, and he just lost it. It came out of nowhere."

Eric leaned back on his heels.

"You look more shocked than I was," Lara said.

He nodded dumbly.

"That's too bad, because I was hoping you'd tell me what to do."

Eric sighed. He moved beside her and leaned against the rail. "I just wish he'd be a kid for a change," he said. "I wish he'd go to parties, or go joy-riding in Atlanta with some friends. I wish Sandy would go on food stamps and give him some freedom. He's never had freedom." They fell silent while Lara wiped at her eyes with the back of her hand.

"What should I do?" she repeated.

"What do you want to do?"

In the porch light, her eyes shone. "I want to take him with me to Washington. I want to get him out of here. Does that sound crazy?"

Eric shook his head. His heart began to pound.

Lara studied his face. "You don't want him to go," she said.

Eric shook his head. "No, I don't." The realization stunned him. Everything Lara had said was right. He sat picking at a splinter on the porch.

"Did I do more harm than good?" Lara asked.

"I don't know." He stood and offered her his hand. She took it and he pulled her up. She raised on her toe tips and kissed his cheek. He smelled bourbon, shampoo, her damp skin. He hugged her tightly. They stood that way for minutes. In the silence, Eric thought of Sterling. He pictured the boy twenty years from now living in Winston, married, with squalling kids and a rundown house, still working at Dairy Queen.

When he finally pushed away from Lara, he'd made up his mind that things had to change. "Are you going to be all right?"

She nodded.

"Okay. Lay off the booze. Make yourself some coffee. I'll talk to him. It'll be okay."

September 14

"LARA'S leaving," Eric said while Sterling stood at the counter leafing through a magazine. The boy froze for a moment, then continued turning pages.

"Hell if I care," Sterling muttered.

"Funny, that," said Eric. "'Cause I kind of think you do." He wandered to the racks and began counting CDs in the A section. "She had a bruise on her face."

A heavy silence came from where Sterling stood.

Eric noted down 15 As and moved on to Bs. "And she was hitting the bottle pretty hard."

An even more palpable silence.

Eric noted down 23 Bs. "I guess you and Dave Grier have more in common than you thought."

"Shut up." Sterling threw down his magazine.

"I guess you showed her. You're a redneck monster. Just like she suspected all along. You don't have to worry about her finding out how bad you are, 'cause now she knows. And you don't have to worry about college 'cause, clearly, you ain't good enough to go."

"It ain't like that."

"Hell, yes, it is. I mean, what's been going on with you lately? You're turning into your own worst nightmare. You like to blame it on Lara, but I think you're just using her as an excuse. You're scared as hell, and anything that doesn't go your way, you freak out. Well, welcome to life as an adult, Sterling. Welcome to having to make hard decisions without knowing exactly what the right choice is. Welcome to the joys of a relationship. You feel scared, you feel vulnerable, and half the time you feel like a fucking idiot. That's the way it works for all of us, not just for you.

"Now, unlike some of the kids around here, you have a real chance to be something other than what this town says you are. You've got the brains, you've got the determination, and I think you've got the guts too. But I can't make you do it, and neither can Lara. Which brings me to my last point. If you want to prove to Lara and to yourself that you're not the loser you've been playing, you should talk to her. You should apologize and hope to God she forgives you, because I don't know if I would."

"I can't."

"Why? Don't you even feel bad about it?"

"God damn it!" Sterling glared at him. "I can't fucking sleep for feeling bad about it. But she doesn't want to see me. She doesn't give a damn about me."

"Well, for someone who doesn't give a damn about you, she was pretty upset. She asked about you and talked about you the whole time I was over there. She cried. And even if she doesn't want to see you, you still owe her an apology."

"I ain't talking to her no more."

"Fine," Eric snapped. "Do what you want. Just don't bitch to me three months from now when she's gone, and you wish you'd said something."

chapter thirty-two

November 10

S TERLING didn't know when he'd started wondering about his daddy's gun, but now he thought about it all the time with a longing that bordered on obsession. He imagined the weight of it in his hand, the feel of the black metal barrel cool under his fingers. If he closed his eyes, he could hear the clicking sound of the bullets sliding into the chamber, could feel the solidity of the grip, the hard tastelessness of the barrel in his mouth.

It was so much easier thinking about the gun than about Lara. And the thought of the gun came just as readily to him these days. On afternoons when he was alone in the house, he'd go to the living room and stare at his father's locked gun cabinet, and he'd wonder where his mother had hidden the key. With the dim light slanting through the window, he'd rummage through his mother's underwear drawer, through the hall closet where she hung her clothes, through the kitchen cabinets.

He found keys. Little delicate keys to long-gone jewelry boxes. Thick fat keys to ancient chests of drawers that other people must have owned. Keys to his father's car, spare keys to the rig, keys to their old house in town that had three bedrooms, two baths, central heat, and a back yard where his father would toss him baseballs and where he hit one and broke the kitchen window on a Sunday afternoon many springs ago.

He found the box of bullets behind dull knives and plastic corn holders in a drawer in the kitchen. Cradling the box, he took it into his bedroom and spilled the bullets onto his desk. They were dull and coppery, heavy, cold. He set them on their ends so they pointed upward in rounded peaks. He pretended they were stars and moved them around to form constellations in the August sky. Enif, Markab, the same August sky that still hung on the ceiling in Lara's bedroom.

When he was done arranging them, Sterling sat on his bed and looked at them. He kept the desk covered with bullet constellations like that for three days, becoming half-hysterical when a bullet would fall, roll, knock down other bullets, and he'd have to start over again. Drawing deep racking breaths, trying to keep his hands from shaking, he replaced each star dotingly in its proper position.

The decision to give up on finding the key to the gun cabinet came to him at one of those moments, when his hands were shaking so hard that he couldn't reset the bullets, and he broke down crying from frustration. Suddenly he thought *Why do I need the key, anyway?*

Within a minute he was bashing at the gun cabinet lock with his aluminum baseball bat, using vicious swings that splintered and dented the wood and filled the house with loud hollow thuds.

The lock flew off and the cabinet door swung open. Sterling reached up and felt along the top shelf for the pistol. His hand searched the smooth wood, deep back, up and down. But the pistol wasn't there. He felt like he was in a dream where he had to get something quick but, no matter what he did or how hard he tried, he couldn't find what he was looking for. The rifle was in the long center section of the cabinet. He bent down and rooted underneath it. The rifle wouldn't work; he needed the pistol. Where the hell in the name of God and Jesus was the fucking pistol?

He stood up again on his toes and looked for it on the top shelf. The shelf was empty. Sterling started crying. Why couldn't one thing go right for him? All he wanted was the goddamned pistol. Was that too much to ask? He knew it had been there when they moved, had seen his mother place it on the top shelf and lock the cabinet four years ago, the image vivid in his memory, his daddy's guns left behind, just like he'd left his family behind.

The energy went out of Sterling's legs and he sank to the floor. The room rocked around him while he gulped deep breaths and tried to think. He sat for ten minutes with his mind reeling through a fog of desperation. Where the hell was the gun? Should he look outside? Something nagged at the back of his mind, something he should realize or remember. He sat there trying to pin down that prickling sensation, trying to weave in and out of all his other crazy thoughts and focus. And then, suddenly, he did.

It took him five minutes crawling, because he couldn't find the legs to stand, to reach the door, and from there he staggered to George MacKnight's gas station and called Eric.

CAPTAIN EDGARS fantasized about settling down in the La-Z-Boy and turning on the TV. He dreamed of the familiar groove in the chair bottom, and how he'd push himself back until the footrest popped out and he could prop up his legs. With the drone of Dan Rather in the background and the clinking sound of Mary rinsing supper dishes, he'd close his eyes and doze.

Instead, he sat at his desk, the room around him obscured by the omnipresent piles of paperwork, and he tore open an envelope from Lara's father. Dozens of pieces of paper fluttered out, copies of e-mail Lara had written to family and friends, opened envelopes with her letters, all containing information Mr. Walton thought might be relevant. It would take Edgars hours to go through this stuff, and it was eight already. Mary had long since eaten, and the supper dishes would be clean by now.

He began perusing Lara Walton's e-mail, five copies of the same letter to friends suggesting that they finger Dave Grier if she were to "turn up dead or missing." Next he found a note to her parents mentioning the hole in the basement and how easy it would be for someone to slide through. Edgars thought of the fibers they had collected clinging to the stone around that hole. He cursed the crime lab for taking so long.

Gulping cold coffee, he tried to stop thinking about the crime lab so he could clear his head and move on. He reached for an envelope and examined the front. It was addressed to Lara's parents and bore Lara's name and an address in Arlington, Virginia on the return label. Edgars noticed that it hadn't been postmarked. She must have died before getting the chance to mail it. It was a short letter, and the date on the top read October 11, the day before her death.

Edgars began to read Lara Walton's thin, scrawling handwriting. He got to the eighth sentence, stopped, began from the beginning, and read it again to make sure his eyes weren't playing tricks on him. They weren't. He was halfway to the door when the phone on his desk began to ring. He paused, exasperated; then, striding back to his desk, he snatched the receiver and snarled "What?"

"Sir, there's a call for you."

"Tell them I'm busy."

"It's Eric Teague. He says it's urgent."

Edgars stared at the letter. His heart was racing. "Eric Teague?"

"Yes, sir. He sounded pretty upset."

"Okay, put him through. But after I'm done talking to him, I don't want to be bothered, understand?" A click, and Edgars said "What can I do for you, Mr. Teague?"

"I was wondering if you might come out to my place. Sterling O'Connor is here, and he has something he needs to tell you."

"That's interesting, because I've got some stuff I need to ask him. How about bringing him by the station?"

"I can't. He's not doing too good. Just please come by. You need to hear what he's got to say."

Stretching the cord until it threatened to pull the phone off the desk, Edgars reached for his coat. "I'm on my way, but keep him there. I need you to make sure he doesn't leave."

*   *   *

CAPTAIN EDGARS pulled into Eric Teague's driveway. He'd called three uniformed patrols to wait down the street, and he passed one of them on his way in. This was a strange moment for Edgars. On the brink of solving the case, he was excited and almost happy, but at the same time he felt very sorry for how it was going to turn out. He wondered if some families were just cursed.

Outside, the air was dank and chilly. Dry leaves skitted across the path as he picked his way to Eric's front door. A gust of wind rattled bare branches. Eric had turned on his porch light. Edgars pulled his coat collar tighter around his neck. As he raised a fist to knock, Eric opened the door. Warm light from the living room spilled out behind him. Eric looked drained. He barely glanced at Edgars, then stepped aside so the captain could enter.

"Thanks for coming."

Edgars looked around Eric's narrow living room. The walls were covered with photographs. He peered to his right, into the kitchen. Sterling was nowhere to be seen.

"Where's the boy?"

"In the bathroom," Eric said in a low voice. "He's puking."

Edgars heard the sound of a toilet flushing, and then the bathroom door opened and Sterling stepped out. They boy pressed a hand against the wall like he didn't quite have his balance. Below his weird frosted hair, Sterling's face was bloodless white. He began inching toward Edgars, feeling his way along the wall like a blind man. Eric went to him and reached out, but Sterling hunched away.

"The captain's here," Eric murmured. "Why don't you come on and sit down. I'll make some tea."

Sterling didn't respond, but continued his shaky forward motion, wobbling through the long living room and into the kitchen. While Eric set a kettle on to boil, Sterling sank into a chair at the table, and Captain Edgars sat down opposite him. Edgars thought about the morning of their first interview and how the boy had looked like a caged animal. Edgars thought about how Mary liked this kid and said he was smart and mature. Edgars looked at this poor wasted boy and thought about how well and how smoothly he'd lied.

He wanted to be angry with Sterling. If the boy had just told the truth from the start, it would have saved Edgars a lot of time and energy. Still, looking at Sterling hunched across from him, eyes unfocused, he understood why the kid hadn't said a word. In a town like this, it was so hard to protect yourself and those things you held most dear from public meanness and scrutiny.

The kettle whistled. Eric poured the steaming water into three mugs. Edgars was willing to bet Eric knew more than he ever volunteered. Eric brought the tea, setting a mug in front of Edgars and one in front of Sterling. Edgars leaned over and inhaled the damp peppermint aroma.

"Well," he said. "I'm ready to hear what you have to say, son." He remembered how the boy had objected to being called son, but now Sterling didn't seem to notice as he curled his index finger around the mug's handle and stared blankly ahead.

"Mr. O'Connor. . . ." Edgars urged.

"I did it," Sterling blurted out.

"Whoa, whoa." Eric had been walking to the table with his own mug of tea, but stopped dead when he heard Sterling's proclamation. "Hold on. Sterling, what are you talking about? Captain, this—"

Edgars held up his hand. "Let me hear the boy out."

"But—"

"Mr. Teague, let me hear what he's got to say. Then you can talk." He turned back to Sterling. "Go on, son."

"That's it. I killed her. You can arrest me now."

Edgars squinted at him. The finger that curled around the mug handle was trembling, along with the rest of the boy's hand. Part of Edgars wanted to come clean, to tell Sterling he'd already figured out what happened, but he knew this way was better. Hearing this confession was how it had to be done. "Why'd you do it?" Edgars asked.

"Captain—" Eric began.

"Mr. Teague, let me hear him out, or I'm going to have to ask you to step outside."

Eric sank into a chair next to Sterling and rested his head in his hands.

"Why'd you kill her, Mr. O'Connor?"

"I—I was real confused. Real angry at her."

"Why was that?" Even now, thought Edgars, the boy was choosing his words. "Was it because she was leaving?"

Sterling glanced at him almost gratefully, "Yeah, that was it. She was leaving."

"Why'd that upset you so much?" Edgars took a sip of tea.

"I guess, see, I guess it was because I liked her."

"You liked her? What do you mean?"

"I mean I liked her. You know what I mean."

"You mean you were in love with her?"

Sterling hung his head and nodded.

"So you shot her?"

"Because she was leaving. I got mad 'cause she was leaving."

"Okay." Edgars took another sip of tea. It was hot and burned his lips. "Where'd you get the gun?"

"It was in Daddy's gun cabinet. Mama keeps it locked all the time on account of the girls, but I found the key."

Edgars fished in his pocket for his notepad, then scribbled *gun cabinet.*

"I shot her with a .38 pistol."

"So where's the gun now?"

Sterling gaped as if he hadn't understood the question.

"Did you take it home? Did you throw it away?"

"I threw it in the Oconee river."

"Where in the river?"

"Just, you know, in the water."

"I mean what part of the river?"

"Oh, uh, down near Athens, on that bridge on the Atlanta highway. I drove out there that night and threw it off the bridge."

"So let me ask you this, Mr. O'Connor. Why'd you wait all this time to confess? It's been a long time. Why now?"

Sterling stared hard into his mug. "Guess I was just scared."

"I can't believe this," Eric muttered.

"Scared of going to jail?"

"I guess. Maybe I didn't really remember doing it until just today."

"Didn't remember, huh? So what shook your memory?"

"I don't know. I just all of a sudden remember doing it."

"You do? That's pretty amazing. Sounds like something out of one of them crime thriller movies, huh?" Edgars laughed and Eric glared at him. "So, what do you remember? If you're gonna confess, I need all the details."

"Details?" Sterling glanced desperately at Eric.

"The details. Come on." Edgars began drumming his fingers on the kitchen table. "I ain't got all day, son."

"Okay. I—I," Sterling stammered. "I went over there and shot her."

"How did you get in?"

"She let me in, and we had a fight, and I shot her."

"Where were you when you shot her?"

"In the hallway."

"So you shot her in the hallway because you fought?"

"Yeah."

"And what were you fighting about?"

Sterling paused. He studied the captain as if wanting to gauge whether Edgars believed him or not. "About her leaving."

Edgars shifted in his chair and wrapped his fingers around the mug of tea to warm them. "And she was facing you when you shot her?"

"Facing me? Yeah, I guess so."

"You guess? Don't you remember?"

"Not exactly. Yeah. I think she was facing me."

"And how many times did you shoot her?"

"I don't know. Can't remember."

Edgars felt a headache coming on and squeezed the bridge of his nose between his thumb and finger. "And you're sure that's how it happened?"

"Yessir. I shot her and you can arrest me now." Sterling looked Edgars right in the eye, his jaw set so he looked twice his age. God, Edgars thought, when this kid makes up his mind to do something. . . .

"Can I talk now?" Eric asked.

"Don't do it, man," Sterling hissed.

Edgars fixed Sterling with a sharp look. "Lord, son," he said. In that moment, as Sterling's eyes met Edgars's, an understanding passed between them, and Sterling, recognizing it, slumped in the chair.

"Just arrest me," he muttered. "I want you to. Can't you just arrest me?"

Edgars shook his head. "I can't do it that way. I'm sorry." He pushed himself up and looked at Eric, "You got a phone I could use?"

"What?" Eric looked startled. "You can't arrest him."

"I'm not arresting him." He glanced around the kitchen and spied a phone on the wall. "You got a phone more private than that one?"

"He's lying, you know," Eric said as he led Edgars back to his bedroom.

"Hell, I know that." Edgars stepped into Eric's room and went to the phone on the nightstand. "I know more about how the murder happened than that kid does. Now if you'll excuse me for a minute?"

After Eric left, Edgars called Bill. Keeping his voice low he said, "Get down to the station. Meet me there in twenty minutes. If you get there before me, call Judge Dixon for a search warrant for Sterling O'Connor's house and truck. I need it tomorrow, first thing."

EDGARS hung up and stood for a moment trying to order his thoughts. He needed to get more from Sterling, but he was also worried about the kid. What was the best way to shield him from what was coming? As he opened the bedroom door, he saw Eric in the hall. Edgars motioned him over and whispered "Can you keep him here until tomorrow night?"

"He has to work."

"I'd rather him hang around here. I'm going to search his house."

Eric slumped against the wall. "How'd you figure it out?"

Edgars shrugged. "I got more evidence."

Eric raked a hand over his head.

Edgars looked toward the kitchen. "So you'll keep him here?"

"Yeah, of course. I just won't open up tomorrow."

"If you could give me a few minutes alone with him, I'm going to try to get the truth out of him this time."

Back at the kitchen table, Edgars lowered himself into the chair opposite Sterling and sat for a moment looking at the boy. Sterling's jaw was clenched, his eyes fixed on the table. To the captain, he looked very young.

Edgars' throat felt tight all of a sudden, and he found himself suppressing a wash of emotion, his eyes itching as if he might cry. He gripped the mug of tea and brought it to his mouth, swallowing a few times until the feeling passed. Finally, he took a deep breath, and, folding his hands on the table, said "I'm about to ask you to talk about something that's gonna be hard. I need for you to tell me the truth about Lara Walton. And I promise you I'll do my best to keep the details private. Things might have to come out in court, but I'll do my best to protect your privacy, because I know privacy's been damned hard for you to come by."

chapter thirty-three

October 11

LARA was driving through town when she saw Sterling in the distance, walking balanced on a railroad track. She pulled her car into a deserted gravel lot nearby and waited as he approached. He jumped from one track to the other, waving his arms to keep his balance. Occasionally, he paused to kick at anemic daisies or blades of grass jutting between the ties. An anomaly in the wasted landscape, she thought, this bright kid, frosted hair gleaming white. Lara waited and watched, wondering if he'd see her and be willing to talk.

She remembered the feel of his back under her fingers. How the skin at his hip was so soft. The damp sheets. The taste of his mouth. The sensation of waking up after a long sleep. *I'm alive because of him,* she thought.

Watching Sterling, Lara knew she'd pulled him through that moment between childhood and adulthood just as Dylan had pulled her. She remembered again the fight with her father on the day she'd left home, and crying in Dylan's arms that night.

"Shhh." Dylan had stroked her back. "It's okay. You're an adult now. You don't have to listen to him any more."

But she hadn't been an adult. She'd only been twenty. She'd been starry-eyed from her first love, and naive. Dylan was an older man telling her how mature she was, and she'd been silly enough to believe him.

When Sterling saw Lara leaning against her little white Toyota with the U-Haul hooked up to it, he stopped, took a few steps backwards, and fell off the railroad track. He stepped in a glob of tar that oozed out under his sneaker. When he lifted his foot, the tar sucked at the shoe's sole.

"Shit." He tried to scrape the tar off on the gravel between the ties. Wasn't it just like Lara to make him fuck up a pair of tennis shoes?

"Sterling!" He heard her voice, realized he'd almost forgotten what it sounded like, the flat clipped way she said his name. He looked up and saw that she'd stepped away from her car and stood with her arms limp at her sides. Behind her rose the rickety tower of an abandoned brick warehouse. The wooden roof had caved in, the windows were boarded, the bricks covered with a chalky white film.

"Sterling!" she called again, more urgently and he felt the rumble under his feet. The train was behind him, still a ways off but coming fast. He leaped from the track and backed away toward Lara, as the train's whistle burst the air. In a minute the locomotive passed with a rush of wind, boxcars creaking and rumbling after it.

The train separated the gravel lot from the rest of the world. The old brick warehouse closed the lot in on the other side. The tower cut a long shadow across the gravel, and Sterling stood in that shadow trying not to look at Lara. But all his senses fixed on her so that even the metallic shrieking of the train's wheels seemed quiet.

She moved toward him slowly. He vowed not to look at her, not even to talk to her. How had she found him, anyway? Then he remembered the secretive call Eric had made right as he was leaving the store. It pissed him off. The least Eric could do was to be on his side.

He saw movement out of the corner of his eye as Lara approached. His stomach clenched. He recalled how she'd laughed at his proposal and felt himself getting angry again, aching inside. Another step and she was right beside him. *Trapped,* he thought. *I can't leave, but I can't make myself say anything or do anything either.* He shoved his hands in his pockets and began rocking back and forth. Neither of them spoke until the train had passed.

"If you'll let me, I want to explain why I can't marry you right now," she said.

His heart surged at the sound of her voice. It was the low serious tone she used to comfort him. Only now he didn't want to be comforted. He rolled his eyes to the sky, which was fading from pink to orange. A few thin clouds floated overhead. He tried to think about how there were more clouds now that fall was coming.

"Will you let me explain?" she said. "Because I don't want you to think it meant nothing to me."

Damn, he wished she'd just admit it, admit that she didn't love him, that all she'd wanted was someone to make her forget about the dead guy in Washington. Sterling thought he'd tell her what a horrible person she was, how he hoped she'd go away and never come back because he'd never think about her again without feeling sick. But then he looked at her.

The bruise on her cheek was gone, but Sterling could imagine it like blood on snow.

Lara's pretty mouth hung open as she waited for his answer. Tiny beads of sweat stood out on her forehead and upper lip. It hurt to look at her, so Sterling turned away. The sun was sinking, and shadows began to fold out from the buildings lining the tracks. The lot became a checkerboard of shadow and light.

"When I was twenty, I fell in love with a man who was nine years older than me," she said. "And we were good together, but he died. And then I realized that I was so young when I met him, I never figured out who I was, or what I wanted. Between him and my father, I don't know if I ever made an adult decision on my own. And when he died, I just fell apart. I'd never been alone before. I had no idea what to do."

She fell silent. Sterling's mind raced forward, trying to anticipate where she was headed so he could brace himself.

"I'm scared of doing the same thing to you." She looked down at her feet. "You're young. You've got all this potential, all this stuff you could do. When you asked me about getting married, well, I laughed because I didn't think you were serious. I couldn't believe you'd want to be tied down to anyone, least of all me."

He didn't know what to do. Her mouth puckered and her eyes grew damp. Her lashes clumped to sharp wet points. "I never wanted to hurt you," she said. "I meant what I said about loving you. But I can't get married right now. I'm too much of a mess. I've still got a lot to work through, a lot of growing up to do. And you do too."

Sterling suddenly understood that Eric was right; relationships made you feel vulnerable and scared. Lara felt scared and unsure just the way he did. Sterling's mouth began trembling. He tried hard to keep it still.

"I'm sorry for hitting you," he croaked. "I shouldn't never've done it. I just. . . ." He turned his face away, ashamed that he was crying. She took his hand, and they stood silently looking down the tracks at the train, which had become a small speck in the distance.

Lara leaned her shoulder against his. "The thing is, I miss you. I don't know what to do. I don't want to let you go." She paused. "I think, I don't know—I think maybe I don't even deserve to have you."

Sterling put an arm around her shoulders. In the silence that followed, he thought about himself. About how many years he'd lived worrying that there was something wrong with him. Something horrible no one would tell him about. Something that drove people away. Now, standing beside Lara, he realized that everyone felt that way sometimes.

"Don't be sad," he said to Lara, only he was saying it to himself also. "You didn't do anything wrong. There's nothing to be sad about."

He lowered his face to hers, feeling her warm breath, smelling her baby powder smell. He kissed her to comfort her, to comfort them both. And she kissed him back the same way. He got lost in kissing her. The familiar taste of her mouth, the way she moved her lips against his so it tickled.

Someone honked.

A few cars crossed the tracks, the drivers gaping.

"We're making a scene," Lara breathed.

"I don't care." He kissed her again, pressed himself hard against her, not able to get enough of how her body felt. He didn't want to stop or let go because she had the U-Haul and was leaving soon, but another car honked and he pushed away. More traffic passed, more drivers stared. Someone yelled his name. Behind Lara, his little town looked depressing. Even the cracks in the sidewalks, the old dogs draped across porch steps, made him feel tired and sad.

In that instant, he knew he'd ask to go with her and that she'd let him. He took a breath. "Eric said you're leaving tomorrow."

"I meant to talk to you about that, I—"

"Thing is," he interrupted. "I want to come along."

THE girls had already eaten by the time Sterling got home. They came padding in from the living room while his mother silently dished up biscuits and fried potatoes, then set them in front of him. He tried hard to eat, knowing that it softened her up, but his mouth had gone dry, and the food felt thick and sticky so he could barely swallow. He took a bite and wrestled it down his throat, then took a sip of tea and said to himself *okay, now, tell her.* But he got scared.

The girls were sleepy and hung around his chair for only a few minutes before returning to the living room to watch TV. *Say it now,* he told himself, but couldn't. Instead, he finished dinner, and she took his plate to the sink and began washing it.

With her back turned to him, it seemed easier.

"See," he faltered. "See, Mama, the thing is that I'm leaving tomorrow."

She kept on washing at first, like she hadn't heard.

"I'm going out of town. I found this job, out of state, and it pays real good so I could send more money home, but I gotta leave to work it."

Still she kept washing that one plate, scrubbing hard even though it was already clean. Finally, she said, in a low voice, "Half the town seen you kissing that woman today."

"Mama, I'm going away and I'm gonna write and send you all money. I can't stay here forever. I'm not going to. I got some money saved up, and I'm giving you all of it. It should hold you until I can send my first paycheck."

His mother began to sink like a balloon with a leak, wrinkling and going soft. Her legs crumpled and she slumped to the floor. Sterling sat rooted in the chair, watching her curl into a ball. She began to sob, silent racking sobs with her mouth hanging open. He felt his own throat closing up. For the first time, it really hit him, what he was doing. He was leaving them. He wouldn't be there to look after them any more.

Sterling stood, walked over, and knelt in front of her. He tried to think of something to say, but couldn't.

He should stay. It wasn't right to leave. But then he thought about Lara and Washington, D.C. He thought about college, and it seemed he couldn't decide anything one way or the other, so he just knelt there. His mother began a low wailing that brought the girls from the living room, wide-eyed and pale. They came to stand beside Sterling, and he wrapped an arm around each of them and hugged them close.

"Mama?" Darlene asked.

"It's okay," said Sterling. "Mama's sad right now. Y'all just let her be sad."

"Why are you sad, Mama?"

"She's sad 'cause I'm leaving," Sterling said. "I'm going out of town for a while, but I'm gonna write you two every day and I'm gonna send you presents, and I'll be back to visit at Christmas time."

Their mouths turned down, and Darlene began to cry.

Sterling stood, his stomach churning. "I'm gonna go pack, Mama. I'm leaving tomorrow morning, first thing. I ain't told the folks at Dairy Queen yet, but I'll talk to them tomorrow on my way out of town. Eric already knows. I'll get him to give you my last paycheck. It may be a while before I can get another one to you, but I'll send one as fast as I can." He started down the hall, then turned and came back. "I'm sorry. I love you guys, you know."

He left his sisters huddled against his weeping mother and closed the door to his room. He began packing, feeling as low as he'd ever felt, thinking he should stay. But deep inside, he knew he couldn't.

Sterling pulled some T-shirts from the bureau. Half of them were too small and he put them back. He felt like a snake sloughing its skin, shedding the trappings of a life he'd outgrown. At that moment, he didn't know quite who he was. But he understood that if he stayed in this town one day longer, he'd never get away, and all he'd ever be was Sandy O'Connor's bastard son.

After he packed, Sterling lay on his bed, wanting to talk with the girls one last time. But he couldn't stand to see their sad faces, or his mother's, so he remained in his room.

He fell asleep at ten-thirty, an exhausted sleep where he dreamed almost nonstop, dreamed about the warehouse and the railroad tracks, dreamed about Lara walking away, and he didn't wake up until he heard the pounding on the door, and thought it was Lara come to get him. Two hours later, he sat in the police station interrogation room trying to remember the first time he'd seen Lara, while, across from him, Captain Edgars waited.

chapter thirty-four

November 10

WHILE Eric and Captain Edgars talked in hushed voices in the living room, Sterling sat at the kitchen table, remembering his last night with Lara.

After he was through helping her load boxes, he drank two glasses of lukewarm water, then headed toward the front door. The idea of telling his mother about leaving weighed on him. Lara followed him silently, and they paused in her foyer. The rose-colored light from the street lamp outside streamed through the open door behind him. Lara stood in his shadow. The shell of a house was even emptier now, but the pink light glowing on the walls made it seem enchanted.

With her body in shadow, surrounded by the soft glow, Lara seemed enchanted too. As he stood looking at her, for the first time ever Sterling didn't want sex. He felt close to her in a different way. He reached out and she did too, bridging the distance between them with their arms. He gripped her hand, brought it to his lips, and kissed it, her fingers pale in the dim light. He remembered how she stood with her arm reaching toward him, her white fingers stretched wide. Then he turned around and walked out the door.

He hadn't said goodbye.

"Sterling," Eric called.

He wanted to scream with frustration. The vision of Lara standing with her arm outstretched had seemed so real that Sterling could almost remember what it felt like to touch her.

"Sterling," Eric repeated. "How about staying here for a few days?"

Sterling looked at Eric and the captain who stood in the living room. The captain frowned. Eric looked worried. It brought the cold weight of reality down on his shoulders again. There was no running away from this. He set his jaw.

"I want my sisters here," Sterling addressed Edgars. "If you arrest Mama, I want my sisters with me."

T HE search warrant was ready the next morning, and Edgars himself went through Sandy's things. He found a key to the busted-open gun cabinet inside a sock in her underwear drawer. On the floor of the closet, he found a size seven woman's shoe, the print exactly matching that found outside Lara Walton's house.

Edgars didn't want to embarrass Sandy, didn't want to make a scene, but he had to have officers with him just in case. He tried to pick a time in the mid-afternoon when there wouldn't be many people at the Quickie Mart. He arrived there first, pulling his car onto the new blacktop, waiting for two cruisers to join him. Sandy wouldn't know they were arresting her, because they came in like this for coffee almost every afternoon.

After the officers arrived, Edgars walked through the door, and, as he'd done so many times before, saw Sandy behind the register. She was wiping off the countertop with a dingy rag. She looked at him and smiled weakly.

"My boy's gone missing," she said. "You ain't seen him, have you?"

"He's at Eric Teague's place, along with your girls."

Sandy looked startled. She studied his face and something in his expression must have told her everything, because her head dropped and she pressed her hands against the counter to steady herself.

"Oh," she said.

Edgars had expected something from her—an excuse, a justification, tears, denial—but Sandy fell as still and silent as a corpse.

She confessed everything at the station in a quiet, resigned way. She didn't ask about Sterling or the girls. Didn't do anything but answer questions in a monotone with details so precise that Edgars was left with no doubt as to her guilt.

She had gone to Eckerd's at around eleven. She'd bought cough syrup, the nighttime kind that was supposed to help you sleep. Then she went home and gave the girls enough to knock them out for a while. She wasn't worried about Sterling waking, because, as she'd told the captain, he always slept hard. Sometime around one-thirty, Sandy had driven the truck to Lara Walton's house. The light from the street lamp out front, and Sterling's descriptions of the place, were enough to allow her to find the hole in the foundation. She'd pulled on a pair of rubber washing gloves, slipped through the hole, and stood in the knee-deep water waiting for her eyes to adjust to the dark. A few slivers of light shining through cracks in the floorboards above had allowed Sandy to find the basement stairs. She ascended them and stood in the hallway on the first floor.

The hall light was on, and, through the second-floor stair rail, she could see a dim light shining above. She climbed the risers and crept toward the light. Getting the gun ready in her right hand, she peeked around the corner into Lara Walton's bedroom. Lara was asleep with the light on, her back to the door. It was an easy shot—Lara was only five feet away—and Sandy took it, emptying the gun into Lara's head and shoulders. She then fled out the back door and down the three blocks to where she had parked her truck. She drove to the landfill, stuffed the pistol in a garbage bag, and hurled it over the fence. When she returned home, the twins and Sterling were still sleeping soundly.

Edgars jotted down the details on his notepad even though the recorder was running. It gave him something to focus on aside from Sandy. She listed the details calmly, but Edgars understood that as she'd leveled the gun at the back of Lara Walton's head, Sandy had believed she had no other choice.

When she was through talking, the captain let his eyes come to rest on her face. "Your boy almost went to jail for what you did," he said.

Sandy fixed her gaze on the table in front of her. "I wouldn't have let that happen. All I ever wanted was for him to be at home for his sisters."

"And for you too." Edgars said.

Sandy paused, then nodded. "For me, too."

Edgars sighed. "That boy's not your husband," he said. "It's a natural thing for boys his age to leave home. A good mother would have let him go."

Sandy hung her head and didn't reply.

November 19

"THERE'S a new rumor going around," Mary said as she sat down opposite the captain at the kitchen table.

"What's that?" Edgars thought about how nice it was to be eating dinner at home again.

"Myrna Lloyd at the dry cleaner said you didn't really solve the Walton murder at all. She said you hired a retired FBI agent from New York to come down and do it for you."

Edgars smiled. "That explains a lot. For a while there I couldn't walk down the street without every other person stopping and congratulating me. That ain't been a problem in the last few days. I was wondering what was going on."

Mary studied him. "So you aren't upset?"

Edgars paused.

"You know, I stopped by Dairy Queen the other day," he said. "I just wanted to see how Sterling O'Connor was doing. The place was packed, more crowded than I've ever seen it, and to a man everyone in there was staring at the kid. I caught his eye, and winked, you know, tried to give him some encouragement. Bob, the manager, said business has been up fifty percent since we arrested Sandy."

Mary stabbed her salad with her fork. "Some people. . . ." she muttered.

"Yeah, well, the town ain't had this much excitement since Sherman came through. So I guess I can handle a little rumor or two. Seeing Sterling O'Connor the other day puts my troubles in perspective."

"I think that boy has lived his whole life putting other people's troubles into perspective," Mary said.

November 22

Dear Mr. Teague,

Thank you so much for your kind words during this difficult time, and for the lovely pictures that you sent. The photographs capture Lara's spirit, and we are grateful to have them. We must also thank you for your candid explanation of the events leading up to our daughter's death. Although Captain Edgars was very forthcoming, we still had many questions, which you helped to answer. Lara mentioned your name in an e-mail she sent to her father, and commented about your warmth and generosity, and your abilities as a photographer. It eases our minds to know that she had such a good friend during her months in your town.

Finally, as to your desire to know more about Lara's funeral, her body was cremated in Atlanta and we brought her remains back to Washington with us. Lara always loved the ocean, and on our next trip to the beach, we plan to scatter her ashes along the Atlantic coast where she spent many happy hours as a child. We have enclosed a copy of her obituary, as well as a copy of her final letter to us (never mailed) which pertains to Mr. O'Connor, and which we feel he might want to see. Please tell Mr. O'Connor that he is now obligated to do something positive with his life, and also to keep our daughter alive in his memory.

Sincerely,
Regina and Hinton Walton.

November 25

E RIC shared only a few details of Lara's obituary with Sterling. He didn't think the boy could handle more than that. Sterling dragged in to work and took care of the girls, but he no longer laughed and barely spoke.

Eric stood in the CD store some days remembering how he'd tried to keep Lara and Sterling apart, and all the things he'd done to discourage Sterling from leaving town over the years.

Two weeks after Sandy's arrest, Sterling and his sisters were still living with Eric. He woke in the mornings to find all three kids huddled asleep on the sofa-bed in the living room with the TV running. He stared down at them, shook his head and thought *I've taken in orphans.*

Sterling ate when he wasn't hungry and pretended to sleep when he couldn't so that the twins would do the same. But then, a few days later, the Department of Family and Children's Services called. Eric watched from the living room as Sterling talked on the kitchen phone, his face dark, his voice rising. "Paula's just their *cousin.* I'm their brother! I'm eighteen. I'm old enough to take care of them!"

Two days later, on a rainy Friday afternoon, Sterling led Dayla and Darlene out of the house, holding one little hand in each of his. The girls clutched small pink backpacks stuffed with their clothes, and already their faces were tear-stained. Sterling's eyes were red, his jaw tight. Eric watched Sterling open the passenger door and help the girls into the truck.

The boy returned alone two hours later. He strode through the living room where Eric lay watching a football game.

"Hey, you okay?" Eric sat up.

Sterling shot him a bitter look, "Yeah, I'm great. I got no one now."

He disappeared down the hall into the bathroom. Eric followed him and knocked on the door. "The girls are just six miles down the road. You can see them any time. And I'm still here."

Sterling didn't respond, so Eric left him alone. He didn't come out of the bathroom for over an hour.

December 7

A week later, the O'Connor house was rented out, and Sterling began boxing up things and moving them into Eric's garage.

chapter thirty-five

March 13

S TERLING was still living with Eric in March and showed no
signs of leaving. He visited his sisters when he could, and continued to work the longest hours he could get. But he wasn't the
same kid he used to be, and Eric was worried.

One evening, Sterling came in and dropped an envelope onto the
coffee table in front of Eric. It was unopened, but black lettering
across the front read OFFICIAL ACCEPTANCE ENCLOSED. Eric put down
his magazine and touched the envelope. The University of Georgia
was the return address.

"You got in," he said.

Sterling turned and walked to the window.

"Hey, get your jacket on. Let's drive to Athens."

"No, man, I don't feel like it."

"I don't care if you don't feel like it," Eric said. "We're going anyway. Come on."

It was a cold, bright Wednesday afternoon and crowded in downtown Athens, but Eric found a place to park. He slid some change into
the meter while Sterling watched from the sidewalk, hands shoved
deep in his jacket pockets as he stamped his feet against the chill.

They passed through the wrought-iron gates that marked the campus boundary and found themselves between white-columned buildings and giant oak trees. Eric glanced at Sterling as the boy fixed his

eyes on the ground and sent an acorn spinning away with a kick. In the center of the campus, the path opened to a brick courtyard where a fountain sprayed out a blossom of water. Here Sterling stopped and collapsed onto an iron bench. Eric sat down beside him as Sterling wiped his nose with the back of a hand and stared at the water.

Eric thought back on the last four years, on all the conversations he'd had with Sterling. All the times he'd helped the boy with homework and lectured him on girls. *Hell,* Eric thought, *I love the kid. I should have made him leave the second he graduated from high school. And maybe if I hadn't been so selfish, and so goddamned scared of what everyone in town would say, I could have helped him more. I should have helped him more.*

Eric looked at the boy slumped on the bench, legs stretched out in front of him. "You know, I don't want to lose my best employee, but you need to do this, Sterling. You need to get your education."

"Don't have the money." Sterling didn't even glance at a group of cute girls walking by.

"There's financial aid. There are scholarships." He paused. "Hell, I have some money set aside. I'll help you out."

"I can't take your money," Sterling said.

"I'm not talking about giving it to you." Eric tried to sound sterner than he felt. "You're going to work it off during the summer." Eric waited for a moment, then said, "So, you start college next fall."

Sterling shook his head. "Naw, man."

"It's not your fault, you know," Eric voiced what he knew Sterling was thinking. "What happened isn't your fault."

Sterling shot him a bitter glance. "If I hadn't decided to go to Washington with Lara, she wouldn't be dead, and Mama wouldn't be in jail. I should have told Lara no. I should have stayed home and looked after my family."

"So you're going to punish yourself, is that it? You have this great opportunity to improve your life and help your sisters, and you're going to blow it, just to spite yourself." Eric felt something catch in his throat. "Listen," he lowered his voice. "I'm making you go to college. I don't care if I have to hogtie you and cart you over here to register. See, you don't have to feel guilty about anything, because I'm not giving you a choice. You're going to college."

Sterling looked startled. Then he shifted and ran a finger along the scrolls in the wrought-iron bench. Eric tried to read the boy's expression, but it had become inscrutable. A heavy silence descended. Finally, Sterling cleared his throat. "I was gonna say you ain't my daddy and you can't make me." He looked at Eric. "But I guess I won't say that."

Eric smiled. He lifted his arm, and for the first time in years let his hand come to rest on the boy's shoulder. "If Lara knew you were blaming yourself, she'd be pissed as hell. I'd hate to see what she'd do to you in the next life."

They fell silent again. As Eric studied the boy's face, he saw a barely perceptible change in its expression, the faintest relaxing of his jaw, a flash in his eyes. Eric knew that something inside Sterling had just given way, for better or worse.

Sterling gave Eric a quick sideways glance. "There is no 'next life.' Religion is just a way to keep the proletariat happy." He inhaled and stretched his arms over his head as if waking after a long sleep. "Religion is the opiate of the masses, man." He winked at Eric, then began looking around at the buildings, the trees. "It's really nice here." Sterling's voice broke, as if he might cry.

"Let's just sit for a while," Eric said. "It's a beautiful day."

❧ acknowledgments ❧

So many people have contributed to this writing effort, that I'm afraid I'll leave someone out of these acknowledgments. For that reason, I'd like to begin with a blanket thank you to all those who have sustained me with their support and humor.

Thanks go to Robert Singdahlsen and Lois Vick, my high school writing teachers. Without their encouragement, I never would have continued writing. James Kilgo at The University of Georgia further nurtured my writing skills. Tom Payton, Judy Long, and Pat Allen gave me an invaluable chance to experience the writing business from the inside.

I would like to thank my agent, Jacky Sach, for her faith in my work and for her unflagging moral support. Everyone at Soho Press has been wonderful, especially my editor, Laura Hruska. Not only are her editorial skills considerable, but she has been infinitely patient in dealing with a "first time" novelist. I have learned much from her.

Two writers groups have been instrumental in helping me with this novel. Thanks to Hubert Whitlow, Janice Pulliam, Donald Harris, Jerry Rogers, Chuck Stammer, Amy Munnell, Marie Mason, Dee Wilson, Julie Cannon, Lisa Knighton, Michael Jenkins, and John Robinson. Special thanks to Nancy Crew. Her tireless rereading and insightful critique have shaped this book from its inception.

My friends Mary Carney, Kristen and Paul Houghland, Rowena Yeung, and Jeanne Dennis have been sources of faith and encouragement. I could not have made it through this process without them.

Thanks to Jonathan Smiley who has been in the trenches with me for longer than either of us care to admit. Even though he was not present at this novel's genesis, Evan Greller has provided much-needed love and support. He has helped guide me literally (around New York City) and figuratively throughout the final stages of this process. Bonnie, Gene and Debbie are also to be thanked for their encouragement. I am glad to have them as part of my extended family.

Above all, I'd like to express appreciation to my family. From my father, Merrell Patrick, who grew up on a tobacco farm in Kentucky, I received the love of nature, of wide open spaces, of the countryside and of its people that inspired this novel. Dad's support and encouragement in this endeavor have been unflagging. From my mother, Cindy Patrick, I inherited a love of books and reading. As a committed teacher born into a family of academicians, she instilled in me an appreciation of culture and of learning, as well as a drive that allowed me to pursue this goal. Her optimism and enthusiasm have been much appreciated. Finally, my brother Ian has been not only the best brother ever, but a friend and an alley. He has helped me maintain a healthy perspective and can always make me laugh, no matter what.